W9-CMF-103

XONE OF
CONTENTION

TOR BOOKS BY PIERS ANTHONY

Alien Plot
Anthonology
But What of Earth?
Demons Don't Dream
Faun & Games
Geis of the Gargoyle
Ghost
Harpy Thyme
Hasan
Hope of Earth
Isle of Woman
Letters to Jenny
Prostho Plus
Race Against Time
Roc and a Hard Place
Shade of the Tree
Shame of Man
Steppe
Triple Detente
Xone of Contention
Yon Ill Wind
Zombie Lover

WITH ROBERT E. MARGROFF:
Dragon's Gold
Serpent's Silver
Chimaera's Copper
Mouvar's Magic
Orc's Opal
The E.S.P. Worm
The Ring

WITH FRANCES HALL:
Pretender

WITH RICHARD GILLIAM:
Tales from the Great Turtle (Anthology)

WITH ALFRED TELLA:
The Willing Spirit

WITH CLIFFORD A. PICKOVER:
Spider Legs

WITH JAMES RICHEY AND ALAN RIGGS:
Quest for the Fallen Star

WITH JULIE BRADY:
Dream a Little Dream

PIERS ANTHONY

XONE OF
CONTENTION

A TOM DOHERTY ASSOCIATES BOOK

NEW YORK

XONE OF CONTENTION

Copyright © 1999 by Piers Anthony Jacob

This book is printed on acid-free paper.

A Tor Book
Published by Tom Doherty Associates, LLC
175 Fifth Avenue
New York, NY 10010

www.tor.com

Tor® is a registered trademark of Tom Doherty Associates, LLC.

Library of Congress Cataloging-in-Publication Data

Anthony, Piers
    Xone of contention / Piers Anthony.—1st ed.
        p.   cm.
    "A Tom Doherty Associates book."
    ISBN 0-312-86691-7
    I. Title
    PS3551.N73X66   1999   99-22200
    813'.54—dc21   CIP

First Edition: October 1999

Printed in the United States of America

0 9 8 7 6 5 4 3 2 1

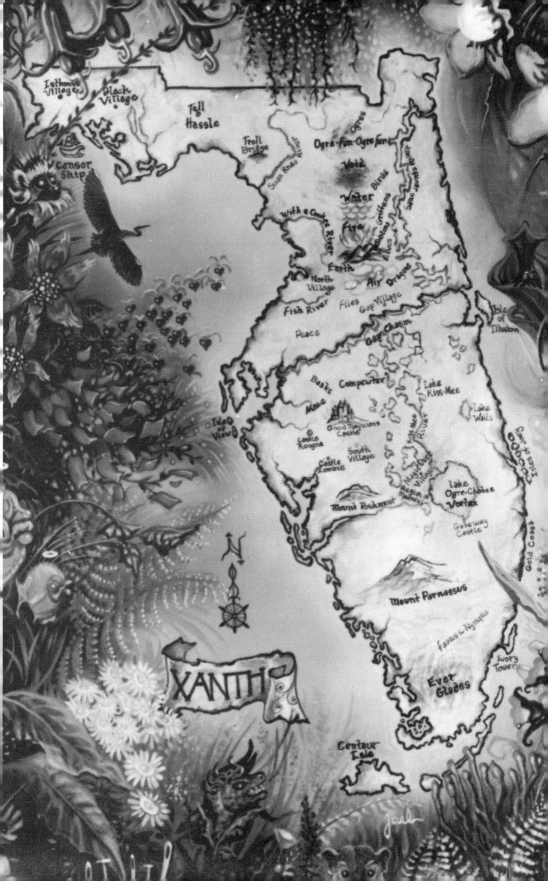

Contents

1
LEMON

Edsel struggled with the program, but it just wouldn't jell. The problem really was in the software, which was unusually unintelligible. How could he make it seem easy and user friendly, when its programmers had evidently labored decades to make it difficult and hostile? This was of course how he earned his living: designing software to make other software seem nice. But in this case he needed to tweak a default in the computer operating system, and access to the key level was barred. That was the fundamental bone of contention.

"Damn you, Macrohard," he swore softly. "Just once, couldn't you give a person a break? I'm not trying to steal Doors from you, just to put a special function on the keypad 'Enter' key so Grundy Golem can work independent of the mouse. There are folk who don't like being chained to the mouse, you know; this isn't Dizzy World. Would it hurt you so bad to let someone have it his own way for a change?" But of course he knew the answer: yes, it would truly pain the company to let a user ever have it his own way. Macrohard never wanted anyone to forget for half an instant exactly who was the master, and who was the least important person in the universe. It couldn't stop third party programmers like Edsel from trying to alleviate things, but it could and did make sure that they were unable to make any significant improvements. So the bone became a whole zone of contention.

There had to be a way around this block. He had all the rest of it figured out—if he could just use this one key. If he could only get in there to redefine it. Without Macrohard catching on. He almost thought he had a glimmer of a way, but he couldn't quite grasp it. He was up against a deadline, and this one aspect balked him maddeningly. This wasn't like his problem with the printer, which Doors refused to allow to use its two paper trays; both had to have paper, but only one could be drawn from, so that he could not have one tray feeding paper while he refilled the other, cycling through without delaying his work. That had been a real aggravation when he had changed to Doors: its deliberate crippling of the useful features of his printer that he had always used before. But what could he do? Doors had become just about the only game in town, and it slammed shut on any fingers it chose. He had survived that aggravation, but he had not been under a deadline then.

Maybe if he took a break, got his mind off it for an hour, the way would come to him. Sometimes it was like that: you had to take the pressure off the gate before you could unlatch it. He remembered his frustration the first time he needed to format a floppy disk, and Doors didn't even list formatting as an option. Their Help feature did tell where to find it, but neglected to clarify that a right mouse click was necessary instead of the left one, to get the proper menu. Macrohard was a genius at providing the necessary function, but effectively disabling it by the selective omission of a key detail, so that most users could not get the benefit of it. Truly fine sadism. So he had wasted precious time before finally finding it by chance. That was too often the only way, as with evolution: time and chance. And that could be wearing on the psyche. While the anonymous Doors programmers surely laughed their nerdly heads off. They evidently loved making working folk waste time, energy, and patience.

Edsel got up and walked to the garage. There was his pride: the Lemon motorcycle. He had had it for years, and it was a great old machine. Just a little off its feed right now, but some tinkering with the carburetor should fix that.

He laid out his tools and got to work. He always felt better when with his fine machine. The nerviest thing he had ever done was to put it up as his stake in a bet with his friend Dug. But it had been important, because he had won that bet, and gotten Pia. The bet had been that Dug, who had hated computer games, would like *Companions of Xanth*. The motorcycle against the girl. Not only had Dug liked the game, he had come out of it with a new girlfriend, Kim, now his wife. So his old girlfriend, Pia, was freed to be with Edsel. A win-win situation for the home team.

Or was it? Now it was seven years later, and his marriage to Pia was in trouble. Somehow they seemed to fight more than they made love. Sometimes they did both together. He was beginning to wonder whether they had made a mistake. Dug and Kim hadn't; their marriage was solid and harmonious. Which was odd, because Kim really wasn't lovely; she wasn't nearly as pretty as Pia, and not half as sexy. She also talked too much. But somehow she seemed just right for Dug. She clearly adored him, and he adored her. Edsel wasn't sure there had ever been a hard word between them. In contrast to the way it was between Edsel and Pia. Edsel had asked Dug about that once: how he had discovered Kim, and how they managed to get along so well.

The answer had been perplexing. "Sure, Kim didn't seem like much. But then she kissed me."

"That was it?"

"That was it. And when there's a problem, she kisses me again."

"When *we* have a problem, Pia won't kiss me at all."

"She's like that," Dug had agreed. That had reminded Edsel how Pia had once been Dug's girlfriend, and he didn't care to dwell on that.

He took down the carburetor, but the problem didn't seem to be there; it was clean and clear. Maybe in the gasoline line? That could get more complicated.

"Edsel!"

He jumped. "Yes dear," he replied, hoping this was not going to be another scene. She looked and sounded furious. Talk about a zone of contention!

"Don't 'yes dear' *me!* What are you doing here?"

"I—"

"Why haven't you finished that *Cuss Companion* program yet? You know you shouldn't be goofing off here when we have a deadline! Can't you finish *anything?* I just got a call from Kim, asking if she can tell the buyer it's in the mail. I'll have to tell her no, because my idiotic husband cares more for his junkcycle than for his job!"

He didn't try to explain. It wouldn't do any good, when she was like this. But he did need to get back to the Companions program.

He looked at his watch. Three hours had passed! He had gotten lost in the Lemon and his thoughts, and spent way more time than he could afford. Pia had a right to be angry.

He reassembled things as rapidly as feasible, and washed his hands. He went to find Pia, hoping to explain, but she was on the phone, giving Kim an earful. It was an irony of the situation that the two women got along great. Maybe that was because Pia was glad Kim was taking up Dug's attention, and Kim was glad that Pia *wasn't* taking his attention. So he went to the office and put the Companions program on his computer, running through its routine. He was rather proud of it, overall.

A little figure, obviously fashioned of wood and rag, appeared. "Hi! I'm Grundy Golem, your Companion of the moment. I speak Basic, C++ and other computer languages, but you don't need to worry about that; I'll translate everything to your tongue. Please check in your name, gender, age, status, and whatever." A check-off sheet appeared. Edsel typed in his name, and checked Male, 23, Married. This part was optional, but it added to the effect.

"That's great, Edsel," Grundy said. "What do you want to know? Click your cursor on one of these words, or Select it by touching Alt and the first letter, and touch Keypad Enter." The figure held up a sign listing a number of popular programs.

Edsel clicked on Macrohard Doors Excess. "Good," Grundy said. "Now before we get into this, Edsel, I must tell you that you don't need to have me as your guide." His voice come through the system speakers; this was a multimedia program. "You can choose any of these others by Selecting or clicking on them." Several pictures appeared. One of them was Pia; it had amused them all to have her be the model for their own program. She looked great, because a program figure didn't put on weight the way a living one did.

Edsel clicked Pia. Her picture came to life. She was wearing a dark blue jacket and skirt, and had small golden earrings representing Pluto, the P planet. "Very well, Edsel" she said dulcetly. "Now how can I help you with Excess? Do you know anything about spreadsheets or databases?" She smiled. She had a nice smile. In fact she had a nice everything, in appearance.

He clicked "No."

"Well, they are both ways of storing and using information," she said. "Would you like me to walk you through the basics?"

This time he clicked No, though she had a lovely walk. She faced him, putting on a cute smile of perplexity. "What would you like, Edsel? Just type it in, and I'll do my best."

He typed "Disrobe."

"If you wish." She opened her jacket and drew it off, revealing a tight, well-filled sweater. She put her hands on its base and began to draw it up, showing a sheer blouse beneath. Then she paused, catching on. "Hey—it's supposed to be the program I'm helping you with, Edsel, not your sex life."

He smiled. He had always liked that part. That was as close as the Companion Pia ever came to quarreling, and farther on in the program she would remove the sweater if asked, and later the sheer blouse too. But it took precise management to get her to remove her bra or skirt, and that only after the user had demonstrated some competence in Excess. Her figure was worth the effort, though. To date they had had only three complaints about that feature, and dozens of notes of appreciation, and the program had sold well. One mother's letter had been choice: "Thank you so much for teaching my thirteen year old son to operate Excess. I don't know how you did it, but he learned it readily when he used your Companions guide, after getting nowhere elsewhere. He even runs through the guide for refreshers every so often, and his friends are learning too. They all say yours is the best." Obviously Mother herself had not caught on to the secret lure, and Junior wasn't telling. Modern teens were not stupid about software of the feminine kind, or about the attitudes of parents.

Edsel canned the program. It was the update for the Discuss word processor he was working on now, popularly known as Cuss. The latest revision of Cuss word was even more complicated and balky than usual, and really needed a good tutorial program. For example, it wouldn't let a file it made end in anything but .doc, as if it were a cartoon rabbit, on pain of horrendous file-trashing threats. Only by chance (as usual) had he discovered that he could get around that by putting his proposed file names in quotes. His tutorial clarified that and other dirty little secrets. If he could just make it work. He *had* to differentiate the two Enter keys, so that the Companions guide could have its own "Okay" key for special effects. But he still couldn't figure out how to free it from Macrohard's malign grip. Dog in the manger: if Macro didn't want to use it, nobody could. That familiar bone of contention, again.

Maybe there would be inspiration on the GigaGrid, or the Mundane Mega Mesh that enclosed the world. He clicked the Mode M site and was on his way.

"That's right—go hide in the Grid, the way you always do," Pia said sourly behind him.

"Oh, go buy another box of chocolates, the way you always do," he retorted. He would rather make love to her than fight her, anytime, but often there wasn't much choice.

She disappeared, and he forged on into the Grid. It was always this way: she had a sharp tongue, and he inevitably responded. Their marriage was on the rocks, and with it, maybe, their business. If it weren't for Dug and Kim, "Companions" might have foundered already. Kim was gregarious, so she was the saleswoman, phoning clients, emailing them, paying personal calls, bringing in the orders that were their life blood. Dug handled the shipping and handling, often delivering the larger orders personally, for he was a handsome man who always made a good impression. Pia handled the accounts, and Edsel, of course, struggled with the programs. He had let them down, this time, by trying for too much, and now he didn't have a finished program for them to deliver. He was the weak link, and he hated that. He was the lemon, this time.

Now he was cruising the GigaGrid, meandering through the Mesh, looking for inspiration. Maybe he could yet figure it out, so that he could complete the program, and they could deliver it late. He whistled in the way he had, smiling, his tongue against the roof of his mouth; it was easier than doing it purse-lipped, and fewer people knew how to do it, a double advantage as far as he was concerned. He liked being different in inconsequential ways.

He became aware that he had drifted into strange territory. There was a sign. THIS IS THE O-XONE. ENTRY TO THE MAGIC MESH REQUIRES THE RIGHT SPELL. PENALTY FOR ABUSE IS A BUNION.

Edsel laughed. This was a joke or a challenge. He liked challenges almost as much as he liked jokes. Pia had been a challenge. So it seemed that someone had set up a Mesh Leaf with a trick mode of entry, and he would see if he could get in. What would be the key?

He tried the usual run of code words and signals, but they didn't work. Then his left big toe began to hurt. It felt like a bunion. He put voice into his whistle, wondering whether this could be coincidence. How could a Mesh Leaf give a person a bunion? What kind of Xone of contention was this?

The sign changed. SPELL ACCEPTED. YOU ARE NOW IN THE O-XONE. FOR ASSISTANCE IN NAVIGATING THE MAGIC MESH, SEE BREANNA OF THE BLACK WAVE.

Spell accepted? What was it talking about? Oh—it must be a joke, the sign changing automatically after a moment, encouraging him to hit on this Leaf. So okay, he could play this game; where was this Black Wave gal?

He walked down the hall, and noticed two things: first, his bunion was gone, and second, what was he doing walking down a hall? This was an address on the Mundane Mega Mesh of the GigaGrid; he was gazing at his computer screen and interfacing with mouse and keyboard. Yet he wasn't; he was now walking down a hall. There were booths along it, each with a picture of a person, and a name. The colors were somehow brighter and clearer than those in his office, and the air seemed fresher.

And here was the name Breanna, under the face of a cute black girl who looked to be about sixteen. She must be the one. So he lifted his knuckle and knocked on the picture.

It came to life. "Ouch! You hit me!"

Startled, Edsel apologized. "Sorry. I didn't mean to."

She looked at him. "What do you mean, didn't mean to?" she demanded with cute severity. "You rapped me on the noggin with your knuckle."

"I—I thought it was just a picture. I was knocking on the door. You know—hitting the site. I never thought it would be literal."

She stared at him. "You're Mundane!"

He was taken aback. "I confess I am. You aren't?"

"Of course not. Not any more. Now I'm Xanthian. In real life, I mean; this is just my Magic Mesh Leaf. How did you get into the O-Xone?"

"There was a sign, saying something about a spell, and a penalty, and my foot began to hurt, and I whistled—and then I was here. So I did what it said, and looked you up."

Breanna seemed mollified. "Okay. Let's start at the top. I'm Breanna of the Black Wave. My talent is to see in blackness. Who are you and what's yours?"

"I'm Edsel of—of Mundania, and I guess my talent is to cruise the GigaGrid. Or to make droll jokes. But I never found this—this Magic Mesh before."

"Of course not; it's barred to most Mundanes." The picture considered. It *was* a picture; just her head and shoulders, animate but flat, like a TV image. Yet her eyes looked at him, and she was responsive to his words. "You must have found a glitch. A spell that wasn't programmed. What exactly did you do?"

"Well, I whistled. Like this." He made a voiced whistle.

The picture wavered and became three dimensional. Breanna's lips pursed. "That's magic, all right; it just enhanced my sight."

"You mean your site?"

She smiled. "That too, maybe. I mean, suddenly I see you rounded instead of flat. Am I the same to you?"

"Yes. But you're still just a head and shoulders. I can't see your rounded portions, though I'd like to."

She flashed another smile, appreciating the implied humorous compliment. "For sure. That's all there is of me in the Leaf. I mean, how could the real me be here?"

"I don't know. The real me seems to be here, though that seems impossible."

"For sure. We'll have to patch that glitch. But you don't seem bad for a Mundane."

"Well, I hope I'm not bad, even if my marriage is patchy." He hadn't meant to say that; he was a little unsettled.

"Too bad you're not in Xanth. Marriages are forever, there."

"I know. My friend Dug went to Xanth and met Kim there, and they have a happy marriage."

Breanna's eyes widened. "You know Dug and Kim Mundane?"

"Sure. I'm in business with them. I was the one who first put Dug onto Xanth. The Xanth game, I mean; I didn't know he'd actually cross over."

"Yeah, he was in the Companions game. I wish I could have been a Companion."

"Oh? Why weren't you?"

"I was too young then, only nine. Anyway, the Black Wave had just come into Xanth then; we didn't know our way around. Sherlock went with Dug and found a good place by Ogre Chobee for us to settle in. So I guess I can't complain. But it sure sounds like fun."

"It sure does," he agreed. "Well, if I'm ever in Xanth, you can be my Companion and show me around." He felt a trace of guilt as he spoke, because he was flirting with this cute girl, and as a married man he shouldn't.

"I can? That's great!"

"Only I can't get into Xanth," he said with regret. "Dug and Kim go there only when invited. There was some kind of trial. Something about a big bird, I think."

"Roxanne Roc," Breanna agreed. "She won. She's just about the most important bird in Xanth now, except for the Simurgh. That's another great moment of history I missed. Bleep, I'd sure like to be in on a Great Moment. Well, I did get to go to Jenny's wedding." Then her picture paused, orienting on him with wild surmise. "Say—maybe we can do each other some good. Maybe you can visit Xanth, and I can be your Companion and show you around, and maybe that will be a great adventure and accomplish something nice, like patching up your marriage."

Edsel realized that Breanna was a creature of dreams. But her enthusiasm was contagious. "I'd like that. But I don't see how."

"I just got this wonderful wild notion. Here we are talking in the Interface. If we could stretch it a little farther, and exchange places, then maybe you'd be in Xanth and I'd be in Mundania. I wouldn't mind visiting it, though I sure wouldn't want to stay." Then she reconsidered. "Well, maybe not you and me changing places, exactly. Maybe I could switch with your wife, and you could switch with my boyfriend Justin."

"Justin?"

"Justin Tree. He used to be a tree—well, he was a man first, then a tree, then we met, and now we're betrothed but we can't marry because I'm too young. We can't even smooch much, because I'm not supposed to know the Adult Conspiracy. I hate that! I mean, what's the point in making him convert early to a young man—he took some youth elixir— if we can't *do* anything? It's driving me crazy."

"I think I know the feeling," Edsel said, though he hardly understood all of what she was saying.

"So maybe if Justin and I could switch with you folk, and get into Mundania for a while, where there's not much enforcement of the Conspiracy, we could at least go from necking to petting. And you folk could do whatever you wanted, in Xanth, and your marriage wouldn't be in trouble, because marriages never are."

This was surely sheer foolishness, but it was wickedly tempting. "I'd do it, if there were a way."

"I'm thinking there could be a way. With the right connection. If nobody objected." She cocked her head. "Do you think sixteen is too young?"

He knew what was on her mind. "I was sixteen when I got together with Pia, and she was fifteen. A girl can be pretty mature at fifteen, and moreso thereafter."

"For sure!" she agreed happily. "And Justin's not young at all. He's about ninety nine, I think."

He thought he had misheard. "Nineteen?"

"Ninety nine," she said carefully. "But he was a tree most of that time. I told you. But now he's been youthened to nineteen, so he'll be twenty one when I'm eighteen. We think that's about right. But he's got these grandfatherly reservations about things. You know, about touching girls. I figure if I can just get him safely alone for a week or so, I can bash down those barriers." She glanced at him again. "Do you think so?"

"Uh, that depends. If—"

"Oh, right, you can't see the rest of me. Well, it's proportional. Especially when I take off my clothes."

She did have adult notions. As Pia had had, at that age. "Then if he's got the body of a nineteen year old male, and you're sixteen, and proportional, you should be able to handle him in about three minutes."

She laughed. "Yeah. That's what I figure. When I get the chance. Anyway, here's how: physical travel between Xanth and Mundania is difficult, unless you have a special pass. Oh, I mean you can do it, but you're liable to come out in some other time or place and be lost. But exchanging bodies—I think that's feasible."

"Exchanging bodies?" he asked somewhat blankly.

"You're a bit slow on the uptake, aren't you," she remarked without rancor. "If I switch with your wife, and you switch with Justin, then the two of you would be in Xanth. You'd be in our bodies, but you'd still be *you*. And you could do what you wanted to. So could we."

"Oh. Yes. That could be interesting." In fact, as he considered it, it seemed more than interesting. If he could embrace Breanna, knowing it was really Pia, so he wasn't being unfaithful . . . ∞ His thought trailed into an ellipsis with a potentially infinite number of dots. Some of them were white dots, like Pia; some were brown, like Breanna.

"So let's see about it. We'll need some magic to handle it, but I think I know whom to check with. I'll have to go out of the O-Xone a moment, though."

"What does the O stand for?"

"Other, I think. Because it's neither here nor there. It's the interface between Xanth and Mundania, a halfway zone. I'm on duty because I remember some about Mundania, so can help folk like you, though we haven't been set up long and you're the first, and you're not even a Character."

"A what?"

"A Character. Xanth folk come here to the O-Xone and pretend to be Mundanes, and I guess Mundanes try to pretend to be Xanthians, mostly in their X-Xone, and maybe soon they can meet halfway. When we get it organized. Sean's working on it."

"Who?"

"Sean Baldwin. He's Mundane, but he's with Willow, who's Xanthian. She's a winged elf, actually. Sometimes he has to stay in Mundania, and she has to stay in Xanth, so they can't be together all the time, so they want a connection, and maybe this will be it."

Breanna tended to provide more information than he could assimilate immediately, but it did help some. He returned to basics. "This business of exchanging bodies—I'm still not sure exactly how that works."

"Yeah, I guess you ought to try it. Maybe you should step into a picture."

"Do what?"

"Just walk on down to one of the scenes, and think yourself into it, and you'll get a sample. That's part of what the O-Xone is all about: sampling the other side. It'll give you a feel for it, though it's really illusion."

"Illusion?"

She frowned. "You *are* slow. Here in the O-Xone the magic's not complete, and illusion's cheap, so we use it a lot. I've got to go check with Nimby, so you take a break in a picture, and we'll meet here again when we're both done. Okay?"

"Uh, okay," he agreed.

The picture lost animation. It was just a picture, again instead of a video.

He turned and walked on down the hall, looking at the other pictures. They were of various fantasy scenes, each painted on a large leaf. One was a fancy castle, with a moat around it and fruit trees beside it, labeled CASTLE ROOGNA. Another was a monstrous gulf, labeled GAP CHASM. Another was a group of centaurs. That made him pause. The males were muscular in their human aspects, with large bows slung across their backs, while the females were—extremely well endowed. They wore no clothing on their bodies, not even halters. Fascinating! But he wasn't ready to tackle anything like that, so he moved on until he came to a scene of a deep, quiet forest. There was a squirrel in the foreground, ordinary except for one thing: it had wings. A flying squirrel, of course.

That should do. But how did he get into that body, even in illusion? There didn't seem to be any instructions. Breanna had assumed he knew how, forgetting how "slow" he was about such things. Think himself into it, as she had suggested?

"I am a squirrel," he said tentatively. Nothing happened. "A winged squirrel." Still nothing.

He stared into the picture, pondering. Did he need to hum-whistle to invoke the magic? He tried that, and the picture seemed to shimmer and expand, but he still wasn't in it. The winged squirrel was still there, with a dark trail wending into the background.

Then, irrelevantly, he remembered a song. It was about a young man who faced a difficult trip through a forest, yet he anticipated it with joy. He began to hum it, thinking the words. "Though the path is long and dark, rocky steep and narrow/Though the wood is dark and cold, this brings me no sorrow." Because in that woodland lived his darling loved one. Edsel was married, but he still liked romantic situations. He pictured Pia in that wood, as lovely as she had been at sixteen.

Then he was in the scene. The forest was suddenly huge around him. He took a step, faltered, and spread his wings for balance. He was the flying squirrel! Could he really fly? It seemed worth a try.

He faced in the direction of a glade, spread his wings, ran on his hind feet, flapped—and was airborne! He pumped his wings frantically, trying to maintain balance while gaining elevation, but overdid it and stalled out. He dropped, landing on his tail. No damage done, fortunately.

But his clumsy effort had attracted attention. Suddenly a monstrous shape was entering the glade. It was a fire-breathing dragon!

Edsel panicked. He got all four feet under him, folded his wings, and scooted for the nearest underbrush. A jet of flame passed over his head, and he realized that the dragon had expected him to take flight, so had aimed high. But because he was really a land-bound creature, he had stayed on land—and maybe saved himself a frying.

However, the dragon wasn't through. It was reorienting, and this time it wouldn't miss. Brush would not protect him from that flamethrower.

Edsel scrambled for the nearest tree, getting behind it just as the flame set the brush on fire.

How could he escape? He peered up the trunk of the tree. The top seemed worlds away, and he didn't trust his claws to hold on, for all that he was a squirrel. The dragon could toast him long before he got out of range. He heard the ground shaking as it tramped toward the tree.

He would have to make a break for it on the ground. Maybe if he ran toward the dragon, that would surprise it, and he could get by it and beyond it before it could turn around. Then maybe he could find a hole in the ground or something.

A giant foot crashed down on one side of the tree. Edsel turned to the other side—and there was the dragon's awful snoot. He was trapped before he even got started.

"I want out of here!" he cried. And there he was back in the hall, standing before the picture, which now showed a dragon crouching by a tree. His heart was pounding. That had been one close escape.

If this was illusion, he wasn't sure he would care to try the reality. He'd better tell Breanna the deal was off. He walked down the hall toward her Leaf.

Then, bothered by something, he turned back to the picture. The dragon was now looking around, evidently having lost the squirrel. That was what Edsel had wanted to know: that the squirrel had escaped. He had not led it into a frying or chomping. He turned away again, relieved.

As he approached the Leaf, it came to life. "Oh, there you are," Breanna's face said. "Did you enjoy yourself?"

"Not exactly," he said, abashed.

"I thought maybe you'd try the one with the mermaids in the pool. I hear they can be very friendly with human visitors."

"I didn't see that one," he said, with real regret. He could have entered a scene with friendly mermaids? He had heard it said that a mermaid had all the good parts of a woman, and none of the bad parts. As if there were any bad parts.

"Or maybe the one showing the Faun & Nymph Retreat. Naturally I'm not supposed to know how they celebrate all day, being underage, but I have a suspicion you'd find it interesting."

More than a suspicion, he was sure. He really should have checked out all the pictures before choosing one. "No, I got into one with a flying squirrel."

"That one? I hope you watched out for the dragon."

"I did run afoul of the dragon. It almost got me. A couple of those fire jets just missed me."

"Yeah, it's enchanted to just barely miss each time. To make it seem realistic. Even if the dragon scored on you, it couldn't hurt you, because it's illusion. A score that didn't work would ruin the effect, but a near miss can be scary."

"Yes." So he had been taken in by illusion, when there was no danger. That gave him new respect for illusion.

" 'Sokay. I checked with Chlorine, and she says it's fine, except that I can't go to Mundania."

"You can't? But that's not fine, because you wanted to visit there, with Justin to—you know."

She shook her head. "No, it's okay. Really. Because I'm getting something better. I'll get to be your Companion in Xanth. And maybe, if there's some slack time, like camping overnight, if I try to stretch the Adult Conspiracy a little—

"I won't even notice," Edsel said quickly. "Or tell. It's your business, nobody else's."

"Yeah," she said gratefully. "Chlorine understands, too. She used to be plain, before things changed."

"Chlorine? Where I come from, we put that in water."

"You aren't where you come from," she said with half a smile. "You'll meet Nimby and Chlorine tomorrow. But there's more: they're going to visit Mundania, by switching bodies with you. They'll need Companions too, to show them around, because Mundania can be just as dangerous as Xanth for strangers. So can you dig up a reliable pair of Mundane Companions?"

"Mundane Companions? I suppose we could ask Dug and Kim—"

"Great! Bring them here this time tomorrow, and your wife, and I'll bring Nimby and Chlorine, and Justin, and we can work it all out. This should be a great adventure."

Just like that? But of course Dug and Kim had had experience in Xanth, so should have good advice. What Pia would think of this he wasn't sure. But it was worth a try. "I'll do that," he said.

"Great!" Breanna repeated. "See you tomorrow." Her picture reverted.

Bemused, Edsel faced the O-Xone exit and walked. As he came to the marked portal, he saw it was a wall. He did his hum-whistle, and suddenly he was out. He could tell, because he was looking at a monitor screen with a cursor blinking in front of him. The hall with pictures was gone.

He exited the Mesh, and then the GigaGrid. He had some talking to do, to several people.

First, Pia. She was every bit as understanding as usual. "Have you been doing drugs?"

"No," he said patiently. "This is a Mesh interface. And maybe a chance for us to get into Xanth for a visit. The way Dug and Kim do."

"Just because they're crazy enough to believe in fantasy is no reason we have to," she retorted. "How could you fall for such a line of crap?"

"Pia, please. I thought it would be good for our relationship. To have a break. A vacation in a magic land. Maybe we could mend fences, or something."

"As if you even care!" she said witheringly.

"I *do* care. I—I'm sorry that things are going wrong."

"Maybe they're going right. Did you ever think of that?"

"Going right?" he asked blankly.

"Maybe it was a mistake, us getting married. Maybe now we're finally catching on. Maybe we're getting ready to set things right."

"I don't understand." But he feared he did.

She softened. "Ed, some marriages aren't meant to be. I think we should consider divorce."

He was stunned. She had said the D word. He had thought she was going to recommend counseling. "I—I don't want that."

"But maybe it's best. To recognize the situation, and take appropriate action. There should be less pain that way."

She was serious. She must have considered this pretty carefully, and that knocked his world for a loop. But what could he do?

He decided to go for double or nothing. "How about this: let's make a deal. You give this fantasy visit an honest try, and if it doesn't work, then I'll—I'll not oppose a divorce. If that's what you want."

She eyed him appraisingly. "You won't fight it?"

"I won't fight it. Though I don't want it. I'd rather make love than war, anytime. But I'll go along with it. If that's the way you feel."

She nodded. "Deal." She extended her hand.

"Deal," he agreed, shaking her hand.

Edsel called Dug immediately. Dug and Kim lived within a mile, and the two couples often visited each other socially as well as for business reasons.

Kim answered the phone. "Yes?" she inquired politely. She had a nice voice.

"Edsel. We—could we come over? Now? There's something we need to discuss."

"Of course. I'll tell Dug." Her tone indicated that she realized that this was not routine.

~~Dug~~ wheeled out the Lemon, and Pia climbed on behind him, putting her arms around his waist. He had always liked riding with her, feeling her thighs against his hips, her bosom against his back. Her body wasn't quite as good as it had been, but still appealed to him. He wondered how he had changed to turn her off, or whether she just had a short romantic attention span.

He started the machine, and the engine came alive. It skipped a little, then settled down. He still hadn't fixed the problem, but it was marginal rather than serious, so far. He guided the Lemon out into traffic. Two things he loved: the motorcycle and his wife. Now the one was weakening, and so was the other. But the game wasn't over; maybe he could save both.

"You should have dumped this junk long ago," Pia muttered. "For a decent car."

"But I thought you liked my bike," he protested.

"Times change."

Painful truth. Her feeling had changed, for the motorcycle and for the man. If only he knew why!

Actually, he feared he did know why: because Pia was as shallow as she was lovely, perhaps incapable of a meaningful long-term relationship. She had always used her looks to get by, and never developed a serious unselfish commitment to anything. Yet he remained smitten. What he truly wanted was perhaps not even theoretically achievable: the looks of Pia as she had been at age sixteen, and the character of Kim. Or at least Pia's present appearance, and an uplifting long term goal. Something she truly believed in, that didn't directly benefit herself.

They pulled into Dug and Kim's drive and parked. Pia got off, but didn't go to the house. She was waiting on Edsel, not from courtesy so much as an indication that this was his stupid notion to present to the other couple.

Kim opened the door. She was tall and lean, in jeans, and her face was garden variety, but she had a contagious enthusiasm for things. She had short curly light brown hair and blue eyes. Edsel wondered for the nth time what Dug saw in her, for Dug had always been just as fascinated by sexy women as Edsel was. She had been a string bean at sixteen, and remained one at twenty three. Pia, in contrast, had lustrous long dark brown hair, sexy green eyes, a cute heart shaped face, and a figure that remained not far short of great. There simply was no comparison between them. Yet Dug plainly doted on Kim. Ever since she kissed him, he said. As if that made sense.

Edsel paused to let Pia enter first. She was in a form-fitting light sweater and a snug short skirt, and her walk was a delight to behold. No mystery what he saw in her.

Dug met them inside. "Sit down," he said. "Kim says it's important."

Edsel sat on the living room couch. Pia did not join him; she chose an individual chair across the room, crossing her legs. That left Edsel with mixed feelings. He would have preferred to have her sit beside him, but he had always been wowed by her legs, especially from this angle. She well knew her power over him, but didn't look at him.

Dug took another chair, facing Edsel rather than Pia. Dug had once been Pia's boyfriend, but he had treated her like a sister ever since Kim came into his life. Edsel suspected that that bothered Pia on some level, though she wanted nothing romantic to do with Dug. The men she dumped weren't supposed to do as well as Dug had.

Kim was left to join Edsel on the couch. She folded her legs beneath her and faced him expectantly.

How to start? Suddenly this seemed complicated. "I—I found a new Leaf on the Mesh. An interface with Xanth, called the O-Xone."

"They've set up the O-Xone already?" Kim cried, delighted. "Wonderful! Now we can talk with Xanth folk without having to go there. Who's there?"

"A black girl called Breanna. She—"

"Breanna of the Black Wave! Of course. She's ideal. She's from Mundania, originally. Great girl."

"Uh, yes. She and I talked, and decided to work an exchange, so Pia and I could visit Xanth, and two other folk could visit Mundania."

"An exchange?" Kim asked, picking right up on it. It was easy to talk, when she was the other party.

"Yes. We would take the bodies of two people in Xanth, and they would take our bodies. So there would be no actual physical crossing, but we'd seem to be in each other's worlds."

"Fascinating," Kim said enthusiastically. "That will make it much easier to visit Xanth. It gets complicated to do it physically, though with illusion it can seem real."

How true! "Yes. But the thing is that we'll need guides, because—"

"Companions!" Kim said. "Of course. Xanth is dangerous for unaccompanied strangers, even when it's all in a game, and I guess Mundania would be just as bad for Xanthians." She glanced at Dug.

"Worse," Dug agreed, on cue.

Edsel envied their camaraderie. They got along so well. Pia, in contrast, was staring vaguely at the ceiling, bored, not trying to help at all. She was letting the world know that she didn't care one way or the other.

"So if you go to Xanth, you'll need good Companions," Kim said. "And the ones who take your bodies will need good Mundane Companions. Dug and I will be glad to do it."

Edsel was starting to catch on to what Dug saw in her. Kim had not only anticipated his awkward request, but agreed to it as if it were the most natural thing in the world. "Thanks," he said, much relieved. "Breanna and someone called Justin will be our guides in Xanth, but I was concerned about imposing on you."

"No problem at all," Kim said, glancing again at Dug, who nodded. "We're glad to help with anything connected to Xanth. This is such a great breakthrough ! We thought it'd be another year before they got the O-Xone set up. Who is coming here?"

"Someone called—" Edsel scratched in his memory. "Nimble, I think. And Corinne." He remembered the name meant something, like a pool cleaner, but couldn't quite recover it, though Breanna had spoken it several times.

Kim shook her head. "We don't know them. But we don't have to; we'll get acquainted soon enough. So they'll look just like you two, but their minds will be from Xanth."

"Yes. I agreed to have us all come in to the O-Xone tomorrow at noon, so we could meet and work out the details."

"That's great," Kim said. "You have worked it out perfectly." Impulsively she leaned across and planted a firm kiss on his mouth.

The world seemed to turn over. Edsel was floating on the elevated side of a Ferris wheel, high among pink clouds, dizzy but happy. Suddenly the rest of the mystery evaporated, and he knew what Dug meant. That was the best kiss he had ever experienced—and it wasn't even serious. If she had wanted to seduce him, she could have done it merely by holding the kiss longer. Of course that was not her intent, and everyone knew it. But what a kiss!

The clouds dissipated, and he became aware of friendly laughter, not shared by Pia. "I should have warned you," Dug was saying. "She kisses." He thought Edsel was merely surprised. That was the least of it.

"Sorry," Kim said, half mischievously. "It's just that it was such a relief. We thought you were going to discuss something awful, like the two of you breaking up."

Now Pia met Edsel's gaze. Then she spoke. "We're considering it. But first we'll try visiting Xanth."

Things got abruptly serious. "You are considering it?" Kim asked, and now there was no mischief or humor in her expression or tone. Edsel realized that she had not forgotten that Pia had been Dug's first girlfriend. Surely she didn't want Pia on the loose again.

"We hope that a change of venue will help," Edsel said quickly. "Like a vacation. Second honeymoon."

Pia opened her mouth, and by her expression nothing sweet or sentimental was about to come out.

But Dug intercepted it. "Xanth will surely do it. There's no place like it. We'll be there tomorrow to meet the others, in the O-Xone." And this time he shot Kim a look.

Kim jumped up. "Right. And we'd better get our work done today, in case that takes some time. Sorry you folk must rush off so soon."

Beautiful, Edsel thought. They were a perfect team, always working together. In a moment he and Pia were out of the house and mounting the motorcycle.

"This had better be good," Pia muttered as they started off.

Edsel didn't answer. He didn't want to risk getting into a quarrel now, lest she change her mind about the deal. It was clear that Xanth was his only hope.

That afternoon he tackled the Cuss word Companions program, and this time found a way to finesse it so he could address the key he needed. After that things fell together, and he completed it in good order. He copied it to a backup disk and took it to Pia. *"Now* you can tell them it's in the mail," he said.

She stared at the disk. "You got it? You're sure."

"I'm sure. Put in it on your system and see."

She hesitated. Then she came to a decision. "Wait."

He waited, uncertain what was on her mind. She phoned Kim. ''The Discuss Companions is ready. Tell Dug we'll bring it to you in an hour, and he can copy it and ship it before the day is out.'' She hung up.

''An hour?'' Edsel asked. ''We can have it there in fifteen minutes.''

She stood, stepped into him, and kissed him. Then she led him to the bedroom.

Bemused, he realized that she was truly pleased to have the program done, so that they would not default on a deadline. And maybe she was jealous of Kim's kiss, too. Pia never apologized, she just changed her mind, like the popular conception of the ideal woman. She had one effective way to make everything right, and he was not about to object. Whatever other problems they might have, they had none in bed when Pia was amenable. He knew that this was merely a gesture of the moment, and that nothing long-term had changed. But it would be one phenomenal moment.

He was correct.

Next day they coordinated by phone, then got on the GigaGrid. Edsel was on his system, and Pia on hers in the other room, and Dug and Kim on their two systems at their house. They ''met'' at a private online site they maintained, checking in. ''Follow me,'' Edsel said, knowing that they would lock on to his name and be carried along with him.

He made his way to the Magic Mesh. When he came to the warning sign, he typed ''Party of four: Edsel, Pia, Dug, Kim.'' Then he did his voice whistle.

The sign shimmered. WELCOME TO THE O-XONE. Then they were standing in the hall of pictures.

''Oh!'' Pia breathed, amazed. She tugged at her skirt, as if not believing that it was real. Maybe it was illusion, as was her body, but it was tangible.

''It's the O-Xone all right,'' Kim said. ''They have done a nice job.'' She checked her own clothing. She had put on a skirt and blouse for this occasion, and looked decent.

Edsel led the way to Breanna's Leaf. This time he did not knock; hitting was too literal here. ''Breanna,'' he said.

The picture animated. ''Good; you're here. This time we're set up for it. Come in.'' The picture expanded as her image fuzzed out, and became an entrance to a comfortable chamber.

They stepped inside. The room seemed larger from inside; in fact it was like a huge living room, with easy chairs around the edge, facing in.

They stood in the center, uncertain whether to sit. Then from a hall on the opposite side a man and a woman entered. The man seemed to be of college age, and the woman of high school age. In fact she was Breanna, this time complete. "You're right," Edsel said, surveying her body. "It's proportional."

Breanna smiled. "You've been kissed recently, Edsel. It shows. So I guess it's okay for me." She walked up to him, embraced him, and reached her face up to kiss him.

It felt real. Not destabilizing in the way of Kim's kiss, or sexy in the way of Pia's kiss, but solid and pleasant. He had never been kissed by a black girl before, and was almost surprised to discover that it was just like any other kiss. She was a very nice little package.

Breanna stepped back. "This is Justin," she said, indicating the young man. He looked quite ordinary. Not at all like a tree.

"This is Pia," Edsel said. "And Dug, and Kim."

"I know," Breanna said. "We haven't met before, but they are well known in Xanth."

"And we know of you," Kim said. "We got a report on Jenny's wedding, and you were there."

"For sure. So are we ready to meet Nimby and Chlorine?"

Kim's jaw dropped. "Who?"

"Those are the names," Edsel said quickly. "I guess I garbled them."

Breanna glanced at him sharply. "You don't know who they are?"

"I never heard of them before yesterday."

Breanna smiled. "Maybe that's just as well. They are the ones you'll be exchanging with. They want to visit Mundania. In fact it turns out they set this up, so they could do it."

"Set this up?"

"Ah, here they are now."

Two more people entered the room. The man was handsome to the point of looking princely, while the woman was so stunningly lovely that it was hard to look directly at her.

"Nimby and Chlorine," Breanna said.

Edsel tore his gaze from Chlorine. "Uh, this is—"

"Thank you," Chlorine said smoothly. "We know. Now there

should be no misunderstanding, so I will spell it out. Nimby is a demon who normally assumes dragon ass form in Xanth, but he can take any form he wants, and give any form to his companion. We will borrow your forms in Mundania, but we think that something else is better for you in Xanth.'' She glanced around the room.

Edsel glanced too, as he wasn't sure what she meant. Dug and Kim both seemed awed, as if they were seeing something miraculous or incredible. What was their problem?

"Better?" he asked blankly.

"This." Then Breanna and Nimby changed forms, becoming exact likenesses of Edsel and Pia, complete to their clothing.

Edsel stared, suspecting that this was a mirror effect. But Pia was standing beside him. His head swiveled, looking from one woman to the other. They were identical; he could not distinguish them. It was evident that Pia had a similar problem with him.

"So you can be yourselves, in Xanth," Chlorine continued. "Except that you will have to have magic talents, because everyone in Xanth does." Then she and Nimby reverted to their original forms, abating the confusion.

Something else occurred to Edsel. "Pia—she's diabetic. Will she be the same in Xanth?"

Chlorine turned to Breanna. "Diabetic?"

"It's a problem handling sugar in the body," Breanna said. She glanced at Pia. "Do you have to take shots?"

"Yes."

Chlorine glanced at Nimby, who nodded. She turned back to face the others. "Yes, she will be the same."

Edsel wasn't sure whether that was good or bad. But it would be nice to seem to be themselves. Still, he wasn't quite satisfied. Where was the catch? "Why are you two acting as if you see ghosts?" he asked Dug.

Chlorine smiled, and the room actually brightened. "I will answer that, in a moment. But you must agree to tell no one else."

Edsel had a programmer's mind. He didn't like open ended processes. "How can we agree, if we don't know what we're agreeing to?"

"I will tell you, and if you then agree, you will retain the memory. Otherwise you will lose it."

He was really suspicious of this. "You can do that? Wipe memories? When we're not even here, really?"

"Nimby can. You are in the O-Xone."

He looked at Dug again. Dug recovered enough to speak. "He can do it," he said. "You'd better agree."

"But nobody can do something like that!"

Now Kim spoke. "Nobody in Mundania."

Edsel shrugged. "Okay, tell us."

"I am an ordinary girl," Chlorine said. "In my natural state I look like this." She became rather plain, with straggly hair and ragged clothing. "Nimby changed me, outside and inside, making me beautiful, healthy, smart, and nice. When I met Nimby, he looked like this." She paused.

The handsome young man became a weird dragon with diagonal stripes of pastel pink and bilious green. His head was that of a stupid donkey. He also smelled like an overripe swamp.

"A dragon ass," Chlorine said. "But when I asked him to change, he assumed a nicer form." The princely man reappeared. "This isn't his real form either, but I am satisfied with these two forms. I like being a damsel with a dragon. Nimby is actually a crafted form of the Demon $X(A/N)^{TH}$ from whom all magic flows. I speak for him, and guide him, because my compass is small enough to concentrate on scenes and events that are for him like ants on a distant slope; it is an effort for him to focus on them. Your friends recognized him, and are properly amazed."

"Well, I'm not," Edsel said stoutly. "You expect me to believe that this donkey prince is the source of all magic?"

Chlorine glanced again at Nimby, nodding.

Nimby reached out with one hand, toward Edsel and Pia. The hand expanded, becoming huge. The fingers closed around the two of them. Pia screamed as they were lifted right out of the Leaf and through the ceiling, which fuzzed away. They soared high above the landscape of Xanth, whose outline looked much like the State of Florida, or possibly Italy, Korea, or some other large peninsula. The hand held them firmly, but the arm trailed into a mere string, as if they were being flown like a kite. Then the whole thing melted into swirling colors. They became two birds, flying toward a castle. Their wings beat in the air as if it were water. They flew into a window, into a chamber, where a woman walked who had a tiny moon circling her head. She glanced up, seeing them as they joined its orbit. But then they flew on, back out the window, and across the landscape to a great lake, where they dived down into the water and became two flying fish, touring a fabulous magical underwater setting where mermaids and mermen were just the beginning. Then back out to air, to the coast, which glistened like polished brass. On to another castle, and into that one, and to a room where six people stood. They landed, resuming their natural forms. They were back in the chamber with the others.

"Who was that woman?" Pia asked.

Chlorine knew whom she meant. "That was Princess Ida, whose moon has all the folk who ever did, ever will, or ever might live on Xanth. She's very perceptive."

"Yes," Edsel said. "She saw us."

"Ever *might?*" Pia asked. "Like whom?"

Chlorine looked at Nimby, then answered. "Like people Xanth doesn't have room for yet. Like Dol, the son of Magician Grey and Princess Ivy, whose talent is to turn inanimate things living. But they already have three children, so he must remain a might instead of an is."

"I suppose that makes sense," Pia said dubiously.

"There are also Xanth Waves from the future hidden on those moons," Chlorine said. "If they came to the Xanth of today, there would be amazing complications."

"For sure," Breanna agreed.

"And that brass coast," Edsel asked.

"In the realm of dreams, or the gourd, there live the Brassies," Chlorine said. "Men and women made of brass. They have set up a vacation resort in Xanth proper, near the Gold Coast, where things are less precious."

It was a persuasive demonstration. It might be illusion, but it had seemed real. "Okay," Edsel said. "We won't tell." He looked at Pia, who nodded agreement. "But just the brief glimpses we saw—would it be all right to use some of them in our software? I mean like maybe an animation of a Xanth theme park, with all the creatures of the land, air, sea, tiny moons, and magic? I think folk would love it, even just in a computer game."

"That would be all right," Chlorine said. "As long as there is no mention of Nimby."

That reminded him. "No mention of Nimby. But why does anyone with this much power want to go to Mundania in someone else's body?"

"There are other Demons," Chorine explained. "Most are associated with what you call planets, though their essence is not planetary but demonic. The demon X(A/N)TH felt no need of a lot of territory, so took only a small segment of one globe, leaving the rest to the Demon E(A/R)TH. But now, with increasing interaction between the denizens of Xanth and Earth, he would like to explore that other region. However, he has no magic power in Mundania, and the Demon E(A/R)TH might do him mischief, being resentful of his status among Demons. So he needs to do it privately. This seems to be an opportunity.''

Edsel was satisfied. "It works for me." He looked at Pia. "You?"

"Yes," she agreed faintly. Not much impressed Pia, but this session evidently had.

"Good enough," Breanna said briskly. "Let's take a week to set things up, and meet here again, when the four of you will exchange, and the four of us—" she glanced at Justin, Dug, and Kim"—will be your Companions, to keep you out of mischief. We'll have to organize special tours, so as to get the most out of it. Okay?" She looked around.

"Okay," Edsel said, feeling exhilarated. If a tour in magic Xanth didn't change Pia's mind, nothing would.

"Okay," Kim said.

"Of course," Chlorine said.

Then the scene dissolved, and the four of them from Mundania were standing at the O-Xone exit. Edsel hum-whistled, and they were back on their linked computers. Back in Mundania. Already it seemed dreary.

2
COMPANION

Pia had to admit that Edsel had come up with something interesting. She had been finding him increasingly boring, and marriage itself boring, but the magic Land of Xanth was interesting. She had privately envied Dug and Kim's ability to believe in it, and to submerge themselves in mutual fantasy. Maybe that was what made them get along so well: there was magic in their relationship.

Pia herself hardly believed in magic. But that demonstration in the O-Xone had satisfied her that there was something there. Maybe not magic, but one hell of a good show, like the effects of a stage magician. You could enjoy it even when you knew it was all trickery.

Best of all, if it turned out disappointing, it still committed Edsel to dissolving the marriage without a fight. That would make it much easier to recover her freedom. Edsel wasn't a bad sort, really, but if you took away that motorcycle, and his software, and his supposed humor, very little was left. She wanted excitement, novelty, fresh romance, and endless indulgence. Dug had come to bore her, years ago, and Edsel had seemed to be an escape from that, but Edsel had turned out just about as boring. While Dug, ironically, had grown more interesting after he got together with Kim. Maybe he had been about to turn the corner, and she had left him at just the wrong time.

But she would give this fantasy adventure a fair trial. She wasn't sure why Edsel thought it might change her opinion of their marriage, but that was his problem. She preferred to get free of him without suffering an ugly scene, and this was the way. Share the adventure, return, go their separate ways. It was a straightforward course, and a good one.

Now if only she could be as readily free of her diabetes. She had long since learned to give herself insulin shots; they really didn't hurt any more, and twice a day was enough. The blood sugar level checks were mere pinpricks, a nuisance, but again, routine. So apart from a certain caution about her diet, she could mostly ignore it. But she would rather be free of it. For one thing, it was likely to complicate things if she ever decided to have children, not that she expected to. Children were such demanding nuisances.

On the appointed day, their business in temporary remission, they sat at their computers again and connected via their modems to the Mode M Mesh. The three others were so enthusiastic that Pia found herself reluctantly carried along. Dug and Kim swore that there was no better land than Xanth, as long as a person was careful about dragons and such. Edsel—he seemed a bit much taken with that black girl, what's-her-name, with her lustrous waist length black hair, green eyes, and pert figure. As if Pia herself didn't have those same things, except that her hair was brown. Well, Pia's figure had filled out some in the past few years. She had to use a corset when wearing a show dress. She hated that, but she loved chocolate, and the two sort of went together. Her malady also tended to add to her weight, because she was constantly balancing sugar against insulin, and it was easier to eat a bit of sugar than to cancel a shot she had just taken. If she anticipated needing less insulin, then she could cut down, but life was full of ugly little surprises. So she was fighting a losing battle of bulge. Edsel hadn't commented, but she could no longer bend him to her whim as readily as she once had, and she figured this was why. Of course there was an age difference between the black girl and Pia, sixteen vs. twenty two, and she remembered how well Edsel had liked that age. Wait till time had its way with the girl, then see how pert she remained. But what was her concern? That girl was otherwise committed, and in a fantasy land, and if Edsel strayed—well, that would make the divorce that much easier.

They reached the O-Xone interface, and Edsel whistled them in. Pia had to admit it was a nice effect, the way it went 3D, making them seem to be standing in a hall. They ought to learn the secret, so they could incorporate it into the Companions software; it would sell a million. Assuming there still was a business, after the divorce.

They walked down the hall and entered the girl's chamber. Breanna—that was her name. Of the Black Wave, as if anyone could doubt her color. But she seemed nice enough, and they'd better get along, because there really *were* dragons in Xanth, and Pia had no idea how to avoid them.

Justin was there, as quiet as before. Then the gaudy dragon man and splashy damsel arrived. The odd thing was that the room didn't seem at all crowded, even with eight people.

"Some things we need to clarify," the damsel said. Chlorine—that was her name, like a chemical treatment—was taking charge, in her pushy manner, as she had before. "We shall need to remain in touch, in case it should prove necessary to end the exchange early. So we must report to this O-Xone each day." She glanced around, but nobody disagreed. "And though Nimby and I will not have magic in Mundania, the two of you will have talents in Xanth. We want you to have useful ones, that will help you get along without being so strong as to attract undue attention. So you, Edsel, will have the ability to create solid illusionary creatures. And you, Pia, will be able to see one day into the future. That should help you avoid problems, as you will be able to change that future by changing your immediate actions."

She would have a magic talent? This was becoming increasingly interesting. She would have to experiment, to be sure she know how to use it.

"Now let's make the exchange," Chlorine said. As she spoke, she and Nimby changed form, becoming exactly like Pia and Edsel. "Take our hands."

They held hands, then separated. That was all.

"So when do we change?" Pia asked, not really trying to mask her impatience with this ritual.

There was laughter, which she didn't appreciate. "Uh, I think we *are* changed," Edsel murmured beside her. "We're on the other side of the room."

She saw that they were facing Dug and Kim, though she was not aware of turning around. Beside them were Justin and Breanna. "But we're the same," she protested.

"I'm not sure. I feel better than I did, somehow."

"We provided you with bodies in perfect health," the other Pia said. "Except for your malady, of course."

Pia suppressed her irritation. Since this was really illusion, they couldn't cure the incurable. She checked her purse: her insulin kit was still there. So she was in her own body. Yet she did feel better. She had a recent scratch on her left foot that itched; it no longer did. She had meant to wash her hair, as it had started to feel grungy, but had forgotten in the distraction of getting ready; it now felt fine. Surely her imagination, yet enough to make her wonder at the power of suggestion.

"This way," Breanna said, turning to the door opposite the one they had entered by.

Edsel and Justin followed, so Pia had to go too. But she wasn't easy with this. Could this all be a fancy joke? Yet what was there to do except play along until it ended?

Breanna turned her head back. "See you here tomorrow for check-in!" she called.

"Got it," Kim called back from the far doorway.

Then they were on their way down a hall. As they proceeded, it gradually lost its square outline, becoming rounded. Soon it resembled a natural cave tunnel. What was the point? To show off the morphing abilities of the program?

The tunnel opened into a regular cave. There was a stream running through it, and a sweetness wafted from the water. Pia sniffed, trying to identify the tantalizing fragrance, and felt distinctly strange.

"Don't breathe too much of that," Breanna warned. "It's from a love spring."

Definitely a joke. But Pia stifled her breathing. She didn't know what the consequence of imbibing from a love spring would be, but doubted she would care for it.

They came to a metallic or ceramic or plastic contraption with a glassy screen.

Welcome, Visitors

"Hi, Passion," Breanna said brightly. "These are Edsel and Pia Mundane."

"Pia Putz," Pia corrected her, using her maiden name. "And my business associate, Edsel."

Edsel glanced at her, but did not challenge her statement. She was choosing to be herself on this excursion, not someone's disenchanted wife.

How very nice, the screen printed.

"And this is Com Passion," Breanna continued. "She is our inter-face connection to the O-Xone. And her mouse, Terian."

A lovely, sultry woman emerged from the shadow. She nodded, then faded back into obscurity.

"Looks human to me," Pia remarked.

Terian stepped forward again. She shimmered, and suddenly was a brown mouse.

"Eeeek!" Pia screamed, jumping back.

"What's the matter with a mouse?" Breanna asked.

"It might run up my leg!"

The mouse became the woman, who retreated again. Pia realized that she had made a fool of herself. She hoped she wasn't flushing.

Would you like to play some solitaire?

"We can't right now," Breanna said. "We have to go out and see Xanth."

Do return soon

"In a day, Passion," Breanna promised. "Thank you so much for helping."

♥ ♥ ♥ ♥ ♥ That was evidently the machine's way of expressing appreciation.

They stepped out into daylight. The sun was shining down on a thickly forested landscape. A pleasant path led away from the cave.

"First thing to remember," Breanna said. "When in doubt, stay on the path. It's enchanted, so that no harm can come to you on it, and it goes where you want to go."

"Suppose a person needs to—to do something private?" Pia asked. She wasn't sure how natural functions would be handled if they didn't take occasional breaks from the program. Her real-life body couldn't sit in front of a screen forever, no matter how realistic the effects.

"There are places along the path," Breanna said. "There's one now." She indicated a side path. "Want to see?"

"Yes." Actually it was about time for her afternoon shot.

"Okay." Breanna led the way down the offshoot, while Justin and Edsel waited on the main path.

Behind a barrier of bushes was an outhouse with a crescent moon painted on the door. Pia approached it and tried to open the door, but her hand passed right through the wood.

"It's illusion," Breanna explained. "Just walk through it."

Pia tried it. She passed through the wood and found herself in a surprisingly modern bathroom. How much of this was illusion?

She felt the toilet seat. Sure enough, it was a mere board with a hole in it, under the illusion. Well, that would do.

She took out her kit and pricked her finger, checking her blood level of sugar. Then she prepared a shot. She untucked her blouse and swabbed the fat of her hip. She always injected in the same place, and was almost immune to pain there. The shot took only a moment. Then she tucked herself back together, and put away the kit. She should be okay until morning, if she didn't overexert herself.

Breanna didn't inquire; she surely thought Pia had been attending to different matters. They returned to the main path, where the men stood.

A ghost loomed up before them. ''Booo!'' it cried.

Pia stifled a scream and stepped back, but Breanna was unimpressed. ''You're practicing your talent,'' she said.

''To make solid illusionary creatures,'' Edsel agreed. ''Justin reminded me. We need to get a handle on our talents, so we won't flounder when we need them.''

The ghost hovered, now properly harmless.

Pia concealed her annoyance at being frightened. ''I thought a ghost wasn't solid.''

''This one is,'' Edsel said. ''I can't make a real ghost, but this is a fake ghost. Go ahead, touch it.''

Breanna reached out and caught hold of the ghost's substance. ''Sheet,'' she said.

''Can you use such language in Xanth?'' Edsel inquired innocently.

Pia was disgusted. Him and his juvenile sense of humor.

Justin looked blank, but Breanna almost let half a smile escape. ''You can when it's a bed sheet.'' She yanked, and the ghost lurched forward. ''OoOo!'' it complained.

Pia touched the sheet. It was indeed solid. She lifted it up and peeked under. There was nothing; it was just material shaped over air.

The sheet dissipated, and the ghost was gone. ''I like it,'' Edsel said.

''You should check yours,'' Breanna told Pia.

''I thought she just did,'' Edsel said, with that feigned innocence again.

''Will you stop that!'' Pia snapped.

''Did he do something?'' Justin asked, perplexed.

''You were a tree too long, dear,'' Breanna said fondly.

"Indubitably. But—"

"First he implied that a word I said almost sounded bad, though it wasn't," she explained. "Then he made a comment that was similar."

"I don't understand."

Pia realized that the man really had been out of touch too long; he was truly innocent about some things. She liked that.

"I was suggesting to Pia that she should check her talent," Breanna said to Justin. "Edsel pretended that I was suggesting that she check her state of—of digestion."

"Digestion?"

"Girls aren't supposed to have digestion."

"Oh." He remained blank.

"You have a long row to hoe," Edsel said to Breanna.

"I'll get there," the girl said. "Now about that talent, Pia—they work different ways. Mine is seeing in blackness, so it doesn't apply in daytime. Justin's is voice projection; for a long time he needed it, because didn't have a mouth. Show them, Justin."

"As you wish," a nearby tree said.

Startled, Pia looked at the tree. It had no mouth. "Oh—ventriloquism."

"Not exactly," Breanna said. "Watch his mouth."

"I am speaking again," the tree said. Justin's mouth was firmly closed.

Pia nodded. "That is impressive."

"But yours should be more useful," Breanna said. "Because you should be able to see any trouble that's going to happen. But all talents have limits, and it's best to understand them thoroughly. What do you see in the future?"

Pia concentrated, uncertain how this worked. She closed her eyes. Then she saw a pretty shore, with pleasant trees by blue water. "It's just a scene," she said. "Trees and water."

"Do you see yourself?"

"No. It's as if I'm doing the looking."

"Okay. There's a limit. You don't see who whole scene, just what your eyes see. What happened before that?"

"Nothing I can see. It's just the scene. Now it's changing. Oh— there's Edsel."

"What about Justin and me?"

"I don't see either of you. Just Edsel."

"Can you hear anything?"

"No. It's silent."

Justin spoke. "This would seem to be purely an ongoing visual talent, perhaps seeing what she will be seeing exactly one day hence. That is indeed limited, but potentially quite useful. Perhaps Breanna and I are walking behind you at the moment. It is encouraging that there is no sign of mischief."

"I suppose," Pia agreed. She was somewhat disappointed; she would have preferred a more versatile vision of the future.

"Sometimes simple-seeming talents turn out to have important aspects," Justin said. "You should continue your exploration. I'm sure Nimby would not have given you an inferior talent."

"For sure," Breanna agreed.

Pia continued to watch, but all she saw was a dull travelogue as she and Edsel walked along the shore. Maybe it would be interesting when they were there, but with the sound turned off, it was like watching a soundless movie. She had done that once on an airplane flight, because she hadn't wanted to get soaked several dollars to rent germ-laden earphones for two hours. The movie had distracted, frustrated, and bored her something awful. This felt like that.

"Perhaps if you attempt to change that future scene, you would ascertain useful information," Justin suggested. He had a vaguely archaic mode of speaking that made him sound much older than he was. Except that he *was* much older, she remembered; he had taken youth potion. So he was after all in synch. But why was young Breanna so taken with the man?

"How do I change my future?" she asked.

"I should suppose that the mere decision to take a different course would be effective. A person's future is naturally determined by his choices in the present."

"All right. I'll do something else." Pia concentrated, determined to do something else.

But the vision of the future did not change.

They pondered that, but none of them could figure out how she could change her future if it refused to be changed. "I suspect we shall simply have to wait until we arrive at that point," Justin said. "Then perhaps we can estimate how we might have changed it, and what might be effective thereafter."

That seemed to cover it. They walked on down the path. "We don't have much of an agenda,'' Breanna said. ''We thought the first day you'd just want to see the local sights. Then tomorrow, maybe we can visit Castle Roogna.''

Edsel perked up. ''I'm not much on the geography of Xanth. But isn't Castle Roogna south of the Gap Chasm?''

''For sure. Chlorine arranged for a roc bird to carry us there. It should be a nice trip.''

''That's tomorrow?'' Pia asked. ''Is Castle Roogna by the shore?''

''No, it's inland.''

''Then why am I seeing the shore, tomorrow?''

That made the girl paused. ''Gee, I don't know. Unless maybe we ask the roc to take us to the Isle of View or something.''

''The what?''

''It's an island named View. Very romantic. Prince Dolph and Princess Electra got married there.'' Breanna smiled. ''I hear it was quite an event, because neither one of them knew how to signal the stork. But they must have figured it out, because the stork delivered twins.''

''I wonder if there's an Isle of View II,'' Edsel mused, his tone indicating that this was supposed to be funny. ''For the second time around.''

Pia figured it out: Isle of View I Love You. And I Love You Too. Romantic by definition. She didn't want to go there with Edsel; he would get ideas. So she would insist on the original tour, to that castle.

She looked at the future again. It hadn't changed. They were still wandering along that stupid shore.

''There's a sign,'' Edsel said, looking ahead.

The sign said RESTLING-BOXING-SOCKER. An arrow indicated another side path.

''That's probably not—'' Breanna began. But Edsel was already heading down it.

''He's like that,'' Pia said with resignation. ''Impulsive to a fault.''

Breanna shrugged. ''The side path's enchanted, so it should be safe. But these diversions aren't always what you expect.''

''This is true,'' Justin remarked.

They followed Edsel down the path. They came to a region where several men, women, and children were lying on the ground. They weren't sleeping, just lying.

''You folk okay?'' Edsel asked.

''Of course,'' the nearest man said. ''We are restling.''

"Wrestling?"

"Restling. We are finding out who can laze around the longest. The winner gets to do it again tomorrow."

"As we said," Breanna murmured.

But Edsel was already going on to the next. This turned out to be a group of people making boxes as quickly as they could. Boxing.

"Have you seen enough?" Pia asked in a moderately withering way.

"The Socker should be better," he said, moving on.

It wasn't. People were hurling stinking used socks at each other. The winner was evidently the one who could overcome the others with the intoxicating fumes. Several people were gasping on the ground, and others had purple faces.

"Go ahead, get in the contest, Ed," Pia suggested sweetly. "You could win hands down. Or maybe feet down."

He shot her a dark look. "You shouldn't try humor; it's not your forte."

But both Breanna and Justin seemed to be possessed of aspects of a smile.

They returned to the main path. There at the juncture was a female form so luscious it seemed like a crime. Edsel's gaze was immediately locked, and so was Justin's.

Pia exchanged a glance of annoyance with Breanna. Men were so superficial.

"Hi," Edsel said, approaching the figure.

"'Lo," the figure responded in a sultry manner. That was all there was; it was swathed in a toga-like wrapping of scintillating cloth, so that only the hourglass outline could be made out.

"What can I do for you?" Edsel asked eagerly. He was such a fool about women.

The figure began unwinding the cloth. Soon the face would be exposed. "I thought I might ask one tiny little favor."

"We're not looking to do favors," Breanna said. "We're a special party touring Xanth. So if it's all the same to you—"

"By no means," the figure said in dulcet tones. "It is very miscellaneous for me."

"It is what?" Edsel asked.

"Unlike, altered, contrary, deviant—"

"Different?"

"Whatever," she agreed crossly.

"The Demoness Metria!" Justin exclaimed. "I have heard of you. The demoness with a speech impediment."

The opening hood turned to him. "You have an obstruction with that?"

"A what?"

"Problem," Breanna snapped. "No, we don't have a problem with that. But we're not in the business of favors."

"Fortunately I wasn't asking you," Metria said, exposing her lovely face. "I was asking these handsome gentlemen."

"Anything," Edsel breathed raptly.

"Not anything," Breanna said. "We have other business."

Pia wondered why the girl was being so negative. The strip tease was annoying, but didn't seem to warrant such emphatic denial.

The demoness unwrapped some more. Her sculptured slender neck came into view, and the first divine upper swell of her gently heaving bosom. "I thought if you were touring Xanth anyway, you could take along my darling Ted."

"Ted?" Edsel asked foolishly, his mind evidently on that swell rather than her words.

"My baby. You have no idea what I went through to get him delivered. But now Demon Ted is three, and wants to explore Xanth." Her rose-petal mouth quirked. "Without his cadaver."

"His what?"

She unwound some more. "Corpse, carcass, deceased, embalmed, bandaged—"

"Mummy!" Pia said, before thinking. "His mummy."

"Whatever," the demoness agreed crossly. She unwound some more, baring an unbelievable bosom barely covered by a translucent halter, and proceeding down to a waist that was three sizes smaller than impossible.

"Sure, anything," Edsel agreed, his eyes spiraling down in concert with the unraveling winding.

"Acquiescence," Justin agreed.

"We're in for it now," Breanna muttered darkly.

"And of course his inseparable friend of the same age, DeMonica," Metria continued as the winding bared her expanding hips.

"Why not," Edsel said.

"What's wrong with three year olds?" Pia asked Breanna. "Not that I care."

"They're half demon," Breanna said tersely. "Ted has a human father and demoness mother, while Monica has a demon father and human mother. They're cute, but worse than any human children can be.''

"Well, let the menfolk take care of them. They're the ones who are slavering.''

"You ever see worse incompetence than a man with a baby?''

"Point made. The job will fall to us.''

"For sure.''

Meanwhile Metria was winding down to her splendid thighs. ''That creature could irk me, if she made the effort,'' Pia remarked.

"And she's not even trying.''

"So you folk will keep good eyes on them, and not let them get into any mischief?'' the demoness asked as her long symmetrical legs appeared. Their juncture was covered by another trifle of haze.

"Yeah, yeah,'' Edsel agreed. Pia wasn't sure, but it almost seemed that his eyeballs were smoking.

"Excellent!'' Metria stepped out of the last winding. ''Just for that, I'll show you my—''

"Don't show them your panties!'' Breanna cried.

The demoness paused. ''Why not? Aren't they of age? They will earn the glimpse.''

"Because it will freak them out, and they won't be able to do the job.''

Metria considered. ''You do have a prong.''

"A what?'' Pia asked, again before she thought.

"Pin, spur, tine, spike—''

"Point?''

"Whatever. So I'll just leave the little darlings.''

The demoness gathered up the strewn winding, dissolved into smoke, and separated into two blobs. The blobs dropped to the ground, dissipated, and revealed two children.

"I'm Ted,'' the boy said. He wore a little frilly pink dress with matching feminine sandals. His blond hair was tied with a red ribbon.

"I'm Monica,'' the girl said. She wore blue shorts and matching sneakers. She had large brown eyes, a turned up nose, and short brown hair.

But they were indeed cute. ''Uh, haven't you gotten something confused?'' Pia asked them.

The children looked at each other. Then they laughed together, and their clothing started to change. Soon he wore the shorts and she wore the dress. Her hair also lengthened to support the red ribbon, while his shortened.

Edsel came out of his haze. "What happened?" he asked.

"A demoness smoked your eyeballs," Breanna said. "Now we have a chore."

"Oh, yeah," he agreed vaguely.

"Let's explore!" Ted cried, dashing off. Monica followed.

"Stay on the path!" Breanna called after them.

Monica paused, looking back. "Why?"

"Because you're half human. If a dragon chomps you, you'll feel it. A dragon can't get you on the enchanted path."

The child made a cute moue. "Awww, okay."

"At least they will listen to reason," Pia said.

"For the moment. We'll have watch closely, though." The girl glanced at Pia. "Sorry about this. I tried to stop it, but—"

"But the men were idiots," Pia said. She liked Breanna better as she got to know her; she was just trying to do her job.

They followed the children.

"Hey, there's a B," Ted said, pointing.

"It's a rate," Monica agreed.

"What are they talking about?" Pia asked.

"The B's make the people they sting emotional," Justin explained. "A B-rate would make a person scold others."

Pia grimaced. "Sorry I asked."

"There's a Joy stick," Ted said, pointing to a little column beside the path.

"No, it's a Sad stick," Monica said. Indeed, the stick did look droopy.

They rushed on, losing interest, while the human party tried to keep up.

"Where are we going?" Pia asked Breanna.

"We thought you'd like to see some of the routine sights of Xanth. Like a tangle tree, a dragon, a centaur—sort of starting out easy."

"That will do," Pia agreed. "Aren't some of those dangerous?"

"Not as long as we stay on the enchanted path."

"Suppose those little demons run off it?"

"That's one reason I didn't want them along. But probably they'll stay close. Otherwise Metria wouldn't have left them. She does care; she has half a soul."

"Half a soul?''

"Demons don't have souls, because they *are* souls," Breanna explained. "When you use your soul as a body, it gets degraded, and you lose its finer aspects. So they don't have much conscience, and they can't really love. But Metria got a taste of what souled life was like, and got a hankering, and finally married a mortal man and got half his soul. It's sort of a convention; a demon who marries a mortal can have the better half. Then she has a conscience, and can love, in a half-donkeyed way.''

"But what of the man? Can he get along with only half a soul?''

"Oh, sure. It regenerates, in mortals. Not right away; I think it takes several months. But in time it will be whole again. It doesn't regenerate in demons, but for one of them, half a functioning soul is infinitely more than what they're used to, so they don't miss the rest.''

"What about the little demons?''

"They're half human, so I think they have whole souls.'' The girl paused. "Though I've heard of a demoness losing her soul when she had a mortal child; the baby gets it. So I guess I'm not sure. Maybe the offspring have quarter souls.''

Pia was curious. "Maybe we can find out. We can ask the children.''

"Yeah.'' Breanna put two fingers to her mouth and whistled.

The children paused in their running. "We didn't do anything,'' Ted protested guiltily.

"For sure. I just want to ask you something.''

They came back, somewhat warily. "Real people aren't supposed to lie,'' Monica said.

"I'm not lying,'' Breanna said. "But it seems that you've been into some mischief I should ask you about also.''

"Oh, no!'' Ted said. "Only one question.''

"The first one,'' Monica agreed.

"I'll ask the second one,'' Pia said. She had never thought of having children herself, but was becoming intrigued.

"Awww,'' they said together.

"You are both half demons,'' Breanna said. "How much of a soul do you have?''

"Which one?'' Ted asked.

"There's a difference?''

"For sure,'' Monica said, mimicking Breanna.

"Okay. How much does Ted have?''

"A quarter soul,'' the child responded. "Half of Mummy's.''

"And how much does Monica have?"

"A half soul. Half of Mother's."

Breanna pondered, then brightened. "I get it. You're each half human, but Ted has a human father and Monica has a human mother. So Ted shared a half soul, and Monica shared a whole soul. Nada Naga's soul must have regenerated after she gave half to Vore, before the stork arrived."

"Vore?" Pia asked.

"My daddy's Prince Demon Vore," Monica said proudly.

"D. Vore," Breanna murmured. "He has a notorious appetite."

"So Monica has twice the conscience Ted does," Pia said.

The little girl scuffled her feet. "I can't help it, you know."

"You sure can't," Breanna agreed. "Give me a hug, you darling creature."

"Okay." Monica hugged her. Pia felt an unfamiliar twinge of envy. Not for the hug, so much as the joy Breanna evidently took in it. She evidently liked children.

"Ugh!" Ted said, looking disgusted.

"Now it's my turn," Pia said. "What mischief is making you two feel guilty?"

Ted turned to Monica. "See? You gave it away."

Monica tried to resist, but it was evident that her extra burden of conscience was too much. "We found something," she said reluctantly.

"What?" Pia asked.

"Nothing important," Ted said.

Pia looked at Monica.

"But fun," the girl said.

"That could be anything from a stink horn to a basilisk," Breanna muttered.

"What's a stink horn?" Pia asked.

"I'll get one!" Ted cried, and dashed off.

"You don't want it," Breanna said. "Find out what they found."

"What is it?" Pia asked Monica.

The girl slowly extended one hand. In it was a small glistening object.

"Beware," Breanna murmured. "It could be something disgusting, like a slime ball."

"What is it?" Pia repeated, realizing that the warning was serious. She knew that regular children could have fun with bugs and goop, and these were half demon children, surely worse.

"A locket," Monica said grudgingly.

"Let me check it," Pia said.

The child handed it over. Pia inspected it. It was very light, only half an inch in diameter, on a silvery chain. She put her fingernail to the snap fastening.

"Caution," Breanna said.

Yes. "Is there something bad inside?" Pia asked the child.

Monica scuffled again, trying to resist her conscience. "No."

Pia opened it. Indeed, it was empty. "So what's so special about it?"

The fight against conscience intensified. The child seemed ready to cry.

"Maybe some compromise," Breanna said. "Dear, why don't you want to tell us?"

"Because you'll take it and we won't have it."

"But it's not dangerous, to you or us?"

"Not," the girl agreed.

"Suppose we make you a deal. Tell us about it, and you can keep it."

"Okay!" Monica agreed gladly, holding out her hand.

Pia gave her the locket.

"It's magic," Monica said. "It holds all of anything."

"But it's tiny," Pia protested.

"I'll show you." The child grabbed a handful of dirt and poured it into the open locket. The dirt went in and disappeared. She picked up a stone that was triple the locket's diameter and crammed it in—and it fitted.

"How do you get the things out again, if they have disappeared inside it?" Pia asked.

"You just wish them out," the child explained. "And you can wish them in, too, so what you have already doesn't fall out when you want to add something. You don't have to open it."

Ted dashed back. "Here's the stink horn!" he called, holding out a horn-like object.

There was a terrible smell, like a festering zombie whale with ballooning indigestion. But Breanna saved the day: she grabbed the horn and shoved it into the locket. Then Monica flipped the lid shut. The smell dissipated.

"Awww," Ted said, disappointed.

"But we'll have the stink horn for when we need it," Monica told him.

He brightened. ''Yeah.''

''But keep the locket closed, after this,'' Breanna said. ''We don't want that horn falling into someone's soup.''

Both children went into titillations of mirth. They loved the idea of such an accident.

''I hope we don't regret this deal,'' Breanna said. ''But that locket is the kind of thing children can really have fun with. It doesn't seem to weigh any more than it does empty.''

''It doesn't,'' Monica agreed. '' 'Cause it's magic. I told you.'' She dashed off with Ted, intent on finding more choice items to collect.

The adults resumed their walk. Edsel and Justin were waiting nearby, having their own dialogue.

''Look, maybe it's not my business—'' Breanna said, pausing artfully.

''Go ahead and ask,'' Pia said.

''I heard from Edsel that you two are married. But when you—''

''I said we are associates,'' Pia agreed. ''Because our marriage is rocky, and we want to get the feel of separation, in case we want to divorce.''

''Divorce! I haven't heard that word since—since I left Mundania. It doesn't happen in Xanth.''

''Oh? What do couples do when they don't get along?''

''But they *do* get along. I think there's magic. When I marry Justin, it will be for ever and ever until we fade out.''

''How can you be sure of that? I understand he's somewhat older than you. Maybe his interests are different.''

''He's about eighty three years older than me,'' Breanna agreed. ''He's from another time, and he knows all about trees and everything else I never heard of. And he's diffident to the point of aggravation. But I love him. That's all that counts.''

''That's *not* all that counts.'' Then, realizing that this sounded argumentative, she added ''In Mundania.''

''Maybe that's the problem—in Mundania. If you lived in Xanth, you'd never break up.''

''Even when the love is gone?''

''It doesn't go. It doesn't matter how different you are, once you love, you stay that way. If you're married.''

''I find this hard to believe. No offense.''

"Well, you're Mundane. No offense."

Pia laughed. Breanna's attitude was refreshing. She wasn't looking for a quarrel, but she simply didn't take any guff from anyone. "I am Mundane," she agreed. "And I don't think Edsel and I are going to make it. We made a deal: we visit Xanth, and if that doesn't change our minds, then we divorce. But I want to feel what it would be like to be single, so we won't be acting married while we're here. I want us just to be associates, and we can date others if we want."

Breanna shook her head. "That's weird. I can't imagine wanting to be with anyone but Justin. My only problem is I can't make it with him already."

"You can't—?"

"Technically I'm under the Age of Consent, so I'm not supposed to know what's in the Adult Conspiracy. But I came from Mundania, and I already knew that stuff before I came to Xanth. So I don't think it should apply."

"You're sixteen," Pia said. "That's old enough."

"That's what I figure. But Justin is of the old school."

Pia considered. "You love him—and he loves you?"

"He does. You can love at any age, or love someone any age. You just can't do much about it, in Xanth, if you're the wrong age."

"I appreciate your frustration. But you know, I was fifteen when I got together with Edsel, and we did plenty about it then. But now—the wonder is gone. I think we went too fast, too young."

"You mean you're siding with the Conspiracy?"

"I wouldn't go as far as to say that. But it does occur to me there might be some reason for it, in some cases."

The girl pondered a moment. "When you were fifteen—if you had honored the Conspiracy—would you be happy with him now?"

"Good question. I suspect things would me much the same, assuming we were married."

"So what would you have gained, honoring the Conspiracy?"

In was Pia's turn to ponder. "Nothing," she concluded. "And lost a lot of early fun."

"So what do you figure I should do?"

"Take him."

"I can't. All he does is kiss."

"Face to face?"

"What else?"

"To use archaic terms: you're necking. You need to get into petting."

"Petting?"

"Necking is above the neck. Petting is below."

"I know that! But I can't get into it, because—"

"I'll bet the Adult Conspiracy offers a bit of leeway in the in-between age. Why don't you try it and see?"

"But what exactly—if he won't—"

Pia realized that for all her professed knowledge, the girl had been stifled in Xanth, and lacked actual experience. She had the concept without the practical mechanics. "Don't *ask* him, silly. Just do it."

"Do it?"

"Get him alone. Maybe tonight. Take off your shirt. Hold his hand."

"Hold his hand?"

"Like so." Pia glanced around to make sure they were unobserved, then took Breanna's hand and put it against Pia's clothed breast.

"Oho!" Breanna smiled with wild surmise.

"I guarantee he won't ignore you. See how far the Conspiracy will bend. I think you will at least make some progress."

"For sure," Breanna breathed raptly. Pia felt good too; it was nice being reminded of the joys of early discovery.

They came to the first of the planned tour exhibits: a tangle tree. From a distance the thing looked like a drooping live oak. But closer in, she saw that it actually had long hanging green tentacles.

"You don't want to get close to such a tree," Justin said.

"But there's a nice little path leading right to it," Pia said.

"Yes. But observe." Justin picked up a small fallen branch and threw it at the tree.

The tentacles came to life. They caught the branch, wrapping around it and snapping it in two. Then they carried the pieces down to the trunk, where a huge wooden orifice opened. It chomped on a branch—then spat it out, evidently disgusted. The two children chortled together, loving its frustration.

"Trees don't like to eat trees," Justin said. "They regard it as cannibalism. I speak from experience."

"You were a tangle tree?" Pia asked, horrified.

"No, merely an ordinary tree," he said. "Sunlight and soil sufficed.

Until I met Breanna. But the birds and the bees kept me informed of the appetites of other tree species.''

"I don't think the birds and the bees informed you enough about flesh folk," Breanna said.

Justin looked uneasy. "Perhaps in two years—"

"Yeah." But the girl was plainly nettled. Pia could see that she had a legitimate complaint. Two years was an eternity to that age.

They resumed their walk along the path. "Next we shall pass a dragon's lair," Justin said. "Don't step out of the enchanted section."

"Why should we want to?" Edsel asked.

"The dragon's smart. It will try to fool you."

Edsel shrugged, figuring he was foolproof. That was part of what nettled Pia about him.

When they reached the lair, the dragon charged out, snorting fire and smoke. Pia stepped back, but Breanna caught her elbow. "Don't cross the line, even on the far side. It will hurdle that path and came after you."

"But the fire—"

"Can't touch you on the path."

Now she saw that there was no smoke crossing the path. It flattened out as if up against an invisible barrier, and wafted over the top well above head height. This was truly a protected section.

Meanwhile the two children were making faces at the dragon. Realizing that no one was going to step out of the safe section, the dragon snorted one last blast and retreated into its lair, as disgusted as the tangle tree had been.

"I am beginning to appreciate the enchanted path," Pia said.

"Folk who know the dangers can go where they want," Breanna said. "But visitors are restricted, for their own safety."

The day was getting late. "Perhaps we should camp, and visit the centaurs tomorrow," Justin suggested. "There is a suitable spot nearby."

They went to it. It was a park-like section, marked by a colored line so that no one would accidentally step out of the safe area.

"This is beautiful," Pia said. She hated to admit it, but this Land of Xanth was beginning to get to her. It was more interesting than Mundania, and it seemed quite real. Her body felt better than it had, as if she had taken a pill to invigorate her, rather than just a shot. She had had some doubt that she had actually changed bodies with Chlorine, but was becoming reassured.

"Yes, we try to keep the facilities pristine," Justin said. "We want all travelers to be both safe and satisfied." He paused. "Will the two of you be sharing a nest?"

"Nest?" Pia asked, confused.

Justin gestured. There was a large, plush nest nestled in the triple fork of a spreading tree. "A roc bird helped. You may be sure it is secure."

"But we are expected to sleep in a *nest?*" she asked, more amazed that dismayed.

Justin looked perplexed. "There is a problem?"

"Oh, that's right, I remember now," Breanna said. "They use beds in Mundania. I didn't think of that. But it's very comfortable, and there's a canopy if you want privacy. Let me show you. Come on in." She climbed up a vine ladder and disappeared into the nest.

Pia shrugged and followed. The ladder was flexible but firm. She was conscious of the two men standing below as she reached head height, but knew she had pretty good legs, so didn't worry about it. When she got to the rim of the nest, she heaved herself over, lost her grip, and tumbled into the center of the nest.

"Fun, no?" Breanna asked. She was sitting on the far slope of the depression. "You can even bounce." She demonstrated, and in a moment was bouncing high, as if on a trampoline. " 'Course you don't want to do that when there's a man watching; might show your panties."

"What's this business about panties?" Pia asked. "You told that demoness not to show them, and she listened."

"They fry men's eyeballs," the girl explained. "They freak out and can't do anything until the sight goes away."

"That's interesting."

"Your tone makes it sound like 'That's a load of dragon manure.' "

Exactly. "Men don't freak out at such sights."

"Not in Mundania."

"You mean they really do?"

Breanna smiled. "I shouldn't, but I'm a rebellious teen, so I'll show you. Watch this."

The girl climbed up the curving side of the nest and stood on the wide rim. "Hey, boys, look at this!" she called. Then she turned, bent over, and hoisted her skirt, showing her black panties. She was mooning them!

There was no sound. Curious, Pia climbed the nest and peered over the rim.

Justin and Edsel were standing below, motionless, eyes bulging, jaws slack. They were, indeed, freaked out.

The two children were giggling. "That's showing 'em, Blackwave girl!" Ted cried naughtily. "Black is the color of my true love's—"

The girl jammed a hand over his mouth before he could say a naughty word. "Wait till we get older, and I'll be able to do that," Monica said, seeming slightly jealous.

"And I'll be able to freak out," Ted agreed.

Breanna did a forward roll into the nest. That took her panties out of sight. The two men returned to life. Justin stepped back, as if catching his balance. Edsel sat down on the ground. Both looked dazed. Their eyes did seem to be somewhat hot.

"You boys okay?" Pia called.

"I guess," Edsel said. "What happened?"

"You freaked out."

"Freaked out? I don't remember anything."

Both children chortled.

Then Justin caught on. "Someone must have exposed her underclothing."

"Not me," Pia said innocently. "Go on about your business." She turned back to the interior of the nest.

"For the canopy, just pull the cord," Breanna said. She reached up, caught a dangling vine, and pulled. A neat canopy of living branches and leaves descended, making contact with the rim. This was now a shrouded round chamber. "Good when it rains, too."

"I believe this nest will do," Pia said. "Are there any sheets or blankets?"

"You harvest them fresh from a blanket bush. I'll show you." Breanna scrambled back up the slope toward the ladder.

"How is it that men are freaked out by panties, when it doesn't happen in Mundania?" Pia asked as she followed.

"It's part of the magic. There are lots of routine magical effects. You get used to them."

"What happens if a man sees a woman naked?"

"Nothing special. Oh, he's interested, for sure, but he doesn't freak out. I mean, nymphs go naked all the time, and nobody thinks anything of it. It's just certain items of clothing that make the difference."

They climbed down the ladder and touched ground. "Is this logi-
cal?" Pia inquired.

"What's logic got to do with sex or magic?"

That answered itself.

"I don't believe you expressed a preference," Justin said as they
passed him. "Will the two of you be sharing a nest?"

What the bleep. "Might as well," she said. Then realized that her
bad word had been censored out, even in her thoughts. Because she was
in the presence of someone below the correct age. Magic was everywhere.

They came to the blanket bush, where they harvested two nice blankets.

There was a swirl of smoke. It formed into a handsome male figure.
"A greeting, lovely ladies," he said, bowing gallantly.

"Oh, hi, Vore," Breanna said. Then, to Pia: "This is D. Vore, Monica's father. He must be here to pick up the children."

"Indeed. Metria brought them, I will return them. We are obliged to
be somewhat responsible, now that we are half souled." He looked at
Pia. "Have I made your acquaintance, luscious creature?"

"She's Pia Mundane," Breanna said. "I mean Putz. Does Nada
know you're flirting with visitors?"

"I'm not flirting," Vore said quickly. "I'm eating."

"Eating?" Pia asked.

"Devouring her with my eyes," he explained.

That was a pun, Pia realized. D. Vore—devour. "The children are
fine," she said. "They're around here somewhere."

"They have a magic locket," Breanna added.

"I will investigate." He vanished.

"Those children really weren't much trouble," Pia said.

"We were lucky, this time. Things could've complicated in a hurry."

They dumped the blankets in two nests. Meanwhile Vore had taken
away the children, and Justin and Edsel had harvested four pies from a
pie tree. They sat down on large toadstools by a glassy table.

"Don't tell me, let me guess," Pia said, observing the way the table
shimmered. "It's a water table."

"Of course," Breanna agreed. "And here's some milk." She set
down several milkweed pods.

Sure enough: the pies were good, and the pods contained fresh milk.

Breanna had chocolate milk. "I wouldn't want my color to fade," she explained.

That reminded Pia of something awkward. "I gather there isn't racism in Xanth."

"Not as such. But there's prejudice. For example, nobody much wants to associate with zombies."

"I should think not," Pia agreed.

"But they should. Zombies are people too, and they serve Xanth well. If you're ever in trouble, and you see a zombie, ask it for help. They're kind hearted. Their hearts are rotten, of course, but soft."

Pia wasn't certain whether the girl was joking, so she played it low key. "Rotten but kind," she agreed.

"Justin and I will be taking over Castle Zombie, when the Zombie Master retires," Breanna said. "Justin's going to be great."

"Breanna is already great," Justin said gallantly.

"You don't know the half of it," Breanna murmured.

He looked at her. "I don't understand."

"You will. We're sharing a nest and a blanket tonight."

"We are? I'm not sure that's appropriate, considering your—"

"My age? Would you want me to huddle all by myself alone in the great wilderness of Xanth?"

"Of course not. But—"

"Good. So finish eating, and we'll turn in."

Justin looked nervous. "I suppose if we sleep on opposite sides of the nest."

Pia kept her mouth shut. It was fun observing the interaction. Justin seemed like a very nice man, but Breanna was right: he had archaic notions.

They finished their meal as dusk closed. Then they went to their nests. "You know, poor Justin really likes that girl," Edsel said as they settled down. "He told me that it's all he can do to keep his hands off her. But she's too young, so he stays clear."

"Sixteen is old enough."

"I know that. You know that. But he doesn't know that. He thinks a girl's not a woman until she's eighteen."

"It's the Adult Conspiracy. But I don't think it's quite tight. I told her how to try to bend it."

"Bend it?"

"As in the distinction between necking and petting. I'm betting that petting's allowed at her age."

"Maybe so. Speaking of which, how about—"

"Forget it. We're estranged."

"Not until we finish in Xanth and you don't change your mind. Anyway, we've always fought, but gotten along great at night."

He had a point. Still, she wasn't sure. "Sorry. I don't feel like it."

He lay back, disappointed. Edsel had his faults, but he was a gentleman about sex. There was silence.

Then Justin's amazed voice carried across the nests. "Breanna! What are you doing?"

"Just holding hands, dear."

"Breanna!" He sounded shocked. "You—"

"Shut up and kiss me, handsome. Or shall I hold both your hands, like this?" After that the sounds muffled out.

Pia turned toward Edsel. *"Now* I feel like it."

He moved over immediately. "Exactly what did you tell her?" he whispered.

"Just how to hold hands."

"That's all?"

"Like this." She demonstrated with his hand.

"He's done for," he agreed appreciatively. "This is just like the old days."

"For sure," she agreed, imitating Breanna. "But remember: we're still officially estranged."

"Tomorrow," he agreed.

$\overline{3}$
MUNDANIA

C hlorine was nervous about this particular adventure, because it was the first one where Nimby—the Demon
X(A/N)TH—would not have his immense power of
magic. But he wanted to explore Mundania, and this was the only feasible way. Because each Demon was jealous of its territory and prerog-
atives, and had virtually absolute power within its domain. The intrusion
of any other Demon would not be welcome. So Xanth was sneaking in
to look around, and if D. E(A/R)TH caught on, there would be awful
mischief. Chlorine had begged Nimby not to do it, but he had insisted,
so now she would do her utmost to facilitate the visit and keep them
both safe. Because she owed everything to Nimby, and his will was
ultimately her will.

They walked to the exit door, and paused. "See you here tomorrow
for check-in!" Breanna called cheerily.

"Got it," the Mundane woman Kim called back. Then they turned
forward, and walked down the hall to the O-Xone Interface exit. They
passed though that—and Chlorine found herself sitting on a chair, with
her hands on a funny kind of board with a number of marked little
squares, staring at a screen resembling Com Pewter's. Her hands looked
wrong, until she reminded herself that she was no longer in her own
body. She was now a Mundane, among Mundanes. She hoped she survived the experience.

Words appeared on it. "Pia—stay where you are. Dug and I will be there soon. Kim."

But Pia was in Xanth. Then Chlorine reoriented. Of course—she was in Pia's body now, and was to be called Pia, to protect her real identity. And Nimby would be called Edsel. Because the Demon E(A/R)TH surely kept an eye on the Great Global Grid, and would soon know if Nimby and Chlorine appeared on it. They were here anonymously.

But Nimby was in another room, and she had to be sure he was all right. She got up and found her way out the open door to the adjacent chamber. There was Edsel, sitting somewhat blankly before his own screen. "Nimby," she murmured. "It's Chlorine."

He turned to look at her, nodding. He almost never spoke to others. He *could* speak, and elegantly, but this required him to focus on minutia, and he preferred not to bother. That was why she had to speak a lot, for both of them. But that was all right; it made her feel important.

"Nimby, remember, we have to be anonymous, here in Mundania. So we must answer to the bodies we are in. You are Edsel, and I am Pia. Our Companions arrived in another house, and will join us soon. All right?"

He nodded. She found it half a smidgen weird to be calling this stranger Nimby, but no weirder that it had been to see him change from dragon to manform the first time.

She sat in his lap and kissed him. "I love you, Nimby. But from now on I will call you Ed or Edsel. Until we are back in Xanth. And I won't mention Xanth, because that might give us away. We are Ed and Pia outside, but inside we are ourselves." He knew all this, of course, but it helped her to express it, making sure there was no misunderstanding.

They looked around the room, noting the distinctly Mundane look of it. Then they explored the house. There was a staircase leading to a second floor, with two rooms with beds, and one small room with odd ceramic or metallic objects that roughly resembled basins or a chair.

There was a muted rumble outside, and a funny box on wheels rolled up. They saw it out a window. Then doors in it opened, and Dug and Kim got out on opposite sides. Oh.

In a moment and a half, Dug and Kim were with them. "Okay," Kim said. "You are Nimby and Chlorine, right?"

"Yes," Chlorine said. "But we will answer to Edsel and Pia."

"Yes, of course." Kim paused, as if organizing her thoughts. "There are some things we need to get straight at the outset, so we don't get into mischief. For example, both of you can speak and understand our language, right?''

"Yes."

"Good. Because usually Xanthians can't understand Mundanian right away. But you're actually using Mundane bodies, so they must provide you with the language. But how much else do they provide you with? I mean, do you know where everything is?''

"We found the bedrooms," Chlorine said. "But there's one room with odd objects.''

"I think you mean the bathroom. You're going to have to get better acquainted with that, and the kitchen.'' Kim paused. "Maybe I'd better take you in, and then Dug can take Nimby in. Only as you said, we'd better not call him that, because—''

"Yes. Call us Pia and Edsel. We understand.'' She knew why Kim was hesitant, despite the prior reassurance: she knew Nimby's nature, and didn't want to insult him.

"Right. Okay, Pia, come with me.'' Kim led the way upstairs.

They re-entered the bathroom, and Kim closed the door. "Now this is the sink. You wash your hands here, or a pair of socks, or whatever. Same as in Xanth. Turn this tap for cold water, and this one for hot.'' She demonstrated. Sure enough, soon cold water was streaming from one nozzle, and hot water from the other.

"I thought you didn't have magic in Mundania," Chlorine said, impressed.

"We don't. But we have technology. Sometimes it's almost as good. In Xanth you just use spells to heat the water; here we use electricity.'' Kim went to the big metallic depression. "This is the bathtub. Its taps work the same way. You run the water first, and mix it, so you don't burn or freeze. I'll help you set it up, the first time.''

"But why bother?''

"Because you can't use a self-cleaning spell in Mundania. You have to take a bath or shower or equivalent.''

"Thank you.'' Chlorine understood the principle of a bath, though she preferred to swim in a magic cleansing pool.

"This is the tough one,'' Kim said, going to the funny ceramic object that looked vaguely like a chair. She lifted the wooden seat, and lo, there was a basin below, half filled with clear water. "This is the toilet. It's like the hole of an outhouse. You sit on it and urinate or defecate.''

"Into clean water?" Chlorine asked, horrified.

"Mundania is barbaric in some respects," Kim said, smiling. "No illusion to cover the sight or smell. Then when you are done, you turn this handle." She turned it.

Water surged into the basin and swirled around, then sucked down and disappeared. Then, slowly, more water came, until the bowl was half full again.

"What happens to the water?" Chlorine asked, repelled.

"It flows along a pipe underground, into the sewer. This is a kind of subterranean river that carries wastes away. No need to be concerned about it. Just make sure to use only this for this purpose."

They returned downstairs, and Dug took Nimby up for a similar demonstration. Chlorine feared he would be appalled, for normally he simply banished all wastes magically, or transformed them into toads. But he had wanted to find out what Mundania was like. This was part of it.

Then Kim took the next step. "Are you hungry? I must explain that there are no pie trees here; food is more complicated to obtain."

Chlorine decided not to struggle with that learning process just yet. "Nim—Edsel would like to see Mundania. The rest of it."

"We can show you. But I think it's best to start simple. There may be pitfalls, just as there are in Xanth." Kim paused. "Outside, I'll just say 'the other place.' You understand."

"Yes."

"We'll take you window-shopping at the mall, and maybe see a movie. I think that will be enough outside experience for today."

"We must purchase windows at a mill?"

Kim laughed. "Not exactly. I mean we'll just mostly look at things. And it's not a mill. A mall is a big enclosed shopping center. You'll see."

They went out to the box on wheels. Dug and Nimby climbed into the front of it, and Kim and Chlorine into the back. There were surprisingly comfortable couches, and they could see out windows all around.

The box came to life, with a rumble and a quiver. Cool air washed through. Then it rolled backward onto the paved road, paused, and rolled rapidly forward.

"This is a car," Kim explained. "Our second-hand Neptune station wagon, just about the safest car we can afford. It carries us where we want to go. No, it's not magic; it's an application of science. But we like it.''

Chlorine stared out in wonder. All around them other cars, small and large, were rolling similarly along the road. Most of the ones in the near side were going in one direction, while most of them on the other side were going the other direction. Every so often most of them stopped and sat still, for no apparent reason. Then they started again. It was almost beyond understanding.

They came to a plain where many of the boxes sat. They found a spot and sat also. They got out, leaving the car behind. ''But won't it wander away?'' Chlorine asked,

''No. It's a machine, and here in Mundania machines do only what they are told. It will wait here for us.'' Kim patted the Neptune on the nose. ''It wouldn't want to leave us anyway; we get along well.''

They walked into an unbelievably big building. Inside was a wide hall, and a big garden and fountain. Even Nimby was surprised. ''Your gardens are inside, while your hard floors are outside?''

Kim smiled. ''Sometimes. This is the mall. It's closed in so people can shop at the stores without getting rained on.''

They walked along the hallway, whose sides were filled with doors and big windows. In each window was a display of things. They looked. This was window-shopping, it turned out: looking without taking. The first window had shoes.

''But why don't they leave them on the shoe trees until someone needs them?'' Chlorine asked.

''There are no shoe trees here. Not the type you know. Shoes have to be made, just as pies have to be baked, and pillows sewn and stuffed, and just about everything else.''

''Mundania is stranger than we suspected,'' Chlorine murmured.

They came to a window with pictures of cold confection. ''Eye scream!'' Chlorine said.

''Ice cream,'' Kim agreed. ''Would you like some?''

Now she was hungry enough. ''Yes.''

They went into the store, and Kim asked the man for four cones. These came with colored balls of eye scream set in the tops. Kim gave the man a greenish piece of paper, and he gave her a few small coins. Oh—money. It had been mentioned somewhere along the way.

The eye scream was good. Chlorine made a mental note to come here for more, next time they got hungry. But she would have to see about the money, because she didn't understand the numbers and pictures on it.

They came to another type of opening. This one had a line of people passing a booth and giving money to a girl locked in the booth. "She is under an enchantment?" Chlorine asked. "Doomed to stay there until a witch lets her out or a handsome dragon-prince rescues her?"

"Not exactly. This is a theater. This is where they show movies."

"They show moves? Like dancing?"

Dug laughed. "I think we'd better let them see the movie. This one is a returning classic: *Stony Scary Painting Tale*. I'd love to see it again. We're just in time to catch the matinee."

"But you've seen it ten times already," Kim protested.

"So this will be the eleventh. It gets better with each repetition."

"It moves better with practice?" Chlorine asked.

"In its fashion," Dug agreed. He walked to the girl in the booth and gave her money, and she gave him four little pieces of paper. Then the four of them walked into the theater. A young man took Dug's four papers, tore them in half, and gave him back four halves. Chlorine took it on faith that this wanton destruction of what had been pretty papers made sense on some Mundane level.

Inside there were hundreds of seats jammed together, about half of them empty. They found four together in the center and sat facing a huge white screen. "Pictures will appear on that," Kim said. "Sound will come from all around. We will watch and listen, and think about how it would be for us to be those people. That's how we get into the story. And remember, it is a story. It's not happening, and it never really happened. But we can pretend."

"A story," Chlorine agreed, not sure she understood.

"A play," Dug said. "Done by illusion."

That made it comprehensible. The Curse Fiends did plays, and illusion was common in Xanth.

Then the light around them faded, and a picture formed on the screen. It was much bigger than life. It showed men riding funny machines with two wheels along narrow dirt trails. "Oh, this is a preview," Kim said. "Ignore it."

Then one of the wheeled machines was zooming right at them, filling the screen, roaring with sound. Chlorine cowered down, but it disappeared. It was, as Kim had said, just a picture. A moving picture. An illusion. She held Nimby's hand. He seemed to be fascinated by the effect, watching the machines zoom across dirt and sail into the air as they rode over hills. Probably he liked the feeling of magic, though Dug and Kim assured them that there was none.

"Well, maybe there is, in a sense," Dug said. "They take shots over and over, and over, to get them right, and they have equipment hidden beyond camera range, so as to catch flying men before they crash into the ground. But it's mostly fakery. Real folk can't ride cycles that way, and live."

Nimby glanced at him. Chlorine wondered what he was thinking of. She hoped it wasn't of riding zooming loud machines.

There were other frightening, odd, or incomprehensible "preview" pictures. One featured a villain hauling the hero high with a pulley, so that he dangled over a cauldron of acid. Nimby seemed fascinated by this too. "That's a geared block and tackle," Dug said helpfully. "It multiplies the pull. See, the villain can work it with one hand, lifting the hero's whole weight. Leverage is great stuff." Nimby nodded, making a mental note. Chlorine thought it was the physics rather than the story that intrigued him. But she wasn't sure. Nimby was interested in everything, and he had an inhuman capacity for assimilating new information.

Then print appeared on the screen. "Now the movie is starting," Kim said. "There are the credits."

Then the screen was filled with storm and rain, as a couple rode in their wheeled box—their car—through evidently unfamiliar terrain. They had to take shelter in a private mansion run by a Doctor Sam Sausage. After that things became more conventional, and Chlorine began to enjoy the story. Others in the theater talked to the screen, and helped things happen in response to their urgings. It surely would have been a lesser story if they had not been acting to enhance it. Chlorine liked their attitude. She made a mental note to try one of the dance steps it so carefully diagrammed. It was just a jump to the left, and other stylized motions, such as placing the hands on the hips. Very nice. She was glad they had seen this.

When the movie ended, they made their way back outside, where the day was unconscionably bright and warm. They got in the car, which was hot, but then it cooled. It rolled back toward the house, somewhat unsteadily. Had it lost the way? Chlorine had understood that Dug was in some way guiding it, as one would a steed. She glanced at him—and was amazed.

Dug was not guiding it. Nimby was. Nimby was sitting in the "driver's" seat, with his hands on the "steering" wheel. Dug was giving instructions from the other seat.

"Red light ahead. Depress brake pedal. Stop. Green light. Depress accelerator pedal."

The car leaped ahead. But Nimby did seem to have it under control, and soon the ride steadied. He turned the wheel when Dug said, and the car turned at the same time. In due course they reached the house.

Chlorine realized that she should not have been surprised. His powers of magic were greatly diminished, but Nimby had enormous powers of comprehension, and he was here to learn about Mundania. So he was learning to travel the Mundane way. He would be learning other things as they went, so as to understand the rules of this land.

Back inside the house, they tackled the kitchen. Under Kim's guidance, Chlorine succeeded in opening and heating a can of beans and spreading jam on slices of bread. Kim did much of the rest, but it was a start. Mundanian ways were distinctly strange, but she was catching on to them.

In the evening Kim showed them what she called the TeeVee. This was a box with a screen on front, and pictures formed on it, and sound came from it. It was like a very small movie. "You can watch news, sports, sitcoms—anything you want," Dug explained. "Or you can ignore it."

Chlorine found herself feeling increasingly vague and awkward. When she tried to stand, she fell back into her chair, unbalanced.

"Pia!" Kim said, alarmed. "Are you all right?"

"I don't know," Chlorine said. "I'm dizzy, and I don't feel good."

"The diabetes!" Dug exclaimed. "We forgot about that. She has to take insulin."

"That's right," Kim said. "She should have had her shot before she ate."

"Can you handle it, Kim?"

"I'm not sure. I know the principle, but I never saw her do it."

"Then I'd better. I used to help her, way back when she first was diagnosed and was learning the dosages and technique." He grabbed for Pia's purse and rummaged in it for something. Then he approached Chlorine. "Your body has a problem. A shot will take care of it. I'm going to have to get rather personal, but this is something you need to have, and to know how to do. Lift up your skirt."

"Lift?" she asked vaguely. This was not the kind of thing a man often asked a woman to do in company. But Nimby, who understood that she now had the same problem he had given her Xanth body, nodded. He knew she needed immediate help.

Kim reached across and pulled Chlorine's skirt up high, revealing her panties. Both Dug and Nimby saw, but neither freaked out. This was Mundania, Chlorine remembered, where things didn't work as they should.

"Ed, you need to know this too," Dug said. "Her medicine is in this ampoule." He was doing something with a needle. "She takes it in the high thigh, where it doesn't ordinarily show. This much, injected this way." He brought the needle down. "Pia, don't move. I'm sorry I'll be clumsy, so there will be some pain, but it must be done. You must trust me."

"I do," Chlorine said. Because she knew of Dug by reputation, during his visits to Xanth. He was sincere and competent.

Kim caught hold of Chlorine, helping her to not move. "Like this," Dug said, and jabbed the needle into her flesh.

Chlorine jumped and tried to get away, not in control of herself, but Kim held her down while Dug depressed the needle's plunger and the fluid went in. He was right: it did hurt. Then he pulled the needle out. "Swab," he said. "We need a swab. Should have used it before, actually."

Kim found something cool and damp, and dabbed the stuck place. The pain had been brief, and not that bad; Chlorine just hadn't been ready for anything like this. She pulled down her skirt. "Thank you," she said, somewhat weakly. She knew the awkward process had been necessary. She had been feeling really odd.

After that they explained in detail what Pia needed, and when, and how. Nimby was paying close attention, and Chlorine knew he understood. He would see that it was done. Already she was feeling better; the shot had indeed fixed her problem. It had also shown her how much she and Nimby needed the guidance of the Companions. Without them, this could have been quite serious.

Things settled down, and they watched the TeeVee and talked. Mundania was almost becoming familiar.

Then Dug and Kim got ready to depart, for their home was elsewhere. "Tomorrow we'll show you how to ride the motorcycle," Dug said from the car.

Nimby perked up. Kim laughed. "Yes, like the ones in the movie preview, only nobody in real life ever rides them like that."

"Ed would have a fit if his Lemon were treated that way," Dug said. "He loves that machine beyond all else."

"What, beyond Pia?" Chlorine asked.

Dug and Kim exchanged a glance. "You might as well know," Dug said. "Ed and Pia are not getting along well. So yes, he may value the Lemon beyond her."

"Their visit to Xanth is to give them a break from routine life, so as maybe to get a new slant on their relationship," Kim said. "We hope it works out."

"They're good friends and good people," Dug said. "Just not wholly compatible."

"Xanth has a way of making things work out," Chlorine said. "Especially romantically."

"We know," Kim said. "We hope it works on them."

Then Dug started the motor, and the Neptune moved out.

"This has been a considerable day," Chlorine said when they were alone. "Mundania isn't as backward as I expected, but on the whole I prefer Xanth. I mean, the other place."

Nimby nodded. But of course he wasn't here to enjoy Mundania, but to explore it.

"You're in a Mundane body, without magic, so you will need to sleep too. So let's get into bed."

They went upstairs and used the bathroom facilities. It was worse for Nimby than for Chlorine, because as a Demon he had not had natural functions, and in manform he had simply used magic to abate those he didn't care for. Now he had no way to escape them. She had to help him with the details. Fortunately, as a Demon, he also lacked a sense of privacy. She did not say so, but she rather liked having him dependent on her for help for a change. He would need help only once, in anything, but there would be a number of things to learn.

Then they got into the bed. "How are you feeling?" she asked by way of invitation.

Nimby shrugged. That left it up to her.

"Well, I'm tired and overloaded by new experience," she said. "But I've never made love without magic, and never in someone else's body, and never to a Mundane man. That's three to two in favor of doing it now. So let's do it."

So they did it. It was surprisingly clumsy and somewhat messy. But Chlorine didn't mind. She had wondered whether things would be as good without magic, and now she knew: they were not. She wondered why Mundanes even bothered to signal storks. But this also meant she would really appreciate it when they returned to Xanth. Now she had a basis for comparison.

"Are you sorry?" she asked him as they relaxed for sleep.

He squeezed her hand in negation. She appreciated that too. For all its negatives, this experience was like a honeymoon.

4
TALENTS

E dsel woke in darkness. He had not availed himself of the privy section before, and now he needed to. Pia was sleeping beside him; she being more sensible about such things, had no problem. What a delight she could be, when she tried! But he knew she was serious: she still intended to divorce him when they returned to Mundania, and he would not be able to protest. So he had to hope that something happened in Xanth to make her change her mind.

Because though his passion had faded somewhat in their years of marriage, he still did love her. She could be selfish and difficult and cutting, but she could also be wonderful. Tonight had been an example. She knew exactly how to please him, and she was matchless when she tried.

He got up and crawled up the side of the nest to the ladder. He was clothed; they had dressed again, after, as neither one of them was quite used to the ways of Xanth, and wanted to be ready for surprises. He climbed down and walked toward the privy. This was just a pit covered by illusion, but it served well enough. He could see, as there was a faint glow from the ground, maybe of magical origin. He liked the ambient magic of Xanth.

He emerged from the privy and paused. Had he heard something?

"Edsel," a voice called from the night.

"Here," he said, surprised. "Who are you? Where are you?"

"I'm Breanna. Here by the path. Come quickly."

He walked toward her. She was standing just beyond the path, in the darkness. "What's up? I thought you were with Justin."

"I was," she said. "But something came up. You must come right away."

"What came up?"

"There is danger. You must leave this place now. Come with me."

"Danger?"

"Yes. Hurry."

This was confusing. "I thought this place was enchanted to be safe."

"Bad magic is coming," she said urgently. "We must be well away before it gets here. At dawn. Far away. We must go."

"Without Pia? Without Justin?"

"Justin is finding a safe place," she said. "Get Pia."

He remained bothered. "Are you sure? I mean, to sneak out in the night—"

"I am sure. Quickly, Edsel. We must go. Be very silent."

"Okay." He returned to the nest. "Pia," he whispered, touching her shoulder.

She was hard to wake. It was her diabetes, he thought; when she went down, it was for the count. But he kept after her. "Pia. Wake up. We have to get out of here."

She stirred. "Huh? Didn't I already take care of you?"

"This isn't sex. Wake up. We have to go."

"You go. I'll stay." She pulled the blanket over her head.

It was a struggle, but he finally got through to her. She got herself together, grabbed her purse, and followed him out of the nest. They descended the ladder and walked across to where Breanna was waiting.

"What's this?" Pia asked. "We can't go outside the enchanted area."

"We must," Breanna said. "Danger."

"But—"

"She says it's coming here at dawn," Edsel said. "Bad magic. We have to clear the area before it gets here."

Pia evidently didn't have the mental coherence to argue. "Then let's get to where I can finish sleeping."

"This way," Breanna said, turning to follow a small side path. Small glowing fungus growing along the sides marked it.

They followed. Edsel didn't like this, but it was the job of the Companions to keep the visitors safe, and he had to trust their judgment. They had been right about everything else.

The path wound deviously through the night. Edsel had no idea where they were going. He wanted to ask, but didn't want to be too obvious about his ignorance. So he tried to lead into it by broaching a different subject. "How did it work out with Justin?"

"Justin is finding a safe place," she said.

She had said that before. "No, I mean last night. You know, holding hands."

"We do hold hands," she agreed.

"Not this way. Petting."

"We pet pets," the girl said. "They are nice."

Something was wrong. "Does this make sense to you?" he asked Pia."

"No. I don't think this is Breanna."

Uh-oh. But he had to find out. "Breanna, exactly what is this danger that's coming? We have a right to know."

"Danger," she said. "Coming at dawn. You must get far away."

"You said that before," Edsel said.

"Before," she agreed. "You must hurry, before the danger comes at dawn."

Edsel stopped walking, and Pia stopped with him. "We're not going anywhere until you answer a question: how did you hold hands with Justin?"

"We do hold hands," she agreed. "Hurry."

"Show me how," he said.

"This way. Down this path. Hurry."

"Hold my hand," he said. He reached out to catch her hand.

His hand passed right through hers without touching. She was illusion.

"It's a spook!" Pia said. "We've been tricked."

"For sure," he agreed. "And you know, she never said 'for sure.' She doesn't know about the hand holding. She's just a programmed image responding to verbal cues. I was a fool not to catch on sooner."

This was Pia's chance to say something suitably cutting, but she passed it up. "Let's get the bleep back to the safe area." He noted with bemusement that she couldn't say a bad word in the presence of even a fake underage person. That Adult Conspiracy was literal minded.

They turned back—but the path was gone. The lights had blinked out, but it was more that that; there was nothing but a thick tangle of briars there.

"I think I've heard of this," Edsel said. "It's a one-way path. See, it's still there, ahead of us."

"So's the spook," she said nervously.

Edsel thought as rapidly and well as he could, considering that his mind felt numbed. "It's a programmed spook. An image, with a few sentences keyed by our statements. We can't go back; maybe we should go forward. You know, pretend to be still taken in. So the spook won't suspect. Until we have a chance to get away."

"Do it," she agreed.

They faced the spook. "Sorry about the delay," Edsel said. "Let's go where we're going."

"We must go quickly," the spook agreed. "Before the danger comes at dawn."

"Yes, we must go," he said. He took Pia's hand, not for any naughty purpose, but because he knew how frightened she had to be, and wanted to reassure her. "The real Breanna and Justin will discover we're gone, and come after us," he whispered. "We just have to play along until then."

"Yes," she agreed, terrified.

They followed the spook down the glowing path. Edsel turned his head to peek behind them, and saw that the path was disappearing as they went. One way, indeed. This was an aspect of magic he would have preferred not to encounter. Even if they got free of the spook, how could they ever make their way back through that jungle? They were no longer protected from dragons or tangle trees.

The path continued interminably. Now Edsel had time to consider other aspects. Why had this trap been set for them? Whoever had set it up had known something about them. Their names, that they were visitors who could be fooled. The names of their Companions, from whom they were to be separated. But who could be behind this? Or *what?*

The path continued, and so did the spook. All they could do was follow. But Edsel kept his eyes open, watching for any escape, or even a hint of what they were caught in.

On and on. Edsel's legs were getting tired, and Pia was stumbling against him. The spook had been right about wherever it was they were going being far away.

The sky began to lighten. Dawn was coming. That was a relief; at least they would be able to see something other than the glowing path. But that would not necessarily be good news. It might merely clarify how bad the trouble was.

"What's that?" Pia asked, squeezing his hand almost painfully tight.

Edsel looked. A jagged line was forming in the sky. It widened and lengthened, and light spilled out. One end was overhead; the other was touching the horizon.

"The crack of dawn!" he exclaimed, catching on.

At that, the crack wedged all the way open, and light poured across the land. The spook faded out.

The path also faded. They were left standing on a brushy plain. Ahead of them was a dark castle.

"I think that's where we are headed," Edsel said.

Pia shuddered. "I don't want to go there."

Edsel looked around. "I see a stream—and a boat. I think we had better borrow that boat and get away from here."

"Yes."

They tramped through the brush to the boat. It was tied to a deserted cabin. "We must mark this place," Edsel said. "So we know where to return the boat." He didn't want to think of himself as a thief.

He untied the boat and held it steady while Pia got in. There were two paddles lying along its bottom. They took these and moved into the stream. Fortunately the current was away from the castle.

The stream carried them along; they needed the paddles only to steer the boat. Soon it debouched into a lake. The castle seemed to be on the edge of the lake, so they paddled the other way.

"There's an island," Pia said, pointing.

"Maybe that's the best place to hide," he said. "Until Justin and Breanna come looking for us."

"Yes." She seemed a trifle encouraged.

They paddled toward the island. "Maybe the real deadline the spook had was to get us to that castle before the crack of dawn," he said. "The way she vanished, and the path faded, when the light came—"

"Vampires," she said.

"But we delayed just enough to be behind schedule. So we escaped. They can't chase us in daylight. So if Justin and Breanna come before then, we'll be all right."

"We were such fools. We should have known."

"My fault. I took her at her word. I really thought it was Breanna, though I see now that she was obviously phony from the outset. Next time I'll know better." Assuming they got out of this fix. Pia's fear was evident in part by her lack of any cutting comments; she lost inspiration when nervous.

The island looked lovely, but Edsel did not trust that. He paddled around it, looking for anything suspicious.

"Oh, come on," Pia said impatiently. "I need to get steady so I can take my shot, use the toilet, clean up, and get the bleep off my feet."

Edsel didn't argue. Pia had to keep her shot schedule, which included checking her blood sugar. She had to have rest after exertion, or she would get out of adjustment. It could be dangerous to mess that up. So he guided the boat to an inlet with a small beach and drove the prow ashore so it would be anchored.

Pia stepped out first. He caught a glimpse of her high thigh as she lifted her leg, but didn't say anything. He still liked such views, though her legs were thicker than they had been. As her foot touched the sand, she paused, then completed her motion. Then he got out—and felt something like a mild electric shock as his shoe landed.

"You felt it too?" Pia asked.

"Yes. Static electricity?"

"Must be." Then she moved off to the bushes to handle her business, while he hauled the boat the rest of the way to the land.

There was a cluster of what looked like stalks of straw sticking out of the ground. Edsel had a notion, so he picked one and bit on the end. Sure enough: it was a strawberry. "We have breakfast," he announced.

"Good. I'm famished."

He sat on the beach and chewed on the straw. He tried to conjure a solid illusion, but nothing happened. He tried again, and nothing happened again.

Alarmed, he called to Pia: "How's your magic talent doing?"

"I haven't thought of it since yesterday, when all it showed me was a walk along a wooded shore." Then she paused. "Oh, no! I just realized that it's *this* shore. I thought it looked familiar, but didn't place it before."

"But that makes sense," he said. "You couldn't change that view—because it wasn't anything you were doing then that affected it. It was the spook in the night. If we'd said no to it, *that* would have changed our future."

She emerged from the brush. "That's right! Sometimes you remind me what I saw in you."

His cleverness in figuring things out, at least if they resembled computer programming in any way. His mind worked in flow charts, this leading to that, that leading to the other, and the whole process leading to a feasible process of software. "But I was a bit late figuring this one out," he said ruefully.

"I feel better anyway," she said, stopping to kiss him briefly. He liked that too; she had friendly little ways. Of course they didn't mean anything, they were just social manners.

"Have a straw," he said, handing her one.

She tried it. "Strawberry!" Then she looked as if she had just swallowed a pun. "And I just walked into that one. I think I could almost get to like Xanth, if it weren't for the abysmal jokes."

"They are more my speed," he agreed. "Not for decent folk. But about your talent: what do you see for tomorrow?"

She concentrated. "Nothing. It's not working."

"That's what I was afraid of. I think we've lost our talents."

"Lost our—how could that happen?"

"I can't be sure, but my guess is that static electricity shock we got. Maybe this island steals talents."

"That's crazy!"

"So is Xanth."

She nodded. "Point made." She stretched—another gesture he liked. "But I've got to rest. Why don't you keep a lookout for Justin and Breanna while I sleep. Then I'll stand watch while you sleep."

"Okay." The business of the talents bothered him, but he wanted to figure it out better before scaring her with his dark conjectures.

She spied a pillow bush, harvested several nice pillows, and set them on the beach. Then she lay down on them, closed her eyes, and slept. She could do that much more readily than he could; in fact he had trouble sleeping in daylight, even when he felt logy. As he did now.

He tried again to make a solid illusion, and failed again. It definitely wasn't working. So probably he was right: this island stole talents. That was why it was deserted; regular Xanth folk would know better than to set foot on it.

He found a suitable tree, sat in the sand before it, and leaned back against the trunk, looking out across the water. Justin and Breanna would have to come by water or air, and either way, this was the best way to see them. At the moment the lake was quiet, and so was the sky. There was just one puffy cloud relaxing in the sunlight, evidently having nothing better to do at the moment.

Idly, he tried to figure out what the cloud resembled. A mushroom? A squashed bug? A human face? No, none of those; it was just a blob. A face would have eyes and mouth and ears. Eyes there and there, and ears to either side, and a bulbous nose. Yes, like that.

Edsel blinked. It *was* a face! But it hadn't been before. It had been largely shapeless.

Could it be? With sudden excitement, he focused on the cloud. *Bug,* he thought. With six legs, and wings, and antenna, and huge bug eyes.

Slowly the cloud shifted, sprouting legs. The ears became wings. Two antenna grew at one end. And the human eyes became bulging bug eyes.

He was doing it! But just to be sure, he tried another form. Something that couldn't be confused for natural. A geometric form. A triangle.

The edges of the cloud fuzzed. The outline changed. It became a triangle.

"I have a new talent," he breathed. "The island didn't steal my talent, it exchanged it." He glanced at Pia, decorously asleep. "And it must have exchanged hers too."

Then he had a sober second thought. What good was shaping clouds? Sure, it could be fun, but it wouldn't feed him or get him un-lost. At least the solid illusions could have helped him scare off a monster. So he wasn't better off.

But maybe Pia had done better. He would have her look for her new talent, when she woke. Maybe it would be more useful than her original one had proved to be. One would have thought that seeing one day into the future would be phenomenally useful, but circumstances had nullified it. Maybe there was a lesson of life there, if he could figure it out.

Meanwhile, he pondered the likely rules of changes of talents. If the exchange happened when a person first touched the island, which seemed likely considering that slight shock they had felt, would it do it again if a person left the island and returned? That seemed likely, because the island couldn't be presumed to be intelligent. It just had this property of switching talents with whoever touched it.

And if the first time switched out his original talent, would a second time bring it back? Well, there was a way to find out.

Edsel got up and went to the boat. He pushed it into the water, then stepped carefully into it. He paddled it out a few strokes, then reversed and came back in. Was that far enough?

He brought it close, and stepped back onto the beach. And felt the shock. So he was right about that much.

He looked at the cloud, which was trying to drift out of range. He concentrated, trying to form it into a square. Nothing happened.

He tried to make a solid illusion. Nothing happened.

He pondered. So there had been an exchange, but not a reversion. So he must have a new talent, essentially random. He would have to figure it out.

So what could it be? He had lucked out the first time, idly watching the cloud. Now he had no idea. But maybe his contemplation of the cloud hadn't been completely random; maybe his new talent had guided him. Edsel wasn't much of a believer in lucky coincidences; usually there were reasons for things whose logic could be discovered by the right sort of search. This flowed to that, which flowed to the other. So maybe he should just let his mind drift, and he would come across it.

He sat down and leaned back against the tree. And the tree gave way.

He jumped up, startled. The tree had sunk a short distance into the ground. How could that be? It was solid; it hadn't done that before.

Unless his talent had done it.

Edsel pondered, then put his arms around the trunk and pushed down. The trunk sank lower.

That was it. He walked to a nearby boulder and put his hand on the top, pressing down. The stone sank.

Interesting, but what good was it? He was not a pile driver. And it couldn't be good for the tree. Could he reverse it?

He walked back to the tree, put his arms around it, and lifted. Nothing happened. So this was a one way talent.

"Sorry, tree," he said. "I didn't mean to do it. I didn't know my own strength."

Then he walked to the boat, lifted one foot to step into it, and hesitated. Would he make it sink into the ground?

He decided not to risk it. He nudged it onto the water, not ever pushing down. The water should keep it floating, as long as it didn't touch ground. He stepped in, and it didn't sink. So it was only when he pushed down with something other than his feet that the talent worked. That was a relief.

He paddled out a stroke, then back to shore. He stepped out. There was the tingle. Good.

He returned to the boulder and pressed down. It didn't budge. He looked up at the cloud, trying to shape it into a perfect circle. It ignored him, and fled beyond the horizon. He tried to make a solid illusion. Nothing.

Okay, he had a new talent. What was it? He returned to the tree and settled back against it, noting its solidity; the tree was now shorter than it had been, but still tall enough to reach the lower sky. So he hadn't done it too much harm.

His mind scanned the scene and the universe. No notion of a talent came to him. He tried guessing and got nowhere. Could he stir up a dust devil in the sand? No. Could he turn the sun green? No. Could he conjure a mint plant? No. Could he make the sand slippery? No. Could he make a protective shield around himself? No. Could he become a super vacuum cleaner that sucked up everything? No, and he was getting a bit crazy.

Suppose his new talent was something really specialized, that couldn't be tested here and now? Like making the evil cloud Fracto assume human form and walk on the ground? In that case he would not be able to identify it now. So he might as well assume that it was not of that type, and keep looking.

Could his talent apply to his mental ability, such as having a photographic memory? That would be great! But when he tried to remember what the scenery was like behind him, without looking, he couldn't. So that wasn't it.

Finally he gave it up. He didn't know what his new talent was, so he couldn't use it, so it was useless to him. So he would just fetch another talent.

He went to the boat, but as he shoved it into the water, his hand slipped, and it drifted out of his reach. "Bleep!" he swore. He would have to splash after it.

He stepped in the water—and his foot found firm lodging. Had he landed on a rock just under the surface? No, his foot was on the water.

Could it be? He put his weight on it, and set his other foot down. It too landed on solidity. He was walking on water!

Now that could be a useful talent. He wouldn't need the boat any more. He could even maybe carry Pia across a stream, if she didn't weigh too much now. So he would keep this one.

He caught the boat, and shoved it back to land. Then he stepped back on the beach himself—and felt the tingle.

Oh, no! He had lost the new talent already. Walking on water had counted as leaving the island, and so it had been exchanged. Bleep!

He tested it, just to be sure. His foot sank into the water.

"What are you doing?" Pia demanded behind him.

He jumped, splashing himself worse. "I was trying to walk on water," he said, shamefacedly.

"I've heard of arrogance, but this is extreme."

"I found out how to change talents. I was just able to walk on water, but I lost it." He went on to explain.

She was interested. "I can learn my talent by just relaxing and checking what occurs to me?"

"Maybe. It worked for me, more or less."

"Breanna told me about twins she knew named More and Less. Morton and Lester, actually. They have a joint talent to turn into humanoid crossbreeds, more or less human."

"Like elves or ogres? I hope we don't have that talent. But you can try for others."

"No need to egg me on." She experimented. Nothing happened. "I can't think of anything," she said, gesturing with the blue egg in her hand.

"Well, sometimes it just isn't obvious. Maybe we should just walk along the shore and see what occurs."

"As I foresaw us doing, yesterday," she agreed. She glanced at the egg. "What do I do with this?"

"Where did you get it?"

"I didn't get it. I—" She stared at it.

"You conjured it!" he exclaimed. "You can conjure things."

"Maybe I can," she agreed, awed. "I did think of an egg."

"You said 'Don't egg me on,' " he agreed.

She concentrated. "I want a pair of hiking boots," she said. Nothing happened. "I want an ice cream sundae." Nothing.

"Try another egg," Edsel suggested.

"But I don't want another egg."

A second egg appeared, in her other hand. This one was green.

"That's it," Edsel said. "You conjure eggs. That's all."

"Bleep." There wasn't even any underage person nearby, but now they were self-censoring themselves.

"But if you step off the island, you can exchange your talent for another."

"I'm game." She set down the eggs, and he helped her get into the boat.

"I think all you need to do is get your feet off the land," he said. "You don't have to go anywhere."

She got out of the boat. As her foot touched the sand, she paused. "I felt it."

"It's the exchange. Now to see what you have."

"I hope it's more useful." She looked around. She concentrated. "It's not summoning eggs, anyway."

"Right. And mine's not walking on water."

She laughed. "If you can walk on water, I can walk on air." She took several exaggerated steps.

Edsel stared.

She glanced down at him. "What are you staring at? My legs?"

"That too," he said faintly.

"Well, stop. I don't—" Then she looked at her feet. They were half a foot above the ground.

"You are walking on air," he breathed.

"Get me down!"

He caught her around the waist and hauled her toward the sand. She seemed to have the buoyancy of a balloon, and wasn't hard to bring down to the ground.

"Oh, I felt the tingle," she said.

"Because you left the island—and returned," he said. "Now you have a different talent."

"Just as well," she muttered.

They walked along the shore, as she had foreseen. When they figured out an unwanted talent, they took turns lifting each other off the ground and getting new talents. Actually, after the first time, Edsel was worried about Pia's strength, trying to haul him up, so he tried jumping. That did it too. Talents were flighty, here in the Isle of Talents.

"At this rate, we won't be able to hang on to talents we like," Pia complained. "We need some way to anchor good ones."

They came to a sign. CONFUSED? TALK TO THE TELLER

"What's the teller?" Edsel asked.

"Here's something," Pia said. She picked up a small disk from a pedestal beside the sign.

"Maybe it's the teller," Edsel said.

She held it up. "Are you the teller?"

"Yes," the disk said.

Startled, she dropped it. Edsel picked it up. "How do you work?"

"I announce your talent."

Edsel glanced at Pia. "This could be useful." Then he addressed the teller again. "What's my talent?"

There was a tingle in the hand holding the disk. "To turn things transparent, so that only their ideas show."

"Ideas?" But the disk was silent. It seemed it didn't qualify its announcements.

Pia took the disk. "What's my talent?"

"To become what is needed, while it is needed, when you know what is needed."

"I don't understand." But the disk was silent.

"This is nevertheless better than nothing," Edsel said.

"I suppose," she agreed doubtfully. "But doesn't it seem rather, well, convenient that we should encounter this helpful sign and disk right when we needed them?"

"You mean, like a path to a tangle tree?"

"Yes."

"Good point. Let's put it back."

She set the disk back on its pedestal and they went on.

"I don't think I like becoming what is needed," Pia said. "That might be a meal for a dragon."

"Or a sex object for an ardent man."

She had the grace to laugh. "That's not a talent. That's the state of being female."

"Then jump and change it."

"Then I won't know what my talent is any more."

"Um," he agreed. "Maybe we do need that teller."

"Maybe so," she agreed reluctantly. "But I feel as if I'm being herded."

"Yes. Let's take it until we get talents we want, then leave it and the island."

"Yes."

Pia leaped, exchanging her talent. But Edsel wanted to verify his. He looked for something to turn transparent. All he saw was the wooden pedestal they were approaching. So he focused on that.

It became transparent. Inside was the wavering image of a tree.

"It's a tree," Pia said. "Or it was. It still has the idea of its nature. That's sad."

"And I suppose if I tried it on a person—"

"Don't try it on me!" she cried, alarmed.

What, indeed, would become of her if he turned her transparent? These talents didn't seem to be reversible. This one could be dangerous. So he ended it by leaping.

Pia picked up the teller. "What's my talent?" she asked.

"To amplify noise."

"I don't like that." She leaped. "Now what's my talent?"

"Making paintings come to life."

She considered. "Maybe that will do." She kept her feet on the ground and handed the disk to Edsel.

"What's my talent," he asked.

"Waxing the moon's green cheese."

Edsel laughed, then realized that the teller was serious. In Xanth, the moon really did have green cheese on the side facing the ground. On the side facing away, he understood, it was milk and honey, because that was not polluted by the sights it saw. Thus a honeymoon was by definition to the far side.

But how was he going to get to the moon, to encase its cheese in wax? So this did not seem useful. He jumped. "What's my talent?"

"Returning things to their original state."

Now that seemed useful. He tried another question. "Where did this talent come from?"

"A boy named Reuben."

Who must have visited the island, and exchanged his talent before he knew. Too bad for him.

"Let's get away from here with what we've got," Pia said tightly.

"Keeping our feet firmly on the ground," Edsel agreed. He tucked the teller into his pocket, in case of future need.

They strode back to the boat, got carefully in, and paddled it away from the island. Edsel felt relief; the island had seemed nice, but eerie in its lack of people or creatures. Now he knew why: they didn't want their talents involuntarily changed. Those who did want change would come only long enough to get a useful one, then would flee, never to return.

"Where are we going?" she asked as they pulled clear of the cove.

He hadn't thought that far ahead. "I guess we had better return the boat. We don't seem to be finding much we want on the lake anyway. Then we can look for the enchanted path, and our Companions."

"They should be looking for us."

"So maybe we'll meet halfway."

She didn't argue, which meant she was as worried as he was. He did not want to get caught out at night. But how they were going to plow through that tangle of briars to get back to the campsite he didn't know.

Edsel felt something in his pocket. "I forgot to return the teller to its pedestal," he said.

"We can't go back now; our talents will change."

She was right. He would just have to keep the teller, at least for now.

They took the boat back to where they had found it, and tied it in place. Apparently no one had missed it, which was another relief.

They walked across the plain. "I think the camp is that way," Edsel said, pointing.

"Where the very thickest brambles are."

"Right. So we'll have to be a bit indirect. There seems to be thinner cover there to the side."

It turned out to be mixed field and forest, rather pleasant. But of course this was day; it might be another matter by night. They passed an apple pie tree and picked a ripe pie, and sat down to eat it.

"I'd better test my talent," Pia said. "But I don't see a painting to bring to life."

"Maybe you can draw one in the dirt," he suggested, half humorously.

"Yeah, sure," she said witheringly. Then she reconsidered. "The way things are literal, here in Xanth, maybe that would work after all."

"Sure." He cleared a place for her, smoothing it over.

She found a stick and drew a crude picture of a rabbit, with two huge long ears and a wiggly nose. Then she focused on it. "Come to life," she said.

The rabbit jumped out of the dirt and bounded away. Then it turned and bounded back, looking at them. It was lopsided, with brown fur, but definitely alive.

"You did it," Edsel said. "You made a living creature."

"See if yours works," she said.

He nodded. He spoke to the rabbit. "Return to your natural state."

The rabbit hopped onto the cleared dirt and flattened into the drawing.

"Oh, you killed it!"

That was an exaggeration, but he didn't argue. "Then bring it back to life."

"I will." She concentrated.

Nothing happened.

"You did focus the same way?" he asked.

"Yes! It's just not working now."

"Weird. I'd better try mine again." He looked around. Would it work on a fallen leaf? He picked one up and focused.

Nothing happened. So he tried it on a dead stick. Nothing. On a stone, with no result.

"Our talents aren't working," Pia said, annoyed.

"Let me verify this." He brought the teller from his pocket. "What's my talent?"

"Summoning birds."

"But that's not what I took from the island!"

There was no answer. The teller was not much of a conversationalist.

"Well, summon a bird," Pia said, somewhat acidly.

Edsel looked into the sky. There was no bird in sight. He tried anyway. "Bring me a bird."

There was a shuddering in the air. A distant cloud vibrated. A shape came zooming toward them. It was a bird, growing larger. Larger. And huge. Huger. And enormous. Enormouser. It threatened to blot out the sky.

"Get rid of it!" Pia cried, covering he head with her hands.

"I don't think that's my talent," he said with more bravado than he felt.

The monstrous bird braked in air, and they were almost blown away by its downdraft. It landed before them. It was bigger than both of them, by far. In fact it could have swallowed the two of them together.

It settled down, rocked a few times, and tucked its head under one wing. Now it most resembled a boulder, twelve feet high.

"It's a roc," Edsel said, catching on. "I summoned a roc!"

"A pet roc," she agreed, recovering.

"A pet rock!" he exclaimed, laughing.

Then she caught the pun too. "I should have known that's the kind of bird you'd summon."

Still, it was dauntingly big. "What say we just let it be," he suggested, slowly standing and backing off.

"Agreed."

They sidled away. The pet roc remained bird-napping. Apparently his talent had summoned it, but did not require that it remain with him.

Once they were well clear of the big bird, he tried again, this time specifying a small bird. Nothing happened. His talent had fizzled.

"Let me try it," Pia said, taking the teller from his hand. "What's my talent?"

"Making things thicker or thinner."

She glanced at a nearby tree. "Thinner," she said, touching the trunk with one finger.

The tree shook, and shrank. Suddenly it was half the thickness it had been.

She went to another tree. "Thicker."

Nothing happened.

"We seem to be blessed with one shot talents," Edsel said. "They change each time we use them. Fortunately we have the teller, so we don't have to guess what the next one is."

"That's the way it was on the island," she said. "But we haven't been jumping."

"I guess the rule is different, off the island. But I don't like this. We can't ever be sure of our talents. If we didn't have the teller, we'd be mostly confused."

"I'm mostly confused already," she said, but she made a quick smile.

Edsel pondered. "Give me the teller. I want to see what I have, and maybe keep it until I need it."

She handed him the teller, but then changed her mind. "Let me try it first. I don't summon dangerous birds."

"That's just the luck of the draw. Anyway, it is what it is; I just need to find out."

"No, I want to find out."

They were both tugging on the teller. "Okay," he said, compromising. "Let's both ask. One, two three."

"What's my talent?" they asked together.

"Making a wish come true," the teller said.

"But that's only one talent," Pia said. "Mine or his?"

There was no answer. The teller was good at that. "This is simple to resolve," Edsel said. "We can each make a wish, and see which one is granted."

"Do we have to wish out loud?"

"I don't know. Let's try silent, and if that doesn't work, we'll try aloud."

They each concentrated.

Edsel's Lemon motorcycle appeared, parked before him. He had gotten his wish!

He turned to Pia—and paused. She had changed. Her clothing had become ill-fitting, but she looked much better than she had.

She turned and saw him looking. "I wished for my sixteen year old figure back," she said, adjusting her apparel.

They had both gotten their wishes. Belatedly, he realized what that meant. "You could have wished we'd find our Companions."

Her eye caught the Lemon. "And you could have wished for something useful."

"I did wish for something useful! We can ride the bike instead of walking."

"On what highway?"

He studied the landscape with new misgiving. It was bumpy and clogged with brush. They could walk through it, but the motorcycle would be constantly balked. "Maybe there's a clearer area ahead," he said lamely.

"And maybe a gas station?"

Fuel! How would he fill the tank? He hadn't been thinking sensibly at all. Still, Pia had wasted her wish too. He was about to say something cutting, but looked again at her figure, and stifled it. She was stunning.

"Maybe something will turn up," he said. He went to the Lemon, checked it, and found it complete. He got on it and cranked on the motor. It roared into life. But he had nowhere to go. This wasn't an off-trail bike, and in any event, this terrain wasn't for any wheeled vehicle.

He killed the motor and got off. But he couldn't just leave the Lemon there. So he took it by the handlebars and pushed it forward. It was heavy, but he could handle it, and the rolling weight wasn't bad on approximately level ground.

"So have we used up our talents?" Pia asked.

"Must have." He took the teller. "What's my talent?"

"Bringing statues to life."

"But there's no statue here."

There was as usual no answer. "Maybe you can make one," Pia suggested. "The way I drew my picture."

Good idea. He parked the bike, took out his pen knife, lifted a stick, and carved it into a crude man form. "Come to life," he said.

The form moved. But it couldn't say anything, because he hadn't carved a mouth. He had wasted another talent.

"My turn," Pia said, taking the teller from his hand. "What's my talent?"

"Glaring daggers."

"It's got you pegged!" Edsel exclaimed.

She glared. A dagger shot from her eye and just missed his ear.

He ducked, alarmed, and the other daggers missed by greater margins. Damn the literal nature of Xanth.

He grabbed the teller. "What's my talent?"

"Controlling the emotions of others."

"Make Pia happy!" he cried.

"You fool," she laughed happily. "You just wasted another talent you should have saved for a mean monster."

She was right. He had once again acted without thinking. She couldn't be mad at him, because he had made her happy, but the damage was done. He handed the teller to her. "Find out yours, and use it sensibly."

"I will." She oriented on the disk. "What's my talent?"

"Summoning a friend."

She smiled. "Breanna!"

A figure appeared in the distance. "Pia! Is that you?"

"Here!" Pia called happily.

Breanna hurried up, followed by Justin. "We've been looking all over for you. We tried to follow your trail, but there wasn't much. Are you all right?"

"I am now. You know the way back to the enchanted path, right?"

"For sure." Breanna paused. "Pia—you look terrific. What happened?"

"I got my sixteen year old figure back. I'm your age now."

"And twice as sexy," Breanna agreed admiringly.

"Oh, I wouldn't say that," Justin demurred.

"Why not?" Edsel asked. But the man averted his gaze, embarrassed. Oh, yes: holding hands.

"We are certainly glad to see you," Pia said cheerfully. "We were lost."

Justin looked at the motorcycle. "What is that thing?"

"That's my old Lemon," Edsel said, with mixed feelings.

"I must say I never saw a lemon or any other fruit like that."

"That's its brand name."

"It was branded?"

This wasn't getting far. "It's a Mundane machine. I got it for a wish, but I can't use it here. In Mundania it could carry two people rapidly, a long way."

"Oh," Justin said, clearly not understanding.

"Let's get moving toward safety," Pia said joyfully. "We can explain everything as we go."

"Yes," Breanna agreed. "And we must check in, so the others know you're all right. It has been a day."

"But it will take time to get back to Com Passion's cave," Edsel said.

"No, we can do it now. I have an ear." She produced what looked like a human ear. "Speak into this. It's connected to the O-Xone."

Pia took the ear. "This is Pia. Ed and I are okay."

The ear quivered, so that she almost dropped it. "Good, so are we," Chlorine's voice came.

That was it. Pia returned the ear.

They walked through the brush. Edsel pushed the Lemon, unwilling to give it up, though he knew that soon he would have to. They caught the two companions up on their recent adventures.

"Oh, the Isle of Talents," Justin said. "I know of it, though never knew its location. But your talents shouldn't keep changing once you leave the Isle."

"We can use them only once," Edsel said. "Then we have to ask the teller to identify the next one."

"The what?"

He showed Justin the teller. The man shied away. "That's a demon!"

"A what?"

"A demon. They aren't all like Metria, you know. They can assume any form. Some specialize in specific mischief. This one must be changing your talents as you invoke it."

"Changing our talents!" Pia exclaimed, her happiness somewhat tempered by outrage.

"Yes. My guess is that it masks your inherent talent, drawing on its power to provide a temporary new one. Get rid of it, and you'll probably have your original talent back."

"Gladly," Edsel said. He dropped the disk to the ground.

It bounced back like a yo-yo, returning to his hand. Angry, he threw it violently away. It curved in air like a boomerang and returned.

He set it on the ground and put a rock on top of it. But when he retreated, it wiggled its way free and snapped back to stick to his sleeve.

"I suspect you can part with it only by giving it to another person," Justin said.

Edsel looked at Pia. They had been handing it back and forth. They had never tried to dispose of it. "There's got to be another way," Edsel said.

"There should be," Justin agreed. "Probably you can return it to the place you found it. That's often the way of such things."

"The Isle of Talents," Pia said. "Bleep!" Her magic happiness was weathering.

"Nevertheless, I believe we should return it there," Justin said. "Breanna and I do not dare to set foot on it, for obvious reason, so you will have to do it yourself. But we will help you in whatever way we can."

That made sense. "Then let's head for the isle," Edsel said. "We know where it is. I want to get this done and get out of here before dark."

"Not to worry," Breanna said. "My talent is to see in the dark."

"I don't want to get near that dark castle," Pia said.

"But there's no castle in this region."

Pia exchanged a glance with Edsel. "It disappeared when the crack of dawn came," he explained. "It may reappear at night."

"Sounds interesting," Breanna said. "But let's take care of the teller first."

"Maybe we can use the teller to help," Justin said. "If you care to run through several talents until a useful one turns up—"

"But why would it help us to get rid of it?"

"Demons aren't necessarily intelligent. Often they do what they do without thought."

So Edsel tried running through talents, and was in luck: he got the ability to find the very best route to any objective. "What's the best route to the boat?" he asked.

"That isn't right," Justin said. "You did not define the boat."

"Any boat will do, dear," Breanna said.

"Not the Censor Ship."

"For sure," she agreed. "But he's already invoked it, so we'll just have to see."

"This way," Edsel said with certainty, facing the thickest brush. "Toward the boat, in a small meander."

"A small meander," Pia said, but didn't protest, because the talents did seem to work.

They turned and cut through the brush toward the place where the boat was, as none of them cared to risk swimming in the lake.

They found a path, and followed it. That made pushing the Lemon much easier. But the path led straight to a tangle tree.

"We should have known," Breanna said. "You can't trust wilderness paths."

"But my talent indicates this is the best," Edsel said, perplexed.

"What's that caught in its tentacles?" Pia asked.

Breanna peered. "That's Para!" she cried. "The duck-footed boat."

"A what?" Edsel asked.

"We met it by the Isle of Women last year," Breanna said. "It was traveling between a pair of docks. It's really nice. We've got to save it."

Edsel appreciated the pun: pair of docks = paradox. "But what good is a—a boat with feet?"

"You'll see. This is the boat your talent led you to, and it's much better than the other. How can we rescue it?"

"Perhaps we can arrange an exchange," Justin said.

Edsel laughed. "How about my Lemon for the boat?"

"We can try," Justin said doubtfully.

Pia helped Edsel move the Lemon into position just beyond the range of the tangle tree's tentacles. Then he stood to the side, while she sat on it and smiled. Pretty girls made anything salable, and she was excruciatingly pretty now.

"Tangle Tree," Edsel said. "How would you like to trade this for that?" He gestured to the Lemon, then to the tangled boat.

The tree considered. Edsel could tell by the way its tentacles twitched. Then it released the boat. The boat promptly got its dozen or so feet under it and ran away from the tree.

"Para!" Breanna cried. The boat ran to her, and she hugged its wooden prow. "I'm so glad we found you in time."

The boat was evidently glad too. It curled its webbed feet and quivered.

"However," Justin said to it. "We feel that one favor deserves another. We have rescued you; will you transport us?"

The boat slapped a foot against the ground, and stood still. That seemed to be agreement.

Meanwhile, Edsel wheeled the Lemon toward the tangle tree. "Here's your bike," he said sadly. "Though I'm not sure what use you will have for it."

The tentacles shook. "Retreat!" Justin called. "The tree is angry."

Edsel quickly backed off. "What's the problem? We made a deal."

"I think I understand," Justin said. "There may have been a misunderstanding. The tree thought you meant Pia."

Oops. Pia had sat on the bike, decorating it, as he gestured to it. The tree would not have had much experience with Mundane marketing techniques.

"But I'm not about to be going to go get gobbled by that monster," Pia protested.

"Then it appears we are reneging on the understanding," Justin said. "That is not good policy."

"For sure," Breanna agreed. "We've got to work something out."

Edsel had a notion. "Suppose Pia uses the teller to get a talent that will protect her from the tree, so it can't eat her?"

"I don't want to stay forever in its tangles either," Pia protested. Still, she took the teller. "What's my talent?"

"Hearing anything close by."

She cocked her head. "I hear bugs talking to each other through their antennae," she said. "But that won't help me. What's my talent?"

"To be ineffably charming."

"That won't help me either! I—"

"Wait," Justin said. "It might after all help. If your talent is to be charming beyond the capacity of mere words to express, perhaps you could charm the tree into accepting the machine."

Pia considered. "Would I have to get within its reach?"

"I regret that you probably would, as the full measure of your charm is incapable of being verbalized."

"No, she could just let it look at her," Breanna said. "That's not words."

"Perhaps so," Justin agreed doubtfully.

"Well, I'll try it," Pia said, just as dubious. She stepped close to Edsel and the Lemon, and struck a pose. It was a charming pose. "Tangler," she said dulcetly. "May I call you that? I was just the decoration for the motorcycle, not the offering. It was a misunderstanding. But you know, that machine is as useful to you as the quack footed boat. I mean, you can't eat either one. But there's nothing else in Xanth like the Lemon, so maybe it would be a tourist attraction or something. So maybe it's a fair deal after all. Doesn't that make sense to you?" She smiled winningly.

Edsel stared. Pia had always been able to turn on the charm, when she wanted to, but this was moreso than she had ever been before. It wasn't just that she was lovely, in her sixteen year old perfect body. There was an intangible aura about her that made her ultimately winsome and sweet. Justin and Breanna felt it too; he could see them watching as avidly as he was. The magic was truly working. She could charm tears from a stone.

The tangle tree was feeling it as well; its tentacles were quivering, their tips curling and uncurling.

"And such a big, strong, handsome tree as you can surely afford to be generous," Pia continued. She adjusted her pose to show more thigh. Edsel wasn't sure that was smart, as it might just make the tree hungry, but he didn't dare interfere. "You wouldn't want to gobble up poor little me, would you?" The tentacles twisted in denial; how could they do that awful thing? "Because I know that deep down inside your vegetable heart you're really a nice creature." She stepped forward and took hold of the end of a tentacle. "Won't you make the deal, and take the Lemon, and let me leave with my sincere appreciation?" She lifted the tentacle to her face and kissed it.

The whole tree quivered and turned vaguely pink. Edsel acted on cue, and wheeled the Lemon forward. Several tentacles reached out to take hold of it, and Edsel retreated.

"Oh, thank you so much, generous tree!" Pia exclaimed, and hugged the tentacle to her fair bosom. The tree seemed ready to melt. Edsel felt much the same way. Pia was an utterly charming creature.

"Well, bye-bye, Tangler," Pia said, turning and walking slowly away. Her rear view was as compelling as her front view, as she well knew. The tree might not care about her sex appeal, however much Edsel did, but her charm was undiminished. The tentacles were limp with appreciation.

"I believe that does it," Justin said. "Very nice performance, Pia." The compliment was obviously sincere, as his eyes were halfway glazed.

"It was fun," she confessed. "Now let's get the bleep out of here."

"For sure," Breanna agreed. They climbed into the boat.

Edsel realized that the charm was fading. Pia had used up the talent. But she remained a lovely creature. How he hoped that this adventure in the Land of Xanth would somehow persuade her to reconcile the marriage.

He got into the boat. The duck feet got moving, carrying the boat and them along. He looked back to see the Lemon disappearing into the green mass of foliage. At least it had turned out to be useful.

5

COVENTREE

Pia turned back to wave at the tangle tree, and it actually waved a tentacle back. So it could see and understand, as many creatures and things of Xanth seemed to be able to do. She rather liked that; it was a considerable contrast to Mundania's perversity of the inanimate. She also liked having her beautiful body back, though she knew she would revert to normal when she returned home. Now if only she could get rid of the diabetes, and stay rid of it in the real world. But of course such fancies were foolish.

Meanwhile, Para the duck footed boat was transporting them to the Isle of Talents. The feet enabled it to cruise over land and water without pause. It seemed to be floating on land. Certainly it was nice to let her own feet rest. Edsel's temporary talent really had steered him right.

"I am curious about one thing," Justin said. "You folk mentioned seeing a dark castle in this general region. But we know of no castle here. Could you be more explicit?"

"It was just a dark outline against the sky," Edsel said. "And it vanished at the crack of dawn. So I think it's like the path: one way, by night."

"Did it seem inimical?"

"Seem what?"

"Hostile," Pia said, translating. "No, it was just there, and scary."

"The phantasm did not seem hostile either," Justin said. "It merely led you on, assuming the guise of Breanna."

"To whatever it was leading us to," Pia agreed. "I knew it was nowhere I wanted to be."

"This perplexes me. Normally the dangers of Xanth are not subtle. If the phantasm wished you harm, it should have done it as soon as you were clear of the enchanted path. Why did it go to the considerable trouble of making a protected path of its own to bring you to an apparent castle?"

"Protected path?" Edsel asked.

"It must have been, because you came to no harm in the night. There are many dangers in the dark."

"Oh, I don't know about that," Breanna demurred. "I like the dark."

"That is because your own talent is to see in blackness, dear girl," Justin said fondly. "So you can go about by night as readily as by day. But normal folk can't see well in darkness, so it is both more frightening and more dangerous for them."

"Are you implying that I'm not normal?" Breanna demanded archly. Pia noted that she was flirting, but could use some tips about how to do it better.

"Dear girl, you will never be normal," Justin said gallantly. "You are uniquely endowed."

"Endowed," Breanna echoed. "As in holding hands?"

Justin spluttered. She had scored on an awkward memory. Pia wondered how that scene had worked out. Probably it hadn't gotten beyond the "hand holding" stage, but maybe that was enough for now.

They passed a small creature, like a squirrel, with pearly gray fur, perched on a bright spot of stone, its little chin held high. "That's so cute," Pia said. "I wonder if it would let me stroke it."

"Don't touch it!" Justin said, alarmed. "That's a chin-chilla."

"A chinchilla? Their fur is—"

"No. It feeds on chili powder, and cools whatever it touches. Sometimes greatly. See the ice around it?"

Now she realized that the stone was actually ice. Just as well she hadn't touched the pretty creature. But they had already left it behind, and were coming up on another creature, that looked almost like a dog. But not quite. "What is that?"

"Laika," Justin replied. "Don't touch it either; they bite when afraid."

"Like a?"

"Yes, that's its nature: to be like a familiar creature, so that no one will hurt it."

Then they passed a region of balls. Some were bobbing up and down, while others were bashing back and forth. "The vertical ones are bowling balls," Justin explained. "They are very courteous. The horizontal ones are not nice at all; they are sock-her balls."

Indeed, one came zooming at Pia, just missing her and striking the side of the boat, and rebounding. It had tried to sock her. She was glad they were now in the boat instead of afoot; this could have been an awkward region to cross.

The boat reached the water, and splashed into it. The Isle of Talents was in sight. It looked as serene and innocent as ever. Which showed how islands were not to be trusted.

Para Ducks was much faster than she and Edsel had been in the other boat, and soon they were at the Isle. "Now how are we going to handle this?" Pia asked.

"Justin and I can't afford to touch the Isle," Breanna said seriously. "We'll have to wait here on the boat. And Para shouldn't touch either; he might lose his ability to float. So you'll have to go ashore on your own, get good talents, return Teller, and come back here."

Pia nodded. "That makes sense. But won't you folk be bored, waiting out here?"

"Sure. So maybe we'll hold hands."

"Breanna!" Justin said, blushing.

"They won't be bored," Edsel murmured. "How about you and I—"

"Forget it." She wasn't mad at him; she just wanted to maintain control. He was ever the opportunist. Anyway, this was hardly the time.

The boat drew up to a rock beside the water. Edsel stepped onto it, feeling his talent change, then braced himself and held out his hand to steady Pia.

They walked to the interior, searching for the teller's pedestal. "Before we leave it, we had better make sure we have good talents," Pia reminded him.

He brought out the teller. "What's my Talent?"

"You can modify or deflect other folks' talents."

"That's worth saving," Pia said.

"Yeah, I guess so."

She took the teller. "What my talent?"

"You can speak things real."

"What does that mean?" But of course the thing didn't answer.

"I guess you'll just have to try it to find out," Edsel said unhelpfully.

"What am I going to do—speak of a mountain of chocolate?"

A mound appeared before them. It was a small mountain of chocolate. She reached out and broke off a piece to taste. It was delicious.

"But now I've used up the talent," she said regretfully. "I can't speak anything else real."

"Sorry about that," he said, breaking off a chunk of chocolate for himself.

Frustrated, she addressed the teller again. "What's my talent?"

"To put wings on anything."

She considered. "How useful might that be?"

"I'm not sure," Edsel said. "There's no guarantee they could make anything fly. Take a person, for example: put wings on him, and he wouldn't be able to fly, because he would not have the muscle or the balance or the experience."

She trusted his logic. "Very well, I'll throw this one away." She looked around, spied a rock, and willed it to have wings.

Wings sprouted. Evidently startled, the rock flapped them wildly. It sailed up into the air and flew away.

"Then again, I could be wrong," Edsel said.

"Now he tells me," she muttered. But she doubted she would have wanted to keep that particular talent anyway. "What's my talent?"

"To know what is inimical."

"That will do," she said. "I won't invoke it now."

"If Justin's right, once we get off the isle without the teller, our talents will stay."

"Yes. Let's do it before we lose them."

They found the pedestal and set the teller on it. This time it stayed. They walked carefully back, never jumping.

In due course they reached the rock. There was the boat a little way out. Justin and Breanna were sitting in it, embracing. Actually she seemed to be sitting on his lap, and one of each of their hands was out of sight. "They are making progress," Pia murmured.

"For sure," he agreed, smiling. "That little girl could hold my hand anytime."

"Oh?" Pia inquired dangerously.

"Look, Pia—you said we should be dating out. Of course I wouldn't touch Breanna, because she belongs to Justin. But someone else—" He shrugged.

He had a point. If they were going to divorce, they needed to be trying other relationships. "Sorry. You're right. You can hold hands with someone else."

"How about a nude nymph?"

He was testing her. "If you can catch her, you can have her." She masked it, but he had succeeded in making her faintly uneasy. He had always been faithful to her, and it wasn't comfortable to give him leave to be otherwise.

They waved to the boat, and it paddled in. Pia braced against Edsel and stepped in first, then he followed. The boat moved out.

"So what talents do you two have?" Breanna asked eagerly.

"Knowing what's inimical," Pia said.

"Modifying or deflecting other talents," Edsel said.

"These are useful talents," Justin said.

"You should have seen the one that got away," Pia said. "I made a mountain of chocolate."

"And you left it behind?" Breanna wailed.

"Not entirely," Edsel said, producing a big chunk.

Breanna took it. "I love chocolate, especially black chocolate." She broke off a section.

"She has a fondness for all things black," Justin remarked. He glanced at her. "So do I, now."

Breanna looked at him. "So does that mean you want me or the chocolate?"

"Both are surely delicious."

She nodded. "Correct answer." She broke off a piece for him, then gave the main mass back to Edsel.

"This is supper, I think," Edsel said. "So we don't have to stop to look for a pie tree."

They pitched in, demolishing the chocolate.

"But we'd better test our talents," Pia said. "To verify, and make sure they don't fade." She looked around. "Anything maybe dangerous around?"

"Deep water's usually dangerous, if there aren't mermaids in it," Breanna said.

Pia dipped her finger in the water. It tingled almost painfully. She jerked it out. A big blue fish snapped at the spot her hand had just been.

"Loan shark," Breanna said. "They'll take an arm and a leg if you let them."

"I see," Pia said, shaken. "My talent did warn me, though."

"Do you still have it?" Edsel asked.

"Well, I hope so." She paused, gazing at her finger. "Oh—you mean the talent."

"That too."

She brought her hand near the water. It didn't tingle. "I'm not feeling anything," she said, alarmed.

"There may be no danger now," Justin said.

"But suppose there is, and my talent's not working?"

"That is an excellent consideration."

Pia's concern for her talent overrode her caution. She lowered her hand and touched the water. Nothing happened. There was no shark.

But after a moment the tingle started. She pulled her hand out, and saw a dark shape glide by below. "It's working," she said, relieved. "But why doesn't the shark go after the duck feet?"

"I think Para's feet are magically protected," Breanna said. "He goes everywhere, even the deep sea, and his feet never get in trouble."

"How do I test my talent?" Edsel asked. "I don't think I should try to mess with any of yours."

"A sensible caution," Justin agreed. "There should be opportunity to experiment in due course."

"So let's get the bleep on back to the enchanted path," Pia said. "I want to be able to relax."

Justin frowned. "It is now nearing dusk. Even with this fine transportation, it will require several hours to pick our way through the jungle, and it will not be safe at night. We would do better to find a place to camp, and make the return trip by daylight."

"I like traveling by night," Breanna said.

"You are competent by night," he said. "In more than one sense. But we others are not. We would blunder and bring danger on our heads."

She nodded. "Sometimes I miss my days of solitary wandering. Okay, let's find somewhere safe to camp."

"I have an idea," Justin said. "However, you may not agree."

Breanna shot two glances at Pia and Edsel. "He's usually not fooling when he says something like that."

"We'd better hear it, though," Pia said, curious.

"We could explore that dark castle."

Pia felt a shock. "You're right: I don't like it."

"What's your reason?" Breanna asked him.

"The phantom who led the two of them astray did not try to hurt them. The path did not lead to a tangle tree or dragon's lair. This suggests that the intention was not necessarily inimical."

"And we can check inimical," Pia said, catching on.

"Yes. It might be that there is something of interest to us at the end of that path."

"With our collected talents, we could try it," Breanna said. "And back off in a hurry if it looks bad."

"But the castle's gone," Edsel said.

"It should reappear at the crack of night," Justin said.

Edsel shrugged. "If it does, let's try it. It's not nearly as scary to me, now that you folk are here."

Pia agreed. The boat carried them rapidly toward the region of the castle as dusk loomed.

They passed a pizza pie tree. "We'd better harvest some of those for supper," Breanna said. "We can eat as we travel."

They paused and took a harvest break and rest stop. Pia, looking for suitable bushes, discovered a low wall or ledge, just the right height for sitting on. So on her return she sat on it—and suddenly all the knowledge in the world seemed to flood into her head. Alarmed, she jumped up and ran back to join the others. "Something—something—" she gasped.

Soon the others were looking at the wall. Justin sat cautiously on it. "Why this is a know-ledge," he said. "It provides much knowledge to anyone who applies his posterior."

"A seat of learning," Edsel said.

"Exactly. I must mark its location, so we can return when we need further education."

Meanwhile, Breanna was exploring the other end of the wall. "There's a window in it," she called. "It—OUCH!"

They ran to join her. "That is a window pain," Justin said. "Made from bad tempered glass, probably shattered in its childhood. It hurts anyone who touches it."

"Tell me about it," Breanna said, holding her hand. But she was not injured.

Then, with a boatful of assorted pizza pies, and several warm blankets and pillows, they rode on.

"Does Para need to eat?" Pia asked.

"Not that I know of," Breanna said. She tapped the side of the boat. "Hey, Para—want a pizza?"

There was no response, other than a slight weaving from side to side. That seemed to be an answer.

And as the sky cracked closed, shutting out the light, the castle reappeared. "There it is," Pia said, perversely glad to be vindicated. "There's the glow marking the path, too."

"Is the path inimical?" Justin asked.

Pia reached out toward it. "No. If my talent is working."

The boat got on the path and turned toward the castle. Soon the structure loomed large. It was on the top of a low hill, with a tiled stone avenue leading up to it. "Got to be illusion," Breanna decided. "Nothing solid could disappear so quickly."

"But why would anyone go to the trouble?" Pia asked.

"That's what makes us curious," Breanna said. "It's too much trouble just to gobble someone."

"Beware," Justin said. "Those tiles are gobble stones."

"I hope that's meant to be funny," Pia said nervously. The boat halted at the edge of the tiled surface; duck feet didn't want to be gobbled either.

"No, that is really their type. But they do not seem to be active at the moment. Does your talent indicate malignancy?"

"No. But I'm not quite sure my talent is working."

Breanna looked around. "There's a snoozing dinomite," she said. "Test it on that."

Pia looked. "I don't see anything but darkness."

"Oh, I forget—you can't see in blackness. Here, I'll lead you to it." Breanna jumped out of the boat.

"But just exactly what is a dinomite?"

"A reptile that blows up when annoyed. But don't worry; we won't annoy it. We're just checking your talent."

Pia reluctantly climbed out of the boat and followed the black girl to the side. There were no glowing stones or fungi here, so she would have been lost by herself.

"Here," Breanna said, putting out a hand to stop her. "Hear its breathing?"

There was a sound like the crackle of a burning fuse. "Yes."

"Reach toward it."

Pia reached toward the sound. Her hand began to tingle. "It's inimical," she said.

"For sure. So your talent works."

"Yes, but—"

"It's asleep," Breanna said. "I can see its eyes closed. Anyway, it wouldn't explode just for two innocent girls." She backed away, guiding Pia.

"So what would it do, if it woke?"

"It would merely chew us up and swallow us."

"What a relief," Pia said. But her attempt at irony was lost amidst her shuddering. Breanna had a nervy way of testing a talent.

"So now check those stones again, just to be sure."

Pia reached toward the path. There was no tingle. She touched a stone. It was inert. "No problem," she said, relieved.

They got back into the boat, and the duck feet waddled forward. The stones remained inert. "I conjecture that the stones become active only when there is a threat to the castle," Justin said. "We are obviously no threat. Most castles are capable of defending themselves when there is need."

"Even illusion castles?" Edsel asked.

"Evidently so." He paused. "But it just occurs to me that if the castle is illusion, so might be the approach. Those are probably not real gobble stones, merely the semblance of them."

"That's right," Breanna said. "You're so smart, Justin."

The man shrugged, pleasantly embarrassed. Pia was faintly envious; those two got along so well, despite their inexperience in romance.

Breanna turned to Edsel. "You said that phantom knew your names."

"Knew my name," Edsel said. "And yours, because she emulated you. But maybe not Pia or Justin's. I think I mentioned them first."

"Knew I was supposed to be your Companion," Breanna said. "So you would do what I said, if I said it was an emergency. Maybe that was about all it needed."

"Yes. I should have been more alert."

"How could you know? *We* should have been more alert. But we were too busy holding hands."

Which was a technique Pia had suggested. So she might have brought it on herself. "Anyway, we followed the spook. It was a one-way path; when we got suspicious, we couldn't go back."

"And one-way paths aren't common," Justin said. "There is formidable magic here."

Meanwhile the boat was climbing the easy slope of the hill. It was too dark to tell, but there seemed to be pleasant gardens surrounding the castle. Pia's talent gave no tingle; this was not a hostile place. Yet its mystery remained: why had they been lured here?

They reached the huge front gate of the castle. The stones of its construction were outlined in faint glow. Breanna jumped out of the boat and approached the gate. She touched it. Her hand passed through. Sure enough: it was illusion.

Then the girl walked into the illusion and disappeared.

"Don't go alone!" Justin cried, pained.

"It's okay," Breanna called back through the seeming wood and stone. "I can see clearly."

"We'd better follow her," Edsel said.

The boat moved slowly forward. The prow disappeared, and then the rest of the craft, as it moved on through. Pia was in the center; she flinched as the closed gate came at her. But the passage was painless; the thing about illusion was that she couldn't feel it.

Inside, the castle was lighted. They were in a long hall leading to a large chamber. Breanna was ahead, approaching that room. Pia felt no hint of danger. This was just an inanimate structure, illusion that it was. But what on earth for?

The boat walked along the hall. Decorative statues of people and things lined it, and there were a number of plants, too. This was a nice building, for all that it didn't really exist. But what was its purpose?

"I see a thyme being," Justin said. "Perhaps it is just as well that it is illusion."

"Just what is a time being?" Pia asked.

"It is a creature who occupies a patch of thyme plants, and is immune to their temporal influence. People will come to leave offerings, in order to obtain the being's help with their problems of time. Sometimes they have too much, sometimes too little. The being can fix that."

They entered the chamber. It was enormous, with tall arches and a dome over the center. The floor was clear, laid out in diminishing circles of stone. In the very center was what looked like a large manhole cover with a ring in the center.

They stopped here, looking down at it. "This appears to be an illusion intended to call attention to a subterranean cavity," Justin said.

"Then let's explore," Breanna said.

Justin and Edsel took hold of the ring and pulled upward. Slowly it came, lifting a hinged circular panel. Below it was a set of faintly glowing steps leading down into the ground.

"This, then, is the reality beneath the illusion," Edsel said. "The whole path and castle are designed to bring folk to this spot. I just wish I knew why."

"It is certainly a curiosity," Justin agreed. "It seems furthermore that it was you it wanted brought here, because the phantom knew your name."

"It couldn't have known me from Mundania," Edsel said. "It must have listened as we walked, and picked it up."

"Does it occur to you boys that the fastest way to find out is to head on down these steps?" Breanna inquired.

"Suppose the manhole cover slams down, sealing us in?" Pia asked nervously.

"Let me try my talent," Edsel said. "Maybe I can modify its magic, if it has any, so that it can't do that." He inspected the lid. "But this doesn't seem to be magic. It has no catch; it can't seal us in."

"Unless someone slides a block over it," Pia said.

"Who would want to do that?" Justin inquired.

"I don't know. I just don't trust this business of going underground."

They considered. "Maybe one of us should remain here," Breanna said.

"I would not recommend that," Justin demurred. "But perhaps if we divided into two parties, it would be secure."

"Which couple goes?" Breanna asked. "Which stays?"

"We can't let them go alone," Justin said. "We are their Companions. We must not let them get separated from us again."

"But then how can we make two parties?" she asked.

"Split the other way," Edsel answered. "Breanna and I can go down, while Pia and Justin keep the rear guard."

The other three considered that, surprised. They sent a glance around. Then a nod traveled the same route.

But Pia had a qualification. "I can check for what's inimical, so I should go where there might be something bad. So Justin and I should go down."

"For sure," Breanna agreed. "We'll watch for stray monsters of the night."

Pia set foot on the top step. There was no tingle. She tried the next. It was clear. She moved slowly down into the ground. This was like heading into a subway station. So would there be a train down there?

Justin followed her down, equally cautious. "Watch yourself with that sixteen year old creature," Breanna called after him.

Pia smiled. She had forgotten; she had her teen figure back. She *was* sixteen, physically. So was Breanna.

Justin, however, seemed flustered. He was not used to such by-play, having been a tree for so long.

They reached the bottom. A passage led past the base of the stairway, so they could go either left or right. Both sides were lighted.

Pia looked at Justin. "Does it make a difference? Neither direction seems dangerous."

"This is curious," he remarked. "It was a one-way path that brought you here, yet now there seems to be a choice."

"Well, let's try one direction, and if it doesn't work, we'll try the other."

"That seems sensible," he agreed.

They bore left. The passage widened, forming an alcove. In it was a picture or a display. It showed mountains covered in ice.

"There are icy mountains in Xanth?" Pia asked, intrigued.

"There are," Justin agreed. "I am not clear which range this would be, but the scene has an aspect of authenticity."

She peered more closely. "There's something about this scene. I thought it was a painting, but it seems three dimensional. It must be a model rather than just paint. Like a museum exhibit."

"A museum?"

"That's a place where things are shown, often in naturalistic settings. So the people can see them without having to travel to the ends of the world. But what's a museum-type setting doing here under an illusion castle?"

"This perplexes me also. I must confess I am having difficulty making sense of any of this."

Pia poked a finger at the scene. She touched the nearest mountain—and her finger passed through it. "It's illusion!" she exclaimed.

"Why so it is," he agreed. "No wonder it is so realistic. I had assumed that the illusion stopped at the surface of the ground."

"This is weird. It certainly seems to be here for us to see. But what's the point?"

"I confess the point eludes me."

"Let's go on. I sort of like mysteries, so long as they're not dangerous."

They walked on along the gently curving hall. Soon it formed another alcove, with another scene. This was of the mountains again, but now much of the ice and snow was gone. A river coursed away into the distance.

Pia touched it. This, too, was illusion. But it was also fine art. "Whoever made this really knew how to make a scene," she said.

"I agree. I have a certain appreciation for nature, having been a natural creature for much of my life. This is extremely well crafted."

"We are all natural creatures," Pia said.

"Why, that is true," he agreed, surprised. "I meant to say—"

"I know what you meant to say. And I agree. This person really knows his stuff."

"Indubitably."

Pia discovered that she was getting to like this archaic man. He was a gentleman in the classic sense.

They moved on, and came to a third exhibit. This was of a lowlands scene, with rolling hills and valleys. It was largely forested, with many odd trees.

"What are those?" she asked, pointing to several grossly fat-trunked growths.

"Beerbarrel trees. Their trunks contain beer. They are rather popular in some circles."

"You mean people get drunk in Xanth?" she asked, surprised.

"Some do. I confess I do not understand what they see in such activity."

"You never drink?"

"I drink water, of course. Or one of the myriad flavors of soda from Lake Tsoda Pop. Or milk, or boot rear, or similar. But I would not care for an intoxicant."

"Me neither," she said. Actually she had had her flings, back when she had really been sixteen. But it had complicated her diabetes, and she had learned better. "That goes double for boys; I won't go near one who's drinking, because he's sure to get ideas."

"Ideas? Of what nature?"

"Of a sexual nature."

"Oh." He seemed embarrassed. Lovely man.

Then she saw a small figure half hidden behind one of the fat trees. "Oh look!" she exclaimed, delighted.

"It seems to be a little man, or an elf, or fairy." He peered more closely. "No, I think none of these. I don't believe I recognize the type."

"It's a leprechaun," Pia said.

"Really? I have never seen one before."

"Maybe they are confined to this particular forest in Xanth. Their range is very limited in Mundania, too. To Ireland, I think."

"Ire Land? Are they bad tempered?"

"No, just very shy."

They walked on to the next exhibit. This scene was the same as the prior one, except that there were some ponds in the low sections.

Pia looked at Justin. "Does this mean anything to you?"

"The exhibit is very nicely done, but apart from that I see no special significance. Perhaps this is after a heavy rainfall."

They moved on to the next exhibit in the gallery. This was the same scene, but with several of the ponds linking into a lake. It was an attractive view, but some trees were being overtaken by the water; the bases of their trunks were covered. The leprechaun was back, and looking worried. "I guess I'm not one to make judgments," Pia said. "But maybe this is too much of a good thing. I mean, ponds and lakes are fine, but this was regular land."

"I agree. It is painful for me to see trees suffer."

The next scene showed a still larger lake, and several of the trees were dead. "If this is meant to be uplifting," Justin said, "it is not so, for me."

"Let's move on."

They did so—and came to the steps to the surface. "We have completed a circuit!" Justin said, amazed. "I was so taken with the exhibits that I didn't realize."

"Me neither. So it's one big loop. Six illusion pictures of two scenes. And that's it."

"I fear I still do not understand the rationale."

Pia agreed. "Maybe I'm too bleeping suspicious, but I can't believe that this is all there is. Do you think it's a test, or something?"

"A test?" he asked blankly.

"To find out just how smart we are. See if we have the wit to figure out the real situation."

"I suppose that could be the case. I confess feel rather unintelligent at this stage."

Pia realized that Edsel probably could have figured it out. He was good at puzzles. She wanted to prove that she could figure out something on her own, before appealing to him for help. "There must be something we're missing. We have to prove we're smart enough to figure it out."

"This may indeed be a challenge. But my mind is not apt at such riddles."

"Let's see: we made a loop and saw six exhibits. They're in a big circle. Could there be something inside that circle?"

"That seems to be a fair possibility. But I saw no access to it."

"Right. No tunnels going anywhere. Just those illusion pictures." Then she had a bright idea—and was amazed to see a light bulb form and flash, about two feet before and above her face.

"You have a bright notion," Justin said.

"Yes," she said, recovering from her surprise. "These pictures are illusion, right? So they're not solid. There could be something behind them."

"Behind them? I should think merely the wall."

"How do we know? There could be another passage. We wouldn't see it, because it would be covered by the illusion."

"Why I believe you are correct. It is certainly possible."

"So let's go look." She forged on toward the first of the exhibits.

Justin followed. "Actually, there could be other passages from this one, covered by illusion. But your notion is certainly viable."

They reached the snowy mountain view. Pia reached into it. The snow wasn't cold; there was no sensation, and no tingle of danger. She lifted a foot and stepped into it. As her head entered the illusion, she became blind; there was nothing but fog in view.

She backed out, and the passage reappeared. "I'm not Breanna. I can't seen in the dark. That scares me. I mean, suppose there's a pit and a pendulum?"

"A pendulum?"

"Never mind. What I mean is that there could be something dangerous in there. Maybe not inimical, but not good to go into blind, like a drop-off. Because folk aren't expected to walk through the illusions. Anyway, it makes me distinctly nervous."

"A sobering prospect," Justin agreed. "It may be unfortunate we lack a rope, so that we could protect ourselves from a possible fall."

"Yes." Pia remained unwilling to give up on it, but what else was there to do? Then a second bulb flashed. "Clothing!"

"I beg your pardon?"

"We could knot our clothes together to make a rope. Maybe not a long one, but maybe enough. I saw that trick in a movie once."

"A what?"

"Never mind. Let's try it."

"I am afraid I don't—"

He was truly diffident, which was one big reason she felt free to try it. "We take off our clothes and tie them end to end to make a crude rope. One of us can hold it while the other goes ahead. So there won't be a fall."

"Why, I suppose that could work. But—"

She understood his reticence. "You feel it would be bad to see each other naked?"

"That is a matter of concern," he confessed.

"You've seen it before, haven't you?"

"I beg your pardon?"

"You have seen Breanna nude."

"Well, yes, actually. Technically. On occasion she has insisted on bathing in my presence. But—"

"I'm much the same, only a different color. Anyway, we'll be in illusion, so won't see much for long. Let's do it. We don't want the others to worry because we're taking too long." She found she was enjoying this. It was a kind of adventure. She was rather proud of her restored body, too.

"I suppose that is true. Perhaps Breanna would understand."

"Sure she will." Maybe too well, but Pia did not find it necessary to say that. She pulled off her blouse and stood in her bra.

Justin's eyes bulged dangerously, but he managed to squeeze them back into shape. That didn't bother her at all; she liked making an impression, especially when it was risk free. He visibly nerved himself and removed his own shirt.

Pia stepped out of her skirt.

Justin froze. He didn't move at all. After a moment, she inquired. "Justin—are you all right?"

He didn't answer. He just stood there, his eyes glazing over.

Then she realized: he had freaked out! She had overdone it, forgetting about the magic effect a girl's panties had on men in Xanth.

What was she to do? They needed all their outer clothing to make the rope. But if he couldn't function while her skirt was off, that wouldn't work.

She remembered something Breanna had said: nymphs ran nude all the time, and didn't freak out men, though they did attract considerable attention. So would Justin un-freak-out if she went all the way naked? Maybe so, but she did not care to risk it. Even if it worked, her purpose could be misunderstood. She did not want to make an enemy of Breanna. So what else was there?

Maybe she could hide her lower body under the illusion. Then he would be all right, until they were through. Once they were through, they could dress again. That seemed to be the best course.

She walked into the picture, centering on one of the mountains. The floor seemed level beneath the picture; her footing was firm. She could see the illusion up to her waist. Now she called again to him. "Justin!"

He blinked, and his eyes lost their glaze. "I beg pardon; I must have been thinking of something else. What were we doing?"

He had no awareness of the freakout. She would not enlighten him. "We were getting out of our clothing so we could knot it into a rope. I tried stepping in, and it seems okay. How about you take off your trousers?"

Justin got out of his trousers. He stood there somewhat blankly.

"Okay, now let's tie them," Pia said. She suspected that though her bra was not freaking him out, it was having some effect, so he needed to be guided. It would probably be best not to lean forward. She rather liked this aspect of Xanth, now that she was working through it; it gave a woman control of a situation.

He knotted the clothing together securely, and had a clumsy kind of rope. "Now give me one end," she said. "And follow me through the illusion."

Pia held on to one end and stepped deeper into the scene. Justin clung to the other end, bracing in case he had to take her weight suddenly.

Her face entered a higher mountain. It was like walking into pea-soup fog. She could not see her free hand two feet before her eyes. But the footing remained firm, and that was what counted.

Suddenly she was out of the fog, and standing behind the illusion scene. She saw the backs of the mountains and glaciers.

Then the rope went slack, and Justin stepped out of the scene. Now it was his jaw that went slack as he froze in place.

Oh, that again. Well, they were safely through, and there had been no pitfall. Pia un-knotted the clothing and slipped her skirt back on.

"Justin," she said.

He returned to animation. "Was I woolgathering again? I must be more tired than I thought."

"No problem. We are through the illusion without trouble, so can put our things back on." She handed him his trousers.

"To be sure." He put on pants and shirt while Pia put on her rumpled shirt. She wondered idly why there was no similar effect on women. The sight of his underpants hadn't freaked her out at all. Maybe women were simply more sensible, or maybe they had better assets. She could see it either way, preferably both ways.

Now they considered what next. There was another passage opening out to either side behind the picture. Probably an inner ring, servicing the six settings. But was that all?

They walked around the ring, seeing the settings from the rear. That was all. "I suspect that we have not yet fathomed the riddle," Justin said.

"I agree. There must be more. But maybe we have established that this is a safe place to spend the night."

"Should we return to the others?" Justin asked hopefully.

Pia was tempted, but uncertain. "How can we be sure this is safe without a rear guard, until we know more about who set it up and why?"

"Alas, I fear you are correct."

"But maybe we should let them know we are working on it."

"Yes," he agreed eagerly.

They walked through the icy mountain scene, not making the rope now that they knew it was safe. Soon they mounted the steps. "It seems safe," Pia said. "But there's more to check. Can you folk hold on a while longer?"

"Sure," Edsel said. "Breanna's fascinating."

"He's just teasing," Pia whispered to Justin. "He does that."

"Oh. Of course."

"Okay," Pia called. "We should be done soon."

They returned to the mountain image, and walked through it to the inner passage. Pia walked along it checking the outer wall, while Justin checked the inner wall, looking for illusion-masked passages. There were none.

"Maybe the ceiling?" Pia asked.

Justin looked up. "I fear it is just beyond my reach."

"And mine, certainly," she said, for he was substantially taller than she. "But I could check it if you lifted me."

"I suppose I could do that," he said doubtfully.

She had a notion why. "You don't want to pick up a girl who's not Breanna. It would seem too friendly."

"This is an accurate observation."

"Well, you could carry me without picking me up."

"I don't understand."

"Let me ride on your shoulders."

"Oh." He seemed not wholly relieved.

"We do have a job to do," she reminded him.

He squatted down beside the wall, and she mounted his shoulders, putting her legs down in front. "You clasp my knees, so my hands are free to reach up."

He rose to his feet, somewhat unsteadily, putting his hands on her knees. She in turn clasped his neck with her thighs. Her dread panties were now in contact with his head, but he couldn't see them, so didn't freak out. It was possible to get around some of Xanth's magical effects, she realized.

He walked, and she reached, sliding her fingers along the smooth ceiling. It was solid throughout; no illusion covered it. When they completed the circuit, they knew that they had failed.

"Squat down so I can dismount," she told him.

Justin just stood there.

"Or lean over so I can jump down," she said.

He did not react.

What was the matter? Couldn't he hear her? She realized that he hadn't said a word since they started the ceiling search.

Then she caught on: her panties were against his ears, or close enough so that he could hear their faint rustling. They had freaked out his hearing.

She wedged her hands down to cover his ears, breaking the contact. "Get down," she said, loudly enough to be heard through the barrier.

"Certainly." He got down, and she climbed off.

"Well, we haven't gotten far," she said. "There just doesn't seem to be any—wait a minute. We didn't check the pictures. There could be a passage there."

"Perhaps so," he agreed, though he sounded weary.

They entered the mountain scene again, this time checking the side walls. There was nothing. They went to the next scene and checked similarly. Nothing.

"I'm getting depressed," Pia said. "But we'd better check the rest."

They checked the next three, and found nothing. One more failure, and they would be done.

Resigned, Pia entered the flooded scene—and found a gap in her wall. "Justin!" she shrieked. "I've found it!"

He made his way to her, and felt the wall. "Dear girl, you are correct," he said. "There is an aperture."

It was about head height on her. Justin boosted her up and she crawled into it. In a moment she was beyond the illusion, and saw that she was in a short tunnel leading gradually down. The sides of it glowed faintly, so she wasn't blind. "Give me a moment to get clear, then follow," she called back. She needed that moment, because she was on her hands and knees, and he would freak out if she didn't get her panties out of sight first.

"My hands seem to have gone numb," he said.

They must have touched her panties during the boost. This was multimedia magic! "Flex your fingers," she called. "They'll recover in a moment."

She reached the base of the curve, and the tunnel debouched into another full sized passage below. "Okay, come on," she called.

Justin scrambled into the tunnel and crawled down toward her. Soon he stood beside her. "This certainly seems to be an avenue," he agreed, looking around. "It must pass under the inner passage, going toward the center of the circles. That would seem to be where the answer to our question lies."

"Yes. Let's find it. Then we can tell the others, and maybe finally get our night's rest."

"That would be eminently satisfactory."

The passage sloped downward, and at the base there was water. It wasn't illusion; it seemed to be ground water that had seeped in and flooded the floor. It wasn't deep; they sloshed through it and come out the other side.

They came to a large chamber, whose ceiling was supported by a number of thick columns. The columns were square, rather than round. The chamber seemed to be curved; in fact it was like the two passages, circling around a huge central pillar. This was the true center of the establishment.

"What *is* this place?" Pia asked, impressed by its magnitude.

"Why, I suspect these are square roots," Justin said, awed. "Cube roots, more accurately. And that this must be a tree."

"A tree?"

"A very large, very special tree. In fact, I believe this is the Coventree."

"The what?"

"It is largely isolated from the regular forests, but has remarkable properties. I know of it only by reputation, but believe the identification is secure. This would be its root system."

Pia looked around with a new appreciation. "All these columns—roots?"

"And the center is the main root."

"So it's a big tree. So what?"

"The Coventree has the power of illusion. Were it human, it would perhaps rival the Sorceress Iris in that respect. That explains why we did not see it in the light of day; it's enormous upper girth was concealed by illusion. But because it is vegetable, it is not considered to be a Magician. Still, it is a plant well worthy of respect."

"By other plants, maybe," she agreed cynically. "Other trees. But—" Then she made a connection. "You were a tree for a long time. That's why you relate."

"True. I have learned appreciation for the way of trees. Yet by what coincidental chance I should find myself here escapes me."

Another bulb flashed over her head. "That spook who called us this way—it was you it really wanted!"

"Me?"

"Maybe it couldn't reach you directly, so it lured us instead, knowing you would follow. Because you understand trees. You relate."

"Dear girl, I believe you are correct!"

"Everything was illusion, including the copy of Breanna. Except the path—and maybe the other plants cooperated to make that. To get us here—and you here. And now you're here.''

''But why would an important tree like this want my presence?''

''Maybe you should ask it.''

''But I can't just ask a tree something. Trees don't speak. Not even this one.''

''That spook who lured us spoke.'' But Pia reconsidered. ''It didn't say anything meaningful. Just about danger, and hurrying. Like a recording. No intelligence there.''

''Trees don't really understand human dialogue. I was a man before I was a tree; it took me some time to learn the ways of trees, and I think it would take longer for a tree to learn the ways of people. So I doubt that the Coventree would be able to speak to me or anyone in intelligible terms. That is simply not its nature.''

''But you do understand its nature,'' she said warmly. ''Better than any other human being. So it must want to talk to you.''

Justin considered. ''I think more likely it simply wants my understanding. But of what?''

''This is a puzzle,'' Pia said. ''Edsel could figure it out better than I could. But maybe I can get it. This whole place—the castle, the tunnel rings, the pictures—they must all be part of it. Something to understand. To figure out, just as we figured the way to get in here.''

''But why would a tree set riddles?''

''Because that's the only way it can communicate. You said it can't talk, it doesn't understand dialogue. But it must have some reason to tell you something. You just have to figure out what it is.''

Justin considered. ''You must be correct. That is the way a tree would do it. But what message could there be in a phantom castle?''

''That's just to mark the place, so we couldn't miss it. I thought that was obvious all along. But the pictures—it didn't want us to get beyond them until we had truly figured them out. I think the pictures are the message.'' She remembered how their Companions software, back in Mundania, wouldn't let folk see the Pia guide without clothing until they had demonstrated mastery over the subject matter. This could be similar, in vegetable fashion.

''But they are, taken as a whole, revolting. Thàt rising water—perhaps mobile animals like it, but it is not good for trees.''

''Rising water,'' she echoed. ''Justin—that could be it.''

"It can't be it. No tree would want its roots flooded out."

"The tunnel here—it's flooded at the low point. It surely wasn't that way when it was built. The water's rising here too, just as it is in the pictures. And that's not good."

Justin stared at her. "This *is* it," he agreed, amazed. "The water is rising, and drowning out the trees. And nobody cares but the trees."

"And the leprechauns, who must have helped with the excavation of this gallery."

"Yes, of course. And with the crafting of the pictures."

Something shifted inside her, and the chamber seemed to change color. "Do you know, Justin, all my life I've been a selfish brat, and it's never made me happy. Now, suddenly, I see a way to do something unselfish. I want to save those trees."

"But no one can—"

"We know what's happening. The snows in the mountains are melting, and flowing to the valley, and it's flooding, and drowning out the trees. They can't stop it, because they're immobile. The leprechauns probably can't go to the cold mountains. But maybe we can. That's why Coventree wanted to bring you here. So you would understand, because you of all people relate to trees, and do something. Before it's too late. And I want to help you. Maybe it will be the one truly decent thing I do in my life."

"But you're Mundane. You have to return to Mundania."

"Yes. So I guess we'd better hurry, and get this done before I leave Xanth."

"I suppose if you insist," he said dubiously. "But this problem may have no ready resolution. The forces of nature may be intractable."

"There must be a way to handle it, or the Coventree wouldn't have asked for help. We just have to figure out how. Now let's go tell the others."

"But they may not agree."

"Yes they will."

"How can you be certain of that?"

"Because Edsel will do it if I ask him to, and with the two of us in it, you two Companions have to tag along to make sure we don't get in trouble we can't handle."

"You seem truly determined."

"I truly am. This is my one chance."

He nodded. "I that case, I feel free to say that I am very much in accord. The thought of trees suffering unnecessarily is intolerable to me, and I wish to do all that I can to alleviate their distress."

"Why didn't you say so before?"

"Because it was not my province to direct your tour of Xanth, only to facilitate it. A mission like this is well beyond the parameters of my assignment."

"Let me see if I have it straight," she said. "You couldn't ask it, but you can support it."

"Exactly."

"You're so archaically ethical that you couldn't even hint at what you wanted."

"True."

"I think it's a pleasure to know, you Justin. Maybe the decade will come when I'll be able to be like that. But right now I'm simply not up to it. I have to go for what I want."

"I would not presume to criticize your policy."

"I can see what Breanna likes in you."

He smiled abashedly. "Then you are able to perceive this more clearly than I can. She is such a wonderful girl, but I am ordinary. There are times when it is all I can do to avoid—" He hesitated. "Touching her."

Pia considered. He evidently didn't realize that she and Edsel knew about this. He hadn't touched Breanna, technically; she had held his hands. "I think she's more touchable than you think."

"But she is too young!"

Pia, flush with the joy of her decision to do something truly decent for a change, realized that there was a bit more she could do. "Justin, things have changed in the last century, in Xanth as well as Mundania. Okay, so maybe the Adult Conspiracy stops you from going all the way. Yet. But there is an in-between stage, and you should pass through it before the Conspiracy ends. So you're not caught flat footed, as it were, when the time comes. I mean, you don't climb a mountain in one giant step, do you? You do it in easy stages."

"I suppose that could be the case. I confess that Breanna surprised me phenomenally the other night. However—"

"So now it's your turn to surprise her. She'll appreciate it. Believe me, she will."

"Surprise her?"

Pia considered, then changed the subject for a moment. "Okay. Let's go tell the others." She paused. "But don't tell them this."

"Don't—?"

"This." She put her arms around him, hauled his face down, and kissed him soundly on the mouth.

He stood halfway stunned. "I, ah—"

"And when you do that to her," she continued, not yet breaking the embrace, "do this too."

"I'm afraid I don't understand."

She caught his right hand and cupped it in her left hand. She carried it around behind her. "This." She squeezed his hand, making his fingers gently pinch her left buttock.

He did not quite freak out, but it was a close call. She put his limp hand back by his side and stepped away from him. Then she led him back toward the entrance. They had work to do.

$\overline{\underline{6}}$
Modemode

In the morning Nimby and Chlorine struggled with new Mundane clothing, and helped each other look presentable. They went downstairs just as their Companions arrived to guide them through breakfast.

"Now we need to show you how to ride the Lemon," Dug said. "But first, maybe we'd better tackle the Modemode."

"The what?" Chlorine asked.

"The GigaGrid. It goes by various names and nicknames. It covers the world, but you need a modem to access it, so we call it the modem mode, or Mode M Mode, or Modemode. Three syllables. We met you there in the O-zone of the magic mesh address of the Mundane Mega Mesh, or mmm, of the Grid. I realize it's confusing at first, but it does make sense in its fashion, once you get the hang of it."

"Zone—mesh—grid—mode," Chlorine said, working it out. "All steps of a stairway."

"Yes," Dug said. "Mdmd://mmm.mm.o-xone.breanna. That's where we found you. Now we need to be sure you know the way back, because if you should ever be in trouble, that's your escape route. You can reach it from any modem, not just this one. So you can travel anywhere in Mundania, and switch back when you have to; no need to do it from this site. But the mesh is fun in its own right, and you might as well enjoy it. So we figure to take you in for the check-in, then give you a small tour of the Modemode.''

They went in. Chlorine sat in Pia's seat, and Nimby in Edsel's, with Kim and Dug standing behind them for guidance. Chlorine followed the labyrinth, picking out the letters on the keyboard, invoking the modem spell, which was associated with something called a browser and a provider, then M D M D : // and on. She had to give Pia's identity, and Pia's password, ''insulin,'' before being granted admission. When she got to the magic mesh, there she was in the familiar hall, and there was Nimby with her.

Breanna wasn't in her Leaf, but they left their check-in message. Probably she hadn't made it in yet, because there were fewer mesh connections in Xanth, and Breanna might have forgotten about the Ear. But Nimby and Chlorine had done their part. The message would respond automatically when the others checked in; the magic of the O-Xone would see to that.

Kim made Chlorine go back to the screen and keyboard in the house, then to the magic mesh again, making sure she knew the route. Dug did the same with Nimby. Then they went exploring elsewhere in the mesh. ''The browser enables you to go places,'' Kim explained. ''We use Exscrape and Mundania Inline.''

''Inline?''

''You have to wait in line often. Sometimes you can't get in at all, but they still charge you plenty. Let's go to a babble box.''

''A what?''

''It's a place where people can meet and talk on the Grid. Friendships are made there, romances flourish, and fights occur. It's a lot of fun.''

''In fact, many people are ensnared in it,'' Dug added. ''Typing their lives away. They can't leave; babbling has *become* their lives.''

Chlorine wasn't sure about Mundane fun or living, but went along. After all, anyone who put eye to gourd peephole in Xanth was similarly caught, until someone else broke the connection. Folk simply had to learn to be careful.

''I know what you're thinking,'' Dug said. ''And you're right: there's even a *Through the Gourd* Home Leaf.''

Kim guided her to ''lumber on'' to a GigaGrid Alternating Babble, or GAB, where the gabbing occurred. They went to GABfest and merged.

She had to assume a persona, and decided on "Poison," because of her magic talent of poisoning water. The interaction was in the form of words on the screen. Kim had to reach in and type for her, because she could not do it fast enough.

She "signed" the guestbook, and it started.

Poison? Someone called Fun Gus typed. **LOL!**

"That means Laughing Out Loud," Kim said. "You'd better come back with some clever rejoinder."

Well I do it only to water, Chlorine replied with Kim's help.

You pee in water?

"Oh, he's one of *those*," Kim said with disgust. "Change the subject."

Chlorine did. **What's your talent?**

I make things fun, Gus replied. **How old are you?**

"Watch it," Kim warned. "He's a prowler."

But Chlorine answered. **Twenty two.** That was Pia's age. **Why do you want to know?**

How about a date?

"Don't get too friendly with this predator," Kim said.

I'm out of dates. Will you accept a pineapple?"

LMFAO!

"Never mind that that means," Kim said. "Dump him."

"No, I want to know." She typed **LMFAO?**

A picture appeared. It showed one donkey mounting another, but the one below was laughing so hard that the other was falling off. "Oh, donkeys," Chlorine said. She had liked them ever since Nimby first appeared to her in the form of a dragon with a donkey head. "But I still don't understand what they're doing."

"Never mind!" Kim said urgently. "Break off this dialogue."

A new name appeared: Moon Shine. **Hi, Poison. I make women look better in the full moon. Is this creep bothering you?**

Don't butt in, fertilizer face! Gus typed angrily.

" 'Fertilizer' isn't exactly the word he typed," Kim said. "The babble box automatically translates any objectionable terms."

No, this is interesting, Chlorine replied.

How about going priv for modering? Gus inquired.

"Don't do it!" Kim said.

"What does it mean?"

"Going private—that is, to some other chamber where others aren't watching—for modem sex."

"Modem what?"

"Where you talk dirty to each other. Having pretend sex. The Grid is clogged with dirty old men of all ages who want to get their verbal or written hands on young flesh. That's what you are."

Chlorine considered. "But it's not real, is it? I mean it's just talk."

"Talk can lead to desire for the real thing. That can put marriages in peril. I don't think Nimby would appreciate your doing that with someone else."

"I suppose not. How do I end this?"

"I'll do it." Kim typed rapidly. **No thanks. Go do it with your laughing donkey.**

That's telling him, Moon Shine said approvingly. **You wouldn't like him IRL.**

"What's that?"

"In real life," Kim said. "Now let's move on."

Nice meeting you, Moon, Kim typed. **Thanks for rescuing this newbie.**

"Newbie?"

"New to the babble box. That's why Gus was hitting on you. None of the regs will touch him."

"Regs?"

"Regular folk of this region. But I don't think we will need to come here again. You've seen how it works."

"I like it. You're right: it's fun."

They exited the Mesh and the Grid, and were back in the house. Dug and Nimby came from the other room. "That was some dialogue you had!" Dug said. "I recognized Kim's touch. She doesn't like Mesh moochers."

"True," Kim said. "If they want it so bad, let them pay through the nose for phone sex."

"Through the—"

"It's expensive," Kim said, frowning.

"Now it's time for the Lemon," Dug said. "Nimby, I mean Ed, you seem to catch on quite rapidly. Do you think you can handle a two wheeled machine after I demonstrate it?"

Nimby nodded.

They went to the garage where the machine lurked. It looked like half a car. Dug wheeled it out and bestrode it. "This is Edsel's Lemon motorcycle. Here is how you start it," he said. He pushed with his foot, and the motor came alive. "This is how it moves." He started it moving, and it carried him down the drive and onto the road beyond. He looped around and returned to the house.

Then Dug had Nimby get behind him, and the two rode off, discussing the ways of the motorcycle. "Ed and Pia ride all over on that thing," Kim said. "I don't feel easy on one of those monsters, but maybe you'll like it better."

"It doesn't look worse than riding a dragon," Chlorine said.

After a time, the motorcycle returned. Sure enough, Nimby was now in front, and seemed to be handling it competently. "Your turn," Kim murmured.

"Oh, I couldn't make it work," Chlorine said.

"Your turn to ride in back," Kim clarified. "To make sure all is well."

Dug got off, and Chlorine got on behind Nimby. The machine started moving. The ride was different from that of a dragon, but she found she could handle it. She put her arms around Nimby's waist and enjoyed the ride.

They went out on the road, and gained speed. The wind took her hair. She was amazed at the velocity; this was faster than a dragon!

They slowed. She saw that it was because of a red light that hung above an intersection. Nimby had learned the rules of the road. "I like this," she said as they resumed motion.

They returned to the house, where Dug and Kim waited. "We can handle it," Chlorine called.

"There's one other thing you should know about on the Mesh," Kim said. "Xanth is there."

"The O-Xone," Chlorine agreed.

"No, this is an emulation Xanth, not magical. It consists of a group of people who assume Xanthly personae, much as the folk in the Babble Boxes have nicknames, only their names are limited to Xanth folk."

"Oh?" Chlorine asked. "Do they have any real connection to their Xanth counterparts?" They had agreed not to refer to Xanth by name, but this did not seem feasible in practice, and maybe it didn't matter.

"They like to think so, but I don't think there's any solid evidence that they do. Come on; I'll take you there, and you can meet yourself."

"But there's only one of me," Chlorine said, not quite pleased.

Kim smiled. "You were not in Mundania to pre-empt the name, so she got it. But be assured that she means you no harm. I just don't think you should challenge her about the name, because you are here anonymously. You'll have to assume some other Xanth name, to enter the Xanth Xone."

"This is ridiculous."

Dug stepped in. "Think of it this way: Xanth natives have the infinite privilege of actually living in Xanth. Mundanes are stuck forever in drear Mundania. This is one of the few ways they can relate, to get at least the trace of a notion what it might be like to be among the blessed. Can you begrudge them that faint fond illusion?"

Chlorine glanced at Kim. "He has a certain talent for persuasion."

"I had suspected that," Kim said with five eighths of a smile. "I think that's why I married him."

"Well, you started it," Dug told her. "When you kissed me."

"Oh, you always bring that up!" she flared, with eleven sixteenths of a smile.

"Yeah. I bet you don't dare do it again."

"You lose." Kim kissed Dug hard and long.

They finally broke. "I don't think I lost," he said, with the remaining five sixteenths of the smile.

"That's your opinion." Kim's expression of mock severity made her look almost cute.

Dug turned to Chlorine. "So you had better be persuaded, or she might kiss *you*."

Chlorine's conviction that she liked these Mundanes was growing. The fact was, Dug was a handsome man, while Kim was an ordinary woman, in appearance, but they both had personality. Chlorine remembered her early life as a distinctly plain and less than ordinary girl, before Nimby had enhanced her into beauty, character, and intelligence. She related to Kim, who clearly had made something of herself. "I'm persuaded. Let's go meet me."

"Pick a name," Kim said.

Chlorine pondered. Who would be obscure enough to be free? She remembered another poisoner, a disreputable female vaguely related to the mermaids, but ugly and gross. No one would choose to be her. "Ella," she said. "Salmon Ella."

Dug laughed. "Salmonella! That will surely do. She must be a real pain in the—"

"Stomach," Kim said quickly with mock primness.

"Close enough," he agreed, patting her on the bottom.

They went back inline, this time just Chlorine, with the three others watching her screen, and Kim giving verbal instructions. They made their way to the Grid and the Mesh, and to the Xanth Xone. There Chlorine registered as S. Ella, and looked up Chlorine. She was not there at the moment, but at least she had learned how to locate her. "You can try another time," Kim said. "The Mesh is quite flexible. Or you can leave a message for her."

Chlorine realized belatedly that she had no idea what to say to the Xone Chlorine, so it was just as well that she hadn't made direct contact. "I'll try again," she said. She would have to think of something suitable to explain her interest in this character.

"But there are plenty others to chat with," Dug said as they exited. "We can go to a GOO."

"A what?"

He laughed. "That stands for Grid Operating Oubliette. GOO for short. It's an off-Mesh inline game where players from all over the world interact. They make up their own characters and participate in an established setting, where they make friends or alliances or enemies. They gossip about each other, or even fall in love and get married, in the game. Sometimes they have fights to the death. They stay at inns, eat good or bad meals, fight monsters—it's actually a real world for these folk, maybe as real as Mundania, and better for them. Some addicts live almost entirely in their GOOs, playing day and night without sleep. But a good GOO polices itself, so there are no vulgar laughing donkeys to harass you."

"Is that a pun?" Chlorine asked.

"Of course it is," Kim said. "Har-ASS, as in donkey."

"It sounded more like 'her ass.' "

"That, too," Kim agreed. "Men think it's funny to slip in references to female donkeys."

"My point being that there are no female donkeys getting GOOed," Dug said.

"That sounds nice," Chlorine agreed, deciding not to explore the matter of gooed lady asses. "How do we get there?"

"I'll take you." Dug took over the keyboard. "I'll use Fishnet on my Trix account. First I have to lumber on by giving my operator name: DM5555. Then my password: 5☆4●3∇2‡1∞. Then when I get to the prompt line, I type the address: fishnet2.aa.whatname.oo.7734. That brings me to the computer where the GOO is, in this case Origin.''

The screen blinked, and then a scene came on, with a forest, field, and castle. ''And here we are,'' he said. ''In this realm, I'm a dwarf ogre, smarter than the average ogre but not as strong. It's amazing how some women go for ogres.''

''Just remember,'' Kim said warningly, ''You don't know what my mergirl character is doing with men who like wet bare bosoms, while you're making time with feebleminded nymphs.''

''Anyway,'' Dug continued, ''this could seem familiar, because some players overlap Xanth. I mean, an ogre or mermaid can be anywhere in fantasy. Maybe some are refugees from Xanth, for all we know.''

''I'll remember,'' Chlorine agreed.

''Now there are still other realms that might relate. The Grid is a pretty extensive realm.''

''No, I think this is enough for now,'' Chlorine decided. ''Let's focus on what Nimby wants.''

Nimby wanted to explore more of the physical Mundania. So the rest of the day was spent in setting up for their ''vacation'' travel. They learned about the uses and denominations of money and little cards called ''credit.'' They learned about maps, and motels, and places to eat. Tomorrow they would really start exploring Mundania.

At one point Chlorine remembered something. ''Didn't you have a dog, Kim, who accompanied you to Xanth when you were on the Roc jury?''

''Yes. Bubbles. I found her floating in a bubble in Xanth the first time I was there, in the Companions game, and adopted her. But she was old, and continued to age in Mundania, and I knew she would die. So I did what I had to do, and made an arrangement for her to return to Xanth, to be with Anathe Ma.''

''Anathema? Did I mishear?''

Kim laughed. ''You fell for one of the Xanthly puns. Her name is Anathe, and she is a very nice, motherly person, though horrendously ugly. She liked Bubbles, and Bubbles liked her, so it just seemed better. Bubbles is much less likely to die in Xanth, because of the magic, as long as she has the sense to stay clear of dragons. I cried for three days, but of course I was away at college much of the time then, so it was better for the dog. I'm sure she's happy now.'' But for the moment Kim looked ready to cry again.

"Maybe some day, if the business gets established well enough, there'll be company again in the house,'' Dug said.

"Maybe,'' Kim agreed, but she did not seem to be much cheered.

Chlorine was baffled. What did this mean, and why the sadness?

Nimby touched her hand, and then she understood. They wanted to have a child, but somehow their signals to the stork had been ignored, and there was a growing fear that something was wrong in that respect. Ironically, there was no question about Pia's fertility, but Pia did not want children. So Dug and Kim pretended that it was simply their business with the software business that held them back.

As they completed the preparations, Dug was looking increasingly thoughtful. That suggested to Chlorine that he had something on his mind. "You have thoughts?'' she inquired.

"Well, I don't want to pry into what's not my business, yet as a Companion I do need to know what's going on, so as the better to anticipate and avoid problems. Especially as we travel out of my most familiar haunts.''

Nimby glanced at him. That meant that this matter should be followed up.

"What is your concern?'' Chlorine asked Dug.

"The real reason for your visit to Mundania.''

"But we told you,'' Chlorine said. "Nimby just wanted to see what Mundania was like, and of course the Demon Earth wouldn't let him.''

Dug shook his head. "The Demons aren't like that. They have no human curiosity, and they hardly care about territory. Their entire existence is wrapped up in contests with each other. Nimby may be learning a lot about human foibles, but he wouldn't take a risk like this without good reason.''

Chlorine realized that he had a point. There must be more here than Nimby had let on. She looked at him.

Nimby reached across and touched her hand. Then she had it straight. "You are correct: there is more. Nimby did not want to burden you with details of Demon interaction, but since you ask, he will. Yes, there is another Demon bet, and that is that Nimby can't enter Mundania and remain three days without being discovered and caught. He has one year to make the attempt or lose by default. If he is discovered, there will be complications. Since the Demon Earth is watching the normal connections between their two regions, Nimby used a special one, the O-Xone. He is also using a Mundane body, further masking his presence.''

"But does it count, if he's not here in physical person?'' Kim asked.

"Oh, yes. Because he *is* really here. Just without his body and most of his magic. That makes him almost impossible to trace. So he suffers the privations of lack of magic, for the sake of succeeding in his endeavor. And he does want to explore Mundania, because he has indeed been learning human traits like curiosity. They don't come naturally to him, but he is studying them, and this experience helps.''

Dug nodded. "That makes sense to me. What would reveal his presence here?''

"If he did something crazy, that no Mundane would do, that would attract attention. But if the Demon Earth happens to look at us—well, they can read our minds, so he would know. That's chance.''

"And the Demon Earth is looking,'' Kim said.

"Yes. Probably routine sweeps, because he's not sure Nimby is here at this time. But he's alert. So we might make no mistakes, and still get caught. Actually the odds of success are crafted to be about 50-50, because that's the way the demons like it: even odds, so there is always a strong element of uncertainly.''

"They are true gamblers,'' Dug said. "The risks mean nothing; all they want is to win the wager.''

Nimby nodded.

"Well, we'll do our best,'' Kim said. "But you know, I have a question too, if it's all right. I don't want to be offensive, and it has nothing to do with the success of this mission, so—''

"So ask,'' Chlorine said. "We won't answer if we don't want to.''

"Well, I understand that the two of you now wander around Xanth, doing spot favors for people who don't know Nimby's true nature. Given that Nimby is who he is, why should he bother?''

Chlorine smiled. "I can answer that without consulting with him. Nimby is trying to learn about all the things he never paid attention to before, and he feels that mixing with ordinary folk is the best way. They think we're just Damsel & Dragon, and that's fine, because then they don't come asking special favors. By studying the problems of folk with little or no power, we learn a lot about human feeling and hope and grief. So that if Nimby ever wishes to go among people alone, without me as a buffer, he will be able to do so without making mistakes.''

"But aren't you worried that—" Kim hesitated, evidently thinking better of the question.

"That he will dump me as no longer useful?" Chlorine said for her. "No, I'm not worried, because even if my association with Nimby ends tomorrow, I will be far better off for the wonderful experience and love he has given me in this time. And of course it would be simple for him to erase all memory of him from my mind, and leave me with some ordinary man who would take good care of me. I would never know the difference." She glanced obliquely at Nimby, teasing him. "Maybe that one we met last month, Rusty, with the talent of making metal rust down to any length. Maybe the stork would deliver babies with rust colored hair."

"As long as Rusty's not gay," Kim said.

"Oh, I would expect him to have a really gay time," Chlorine said, inhaling. On Pia's body, this had good effect.

Kim pursed her lips. "Maybe we have run afoul of a linguistic anomaly."

"But why should the man be sad instead of gay? I'm not exactly minced spleen."

Dug interceded. "In current slang, the term gay now refers to a sexual preference for one's own gender."

"And a person who prefers the opposite gender is called straight," Kim said.

"Oh." That did set Chlorine back a bit. But then she had the answer: "But I would put him in a straight jacket. That would stop the gaiety."

Dug and Kim exchanged a glance. "That should do it," Dug agreed.

"Or maybe I could marry that man Simon," Chlorine continued, with another slice of a glance at Nimby. "The one who said things, and then they happened. He could say I'd be happy."

The three others glanced at Nimby, but he still didn't react. So Chlorine tried one more. "Maybe that sixteen year old Mundane boy we saw in the region of madness. What was his name—Brandon Risner. He seemed nice." She addressed Dug and Kim. "Weird things are found at the fringes of the region of Madness. We were doing a raccoonnaissance, looking for a tailgator—they have fierce teeth in their tails—and we boarded a scholar ship. Each passenger had to submit a written essay, which meant that only educated folk could use it, but it was fun."

"I'd like to sail on that ship," Dug said.

"Yes, you would have liked some of the folk on it. There was Elena

Human from the North Village. Her talent was Literature. She could summon any character from a book, as long as she was holding that book. There was also Polly Esther from the West Stockade, whose talent was to make long-lasting clothing. Some of it was quite sheer when she wore it.''

"He'd like that ship too well," Kim muttered.

"We crossed a lake of Pollux oil, which smelled even worse than Castor oil. Then we docked and rode a defective donkey.'' Chlorine paused, searching her memory. "No, it was an ass fault, very hard and black. Until we came to a toad lily, which was really all together. That's where Brandon was. He was learning to play chess from a chess nut tree.''

"Wait, I think I missed one," Kim said. "I got asphalt, and chestnut, but what's toad lily?''

"You are toad lily stupid about puns," Dug told her.

Had it been Xanth, a mortified light bulb would have flashed over her head. "Oh, you bad boy!" she exclaimed, punching him on the shoulder. "Toad lily bad.''

Nimby yawned. Chlorine decided she had had enough fun with him. Puns bored him. "I hope you never do dump me," she said, kissing his ear. "I like donkey-headed dragons.''

Dug stood. "I think it's time for us to go home.''

"You're just smug because you're one up on me," Kim said. But she hardly seemed loath, as they departed for the night.

7
MOUNTAINS

I'm nervous, having them down there so long," Breanna said. "Suppose they get in trouble, and we don't know it?"
"Then we would have to go in after them," Edsel said. "Maybe you'll be able to see what I can't, and I'll be able to deflect hostile magic so we can rescue them." But he was nervous himself. Justin and Pia had gone down the steps into the ground, and though they had reported back safely once, now time was extending without their reappearance.

"I guess I fuss too much," she said. "It's just that I love him so, and we haven't been together long, physically I mean, and I'm so afraid I'll lose him to a dragon or something before I ever really have him." She glanced sidelong at him. "Do you feel like that with Pia?"

He shook his head. "No, not really. But of course we've been married for four years. The bloom is off."

"Oh, yes, you said that before. But it seems weird to me. How can you lose love?" She shifted her position, sitting cross-legged, and he couldn't help wondering how far up under her skirt he would have been able to see if there had been more light. She was a cute kid, and nicely formed.

But he needed to address her question. "Well, I haven't really lost mine for her, but I'm afraid she's lost hers for me. I'm hoping she will recover it. I guess I feel I have lost her, and I'm afraid I won't recover her. Is that close enough to your sentiment?''

"No. I know I won't lose Justin's love. Just his body, maybe, if something bad happens. I know it's foolish, but it still bothers me. But I hope it works out for you.'' Then she thought of something else. "Do you notice other women?''

How much honesty was appropriate? Well, this was Xanth, the land of literalness. Might as well be candid. "Yes. I notice you. That doesn't mean—''

"Me? What's to notice about me?''

"You're an attractive girl, the age Pia was when I started with her. And you would be freaking me out with your legs if it weren't dark.''

She glanced down. "Really? Without even showing my panties?'' She seemed pleased.

"For sure,'' he said, smiling. Then, to change the subject, he addressed the boat. "Para, how are you doing?''

The boat slapped a webbed foot against the ground in acknowledgment.

"I wish you could talk,'' he said. "I'd like to know your history.''

"You could play Nineteen Questions,'' Breanna said. "Tell him to tap once for yes, two for no, three for uncertainty.''

"Say, yes,'' he agreed. "Okay, Para: would you like to tell us your personal history?''

A foot slapped once.

"Were you born or made? Oops, wrong phrasing. Were you born?''

"Wrong question,'' Breanna said. "Folk don't get born in Xanth; that's a clumsy, messy Mundanian custom. They get delivered by the stork.''

"Oh, yeah, that's right. Okay, Para: were you delivered?''

One slap, which he heard as Yes.

"So no one made you?''

Yes. There was a moment of confusion as they established that the answer was literal: no one had made the craft, because it had been delivered by a stork.

"This is getting interesting,'' Breanna said. "Who could be the parents of a boat with ten pairs of duck feet?''

Edsel zeroed in on the answer. "Was your mother a duck?''

Two foot slaps: No.

He tried other creatures, but none was right.

Breanna got a notion. "A boat! Was your mother a boat?"

Yes.

They considered. It seemed unlikely to be an ordinary boat. What kind of boat could signal the stork?

"A dream boat!" Breanna said, a bulb flashing over her head.

Yes.

"Was your father a duck?"

Three slaps, signifying uncertainty.

"Uncertain because you don't know?" Edsel asked.

No.

"Because it's not exactly a duck?"

Yes.

They tried variations of ducks, and finally Edsel got it: "A quack! Your father was a quack."

Yes. It turned out that the two had blundered onto a love spring, tricked there by Anemone, which was a water creature with a bad attitude—an enemy, in fact. They desperately signaled the stork about ten times before they managed to get clear of that potent water. The stork works had pondered the order for some months, and finally compromised by delivering one boat with ten pairs of duck feet. By that time the quack was long gone, but the dream boat remained, and she showed Para the ways of the water. But he had to learn the way of the land himself, and that was chancy.

Now they wanted to know how Para had come to be associated with the two docks, where Breanna had first encountered him. This was hard to zero in on, but they were making progress—when Justin and Pia returned.

"I'm almost disappointed," Breanna murmured, smiling. She had a very white smile in the subdued light of the illusion castle.

"There'll be other occasions," Edsel said. Then they focused on the others. The four stood beside the boat, catching up. The two who had gone underground seemed oddly animated, as if they had had some transcendent experience.

"We have discovered a tree," Justin said. "The Coventree. This region is safe for us."

"A tree?" Edsel asked, wondering if he had missed the punch line.

"But we've just got to help that tree," Pia said. "It's getting drowned out, and so are its friends."

"But we can't take time to get involved in forestry," Breanna protested. "We have to get Edsel and Pia safely back to the O-Xone."

"I think not," Justin said.

Breanna spluttered. "But—"

Justin turned to his companion. "Pia?"

Pia turned to Edsel. "I would be so grateful for your support. So very *very* grateful."

She never spoke like that unless she really wanted something, and not only could she make him extraordinarily glad to cooperate, she could make him phenomenally unhappy when he did not. "You have it," he said immediately. He didn't need to know what he was committing himself to, just that heaven was better than hell.

"Thank you," she said, and hugged and kissed him. She had her sixteen year old body back, and it put images of squadrons of storks into his fevered imagination. She would make good on the implication, too, when the opportunity came. She always did. The fact was, he loved being wound around her little finger.

"Since they are determined to resolve this matter," Justin was saying, "we are obliged to assist them in whatever way we are able."

"Have you been enchanted?" Breanna asked suspiciously. "What *happened* down there?"

"We'll show you," Pia said. "Come; you must meet the Coventree."

Breanna shot a desperate glance at Edsel, but he was lost. He could argue with Pia, he could exchange insults with her, he could be mad at her, but he could not oppose her when she used her sex appeal to win her way. He knew this did not mean that she would remain married to him, but for the duration of his cooperation in her design, she would be his loving girlfriend. That might be the best he could get, and he was incapable of refusing it.

"I guess we have to do it," Breanna said, clearly not entirely pleased.

Justin embraced her, and kissed her, and pinched her bottom.

"Justin!" she said, astonished. "You got fresh!"

"Something I learned from Pia," he said, looking apprehensive.

"You learned from—what were you two *doing* down there?!"

"He told me that you surprised him," Pia said evenly. "I told him how to surprise you in turn."

"Oh." The girl reconsidered, perhaps remembering the business of holding hands. Then she turned back to Justin. "Okay. Do it again."

Edsel had to laugh. Pia had made quite an impression on those two, first getting Breanna to lead Justin into something, then getting him to initiate something. Physical romance was a process Pia knew volumes about. The Xanthly Adult Conspiracy would never be the same.

Then Justin and Pia led the way down into the nether section. Para followed them, his duck feet handling the steps well enough. Edsel hesitated, then drew the lid down, closing them in; it now seemed safer than advertising where they had gone.

"First the tour," Pia said. "I know you're tired, and we'll rest soon, but this is important."

Actually Edsel wasn't tired, because he had been riding in the boat and then sitting and talking with Breanna. He was curious to know what had gotten Pia so excited and committed.

It was a showing of six museum-style pictures or settings. Illusion paintings, Justin explained. Two were of snowy mountains, and four were of a pleasant wooded valley.

They completed the circuit. They were back at the stairway. "That's it?" Breanna asked. Edsel felt much the same. So there were six somewhat repetitive pictures; so what?

"The snows are melting," Pia said. "The valley is flooding."

Edsel exchanged a glance with Breanna. This time he did the honors: "So?"

"So the runoff from the mountains is flooding the valley," Pia said. "The roots of the trees are drowning, and so the trees are dying."

Edsel shrugged. "It happens. What's your point?"

"Those are good trees. It's not right just to let them die, when we can maybe do something to save them."

"Since when were you ever an environmentalist?"

Instead of retorting with a cutting remark, Pia paused to consider. "Since I met the Coventree."

"Is this a magic tree? Did it enchant you?"

Pia considered again. "I don't think it enchanted me. But if it did, I'm glad of it. I feel—as if I've fallen in love. With a mission."

This was strong medicine, but not necessarily bad. Pia had never before been dedicated to anything other than her comfort of the moment.

"Then maybe we had better meet the Coventree," Breanna said.

"Coming up." Pia led the way into the last picture.

Edsel and Breanna stared. "Oh, that's right," Edsel said after a moment. "You can pass through illusion."

It turned out to be an awkward route, especially for the duck footed boat. They went through a hole in the side wall, down a small tunnel, into a larger cross tunnel, through a puddle of bilge-water, and into a large central cave where squat square columns abounded.

"This is the Coventree," Pia said. "Or rather, its root system. We can camp safely here for the night."

"But we saw no big tree above," Breanna protested.

"Illusion can conceal as well as appear," Justin reminded her.

"So what do we do," Edsel asked. "Can we talk to it?"

"No, this just proves how it is getting flooded out. That water in the passage will rise, unless we stop the mountain melt."

"You mean those pictures are of this area?" Breanna asked. "Or the valley part of it?"

"Yes," Justin said. "They illustrate the problem."

"And we're supposed to somehow stop nature?" Edsel asked.

"Stop the melting in the mountains," Pia said patiently. "That will stop the slow flooding, and save the trees."

He found this hard to believe. "And for this, you will give me—?"

She stepped into him, very soft and exciting. "Yes."

"Then bring on the mountains," he said.

They found nooks, spread out the blankets, and settled down for the night. Pia joined Edsel, and if she had ever been more desirable or ardent, he could not remember when. All this, to save some trees? He had to be missing something. But meanwhile, he had a piece of heaven.

In the morning, by his watch—the fungus light down here was unchanged—they stirred and got organized. They ate more pizza for breakfast and prepared to set out on their new mission.

Overnight, perhaps in his dreams, Edsel had pondered the flooding problem. Evidently it was a chronic thing, not merely seasonal. Mountain glaciers normally melted some in summer and re-froze in winter, staying in balance. Only a larger pattern of heating, a climate change, could make them melt continuously. What was causing that?

Pia had brought him into this, but now he was getting into it in his own fashion, as a challenge. He liked solving mysteries, and perhaps this was a worthy one.

Justin went to touch one of the square roots. "We will try to address the problem," he told it. "We will do our best."

Pia went to another root. "We really will," she said. Then she leaned forward and kissed its rough bark.

The faint glow around the cave brightened. Whether that was in response to the promise or the kiss Edsel wasn't sure; both were surely potent.

They turned to the exit passage—and there across it was an illusion picture. It showed the valley, with no lakes or ponds, the sun shining brightly. The Coventree understood their mission, and was acknowledging in its fashion. Edsel realized that the tree could not respond in animate fashion, but could at least make pictures, which it probably had to grow in the course of hours. It must have been working on this one overnight.

They walked through it, suffering no blindness, as this illusion was paper thin. Beyond it was another. This one was a map, showing the local lay of the land, and the placement of the snowy mountains. Now they knew exactly where to go.

They made their way out through the passages and illusions, and emerged to the daylight above. The castle was gone; the region was flat. With one significant exception: there was the Coventree, rising above the region where they had seen its great central root. It was a huge tree, larger than Edsel had ever seen before, stretching toward the clouds. The illusion castle must have been formed around it, concealing it at night. But by day, freed of its protective illusion, it stood out in all its grandeur. It would indeed be a shame to let such a tree die.

They got in Para, and the boat set off. Justin and Pia rode in front, eager to see the way ahead, leaving Edsel and Breanna to the rear.

"So did she do you last night?" Breanna inquired.

"Am I allowed to answer without violating the Adult Conspiracy?"

She laughed. "That's answer enough. You know, I can see how Justin would relate to the welfare of trees, and I don't blame him at all. But Pia surprises me; I never figured her for the type."

"She surprises me too," he admitted. "I love her, but she has always been self-centered. I don't see any way in which this intermission can profit her personally."

"This what?"

"Intermission. A mission inside a larger mission."

She considered that. "Quest."

"What?"

"It's a quest rather than a mission. More éclat."

"Quest," he agreed, liking the concept. "But not her type. If there were the promise of a bag of pretty gemstones at the end, I could see it. But just to save some trees: She never cared about trees before."

"There must be a reason."

"There must be," he agreed. They had speculated about enchantment, but it didn't seem to fit.

A shape flew out of the background. It was large, and somewhat clumsy. "Beware," Breanna said. "That's a harpy."

"Have no concern," Justin called back. "That's Handi. I know her. She's clean and intelligent."

"Trees get to know many flying creatures," Breanna said. "I suppose I shouldn't be jealous."

The harpy had the wings and talons of a buzzard, and the head and breasts of a woman. Edsel had understood that they were always ugly, but this one wasn't.

"What is the nature of your quest?" she called. Her voice was not a screech, either.

"Hello, Handi," Justin called. "Come and perch for a bit."

The harpy was surprised. "You know me?" She hovered doubtfully.

"And you know me," Justin said. "I'm Justin Tree, in manform."

"Justin!" she cried. "That is your voice." She came in to perch on the side of the boat. "But what are you doing with three Mundanes?"

"Two and a half Mundanes," Breanna said, nettled. "I'm a permanent Xanth resident. Breanna of the Black Wave. And Justin's my man."

Handi turned to eye her. "Well, he used to be my tree. He had the nicest foliage. I would perch on his firm warm branch and we discussed nature."

"We are going to the mountains to find out why the snow is melting," Justin said.

"That's important?"

"The melt-water is drowning out the Coventree."

Handi nodded. "That's important. That's the finest tree in all these parts." She preened a feather. "Well, I must be off." She spread her wings and lifted into the air.

Breanna watched her go. "Was I too bleepy?" she asked.

"Not at all," Edsel reassured her. "You hardly spoke."

"I hate being jealous. But the thought of Justin talking about nature with bare breasted birds just drives me crazy."

"She does have nice—" He caught himself. "Completely understandable. But how could a man have any future with a creature with no human legs?''

She considered. ''I never thought of that. He really couldn't, well, whatever. I don't have to be jealous of harpies at all.''

He spied another creature. It might be a dragon, but it wasn't threatening them. ''What's that?''

She looked. ''Oh, that's a firedrake. They have iron lungs.''

That made sense, he realized.

The level floor of the valley tilted, providing some leverage so the river could rise toward the distant mountain range. Edsel had never been much for watching scenery, but there wasn't much else to do. Justin and Pia were chatting amiably at the other end of the boat; they seemed to be really hitting it off, after their exploration of the underground gallery. Edsel hardly minded talking with Breanna; she was cute and vivacious. But there was absolutely no prospect of a romantic association there, and he had never had much to do with girls who were not romantic prospects. So he was stuck with the scenery. Fortunately it was varied and interesting.

They passed a woman who was working in a vineyard. But the vines were odd. They seemed to have eyeballs. ''What are those?'' he inquired.

Breanna looked. ''I think they are eye-queue vines. Put one on your head, and it makes you smart.''

''Really?'' he asked, amazed.

''Well, I'm not sure. Maybe they only make you think you're smart. I'll find out.'' She waved to the woman. ''Hi! I'm Breanna of the Black Wave, my talent is seeing in blackness, and I have a question.'' The duck-footed boat obligingly drew to a halt so she could have the dialogue.

''You wish to know whether these vines provide the illusion or the reality of high intelligence,'' the woman said.

''That's right! How did you know?''

''Because I am Jeanie Yus, and long association with the eye queue has made me quite intelligent. In fact, that's my talent.''

''Intelligence, or cultivating vines?'' Edsel asked.

''Yes. And you are evidently a lascivious Mundane.''

''Only when looking at lovely women,'' he said. Actually Jeanie looked smart rather than pretty, but he was a fair hand at dialogue with women.

She nodded. "False flattery can indeed be charming. The answer to your original question is that the effect of these vines varies with the person. They do enhance the appearance of intelligence, but only in restricted ways relating to observation of details rather than substance, obscure vocabulary rather than effective communication, spot memorization of numbers backwards, superficial analysis of pictures, general information of a selected cultural nature, and trick questions. But not only do they make those who use them think they are more intelligent than they are, they also make school administrators think so."

"They have schools in Xanth?" Edsel asked.

"Indubitably. We have a fine school of fish right here in the Melt River."

Breanna was interested. "What effect would such a vine have on someone like me?"

"They tend not to greatly enhance the seeming strengths of folk like you," Jeanie said. "On a basis of one hundred, they would make you seem like eighty five."

"But how can they do that?" she asked, annoyed.

"They relate only to the qualities to which they are crafted to relate. They ignore all others, such a creativity, artistic ability, musical sensitivity, special qualities of character like integrity or compassion or perseverance, or specialized knowledge in diverse areas. They assume that intelligence is an entity represented by a single figure, and that that figure is the only relevant one."

"But why would they assume that?" Breanna asked.

"Because if they did not, their prophecy would not be properly self fulfilling."

"I don't understand."

"Naturally not," Jeanie said with a superior attitude.

Breanna seemed about to jump out of the boat to tackle Jeanie. Edsel grabbed her, getting a faceful of her lustrous black hair. "Para!" he cried. "Get your feet moving."

The boat lurched forward, carrying them away from the vineyard. He hung on to the struggling girl until she relaxed. Then he released her, aware that his embrace could be misinterpreted. Justin and Pia were looking back in surprise, but then returned to their dialogue.

Breanna looked at him. "I guess you didn't do that to grab any quick feel."

"True," he agreed. Then, to defuse it: "Oh, I don't mean to imply that you don't have things worth feeling. You are a very nice little package. If I ever had a legitimate excuse, I'd revel in feels."

It worked. She smiled. "For sure. That woman made me so mad—"

"I think it was unconscious arrogance. She called out the weakness in her vines without realizing that it applied to herself. She really does think she is smarter than you."

"But why?"

"Because you are of the Black Wave. That is most of what she felt she needed to know about you."

"Self fulfilling prophecy," she said musingly. "If you figure the color of your skin makes you better than someone else, the tests you make will reflect that."

"You will make sure they do," he agreed. "In the name of objectivity, ironically. But it's not worth arguing with an attitude like that. It would be like getting into a mud fight."

"I used to like mud fights."

"You know what I mean."

She considered. "What do you think of zombies?"

He was startled by the irrelevance. "Why, I don't know any zombies, but I wouldn't want to embrace one."

"For sure," she said, turning away.

Edsel found himself vaguely nettled. "Am I missing something?"

"Those eye queue vines would make a zombie be about ten on a scale of one hundred. Their brains are rotten."

He was baffled. "I *am* missing something. I feel sort of stupid."

"No, just from another culture. Maybe some time I'll tell you about zombies. Meanwhile, I'll apologize for confusing you. It wasn't fair."

"Oh, that's all right," he said, still wondering what was going on in her mind.

Then she caught him about the shoulders, drew him close enough to be well aware of those things she had worth feeling, and kissed him so soundly that it felt as if the boat were tipping over the brink of a waterfall.

When she released him, he put his hands on the sides of the boat to maintain his balance. "Why?" he gasped after a moment.

"Two reasons. First, you saved me from making a fool of myself, back there. Second, those two up front owed us a kiss. And maybe a feel, but I think you got that too."

Indeed. "Owed us a kiss?"

"Your woman kissed my man, underground, and gave him a feel. I can tell. Now that score is even."

He wasn't sure of the logic, but it had been such a good kiss that he didn't question it. Breanna kept her own particular social accounts. She had kissed him in the O-Xone, because she had said that someone else had done it and it showed. Someone else had: Kim, and Pia. Apparently if anyone else got a kiss, Breanna felt entitled. "You said something about an apology, then you kissed me. Is there a connection?"

"Yes. I gave you a gourd apology. That's like that."

"I think I could get interested in the gourd."

"For sure!" she laughed. "All in good time. You know, I think I could get to like you, if I tried."

"Ditto here. But I think we had better not try too hard."

"We're pushing it," she agreed. "Maybe we're a little jealous of them." Her gaze flicked momentarily toward the front of the boat.

"They have found a common interest," he agreed. "Pia has become an environmentalist. I would never have expected that."

"Justin is already. Because of his several score years as a tree. I like that in him, but I have sort of left it to him, same as he has left civil rights to me."

"Xanth has a civil rights problem?"

"It does with zombies."

"You're representing the zombies!" he exclaimed, catching on.

"Yeah."

"How did you get into that?"

"Well, it started with King Xeth. He—"

She broke off, because at that point they were approaching an odd couple. It was a centaur, the first Edsel had seen in the flesh, and on its back a girl. The girl had brown hair, wore blue jeans, and would have been rather short if seen standing on the ground. But as it was, her head was high enough.

"Hello," Justin called from the front. "I am Justin Tree. Is this the best way to the snowy mountains?"

"Hi," the girl replied. She wore a hat that said Tom, but maybe she had borrowed it. Unless she was a tom boy. "I'm Heather. I'm ten, and my talent is relating to dragons. I'm looking for one who's not hungry at the moment. I don't know the best way to the mountains, but I'm sure Shaunture does."

The centaur seemed reluctant to talk. He merely pointed upriver.

"My concern is that the river may meander, and we would like to reach the mountains expeditiously," Justin said.

Heather looked down. "I guess you'll have to answer, Shaunture," she said.

Now the centaur spoke. "The river does not measure, but—" He paused, for a measuring tape had appeared in his hands.

"Meander," Heather said. "It does not meander."

"Thank you." The tape disappeared. "But you will want to avoid the colored people."

Breanna sat up straight. Edsel put a cautioning hand on her brown arm.

"What is the problem with colored people?" Justin asked.

"Their talents. They were originally Mundanes, and their form of greeting is to shake hands. When they got magic, thanks to the curse of a passing demon, it was inconvenient. They are named White, Green, Brown, Black, Grey, and other collars, and—"

He paused, for a huge horse collar had appeared around his neck.

"Colors," Heather said. "Other colors."

"Thank you," the centaur said, as the collar faded out. "Not only are they those colors, but anything they touch becomes those colors too."

"So they really are colored people," Edsel murmured. "Literal Xanth strikes again."

"For sure," Breanna murmured back. "I should have known."

"I appreciate the problem," Justin said. "We shall not wish to shake hands with these people."

"Yes," the centaur agreed. "Their Mundane costume is quaint, but—" He paused, for now a clownish costume had formed around him.

"Custom," Heather said. "Their Mundane custom of touching hands."

"Thank you." The costume dissolved.

"I begin to see why he doesn't like to talk," Breanna said. "Every time he makes a mistake, it takes form."

"Is there a detour we can take to avoid them?" Pia asked.

"If you take a slightly different angel, you can—" The centaur paused, for an angel had appeared hovering before him, complete with glowing halo and white wings.

"Angle," Heather said. "A slightly different angle."

"Thank you." The angel faded. "You may then pass the home of a center Magician who—'' Now a small building appeared before him, with arrows pointing to it, making it the center of the illustration.

"Centaur," Heather said. "Centaur Magician."

"Thank you. He will be able to direct you further."

"Thank *you*," Justin said. "You have been a real help. So has Heather."

"Yes, she is invaluable," Shaunture agreed. "I dread the day when she finds her dragon and departs with it."

"Well, it doesn't take much brains to be a damsel for a dragon, so I'm qualified," Heather said. "Though I'll hate wearing a skimpy dress."

"I have no concern what she wears," Shaunture confided. "I would like to give her a bucket of—"

A bucket appeared on the girl's head. "Mmmph, mmph!" she cried, unable to make herself understood. She tried to lift it off, but it seemed glued in place.

"Bouquet!" Edsel called. "A bouquet of flowers!"

"Thank you," the centaur said as the bucket faded. "I shall stop speaking now."

"This is understandable," Justin said. "We nevertheless remain appreciative."

"Heather, I think your talent is relating to creatures, not just dragons," Breanna said to the girl. "Maybe you should stay with Shaunture, who really needs you."

The girl's mouth dropped open in surprise. "Really?"

"Really. You always know what he means to say, and that really helps him."

"Well, he says I help, so as not to hurt my childish feelings. But centaurs are way too smart to associate long with dull kids like me."

Breanna seemed to be digesting an internal thought. "Intelligence isn't always what you think. Ask him."

Heather looked at Shaunture. He nodded. "Oh, Shaunture," she cried. "I'd love to stay with you! I know you'll never chomp me."

The centaur looked at Breanna. "I must speak again after all. I am grapefruit for—" He became a huge grapefruit.

"Grateful!" Heather cried joyously, perched on the top. "For her insight."

The centaur resumed his natural form. He spat out a grapefruit seed and shut his mouth firmly.

Para moved on. "I like your boat," Heather called after them. Para made a dip of appreciation without breaking stride.

"That centaur reminds me of someone," Pia remarked.

"Demoness Metria," Justin replied.

There was a swirl of smoke. "Oh, no," Breanna muttered.

The smoke formed a mouth. "Did someone mention my name?"

"It was an accident," Breanna said.

The smoke coalesced into a lovely buxom form, bound by an elastic halter stretching almost to the snapping point. "And you found the foul footed boat."

Para quivered with indignation.

"What kind of foot?" Edsel asked quickly.

"Avis, feathered, game, bird, domestic—"

"Fowl?"

"Whatever," the demoness agreed crossly.

The boat relaxed.

"I'm sure the children will love to ride in it," Metria said. "Thank you so much for offering." She fuzzed back into smoke.

"We didn't—" Breanna started, but of course it was too late. The smoke formed into Demon Ted and DeMonica. They were stuck for another round of babysitting.

"Maybe the two of them will one day grow up and marry each other," Pia muttered. "And the stork will bring them children *they* have to baby-sit."

"Named Tedmon and Monted," Breanna agreed. "And there'll be no Mundanes visiting who are foolish enough to do it."

"Whose *menfolk* are dazzled into volunteering," Pia said. They both laughed. "Actually the children aren't all that bad, and the dazzleability of the menfolk make them more readily handleable."

"For sure."

Justin turned his head to exchange a glance with Edsel. The girls were having their bit of fun.

They departed from the river at a slight angle, so as to avoid the colored people. Soon they came to a boy who stood by the side of the path they were following, with his right thumb lifted.

"Same to you, jerk!" Ted called.

"Shush, that's a Mundane!" Pia exclaimed. "Hitchhiking."

"We do have room for another passenger," Justin said.

"First things first." Pia cupped her hands and called to the boy. "What's your name?"

"Gabriel," the boy called back.

"So he's not one of the colored people," Pia said. "He can ride with us."

"What's wrong with colored people?" Monica asked.

"Nothing," Edsel said, forestalling trouble.

The boat stopped, and the boy climbed in. "Do you know a safe way to the snowy mountains?" Pia asked him.

"Oh, sure. Right the way you're going now. But you don't want to go all the way there. They're cold."

"We'll chance it," Pia said, and resumed her private dialogue with Justin. She had tuned him out, as was her custom with folk she had no immediate interest in.

So Edsel and Breanna took up the slack, lest the children do it. "What are you doing in Xanth, Gabriel?" Breanna asked. "Because you're obviously Mundane."

"I guess it does show," Gabriel said, abashed. "I'd like to live in Xanth. I made a deal: I can visit Xanth for a week. I can stay here if I can find a family to adopt me or a girl to marry me. Otherwise I must return forever to drear Mundania."

"How old are you?" Breanna asked.

"Fourteen."

"That's what I thought. You're younger than I am, and so you are still mired in the Adult Conspiracy. You can't marry a Xanth girl."

"I could marry one who is eighteen or over," Gabriel said. "If she wanted to. If she didn't break the Conspiracy."

Both children perked up, evidently intrigued by the prospect of breaking the Adult Conspiracy.

"But you already know all that stuff, don't you?" Breanna asked.

"Sure. But in Xanth—"

"I know. And you'd rather put up with that, than go back to Mundania."

"Yeah. Do you think I have a chance?"

"To find a girl, no. To find a family, maybe." Then Breanna brightened. "Does it have to be any special kind of girl?"

"I don't think so."

"How about a nymph?"

Gabriel smiled. "I'd love a nymph. But she'd break the Conspiracy in the first five seconds."

The children squealed with laughter. Ted grabbed Monica, and she flung her hair around and kicked her feet up in a parody of a nymph.

"For sure," Breanna agreed ruefully. "Bad idea. But maybe there'll be a family."

"Maybe," he agreed hopefully.

There was a fairly sharp turn in the path. Para, traveling rapidly, was off-balanced by the extra weight, and his side scraped against a sad looking tree. It emitted a sighing sound.

"What was that?" Edsel asked as they moved on.

"A sigh-press tree," Justin called back. "They sigh when pressed."

Now they came to another person. It was a somewhat portly woman. "Are you looking for a ride?" Pia called.

"I'm looking for a lake," the woman replied.

"There's a lake on the river not far ahead," Gabriel said.

"How do you know?" Edsel asked.

"Because I saw fire ants near a fire, and earth ants near earth, and air ants near air. I saw water ants here, so there must be water near."

Edsel nodded. "That works for me."

"Then get in and we'll take you there," Pia said to the woman. "Para could use a swim."

"A swim!" Ted cried, clapping his little hands. Monica's dress became a two piece swimsuit.

The woman climbed in, and there were introductions. She turned out to be Alexandra.

"What's your talent?" Breanna asked.

"I'm a were-dolphin."

"I never heard of that!"

"I think I'm the only one. I've been searching out stray lakes, hoping to find another of my kind, so far without success."

"Why do you want another of your kind?" Gabriel asked.

"I'm lonely. I don't like swimming alone."

"But you don't need another of your kind just for company," Breanna said.

"I think I do. Who else would want to stay with someone who's half in and out of the water?"

"I would," Gabriel said.

Alexandra looked at him. "You look young and wild. Surely you wouldn't want to settle down to a dull lakeside life."

"Life would never be dull, in Xanth."

"Not if we kept you company," Ted said.

"We're younger and wilder," Monica agreed.

Edsel exchanged a glance with Breanna. "Would you consider marrying a boy without violating the Adult Conspiracy?"

Alexandra considered. "That depends on how good company he was."

"Why don't you talk with Gabriel, here?" Edsel suggested.

The two half demon children lost interest, and peered out of the boat.

"I could be great company, I think," Gabriel said. "If that meant I could stay in Xanth."

The two started a dialog, sitting in the center of the boat. Edsel, as a matter of courtesy, tuned them out. "There seem to be a number of interesting people in Xanth," he remarked to Breanna.

"Every person is interesting, when you get to know him," she said. "I'd like to meet every person in Xanth. But there are too many."

Surely so. "What do you think we'll find at the mountains?"

"Melting snow. I've wondered how there can be such a cold place in warm Xanth."

"Well, it's because the temperature drops with elevation."

"That's in Mundania. Here in Xanth you can fly way above the mountains, and not be cold. I've been up there. So there must be magic."

He realized she was right. Xanth did not follow Mundane rules. "What kind of magic?"

"Well, once I met two brothers. One could turn himself into ice. The other could turn anything else to ice. Maybe those brothers live in the mountains."

"Maybe so," he agreed. That seemed just crazy enough to suit this magic land. "But you know, there seems to be an awful lot of fortunate coincidence in Xanth. Like the way certain people meet." Without moving his head, he flicked his eyes in the direction of the youth and the woman in the center of the boat.

"For sure. I've thought about that. I think maybe the Land of Xanth is female, so she does nice things for her people."

"But the Demon X(A/N)TH is male."

"Yes, mostly. Actually demons are any gender they want to be. But the Demon is not the Land. The Land is more like his daughter."

Edsel nodded. "Now that makes sense. Maybe that's why marriages last forever in Xanth."

"For sure. If you could arrange to stay in Xanth with Pia—"

"I don't think so. We have obligations in Mundania, and these are borrowed bodies. But sometimes it rubs off on people. Dug and Kim are just as much together now as they ever were, and they don't spend much time in Xanth."

"Maybe they drank some love elixir."

"If that's magic, it shouldn't work in Mundania."

She nodded. "Maybe not. Still, it might be worth trying. If we pass love spring, you might save some of its elixir, and try it on her. I hear that diluted love elixir and a finder spell can enable a person to find her true love."

They came to the lake. "Oh, wonderful!" Alexandra exclaimed. "I'm so dry." She jumped out of the boat, ran to the water, and dived in. As she struck the water her clothing disappeared and her body became roughly fishlike. She had assumed her dolphin aspect.

Gabriel ran after her. "I love to swim," he said.

"But there might be sharks or serpents in that water," Breanna warned him.

"They won't bother me," he said, pausing at the edge to rip off his clothing. "Not with a dolphin friend protecting me."

"He's got a point," Breanna said.

"You're not supposed to look," Edsel said, smiling.

"I meant—" She paused. "Oh, you're doing it again. You rogue."

Para moved to the lake, and into it without pause. Now there were three of them swimming: dolphin, boy, and boat.

"Our turn!" Ted said. He was now in trunks, and Monica had a shower cap.

"No, wait," Breanna said sharply. To Edsel's surprise, they obeyed.

"There's a shark!" Pia cried. She was especially nervous about them, since one had snapped at her hand.

Then the sleek dolphin circled, intercepting the shark before it could reach the boy. The shark veered away; it knew better than to tangle with such a foe.

"Isn't she great?" Gabriel called. "What a creature!"

"I think this is going to work out," Breanna said.

"Now you can swim," Breanna told the children. Even as she spoke,

they were leaping off the side, making small cannonball splashes. "But stay close to the boat."

Para paddled joyfully around, then moved back toward land. A centaur stood there.

"Hello," Justin called as they walked out on land. "Are you the centaur Magician?"

"I am," the centaur replied. "My name is Rempel. My talent is to know the talents of others."

"I thought all centaurs had names with CH sounds," Edsel said.

"That is the custom, not the rule," Rempel said. "We who are outside the norm do not necessarily follow it."

"Outside the norm?"

"Conventional centaurs do not have magic talents," he said. "Let alone strong ones."

"They consider personal magic obscene," Breanna murmured.

Something moved through the grass. "What's a shark doing on land?" Pia cried, alarmed.

Rempel looked. "Those are a variety of shark called skates," he said. "They are harmless to ordinary folk, unless stepped on."

Now Edsel saw that the creatures were forming hoops and rolling along the ground. "Skates?" he asked.

"Roller skates."

He should have guessed.

The boat halted by some sweet smelling rose bushes. The roses were all colors. Breanna had hauled the children in; now she got out and went to smell a brown one—and suddenly floated into the air above it. There was a shrill of laughter from Ted and Monica.

"Beware," Rempel said. "Those roses have the talent of levitating things their own color."

Edsel went and caught Breanna's flailing arm. He drew her away from the rose, and she fell back to the ground. "I'm getting in trouble, just like a Mundane," she muttered.

"Maybe it's contagious," Edsel said.

Breanna looked around. "What's that? It doesn't look quite like a centaur."

Edsel recognized the creature immediately, but decided not to speak.

Rempel smiled. "Indeed, it is not. That's Ally, short for B B Allusion, a chestnut copper mare, just visiting." When Breanna still looked blank, he said "A horse. A member of one of my ancestral species."

"Oh," Breanna said, embarrassed. "Like a night mare, only less magical."

"For sure," Edsel agreed.

Rempel suddenly galloped to the edge of the lake. "Away! Away!" he cried, splashing the water with his forehoofs.

Edsel and Breanna walked across to see what was going on. There was only a rather blobby sea creature feeding on what looked like weeds at the edge.

"This is Hugh," Rempel said. "He is a manatee. Sometimes the sharks come after him. Then I have to drive them off."

"Awww," Ted said. His sympathy was for the sharks.

"To save Hugh Manatee," Edsel said.

"Precisely." Then the centaur paused thoughtfully, glancing at Edsel.

"He does that," Breanna said. "At least it bypassed the children."

Alexandra and Gabriel emerged from the lake. She changed to clothed human form in one motion; clothes seemed to be part of her magic. Thus she wasn't violating the Adult Conspiracy by showing him any panties. Gabriel had to clothe himself the ordinary way, but since Alexandra was of age, it didn't matter what she saw.

They walked toward Edsel, Breanna, and Rempel. "I'm going to have sore muscles," Gabriel said. "I haven't swum like that in a long time."

Rempel trotted a short distance to pick something from what looked like a pea plant. He brought it back and gave it to Gabriel. "Try this."

"What is it?" the boy asked doubtfully.

"A thera pea. It is good for sore muscles."

The children tittered. "I thought it made you p—"

"Demon Ted!" Breanna snapped, silencing the boy. It occurred to Edsel that some day she would make a good mother; she had the maternal reflexes.

Gabriel popped it into his mouth. In a moment he smiled. "The soreness is gone!"

Rempel shrugged. "It is convenient to know the talents of things. I can show you a lie-lack bush if you wish; a person near it can't tell a lie. Or a ruler; that writing device takes control of the person who uses it."

"Why is it that you are out here in the wilderness?" Edsel asked. "Surely many folk would like to have you and your talent near."

"I prefer nature."

Edsel nodded. "I can appreciate that." He looked at Breanna. "I suppose we had better be getting on, if we want to reach the mountains today."

"If you plan to spend the night in the mountains, you will need much warmer clothing," Rempel said. "Unless your love keeps you very warm."

Edsel realized that there was a natural confusion. "Breanna and I are not a couple. Our significant others are the other two." He gestured toward the boat, where Justin and Pia were talking and looking around.

"I apologize," Rempel said. "The compatibilities seemed otherwise."

"Opposites attract," Breanna said. "So I'm attracted to Justin Tree. I'm young and he's old." She glanced around. "And we are involuntary baby-sitters for these two half demon children."

"For sure," Monica said, mimicking her.

"Do you have any advice on the best route to the mountains?" Edsel asked.

"The path forks," Rempel said. "You will want to take the right path, to avoid mischief and find warmer clothing."

"For sure," Breanna agreed, as the children tittered. "Thank you."

"If you get on the wrong path, you will need both your talents, for there will be darkness and magic to be deflected."

"Thanks," Edsel said. They walked back to rejoin the others.

"This is a beautiful place," Pia said. "Justin has been pointing out its novelties. For example, there's a chemis-tree."

They looked. The tree's fruit seemed to be in the form of colored fluids in little beakers.

"And a water chestnut tree," Pia said, indicating another. The nuts were in the shape of damp little chests.

"You are becoming a naturalist," Edsel remarked.

"I really am," she agreed. "I never cared, before I met Justin. He's teaching me so much."

"We have to get moving, if we want to catch the mountains today," Breanna said. Her voice seemed just a trifle tight.

Justin called to Gabriel and Alexandra. "Do you wish to ride farther with us?"

"No thanks," Gabriel called back. "We like it here."

"Maybe we'll get married," Alexandra agreed. Then the two of them dived back into the lake.

"It's definitely working out," Pia said. "In the Xanthly way."

They got into the boat. The duck feet carried them along the path up the river. "We need to take the—" Edsel began.

"Oh look!" Pia cried. "There's an adder." She reached for a nearby snake.

"Oooo, great!" Monica exclaimed.

"But that's poisonous!" Edsel protested.

Too late. Pia caught the snake and lifted it into the boat. Edsel looked desperately around for a stick, but there wasn't even a paddle.

"What's two plus two?" Pia asked the snake as the children crowded close.

The adder struck at the side of the boat. There was the sharp bong of a bell. Now there was a mark on the wood: the number four.

Edsel relaxed. It was after all harmless.

Pia lifted the adder and set it outside the boat. It slithered away. She glanced back at Edsel. "What were you saying?"

"Just that we should take the right path."

"Did we take the wrong one?" Justin asked. "There was a pitchfork back near where we saw the adder."

"A pitchfork?" Edsel asked, concerned.

"From a pine needle tree, technically. The smallest needles make tuning forks, the middle ones make pitchforks for farmers to use, and the largest make forks in the road. They are all sizes of pitchforks, really."

So a pine needle tree could make a fork in the road. Now he got the punnish logic of it. And they had passed right through that fork while distracted by the adder. Should he ask Para to go back and check that fork?

An awful shape loomed behind them. "Haaa!" it roared. It looked like a centaur, except that it had black horns, bat wings, red skin, and green stripes.

"What is that?" Edsel asked, more than concerned.

"It's a demon centaur," Breanna said. "This is mischief." She faced forward. "Get moving, Para; we're in trouble."

"Great," Ted said.

"No it isn't," Monica said. "They chomp children."

The boat accelerated, but the centaur was in full gallop and still gaining. "Haaa!" it repeated, just in case they hadn't heard the first time. "I am Dyrak, scourge of mortals, and you are on my path."

"I think we took the wrong fork," Edsel said.

"For sure! Duck feet can't outrun that thing. But maybe if we can reach water—" She looked desperately from side to side. "Para! Take that detour ahead! It leads toward the river."

The boat slowed around the sharp turn and plunged into an offshoot path. The tree branches closed overhead, forming a canopy, making it seem like a hall. The demon centaur's hoofs screeched to a halt; he did not follow them. "You'll be sorry!" he called.

"Oh, pooh!" Monica called back.

"Yeah, poop!" Ted agreed.

Now Edsel saw creatures standing between the trees that lined the hall. They had the lower portions of men and the upper portions of bulls. They looked ferocious, but they weren't moving. "What are those?" he asked.

"I think they're hall minotaurs," Breanna replied. "They keep order in halls, but I hear that folk seldom like the order they keep."

"They don't seem to be doing anything," Edsel said.

"That's because we're going the way they want," she said darkly. "They'll step in if we try to escape."

Edsel glanced at the children. They looked nervous. That made *him* nervous. "We can't get out of this?"

"Rempel said we'd have to use our talents."

Edsel concentrated. What was his talent? Ah, yes—to modify or deflect other talents. He hadn't tried to use it, but this must be the time.

Breanna peered into the deepening gloom surrounding them as the foliage of the trees became thicker. Edsel remembered that she could see in blackness. "Worse coming," she said tersely. "Ugly folk. I wish I had a pair of bi-noculars."

Edsel knew better than to guess. "What are they?"

"They help you to see in the dark, twice as far."

The boat slowed. The way ahead was being blocked. "Don't stop," Breanna cried. "Plow on through!"

Para tried, but hands were grabbing onto his sides. They were gnarly, warty hands. They belonged to people clinging to the boat, trying to climb in.

Edsel reached for a hand, about to rip it off the boat. "Don't touch them," Breanna said. "They look poisonous."

"Who are you?" Ted asked a horrendous male face as it drew up over the rim.

"E Coli," the face answered.

Edsel didn't like the sound of that.

"Who are you?" Monica asked a disreputable female face.

"Salmon Ella."

The sound of that was no better. But could his talent help? Edsel leaned over E Coli. How did his talent work? Did he have to touch, or speak?

Then Coli heaved himself up and sprawled half in the boat. Edsel put both hands out to push him back, recoiling at the touch.

And the man turned green and lumpy, and fell away. What had happened?

"Great," Ted said. "You turned him into Broc Coli!"

Now Salmon Ella hauled herself into the boat. Edsel pushed her back. She turned into a sleek fish and fell away.

"Ella's a salmon," Monica said.

So that was how his talent worked, in true Xanthian fashion.

The dark path lay right under an innocent looking tree, beyond which was open water and light. "Don't go there!" Justin called, and the boat veered to the side, crashing through brush.

"Why not?" Edsel asked.

"It's a captivi tree."

Oh. Of course Justin knew his trees.

Now the boat shot out of the gloom and splashed onto the water of the river. They had won through.

"That was fun," Ted said. "Let's do it again."

"Isn't it about time for your nap?" Breanna inquired.

"We don't take naps," Monica said.

"You do now," Breanna said. She unfolded one of the stored blankets and draped it over them. It was decorated with pictures of tires.

"Look out!" Ted cried. "She's making a bed."

"It's part of the Adult Conspiracy to subjugate children," Monica said, appalled.

Then, to Edsel's surprise, the two children settled immediately into nap mode. "What kind of blanket is that?" he asked.

"It's a tire."

"It's attire?"

"A tire. It makes children tired." She shook her head. "I must confess, at times the Adult Conspiracy is convenient."

"You mean, naps really is part of it?"

"As far as they know." Breanna smiled mysteriously. He realized that she, being underage, was not yet officially part of the Conspiracy. She had been bluffing.

Now that they were on the water, it seemed to be clear sailing. Edsel relaxed. That last session had demonstrated that Xanth was not necessarily benign. "Say, we should check in," he said, remembering. "Another day has passed."

"For sure." Breanna produced the Ear and handed it over.

"Edsel Mundane here," he said into it. "All is well for the moment."

"That's fine," Chlorine's voice returned. "Same here."

He returned the Ear. "I feel a bit guilty for that, but there's no point in worrying them."

"Oh, look—Siamese triplets," Breanna said, pointing to the shore.

"Wha?" Then he saw them: three identical cats.

But they had not escaped cleanly. One of the monsters had poked a hole in the boat. Water was leaking in, forming bilge. Edsel looked for a cup or container to dip it out. The leak wasn't large, but it could not be ignored.

Then a water creature swam toward them. It dived under the boat. Suddenly the leak stopped. It had been closed up or patched over, and now the hull was tight. The swimming creature must have done it.

"What was that thing?" Edsel asked.

"A seal, of course," Breanna answered.

A seal had sealed the boat. Of course.

Now they made good progress upriver. "Was there some reason we didn't travel on the river before?" Edsel asked.

"Maybe Justin knows." Breanna lifted her voice and called to the front end of the boat. "Why didn't we use the river before?"

"The rapids," Justin called back. "And the slows."

Edsel worked it out: the rapids would be too fast for comfort, and the slows would be too slow. Everything made sense, in its fashion.

But soon they had to return to the land, because a storm was coming. The clouds loomed massively. "I don't like the look of this," Breanna said. She lifted the blanket, and the children woke up, refreshed. "Stay close; we'll have to take shelter."

"Storms can be uncomfortable," Edsel said. "But it's only water."

She shook her head. "Every time you start seeming normal, you say something stupid."

They pulled off the path, and Edsel and Justin lifted the boat and turned it over. The duck feet lay flat against the hull. They all got under that shelter.

Just in time, for now the storm struck. Objects the size of footballs struck the ground with sickening thuds. Then one splatted against the boat. Part of the blob dribbled down to plop before Edsel's nose. It was gray and wrinkled.

"What kind of storm *is* this?" he demanded.

"A brainstorm, silly," Breanna said. "I hate them."

He could understand why. Only in Xanth!

Soon the storm passed. They got out, righted the boat, and resumed their travel toward the mountains.

The grade steepened, and the temperature dropped. They had to wrap blankets around them to stay warm, because they had forgotten to get better clothing. Justin and Pia shared a blanket in front, and Edsel and Breanna shared one in back. The two demon children did not seem affected by the cold.

"I wonder whether we should change partners," Edsel murmured.

"No, I don't think you two men would want to share a blanket." But Breanna's brown face was serious; she was concerned. Pia was a mighty fetching figure of a woman.

"For what it's worth," he said, "I know Pia. She goes for what she wants, and there's not a romantic bone in her body unless she chooses to put it there. She wants information, not Justin."

"And he's thrilled to a convert to the interest of trees," she agreed. "I guess I don't have reason to be jealous. It's just my nature." Then she turned to him. "Maybe they should be jealous of us."

"Uh—"

"Tell me more about this in-between stage you call petting. Better, show me."

Treacherous ground, partly because he did feel himself attracted to her. "I—think you already know enough."

She laughed softly. "Just teasing, Ed."

Was she? He had no doubt of her loyalty to Justin, but she could be as single minded as Pia about getting what she wanted. She wanted experience.

"Awww," Ted's voice came. "Aren't you going to even goose her, like this?" He reached under Monica's skirt.

"Eeeee!" Monica screamed, sailing high into the air.

Then they both dissolved into laughter. They must have rehearsed that little charade. Obviously they did know something of the secrets of the Adult Conspiracy, and thought they were hilarious. Edsel was abruptly glad for another reason that he had not done anything with Breanna, aside from her age and commitment to her fiancé. He had not realized how closely they were being watched.

The boat rounded a turn in the trail, and there, suddenly, was The Scene. "The illusion picture!" he exclaimed. "This is it."

"This is the reality," Justin called back.

They got out of the boat, each swathed in a blanket, and studied the situation. The mountains were indeed only half clothed with snow, and their middle and lower reaches were still draining into the river.

"Obviously there is a warming trend," Justin said. "But what is causing it?"

There was a swirl of smoke, larger and more ominous than Metria's. It formed into a giant diffuse demon. "I am causing it," the demon announced proudly. "Do you have a problem with that?"

Edsel hesitated. Caution seemed best. This could be an ugly customer.

"For sure," Breanna said. "It's flooding out the valley."

So much for caution. The demon swelled to a larger size, glowering down at her. "And who are you, dirt face?"

Uh-oh. Breanna didn't like being put down.

"I'm Breanna of the Black Wave," the girl said boldly. "And who the bleep are you, hot stuff?"

The demon swelled another size. "I am the Demon CoTwo, and I like warming air. I hate ice and snow."

"Then what in Xanth are you doing here by the snow mountains, airhead?"

Edsel opened his mouth to interject something, but nothing came to mind. He saw Justin and Pia similarly stymied. Breanna's mouth had been too quick for them.

CoTwo expanded another notch. "You dare to question me, you burned up urchin? I mean to abolish all cold air in Xanth, starting with the coldest. That is here. After all the snow and ice is gone, I will look for other ice to melt, until the whole land is warm."

"We don't like that, foghead," Breanna said.

The demon swelled to yet more horrendous girth. "And what do you propose to do about it, toasted gamine?"

"We propose to stop you, gas-brain," she retorted.

The Demon CoTwo opened his mouth until it was wider than his head. "Ho, ho, **HO!**" he laughed. "And how to you propose to do that?"

Now Breanna hesitated. "I'm not sure. But we'll do it."

"And here is what I will do," CoTwo said. "I will blow you away. And if you ever return, I will treat you unkindly."

"You don't scare me, you quarter-wit," Breanna said.

"Uh, Breanna—" Edsel murmured.

But it was too late, as it usually was in such situations. CoTwo bloated to gargantuan proportion, then aimed his big mouth and them and blew. The wind was horrendous. It picked them up and literally blew them away. They sailed heels over head through the air. Edsel didn't have time either to be scared or to try to catch a naughty glimpse of one of the women.

They landed some distance downriver, in the cold water, unhurt but shaken. Para was inverted, his duck feet waggling frantically in the air. The supplies had gotten dumped or soaked.

"That was fun," Ted exclaimed.

"Let's do it again," Monica agreed.

The adults shared a sigh as they helped right the boat and then dragged themselves out of the water. At least they had found out what was causing the problem of rising water. What they would be doing about it was a work still in progress.

$\overline{\underline{8}}$
GOOD MAGICIAN

P ia shook herself off. She hated getting soaked in her clothing. She was shiveringly cold, and their blankets were also
hopelessly wet, and dusk was closing. What a mess! Para,
the duck footed boat, was the only member of their party who seemed
satisfied; he was resting on the water, untouched by the chill and undis-
mayed by his dunking. He was evidently not the smartest of creatures,
and liked being of service.

Well, she had never been one to mope ineffectively. "We need a
fire, a tent, and food," she said. "Then we can strip and dry our clothes
while we eat in comfort."

"I can find some fireweed," Justin said.

"I can make a tent from the blankets," Edsel said.

"I can roust out some chocolate spiders," Breanna said, peering into
the darkness.

"Spiders!" Pia said, alarmed.

The girl shot her a dark glance. "You're a vegetarian?"

"No, but—" She realized that she was in danger of looking like a
squeamish female. It was true; she was plenty squeamish about bugs and
other noxious notions, but she didn't like admitting it. Maybe someone
else would balk at eating spiders, and then she could safely do so too.
"Okay. I'll make a hearth."

"We'll fetch wood," Demon Ted said.

"And pillows," DeMonica agreed.

The children were getting helpful? Pia distrusted that. But maybe such chores were their idea of fun.

The others scattered. Justin and Breanna disappeared into the darkness, while Edsel scouted around for sticks of wood suitable for ridgepoles. He was good at things like that. He used a rock to pound forked sticks into the ground, put the ridgepoles into the raised forks, and then set about stretching the sodden blankets across them. The blankets would drip dry as time passed, and should provide shelter.

Pia used a stick to scrape a section of ground clear, then carried in stones to make a circular hearth. The effort warmed her, but not enough; her teeth were still chattering.

Ted brought in a number of dry sticks for the fire, and Pia thanked him. He stepped on his own toes and almost blushed; he didn't know how to handle thanks from an adult.

Monica brought pillows. They were dry, and promised to be useful for sitting on, and for sleeping on later. Pia thanked her also, and she reacted much the way Ted had. They were not bad children, just active and sometimes impertinent.

What was interesting was the way they brought these things: each in turn held the locket they had found before, and spoke to it: "Out, sticks," or "Out, pillows," and the things had abruptly appeared before it. That was a most useful and capacious locket.

Justin returned with the fireweed. This was dull green stuff. But when he laid it in the hearth and said "Fire," it burst into brightly colored flame. The light radiated out, blessedly warm.

Then Breanna returned with an armful of dark brown leggy substance. It was hard to tell where she left off and it began. Pia forced herself to look. And smell. It was chocolate in the shape of spiders. Oh. She was glad she hadn't made a scene about that.

Then one of the spider legs moved. Pia stifled a scream.

"Oops, I got a live one," Breanna said. She picked it up and carried it to the fringe of the glade. "They slough off their old skins as they grow, and those are pure chocolate. But I wouldn't care to eat a live one."

"For sure," Pia agreed weakly. The two children tittered; she wasn't sure whether they were laughing at her imitation of Breanna, or her alarm about the spiders.

They sat around the fire and warmed. But their clothing remained clinging and clammy. The others did not look any more comfortable than Pia felt.

She would have to take the initiative. "Let me make sure I understand," she said, standing up. "The Adult Conspiracy decrees that no child shall hear any bad words or see panties. Is that right?"

"That is correct," Justin agreed.

"And no child shall be told or shown the secret of summoning storks."

"Correct." But he looked a little nervous, as if distrusting what she was leading up to.

"Well, none of us will be doing any of those things," Pia said. "But we do need to clean and dry our clothing. So I am going to wash mine." She reached under her blouse and unfastened her bra. Then she drew blouse and bra off together.

Naturally both men stared at her bare upper torso. But no undergarment had been shown, so they did not freak out. Of course she knew from her subterranean experience with Justin that bras alone did not do it, but she didn't care to speak of that. The children looked also, but immediately went back to eating chocolate; there was nothing interesting to see.

Pia removed her shoes, then drew down her skirt and panties together. The eyeballs of the two men expanded by five per cent, and their jaws dropped by a similar amount, but again no undergarment had been exposed. There was no freak-out, and the children remained bored.

"Now I shall do my laundry," Pia said, privately relieved. She hadn't been quite sure that she would get away with this, and wasn't sure of the penalty if the Conspiracy stepped in. "Then I shall retire to a tent, with Edsel to keep me warm." She carried her clothing to the bank of the river.

There was a pause. Then she heard the reaction. "For sure! No violation." And in a moment Breanna joined her, carrying her own bundle of clothing.

Then at last the men, oddly most reticent, did the same. The children, being half demon, formed their clothing from their own substance, so didn't need to wash it separately.

There was a swirl of smoke. For a moment Pia was afraid that their fire had spread out of control, but then a pair of eyes formed, and it

coalesced into Demon Vore. He looked at the four adults, and his eyeballs too expanded a size as he surveyed the girls, but he made no comment.

"About time," Ted said.

"It's really boring here," Monica agreed.

"So I see," Vore replied. "Tomorrow Metria will take you to visit
Robota."

Both children clapped their little hands in delight. Then Vore swept
them up and puffed into swirling smoke. One swirl was white, another
brown, and their shapes were oddly suggestive as they dissipated.

"Did you see his eyes?" Breanna asked. "One reflected a white
nymph, the other a brown nymph."

"I wonder who those could have been?" Pia said. Then they both
laughed.

The men came up behind them. "If I heard correctly," Justin said,
"We shall not have to baby-sit the children tomorrow."

"That's a relief," Pia said.

"However, we have a small problem," he continued. "We have just
two tents, and while Edsel and Pia can share one for warmth—"

Time to stifle this. "The Conspiracy frowns on stork summoning
when one of the parties is under eighteen," Pia said. "But I don't believe
it says anything about sharing warmth. Does it?"

"Ah, no, but—"

"So until your clothing is dry, you had better stay close to Breanna.
For warmth, after you both have suffered a chill. This is merely routine
common sense."

"True. But—"

Pia turned a severe glance on him. "You are not going to summon
any stork, are you?"

"Of course not! But—"

"So there is no problem, is there?" When he hesitated, she repeated:
"*Is* there?"

"For sure not," Breanna said eagerly, and hauled him off to a tent.

Edsel joined her in the other tent, and closed off the ends. "Sometimes I think I could get to like your style," he said, "if I didn't already
love you."

"Shut up and warm me," she said. But she was pleased. Their tacit
deal required her to make him deliriously happy for the night, and she
knew exactly how to do that, and was doing it now, but sometimes she

liked doing it better than other times. She appreciated his recognition of the way she had solved the problem of wet clothing.

He spoiled it by only one comment. "I wish I could win you back."

"We're not yet out of Xanth," she replied, hinting that his ploy was not yet lost. But it was a mere courtesy; she still intended to divorce him after this was over. Then she would see about studying Mundane environmentalism. Justin was a continuing font of information and insight into all things natural, but the things here were mostly magical. She would need to learn the non-magic variants.

"Poor Justin," he said. "He can't do this, and he wants to so much."

"Maybe I can educate him." For she could say things to the man that Breanna could not. Because despite her sixteen year old body, she was not sixteen, and there was precious little the Adult Conspiracy had left to show her.

Sixteen: she loved being physically sixteen again. The merest twitch of this body could make a man flip.

She twitched. Edsel flipped. Ah, there was true power. He was completely unable to resist her. And, with the magic of this land, she could freak him out whenever she wanted to, just by putting on the right bit of clothing. He thought he was having his will of her, but she was having her will of him, making him perform with desperate enthusiasm, thinking every notion was his own. How little he knew! How little men ever knew.

In due course Edsel wore himself out, and she was able to relax. She had not thought to bring any Mundane stork signal interrupters, but there were other ways, if she were unlucky. And it did guarantee Edsel's complete cooperation on the quest.

She wondered idly what it would be like to seduce Justin. She could surely do it, if she chose. But it would not be ethical, and with her appreciation of the need to save the trees had come an appreciation of the rules of that game. Strictly hands off the Companions. Anyway, Breanna was her friend.

Still, it had been fun making both men stare. She did not merely love this, she actually reveled in this sixteen year old physique, and wanted to show it off while she had it. Once she returned to Mundania, she would revert to her real body. That one was not as good; her necessary consumption of sugar, to counterbalance the insulin shots, had led to some weight gain. If this body was a 10, that one was an 8, and descending. But maybe she would now have the stamina to do the dieting and exercise required to whip it back into shape, working around her condition.

She slept, surprisingly comfortable on the pillows, in the warmth of the tent and Edsel's proximity. Their session had really heated him up, and that in turn warmed her.

In the morning she disengaged from Edsel's too-fond embrace and went out to recover her clothes. They were where she had left them, hanging on sticks by the gently blazing fire, and quite dry. Someone must have tended the fire during the night, for it was in good order. She put on her bra and panties, then reached for her skirt—and saw Justin. The man had evidently been out gathering more food, and come upon her unawares, and freaked out. He was fully dressed, standing frozen.

Well, she knew how to handle that. Interesting that the sight of her underwear itself had not affected Justin when he tended the fire in the night. It was only such apparel *on the body* that did it. As was the case, to a lesser extent, in Mundania. Like soda and ice cream, it took a combination to do the trick. What would be the effect of panties on a dressmaker's mannequin? There had to be some special magic, because Edsel was also affected, as Breanna had demonstrated when she mooned both men with her black panties. Edsel had seen similar sights many times before, both from her and the steamy movies he liked. Yet in Xanth he had completely freaked out. So was it something in the air?

She donned the rest of her clothing, then snapped her fingers. The man recovered. "Hello, Justin," she said cheerfully, as if there had been no break.

"Hello, Pia," he answered, unaware of his time out. He set down the armful of pies and milkweed pods he had foraged. They would have a good breakfast. "Did you sleep well?"

No need to go into the first half hour. "Very well. And you?"

He fidgeted. "I—I have never before been that close to a—a—"

"Naked girl?"

"Whatever," he agreed, halfway emulating Metria. "I very much admire and love Breanna, but I was so sorely tempted to—to—"

His diffidence was charming, but probably pointless. "Let me ask you some things. If two people both know the content of the Adult Conspiracy, and both wish to indulge in an aspect of its mystery, is there any reason they should not?" She took one of his pies and began warming it over the fire.

"Well, that depends on their ages. If one—"

"But *does* it? Doesn't the Conspiracy govern what they may learn or say, rather than what they actually do?"

"Why, surely it governs also what they do. I—"

"Breanna mentioned a man called Ralph, who was supposed to guide her to the Isle of Women last year, who attempted to summon the stork with her."

"Why yes," he agreed. "I was with her at the time, in her mind. She kicked him into Para, who carried him hastily away. That was an ugly scene."

"Why did she have to fight him off? I mean, if the Conspiracy is enforced in actions, why couldn't she have just lain there, and he would have been unable to violate it? The same way we are unable to say bad words in her presence, like bleep?" Her pie was warm enough; she took a bite.

He stared at her. "I never thought of that. I don't know what would have happened."

"I do. She did need to fight him off. Which means that aspect is not magically enforced. Some things can be done, but not spoken of, such as natural functions—which this happens to be." She couldn't identify the flavor of pie. "What kind is this?"

"Brownberry. Similar to blackberry, but less so, and with a mocha flavor." Then he returned to the other subject. "But surely it must be enforced, because—"

"Because it is enforced in every other respect. Maybe you are right. In which case, you don't need to worry. Next time you are with her, don't hold back. The Conspiracy will stop you." She decided that there was indeed a hint of chocolate and coffee flavor in the pie.

He was clearly nonplused. "But suppose—"

"Suppose it doesn't. Then it must be because it doesn't apply to two people who are knowledgeable and willing, and who love each other. At least when both are at least sixteen. Doesn't that make sense?"

"But I've always believed—"

"I've always believed that magic doesn't exist," she said. "Sometimes long-held beliefs are mistaken. I think the practical thing to do is to try a thing to see whether it works." She sucked on a milkweed pod, getting the fresh milk.

"Possibly you are correct," he said dubiously.

"Justin, you know an enormous amount about nature, but not much about romance. So don't take my word; just let yourself be natural with her, and see what happens. Whatever happens must be right. Isn't that so?''

''Perhaps it is,'' he conceded.

She had finished her pie. She was satisfied; she had set out to educate him, and might have done Breanna a considerable favor in the process. It was quid pro quo: Pia was monopolizing Justin by day, so she was enhancing him for Breanna by night.

The flap of a tent moved. Breanna emerged. ''Oh, I must have overslept,'' she said.

''It happens,'' Pia said, not deceived. The girl had been listening, and she was no fool. Justin would be in for the night of his long life, tonight.

Breanna had no clothing. She fetched hers and took it back into the tent. She emerged a moment later, dressed. Justin had been with her all night, without clothing, but this was daylight; he seemed about ready to faint. And of course the girl had done it deliberately; she could have called for her clothing to be passed into the tent. No fool, indeed.

Then Edsel emerged from his tent. ''What, am I the last one up?'' he asked. ''Oh, the shame of it!''

He was too theatrical. He had been listening too. Pia grabbed his clothing and tossed it to him before he could come out.

The others ate, and then they took down the tents and put the blankets and pillows in the boat, together with the rest of the pies. They were ready to travel.

''But where should we go?'' Edsel asked. ''We know what the problem is, but not what to do about it.''

''The Good Magician's castle,'' Breanna said. ''We'll ask him. He always has the answers.''

''However, there may be a complication,'' Justin cautioned.

''For sure,'' Breanna agreed. ''It's a challenge to get in, and he charges a year's service or the equivalent for each Answer.''

''But he does deliver,'' Justin said.

Pia considered. ''We can't do any year's service. We're here for only a few days.''

''Perhaps, considering the importance of the mission, he will make an exception,'' Justin said.

''Also considering who else is involved in this exchange,'' Breanna said. She meant Nimby, the Demon $X(A/N)^{TH}$.

Justin nodded. ''Pertinent thought.''

"So let's go there," Pia said. "Do you know the way?"

"For sure. That's our job—to take you safely where you want to go."

They got into the boat, and it paddled off downstream. That was faster than the upstream trip had been. Soon they came to the slows and the rapids. They moved out onto the land. That was the nice thing about this boat: it wasn't limited.

"We had better check in," Edsel said. "It's that time."

"For sure." Breanna gave him the Ear.

"Edsel and Pia checking in," he said into it. Then he put it to his own ear, to hear its reply. He looked surprised. "Nimby and Chlorine didn't check in yet? Well, maybe they forgot. We'll check again, later." He returned the Ear.

"Do you think they're in trouble?" Pia asked.

"Com Passion doesn't know. There was no indication of trouble yesterday, so maybe they're just late."

"Maybe," she agreed. But this made her uneasy.

Then the boat stumbled and stopped moving. They hastily piled out, and Justin looked. "You are missing some toes," he said, appalled.

Para bobbed, his way of nodding.

"But that's not supposed to happen," Breanna protested. "His feet are magically protected."

Justin looked around. "No wonder," he said, advancing on a patch of milky white weeds. "You walked over lack toes. It's extremely intolerant. Even a protective spell may not suffice to counter it."

"And if we had been walking, we'd be lacking toes too," Breanna said, shuddering. "We must help Para get his toes back."

Especially considering that riding in the boat was an awful lot easier than walking. But Pia kept her mouth shut; it wasn't a worthy thought.

"Doesn't Xanth have healing springs?" Edsel asked.

"Yes, but none close by here," Justin said. "However, I believe there is a quack doctor in the area."

Pia started to laugh, then realized that he wasn't joking. So she stifled it.

"Para's father was a quack," Edsel said.

"And his mother was a dream boat," Breanna said. "So a quack doctor should be fine."

"Perhaps we can get directions," Justin said.

At that point a young man came from the path ahead. He wore a loose shirt and saggy trousers. Pia was closest, so she hailed him. "Hello!" She smiled winningly.

He paused. Young men tended to, when she hailed them and smiled.

"I am Pia, and I would really like some information."

"I am Don. My talent is—"

"Yes, of course. Do know where the quack doctor is?" Then she stopped to stare.

For a young woman now stood where the man had been. She wore a shirt that was tight across the front, and trousers that were tight across the back. "Changing gender at will," she said. "That's his story. I am Dot."

"You—you're the same person?" Pia asked. She had seen some amazing things in Xanth, but nothing quite like this.

The man reappeared, with the clothing losing its spots of tightness. His hair was tied back in a ponytail that could have applied to either gender. "Yes. I do know where the quack doctor lives. That's her story. Right this way."

He turned, and his hips flared: he was becoming the woman again.

"History—herstory," Edsel murmured as they followed. "I get it—I think."

"I guess she can see his story, and he can see hers," Breanna said. "No battle of the sexes there."

"But it does give new meaning to the term gender-bender," Edsel said. He would.

They followed Dot/Don along another path. Pia verified that the person's clothing did not change with the gender; it was a unisex outfit that filled out in different regions according to the body beneath it. Probably a tunic would have been better, because it was more naturally pliable. She wondered what it would be like if Don/Dot wore no clothing. Edsel's eyes would inflate at sight of the woman, and deflate at sight of the man. What kind of a romantic life would such a person have?

They passed a handsome tree. Edsel was about to touch its trunk, but Justin stopped him. "No! That's reverse wood!"

Edsel paused. "Does that mean what it sounds like?"

"Yes," Breanna said. "Think of antimatter."

Edsel abruptly stepped well back from the tree. "Antimatter—touch that and it's total destruction."

"Not that extreme," Justin said. "But reverse wood is never to be taken for granted. It reverses magic, and you can seldom be sure what form that reversal will take.''

Dot looked back. ''I was delivered near that tree. I think it accounts for my talent. The first time I touched it, it reversed me from a boy to a girl, and the second time, the other way. After a while I got so I could do it on my own,'' Don concluded.

''I don't want to touch it,'' Pia said. ''I'm satisfied as a girl.''

''For sure,'' Breanna agreed.

''Reverse wood does not necessarily reverse gender,'' Justin said. ''It may have no effect on a person, and merely reverse some thing a person touches it to. But I agree that we do not wish to experiment. I am surprised to discover it here; I had thought most such trees were destroyed some time ago.''

''That reminds me,'' Don said. ''When I was really little, this tree was a rotting stump. Then it formed into a gnarly old tree. Now it's a mature tree, healthier.''

''It is living backwards!'' Justin said. ''Reverse wood lives backwards. That makes perfect sense, though it had not occurred to me before.''

They moved on, and soon came to a shack where a number of ducks flocked. An old man sat on a stool, bandaging a duck's sore foot. This was obviously the quack doctor.

''Someone to see you, grandpa,'' Dot said.

The man looked up. ''Hello. I'm Owen Cossaboon, quack doctor. What can I do for you?''

''You're Mundane,'' Breanna said.

''Yes, I have no magic. That's why I'm a quack. But I do what I can.'' He turned the bandaged duck loose.

''We have a patient for you,'' Pia said. She beckoned to Para, who had hung back. The boat limped up.

''Oh, you ran afoul of the lack toes,'' Owen said sympathetically. ''I thought we had cleaned out that patch, but it must have grown back.''

''Can you help?'' Pia hardly relished the notion of walking a long way instead of riding.

''No, but maybe my daughter can.'' He turned his head and called ''Sharon!''

A woman in her mid 30's emerged from the house. ''What—oh, look at that boat!''

"Para," Pia said. "That's his name. He lost some toes."

"Has he eaten anything from around here?"

"No," Breanna said. "Para doesn't eat."

"Yes, I can help," Sharon said. She came and kneeled by the boat. She picked up an injured foot and massaged it, and its webbing extended.

"You're healing it," Pia said, surprised.

"Yes, but it's not much. I can heal only other folk's injuries," Sharon said. "A few drops of healing elixir could do the same." She picked up another foot.

"It's enough," Pia said. She had seen a good deal of magic in Xanth, but it still could surprise her.

Soon all the duck feet were whole again. "Thank you," Pia said, much relieved. "What can we do for you folk in return?"

Owen glanced at her. "We don't seek any return favors. Just being useful is enough. Just being in Xanth is enough. And that's one remarkable boat."

"Well, I'll give you something anyway," Pia said. She leaned down and kissed him on the ear.

Owen blushed. That pleased her; it meant that she still had it, and it worked on strangers. While she would have bridled if anyone had called her insecure, she did appreciate evidence that she was as pretty as she had ever been. There was power in prettiness.

Edsel fidgeted; something was on his mind. "Maybe I'm missing something," he said. "But if Sharon can heal a duck's feet, why did you have to bandage that other duck?"

Owen glanced at his daughter.

"I can't heal local creatures," Sharon said. "I think it's because of the ambiance of the reverse wood tree. Any creature who has eaten something here is immune to my healing. But Dad helps them. It just takes more time."

They got into the boat. "Well, thanks again," Breanna said. "We have to move on to the Good Magician's castle."

"You will have to get across the Gap Chasm," Owen said. "That may be a problem, unless Para can sprout wings."

"Oops, I hadn't thought of that," Breanna said. "But maybe we'll be able to find the invisible bridge."

"Invisible?" Pia asked, not at all sure she liked the sound if it.

"You'll see," Breanna said cheerfully. "Or maybe won't see, as the case may be."

They moved out. Pia had to admit it to herself: Xanth was getting to her. She liked it, and she liked the people she was encountering here. It was Edsel who had made the deal to get her here, in the hope that it would change her mind about their marriage. She had deemed that a forlorn hope of his, but his chances no longer seemed quite as remote. If she could just keep her nice body—but of course this wasn't really her body. It was a borrowed body, better than her own.

They returned to the main path and headed south. Soon it fed into one of the enchanted paths, so that they could relax; they would be safe as long as they stayed on it.

By about noon they reached it. The Gap Chasm was an enormous cleft in the land, dropping awesomely far down. Pia felt a bit dizzy and ill peering down. The thought of crossing an invisible bridge hardly appealed; how would they know where the edge of it was?

They ranged along the brink. "The bridge isn't right by the path," Breanna said. "This may be a long search."

Pia was getting hungry. "Is it safe to forage here?"

"Perhaps I should accompany you," Justin said diplomatically.

"Fine." He was always such a gentleman that she wouldn't have minded his company even if she wasn't trying to learn all about nature.

They walked a bit away from the chasm. "Those berries look good," Pia said.

"They are excellent, but not for eating," he said. "Those are thimble-berries, useful for sewing." He picked one, showing how it was hollow and fit over the tip of the finger.

Then she saw what looked like pies growing, except that they had projections on the sides. "How about those?"

"Now that's interesting," he said. "Those are the very first of that variety I have seen in Xanth. I know them only from a description. They are Pie & Ears. Note the ears on the sides."

So that was what they were. "Are they edible?"

"Oh, yes, certainly. But best to stay with the ones with ears."

"Why?" she asked, picking one without looking.

"Because when they have legs, they—"

She looked. A pair of legs hung down from the one she held. Suddenly the legs moved. Alarmed, she dropped it—and the pie ran away into the brush. "They run away," she said, understanding.

"Yes. Or—"

She was picking one with a smily face on its surface. She lifted it to her opening mouth. The pie's eyes went round and its mouth formed an O of horror.

She set it down. "Point made." She picked one with ears. They might hear, but they didn't protest.

The others came for pies of their own. Then they settled down to do a thorough search for the invisible bridge. But before they got far, there was a distraction.

First there was the sound: a raucous screeching. Then there was the smell, as of week old garbage. "Uh-oh," Breanna said.

"Perhaps it would be expedient to hide," Justin suggested. "We are after all some distance from the enchanted path."

"What is it—a sick dragon?" Pia asked.

"Worse," Breanna said.

They hurried into the brush, but before they could get out of sight, the horror arrived. It was a flock of big ungainly birds. No, not birds—they had human female anatomy. They were harpies, but not similar to Handi Harpy. These were foul of mouth and feather.

"Look!" one screeched. "Men!"

They flocked to gawk at Edsel and Justin. Pia realized that harpies, having very few males of their species, must be very hungry for male company. That was probably why Handi had been so nice to Justin. But these ones were so foul-mouthed and filthy that they would drive away most males of any species.

"Beware," Justin cried. "We have found a nest of sting-rays."

"You're bluffing," a harpy screeched. She hovered, evidently about to fly at him. Pia wasn't sure what the dirty bird would do when she reached him, but strongly suspected he wouldn't like it. Any more than the average girl liked being sexually harassed by men.

"Perceive it for yourselves," Justin said, gesturing at a large glowing hive.

The harpies retreated. Evidently this was an effective threat.

"What's a sting-ray?" Pia asked, knowing that it would not be the same as the sea creatures she knew of.

"A crossbreed between a bee and a sun ray," he explained. "They sting with laser beams, so can't be readily avoided. An aroused nest is a thing devoutly to be fled." He stood by the nest, holding a stick.

Pia pictured a swarm of angry bees. These might well be worse. They would surely rout the harpies, but what would happen to the humans? She hoped the harpies did not call Justin's bluff.

"How could a bee and a sun ray interbreed?" Edsel asked.

"Remarkable things occur at love springs."

That must account for all the crossbreeds of Xanth. Pia made a mental note: be wary of love springs.

Then she thought of something else. "You know, those harpies could be useful."

"Not in any way I know of," Breanna said.

"We need to cross the chasm, and we can't find the bridge. They could carry the boat across."

"And us in it," Breanna agreed, catching on. "But it would be one stinking trip."

Pia glanced at the daunting crevasse. "Maybe we could stand it, for a while."

"Excellent point," Justin said. Then he called to the harpies. "We would like to make a deal."

"Are you threatening us?" a harpy screeched.

"By no means. We wish to cross the Gap Chasm, and we haven't found the bridge. Could you carry our boat and us across?"

Several harpies spun about to stare at the boat. "We could. Why should we?"

"What would you like in return?"

There was a brief hubbub. "A million kisses."

Justin was ready for that. "My fiancée would object to that." Diplomatically phrased; the harpies could assume that it was jealousy.

The dirty birds reconsidered. "We're going to the cir-cuss," one screeched. "But it moved and we can't find it."

Justin smiled. "As it happens, I know its schedule. I can tell you where it is this year."

They distrusted this. "This isn't the kind of thing you clean folk like. We have our cussing contests there."

"I am aware of that. It is where you and the goblin males settle who has the foulest mouth in Xanth."

"That's it," she screeched in agreement. "The fowlest mouth."

"Carry us across, and I will direct you to it."

"No you don't," the harpy screeched cannily. "Tell us where first."

Justin considered. "It is not inordinately far from our destination. Carry us, and I will show you where. Then you can set us down and we shall go our way."

The harpies exchanged a dirty glance. "Done!"

The humans got into the boat, and the harpies settled along its sides, their soiled talons taking hold. It was a good thing the wood didn't have nerves, Pia thought. The smell alone was bad enough. The creatures spread their dungy wings and heaved upward. The boat lurched into the air and out over the precipice. Pia fixed her eyes on the boat's floor, not wanting to see just how precarious their situation was.

But after a while she nerved herself to look. They were high over the depth of the chasm. Maybe the smell was numbing her wariness of heights, because she found she could handle the view. It looked clean and fresh. "What's down there?" she asked.

"The Gap Dragon," Justin said matter of factly. "He eats most creatures he catches, and he catches most that venture into his domain."

"The Gap Dragon," Pia repeated weakly.

He took this for a request for more information. "He's Stanley, a steamer. He breathes steam rather than fire or smoke. That cooks his meals before he chomps them. He has six legs and vestigial wings. He's Princess Ivy's pet."

"Her what?"

"It is a long story. Briefly, he was youthenized when they met, and they became friends."

"Is that euphemized or euthanized?"

"Youthenized. Or youthened. Made younger, because of an overdose of youth elixir. He was a baby dragon. So they grew up together; it's one of the better friendships of Xanth. He won't eat anyone she asks him not to."

"This princess sounds like quite a girl."

"Oh, she's a woman now, with triplet daughters."

There was a jolting crash, as if they had stuck a barrier. Pia clutched the seat, gazing wildly about—and seeing nothing. "What happened?"

"We hit a wall," a harpy screeched.

"In the *air?*" Pia demanded.

"A wall of air. We're trying to fly around it."

"I know of a couple called Waller and Wallette," Justin said. "They build walls, and their daughter Wallnut makes wallpaper. But I hardly think they would be working up here."

There was another crash, on the other side. Several feathers flew. "Another wall!" a harpy screeched indignantly.

"Now I think I know what it is," Justin said. "It's an air compressor.

The walls of air squeeze things between them, and drop them into the Gap.''

"Now he tells us!'' a harpy screeched. "What can we do?''

"Drop down as if squeezed out,'' Justin suggested. "Then fly again when free of it.''

"Dead stick landing!'' a harpy screeched. Suddenly they all folded their grimy wings, and they and the boat plummeted. Pia felt as if she were floating, and she hated it.

"Not too far,'' Justin cried.

"Spread wings!'' a harpy screeched.

Together they spread their wings. Suddenly the boat was braking. Pia's stomach sagged down toward her feet. But it was better than crashing.

"Forward!'' another harpy screeched. The boat surged ahead. Pia waited anxiously for another crash, but it didn't happen. They must have dropped free of the air compressor.

She pried open an eye—and almost wished she hadn't. They were flying toward a nearly vertical cliff. It was the far wall of the Gap. They had descended into the chasm.

The wind of the harpies' wings dislodged a small object rolling along the brink. It dropped down into the boat and danced about as if hyperactive. It looked like a small tin can. "What's this?'' Pia asked, for the moment distracted from the menace of the looming cliff face.

Breanna looked. "Oh, that's a teenage can.''

"A what?''

"You know, a canteen. Throw it back.''

Oh.

Then the boat lifted, clearing the edge. They were out, and back over normal land. Pia picked up the little can and tossed it to the nearby ground. She was relived to be across the chasm. "Where?'' a harpy screeched.

"South,'' Justin said. "Go toward the Good Magician's castle.''

"Just how good *is* this Magician?'' Pia asked.

Justin smiled. "He is not a Magician in the sense you may believe. He is called good as contrasted to evil. He's the Magician of Information. He has a big Book of Answers that can answer any question.''

"Well, I hope he can answer ours.''

"One problem is that his answers are not necessarily intelligible at first. They are always correct, but sometimes a recipient does not understand until his adventure is over.''

''And for that they pay a year's service?''

''After struggling to get into the castle,'' he agreed.

''Why does he make it so difficult?''

"It is his way of discouraging frivolous inquiries. He prefers not to be bothered.''

''Maybe we're wasting our time, going there.''

''No, I suspect it is the only way. Ordinary mortals are unable to deal with a surly demon.''

She remembered the Demon CoTwo, and had to agree.

''And there is the castle,'' Justin said, pointing ahead. Then, to the harpies: ''Just south of here. You will see the burnt foliage of the swearing-in ceremony at any moment.''

Sure enough, a blighted section of forest appeared below. The harpies descended.

''How can they cuss so villainously, when our bad words get bleeped?'' Pia asked.

''They are largely immune to the Adult Conspiracy,'' Justin said. ''In any event, they are all adults, so have no reasonable limits.''

''But I'm adult, and I can't say bleep.''

''You have the body of a sixteen year old girl, which may affect you, and you are in the presence of a true sixteen year old, so can't speak with complete freedom.''

Pia nodded. She had been speaking rhetorically, having already caught on to this particular idiocy. It made a certain nonsensical sense, but she still preferred to argue the case. ''But I've been telling you how to test the limits of the Conspiracy. Why am I not stopped from doing that?''

''The Conspiracy is very literal. To a considerable degree, words are more important than actions. So there are things you can do but not speak.''

He was echoing what she had told him that morning, perhaps having forgotten in his distraction. So she argued the opposite case. ''That's ludicrous! Actions have to be more important than words.''

''Breanna shares your sentiment. She feels that the Adult Conspiracy is a vestige of idiotic misguided censorious foolishness. But it has the staying power of almost universal acceptance, so can't be ignored.''

''For sure,'' she said, smiling. He had now almost openly questioned the validity of the conspiracy. Breanna would follow that up with a vengeance, tonight.

The harpies landed. The boat bumped on the ground. "Thanks, chumps," one screeched.

"You are indubitably welcome, fair creatures," Justin called back as they took off.

"Do they understand irony?" Pia asked.

"If they don't, they will be truly annoyed, because beauty is no compliment to a normal harpy."

"But they did help us," Edsel said. "And they're not bad birds. They could have dropped us when we had that trouble over the Gap Chasm."

Pia hadn't thought of that. "Not bad birds," she agreed weakly.

Para knew the way, and was heading north toward the nearby castle. "I guess it will be up to me to get into that castle," Pia said. "Since it's my quest."

"It is true that Breanna and I are otherwise engaged, as your Companions, and have already been there," Justin agreed. "In fact that is where we first met." He rolled his eyes reflectively. "What a dear girl."

"What kind of challenges did you face?"

"Mare Imbri put us together, my mind joining hers in her body, and we tackled them together. We used parallax to locate the castle itself, as it was concealed by illusion. Then we navigated a sticky situation, answered some awkward questions, and rescued Mare Imbri from a dream catcher. The main challenge was figuring out the actual nature of the challenges we were encountering."

"But I gather they won't be the same challenges this time."

"That is true. There are always three, of different natures, tailored to the querent."

"Querent?"

"The person or persons seeking an answer to a question."

"Querent," she agreed. "Since I'm Mundane, just about any magic thing will be a considerable challenge to me. Will I be able to get through?"

"They are crafted to be possible to pass, but they are never easy. Wits rather than power seem to be the operative factor."

"I'd better have Edsel along; he's sharp with puns and riddles."

"We will all come along, including Para. But the challenges will surely be directed at you."

The boat approached the castle. It looked conventional as such things went, with a cleared region, a moat, and an inner wall. ''It looks peaceful enough,'' Pia said.

''That would be deceptive.''

A toothy head on a serpentine neck rose from the water of the moat. ''Oh, look!'' Breanna cried, delighted. ''The moat monster.''

''You like moat monsters?'' Pia asked her.

''Sure; they're an endangered species. There are only three castles in Xanth with formal moats, and one of them is Castle Zombie, which isn't suitable for a living monster. So it's between Castle Roogna and the Good Magician's castle. Soufflé shuffles between them. But this is a different one. Probably because I know Soufflé wouldn't really eat a person, so the moat wouldn't be secure.''

''This one will eat a person?'' Pia asked, feeling slightly unwell.

''For sure. Isn't it great?''

''Breanna favors the classic elements,'' Justin explained. ''So much is changing in Xanth that it's nice to see some old conventions retained.''

''Like people getting eaten by moat monsters,'' Pia said, with attempted irony.

''Precisely. This merely means we must not venture into the moat.''

''The drawbridge is down,'' Pia said.

''Yes, that is the obvious crossing point.''

''So something will stop us from crossing it?''

''That seems likely.''

''I wish we had a handbook with instructions,'' Pia said.

Edsel reached out to pick something up. ''Maybe this is it.''

She looked. It was a book—made of hands. There was no print in it. She opened her mouth.

''I know,'' Edsel said quickly, setting the book down. ''Sick joke. Can't read it. I guess it makes me an ill literate.''

She had to smile. It was hard to stay mad at him. ''Well, let's just keep going and see what stops us.''

Para advanced toward the bridge. But then a barrier of sorts appeared. It seemed to be a low table with plates and bread set on it. The butter knives were yellow. In fact they seemed to be made of butter. That figured.

The boat stopped, as the table crossed the path and was a bit too high for the short duck legs to navigate. In any event it wouldn't do to walk on a dining table.

Pia looked to the sides, but they were steep and apparently slippery banks, not suitable for walking across. The way was straight ahead. Beyond was the bridge, which remained lowered.

Pia climbed out of the boat. The others joined her. "Has Breanna been explaining this to you?" she asked Edsel.

"For sure," he said, with half a smile. "They've been through it before, so it's really us who will have to handle three Challenges this time. We'll need to keep our wits about us."

"This table blocks the way, so it must be a Challenge. What do you make of it?"

"It looks like lunch at a restaurant. But somehow I don't think we're supposed to eat those tarts."

"They're not tarts. They're bread rolls."

"Roll, roll, roll your boat," he said in singsong. "Gently down the stream."

She stamped her foot. "This is serious, Ed. What do we do to pass the Challenge?"

"What's the Challenge?"

"I don't know!"

He decided he had teased her enough. "There must be some hint of a problem, and of a solution. We just have to see it."

"For sure," she said somewhat acidly.

"Let's experiment." He sat cross-legged by the table and reached for one of the pieces of bread.

It put down legs and ran away from his hand.

Pia was less surprised than she would have been had she not seen the Pie & Ears by the Gap Chasm. The inanimate all too often became animate in Xanth.

"So you're not for eating," Edsel said. "What *are* you for?"

The things on the table came to life. Rolls of assorted types and sizes walked to the center of the table. Then one sprouted hands and picked up a little pastry cowboy hat, putting it on. The bread strutted around in the manner of a tough cowboy. A second one picked up a fancy lady's hat, preening. A third found a crown, and started lording it over the other bread.

"They seem to be playing a game," Pia said, mystified. "Acting out parts."

Edsel looked at her. "By George, I think she's got it," he said.

"Stop clowning around."

"These breads are playing a game," he said carefully. "A roll-playing game."

"Stop joking!" she snapped. "This is serious."

"No joke, Pi. See, they have settled down."

It was true. The bread was inert again, without arms or legs. Edsel's stupid comment must have satisfied a requirement.

But the table remained. "It must be my turn," Pia said. She sat down by the table, folding her legs carefully under her so as not to show more than was proper. She reached for a roll.

It rolled away. Was that a pun—a roll rolling? So she put out both hands, attempting to corral another one. It sprouted legs and ran away before she could catch it.

"All right," she said, "What are you for?"

The bread came to life. One roll picked up some cloth and draped it around itself. It walked across the table, turned with flair, and walked back. Then another took the cloth and walked the same way, with exaggerated steps.

"It's almost sexy," Edsel said.

"Don't be coarse." But his crude remark triggered a revelation. "They are models," she said. "Roll models."

All the rolls went inert. The table settled into the ground and disappeared, leaving the breads strewn across the path.

"I think that did it," Breanna said. "You each figured out one of the buns. I mean puns. Now we can eat the bread." She picked up a roll and took a bite from it. There was no protest.

Pia felt uneasy about it, but tried it herself. The roll she picked up was just that: inanimate bread. She picked up the butter knife, inserted the blade, and broke it off inside the bread, thus buttering it. She nibbled, and it tasted fresh and good.

"Maybe the animation was illusion," Edsel said. "This is good stuff."

"There is a lot of illusion in Xanth," Justin said. "It can be extremely useful."

"It wasn't what I expected," Pia said, "but it was indeed a challenge."

"For sure," the other three said together.

They ate the rolls, then moved on to the drawbridge. It remained down, and the way across the boat seemed clear. Except for one thing:

the moat monster's head was now beside it, looking down. The monster could readily snap up something that tried to cross.

They halted just shy of the bridge. Pia did not like the look of this. "Maybe the challenge is to distract the monster, so we can pass unmolested."

"That might work," Edsel said. "But how does the last one across do it?"

"Someone will have to stay outside," Pia said. "Maybe Para. Maybe he can swim in the moat, after the challenge is done."

"It works for me," Edsel said. "Okay, you cross while I distract." He walked beside the moat until he got a fair distance away. Then he jumped and waved his arms. "Hey, snoot-face! Come and get me!"

The moat monster glanced at him, then turned back to the bridge. It didn't move.

Para waddled out the other way, then entered the water. The monster glanced, but made to motion in that direction. It didn't care who shared the moat.

"Maybe we can swim," Edsel called. "Instead of using the bridge." He put a toe to the water.

The serpent whipped around. It swam lithely through the water. In half a moment it was there. But Edsel had hastily withdrawn his foot. "Just testing," he said, sheepishly.

The monster writhed sinuously, reorienting on the bridge. It was clear that it could get there before a person could walk all the way across it.

Edsel returned to the bridge. "But you know, it might work if a person *ran* across," he said. "It seems it is only humans the monster is after."

"Justin and I could distract it, while you two raced across," Breanna suggested.

"Wouldn't that be cheating?" Pia asked.

"If it is, you won't get across," Justin said. "The Good Magician's Challenges can't be avoided by ruse or fraud."

"But could be you'd be alone in the castle," Breanna warned. "Which is maybe okay, and we'll wait for you, but you need to be ready."

Pia exchanged a glance with Edsel. "Let's try it," she said.

They tried it. Justin and Breanna went to the side and splashed the water. The monster went after them. They stepped back.

"Do we risk it?" Edsel inquired.

"I—" She hesitated, not at all sure this was worth the risk. Then a bulb flashed before her face. "I get it! It's another pun. The human race."

"We're human—we race across—a human race," he agreed. "So it must be okay; you cracked the code."

"Last one across's a rotten egg!" she cried, and sprinted for the far side.

He followed, and soon overhauled her. But he didn't run ahead; he simply paced her, glancing to the side.

She looked. The moat monster was swimming toward them, its course about to intersect. It was going to be close.

She couldn't speed up; she was already doing her best, and panting, and she had a side stitch. She just wasn't used to exertion like this.

"I'd help you," Edsel puffed. "But then it wouldn't be a race."

And it had to be a race. She nodded and struggled on.

The monster's head struck. She heard its teeth clash right behind her. Then they were across, and she felt herself falling, but couldn't stop.

Edsel caught her and held her up. "We made it," he said. "I don't think the monster really tried. It knew we had solved the pun."

She just hung in his arms and panted. There were times when it was nice to have his physical support. As her bleary gaze wandered across the moat, she saw the monster sink under the water. Its job was done.

Justin, Breanna, and Para crossed the bridge, unmenaced. They were not a true part of the challenge.

Pia caught her breath and her balance, and turned to look at the castle from up close. The detail differed from what she had thought, or maybe it had changed. The stone wall was now rounded, probably circling the castle, and had arched doorways every few feet. This seemed remarkably porous for a defensive rampart.

She looked at the moat. There were docks extending into it all along, as if ready for many boats at once. Some were tall, standing well above the waterline; others were barely above the water. "Why the difference in height?" Pia asked.

Edsel shrugged. "Must be high piers and low piers, for tall and short ships."

"Ships? Here? It's a *moat,*" she reminded him witheringly.

He nodded. "In any event, we are past the moat, so I don't think it's a challenge."

"Maybe the third Challenge is farther in," Edsel said.

"We may be certain that it will manifest in its own manner," Justin said. "I think that Breanna and I had better wait here while you explore."

Pia walked to the nearest archway. As she reached it, a centaur appeared, with a man on his back. The centaur had a bow, and the man had a spear. "You shall not pass," both said together.

Pia retreated. "I think it just manifested," she said.

"For sure," Breanna agreed.

"Let me try," Edsel said. He walked to the next portal beyond.

There was the centaur, without the man. "I regret to say that you are not permitted to pass," he said politely.

Pia walked past that one and tried the third aperture. The man appeared. "Forget it," he said gruffly.

"Who are you?" she asked, striking a winsome pose.

"I am Christopher Christopher. And you are?"

"I am Pia Putz." She smiled, and saw him soften. "Are you sure we can't pass?"

"Very sure," Christopher said regretfully.

"Not even for a kiss?"

The man looked truly reluctant. "Not even for that."

She walked on to the next portal. There was the centaur again. Or was it really the same one? "Who are you?"

"Cy Clone," the centaur growled. "Now get out of here before I throw you into the moat."

She retreated. The centaur looked the same, but didn't sound the same as the one who had braced Edsel.

She rejoined Edsel. "There seems to be a man or centaur blocking each passage. They look the same, but I'm not sure they are."

"Right. They don't talk the same. Maybe they're twins or triplets."

"They don't attack, they just warn us away," she said. "Maybe we should check the other arches."

"You go one way, I'll go the other, and we'll meet on the other side."

She nodded, and set off.

Every portal was blocked. There were two centaurs and several similar men. The centaurs were shy and bold, respectively, or peaceful and violent. Evidently they trotted to whichever portal she was headed for.

Maybe there was just one man, but he was everywhere, either by himself or with a centaur.

She met Edsel on the far side. "All blocked," she said. "More men than centaurs."

"Christopher throughout," he said. "Cy Centaur and Cy Clone, the mean one."

"The same ones I saw," she said. "I suppose the centaurs could alternate sides, but how could the man get around so swiftly? He never looked out of breath."

Edsel was thoughtful. "So is it one man, or several with the same name?"

"And two centaurs, or more than two?"

"I think this is our riddle. Do you think there's a pun we're not getting?"

"From what Justin told me, the Challenges don't have to be puns," she said. "But if it's not a pun, then what?"

"There must be something about these people we need to understand."

"Like how many of them there are, really."

"Maybe we can narrow it down," he said. "Let's go until we find two of them together. Then—"

"Got it," she agreed.

They circled together, back the way she had come. When they came to a man/centaur combination, Pia stayed to talk with them, putting on her winsome air and holding their attention. She had always been good at this sort of thing, and with her lovely sixteen year old face and figure, she was better, because she knew exactly how to use these assets. She had never tried fascinating a centaur before, but they had enough human attributes to be subject to some wiles. She smiled, she moved her hips, she gushed over their masculine appeal, she lifted a leg to adjust her shoe, and leaned well forward, showing just enough thigh and breast to guarantee continued attention. It was a science that worked well enough in the land of magic.

Meanwhile Edsel faded away. She gave him as much time as she could, keeping the two males anchored in place.

Then Edsel returned. She bid the males farewell with a last smile and jiggle, and stepped back. They departed the archway and were no more.

She turned to Edsel. "What's the story?"

"There's another set four arches down. Christopher and Clone."

"The mean centaur," she agreed. "I had the shy one. I almost made him blush, once."

"So there are two different centaurs, and two of the same men."

"We have established a minimum," she said. "Could there be more?"

"I think there could be. But how can they be the same?"

Something was nagging at the edge of her mind. Suddenly it connected. "Clone!"

"Clones!" he repeated, catching on. "One centaur, one man, but they can send clones out to intercept any doorway. They might be illusions, looking and sounding just like the originals."

"But they certainly seemed solid," Pia said. "We could walk right through illusions, but I wouldn't want to try it with solid folk."

"For sure," he agreed with a third of a smile. "I'll bet the clones cover every portal instantly, then the solid originals come to replace them as we talk. That way, just two can block a hundred entrances."

"So when we see both together, and talk with them, they become the originals?" she asked.

"I think so."

"Then how were we able to talk to both, in two different places, simultaneously?"

He looked at her. "Sometimes I think you're not a complete idiot." That was his way of saying that she had caught him in an error.

"And sometimes I think you're not completely ugly," she said, returning tit for tat. "But how do we rise to the challenge?"

"There has to be a way," he said. "I think that if we could fix the two originals in one place, we could walk right through the two clones elsewhere. Because they can't really be in two places at one time. Only the illusion clones can zip instantly to new doors."

"Except that we both talked to them both," she reminded him. "Or can an illusion clone talk?"

"Without a solid mouth or lungs? I doubt it, though with magic anything's possible. Maybe one of each pair was the original, and the other was a clone."

"I wonder," she said, getting into the problem. She was exercising her intellect, and Edsel wasn't disparaging it. She liked that. She had never been known or valued for her mind, limited as it was. "You know those old cartoons, where only the person who is speaking or doing something is animated, and the others are just still pictures? Could they be like that? So we can tell who's the clone?''

"Pia, I'd kiss you, except that you wouldn't like it by daylight.''

He meant when she wasn't honoring their deal, giving him everything at night in return for his complete support by day. Part of what turned her off was his clear superiority of brain. But now they were thinking together. "I'd like it now,'' she said.

He was wary. "What's different now?''

"You're treating me like an equal.''

He laughed—then quickly sobered, realizing that it wasn't a joke. "Have I been a fool all this time?''

"Tit for tat. You wanted the one without giving the other.''

"For sure,'' he agreed, without any trace of a smile.

She waited, and after a moment he embraced her and kissed her. He didn't try to grab a feel. She gave back, making him melt.

He released her. "Oh, Pia—''

She liked him a lot better this way. Her emotion was stirring, after being in remission for some time. She had always known that her body was her main appeal, but she didn't like being considered *only* a body. However, this was not the time to get into this. "We have a challenge to surmount.''

"More than one,'' he said. He reoriented. "One original, one clone, for each door. Which one were you talking to?''

She focused on the memory of her recent dialogue. Now she realized something she hadn't noticed at the time. "The man, Christopher. He reacted, he talked. The centaur just stood there. I thought he was reacting, but now I realize he was just there.''

"You adjusted your shoe?'' He was of course well familiar with the move, and loved it. Sometimes she thought he would rather sneak a peek under her skirt than see her all the way naked.

"Yes. I think my panty showed at one point, but they didn't freak out.''

"They must be immune, for the purpose of this challenge. The Good Magician must have had lovely girls try that dodge before, to get past male defenders.''

"But I did hold their attention. The man's attention, anyway; Cy Clone just kept looking as before. I thought because he didn't look away, that I was fascinating him, but he was really a cartoon still figure.''

"I talked to Cy Centaur. He's smart, and interested in mundane technology. The man was there, but I don't think he ever spoke. So I think he was the clone image. We each talked to one real person.''

''And we could have walked through the clone,'' she agreed. ''Except that the real one would have stopped us.'' But something bothered her. ''We figure chances are that the first one we see in a doorway is a clone, and that as we talk, the original comes to take his place?''

''That's my theory. The clones can go instantly, spotting us. Then the real ones come to stop us. Probably pretty soon, so we couldn't just walk through the clones.''

''But they are responsive from the start. Doesn't that mean that the clones can be animated?''

Edsel paused. ''May I kiss you again?''

''Kisses for sex appeal I can handle. Kisses for respect I like.''

''Then you'll like this one.'' He kissed her again, and there was indeed a special kind of passion in it.

Then he worked it out. ''It must be that they can focus on their clones, seeing what the clones see, and making them move and talk. But I'll bet they can do a meaningful dialogue only through one clone at a time. They must do it while they are closing in on that one, to take its place.''

''And we don't dare gamble that we're talking with clones,'' Pia said. ''Lest we get smashed.''

''I suspect they wouldn't smash us, but we'd fail the challenge, and never get in to see the Good Magician. So we don't want to gamble. Now if we could just attract the originals, then hold them in place while we went through a different door.''

''The moment we moved over, so would they,'' she said. ''But I wonder—could they be anchored through their clones?''

''Anchored?''

''Pretend you're one of them,'' she said. ''When I say 'go,' you turn around, walk in a circle, or something.''

''That's no problem. But I don't see—''

''Go.'' She drew up her blouse, showing her bra.

Edsel stared, as he always did. After a moment, he started to turn.

She leaned forward. He froze. After another moment he tried to turn again.

She lifted a leg. He froze again. When he started to recover, she lifted her leg farther. His eyeballs began to glaze.

She resumed her normal posture. His expression cleared. "Point made," he said. "Here in Xanth, you have power."

"Maybe I can't freak them out, but I might anchor them in place for a while," she said. "So they couldn't walk across to join the clones."

"Good notion. But maybe you would catch only one, and the other would avert his gaze when he saw the other freeze, and move in."

"Then you can take out the other. Let me do the man, and you do the centaur."

"But nobody would freeze if I did a striptease."

"With your mind," she clarified. "Say things so fascinating that the centaur is entirely distracted."

"Body and mind," he agreed, smiling. "Let's try it. First we'd better get them both to one door. Then when we figure they're there in the flesh, we can go to a random one and go into our act. I think you have figured out the key."

"Agreed." She kissed him. If he had always been like this, working with her instead of treating her like an object, their marriage might never have been in trouble.

They walked to the nearest archway. Cy Centaur appeared. They walked on to the next. Christopher appeared. They went on to the next. Both man and centaur appeared.

"Now," Pia breathed. "Anchor site."

"How are you doing?" Edsel inquired of the centaur.

"You shall not pass." It was Cy Clone, speaking without moving.

"Now is that nice of you?" Pia asked the man.

"It's our assignment," Christopher said, taking in her trim figure. But otherwise he did not show animation. These were clones, being operated by remote control.

"We believe we have figured out the key to this challenge," Edsel said.

"I doubt it," Clone said gruffly, flicking his tail in a disdainful manner. Now he was real.

"Oh, but we do," Pia said, smiling at the man. "It has been such a pleasure to meet you, however."

"That's nice," Christopher said, leaning forward to take in more of the smile. He was real too. So now it was clear where the originals were.

They stepped to the left, beyond the archway. The two figures therein faded.

Then they ran back around the archway and on to the right, trying to fake out the guardians about the direction they were taking. They ran by several arches, then paused close to one. The man appeared, a still image.

They ran on. About four more arches later they found a set: Christopher and Cy Centaur. "Go," Pia said. She was a trifle breathless, but that would be no liability for this.

They stepped close to the still figures. "Hello, Chris," Pia said, opening her blouse. She saw that she had his immediate attention.

"Cy, I want to tell you about quantum theory," Edsel said, earnestly meeting the centaur's fixed gaze. "It has some fascinating properties. I had thought the theory of relativity was challenging, with its insistence that nothing could exceed the speed of light in a vacuum, and its permutations of time in gravity, but quantum physics is truly weird. Almost like magic."

The gazes of both man and centaur remained fixed. They were still clones.

Pia stepped forward, slowly removing her blouse. She saw that Edsel didn't look, because the moment he did, he would lose his thread of dialogue. She liked that too. Peripheral vision was more than enough. Meanwhile, he continued talking, doing his part.

"You see, Cy, according to quantum theory, you can't know both the position and the velocity of a given particle. The mere act of looking changes things. So if you take a snapshot, as it were, and fix its position, it is impossible to know its velocity. Sort of like a clone not moving if you know where it is. Isn't that weird?"

"Absolutely fascinating," Cy said, unmoving.

Meanwhile Pia was nudging forward, in a kind of dance step that made the upper contour of her bosom jiggle. There was a certain art to the effect. Christopher remained fixed.

"Another quantum effect," Edsel continued, "is that two particles separating from a common source are linked. If something happens to one, it also happens to the other, though there is no seeming connection between them. Does this make sense to you?"

"Amazing," Cy said, without animation.

Pia, having used up about as much of her top as she cared to, hiked up her skirt, showing increasing amounts of leg. The man's eyes remained riveted, though nothing else moved. He was still the clone, seeing what the clone saw, but not there physically.

"It makes sense if you figure that when you measure a property of one particle, you are actually choosing between realities. Selecting the universe wherein both particles are the same. New universes are thus constantly fissioning off. It's a mind-bending concept. They are now making quantum machines that can do calculations much faster than anything else," Edsel continued. "They are very good at probabilities. But the boundary between the realm of quantum effects and that of the ordinary world we know remains elusive. Still, study continues. Relativity relates to gravity, while quantum theory relates to the other three fundamental forces of the universe. Some day it may be possible to combine them into one great Theory of Everything. Perhaps the Superstring theory will accomplish that."

"Did you say four forces, total?" Cy asked.

Pia was now passing Chris. She was up to her panty line, but as they had conjectured, he was not freaked out. She did however have his whole attention. She wiggled her bottom.

"Yes, of course," Edsel agreed. "Gravity, the weak atomic force, the strong nuclear force, and the electromagnetic force."

"But what about the fifth force?"

"What fifth force?"

"Magic."

She was past Chris. Edsel was now largely past the centaur. "Oh. I meant the forces of Mundania. They don't know about magic there."

"That would seem to explain it. Xanth could not endure without magic."

"I agree. It's what distinguishes it from the dreary realm beyond."

It was time to wrap this up. "Psst," Pia whispered. "We're through."

"Through?" Edsel asked, dismayed. "I thought we were getting along so well together."

"Will you stop it? Through the challenge."

The two clones faded. Pia and Edsel were indeed inside the castle. "I thought—"

So he had been genuinely confused, rather than making one of his sharp remarks. She liked that as well. She stepped into him and kissed him. "You did well."

"So did you. I didn't dare look. I would have freaked out."

Exactly. "Let's go ask the Question."

9
XONE

Chlorine rode behind Nimby on the Lemon cycle, enjoying it. He was quite competent now, and obeyed all the obscure signs and signals of the road. Dug and Kim drove their car behind, there to come to the rescue if there were any problem. Exactly as Justin and Breanna would be traveling with the real Edsel and Pia through Xanth, keeping wary eyes out for mischief. Indeed there was mischief to avoid, because the drivers of other cars all seemed to believe that the whole road belonged only to them, and that all others were illicit intruders. They honked their horns and nudged in too close at high speed and made hand signals that Chlorine discovered related to stork signaling in a negative manner. But Nimby, forewarned, ignored them and stayed out of their way. That seemed to satisfy them; they roared on by. Kim had said there was something called a speed limit, but Chlorine must have misunderstood, because no vehicle on the road was honoring any possible limit.

They were traveling north to the Apple-aching Mountains, where they could see the sights and camp for the night. Dug and Kim had camping equipment in their car. But the first night they would stay at a motel, so as to be able to find the best place in the mountains the next morning.

After several hours, Chlorine's thighs were getting tired of the unfamiliar bouncing. She knew how to ride a dragon, but this cycle had a different feel, and there was less leeway to fidget. She was glad when the mountains loomed, knowing the trip was nearing its end.

They pulled into the Mundane Motel, and saw about getting a set of rooms, which turned out to be nice enough. They would go out to a fleet fare place for a meal. But first Kim set up her notebook computer so Chlorine could check in. She had done so in the morning, but that had been early, and there might be a response now.

She navigated the Grid and Mesh, but then had a problem: she couldn't get into the O-Xone. She got an Error Message.

NOT AVAILABLE AT THIS TIME.

"Let me see that," Kim said. She tried it, and got the same message. "Must be a problem in the Mesh. These things happen. We can try again after eating."

They went to the eatery. It was shaped like a vehicle called a bus, but was larger. Signs all around proclaimed the wares. They got really weird long sandwiches called submersibles, stuffed with every kind of oddity. But they tasted good enough.

Back at the motel, they tried the Mesh again. They still could not get past the error message. Kim tried to query the Mesh Server, but couldn't get a coherent response. "They don't believe in magic," she said, grimacing.

Nimby looked unsettled. Chlorine knew what was on his mind. He didn't like having his contact with Xanth cut off. He wasn't sure it was coincidence.

"These things happen all the time," Dug said. "Sometimes a server gets overloaded and is down for hours or days. There's no malice in it, just inadequacy for the demand. Or there can be a hardware or software hitch. Nobody likes it, but soon enough service is restored, and the Mesh proceeds as usual."

Nimby made a trace shake of his head. That was enough for Chlorine. "Nimby has very little magic here in Mundania, but he's very smart, and he can tune in on much that is going on around him. That's why he can avoid bad drivers. He believes that this is not coincidental mischief."

Dug frowned. "We need to get this straight. Kim and I can handle routine Mundane problems, but if there's something else, we'll have to be more careful. Just how sure is Nimby about this?"

"And just how much of what kind of magic does he have in Mundania?" Kim added.

Chlorine had ascertained this soon after they arrived in Mundania, but hadn't thought it relevant. "He has no direct power of magic here, but can do just a little thought projection, enough to let me know what he wants when he touches me, and can extend his awareness some distance out. He can judge whether a thing is natural or contrived. The interruption of the O-Xone interface is beyond his range of certainty, but is suspicious."

"What makes it suspicious?" Dug asked.

"Each Demon is fiercely jealous of his territory, when it is part of a bet, and guards it rigorously, even if he doesn't care about the welfare of the creatures within it. If the Demon $E(A/R)^{TH}$ realizes that Nimby is here now, he will surely try to embarrass him in some way. The O-Xone interruption could be the first step in such an embarrassment."

"Embarrassment?" Kim asked. "Like saying 'Ha-ha, I caught you!'?"

"No. Like trying to trap Nimby here, so he can't return to Xanth right away, and will lose the bet. That would mean that Edsel could not return to his body in Mundania, and probably that Pia and I could not exchange places either. Not until the contest is done."

"Just what form would a confinement-to-Mundania contest take?" Dug asked. "I mean, it can hardly go on forever. There must be some limit."

"Three days after the challenge is made. The demon $E(A/R)^{TH}$ would seek to hold Nimby that time, and Nimby would have to return to Xanth within that time, or lose."

"What would that do to Nimby?"

"A Demon can't be physically hurt, but it would prevent him from defending his status among Demons, and that would be a penalty sacrificing what has taken him a thousand years to achieve. The Demon $E(A/R)^{TH}$ would assume his status and become the—the closest analogy would be the leader—of the Demons."

"I thought I had this figured out, but maybe not," Dug said. "How far would the Demon $E(A/R)^{TH}$ go to accomplish this?"

"We're not sure. It depends on his judgment of the likelihood of success. If he tries to trap Nimby, and fails, he would lose significant status himself. More than if he just lets Nimby escape without challenge. So he is likely to mask his effort, making it seem like chance mishaps, so that if he fails, there will be no consequence to him. He will play it that way until he discovers a better opportunity to succeed. Then, if assured of success, he will do what he judges necessary to accomplish it. That could be severe."

"Just how much power does he have?" Kim asked. "Can he do magic too?"

"No magic. He uses science. He can't make people do things, but can affect earth processes, such as the weather."

"He can make thunderstorms?"

"At least."

"But a storm shouldn't stop Nimby from returning to Xanth," Dug said.

"That depends on the storm."

Kim pursed her lips. "You don't mean just rain. You mean like hurricanes."

"If those are very big storms, yes. And shaking of the ground."

"Earthquakes."

"Yes. And similar effects. It could get awkward for local residents."

"Such things *kill* local residents," Dug said.

"I doubt the Demon E(A/R)TH would care. So it will be better if it doesn't come to that. And the best way to see that it doesn't, is to ensure that Nimby can return to Xanth at will, so that there is no point in trying to trap him here."

"Got it," Dug said. "So maybe this Xone interface problem isn't the Demon E(A/R)TH's work, but just in case it is, we need to explore our options. Are there other ways to return to Xanth?"

"Other than through the Grid and Mesh? I think so."

Nimby touched her hand. Information flowed from him. "And there are other ways within the Grid," Chlorine amended. "Those would be easier."

"Other ways?" Kim asked.

"Through the Xanth Xone," Chlorine said, assimilating Nimby's plan.

"But those aren't real Xanth people," Kim said. "They're Mundanes with pretenses."

"Not entirely. They can't use Xanth identities without the assent of the real folk there. There has to be an affinity, or it doesn't take."

"Hoo, boy," Dug said. "You mean there really is a connection between, say, the Xone Irene and Queen Irene?"

"A tenuous one. It's—" Chlorine concentrated, trying to handle a concept that was well within Nimby's scope but somewhat beyond hers. "Like quantity physicals, the Halloween connection between the two aspics of a dividend photo."

Dug angled his head, working on that. "May I?" he asked after a moment, extending his hand toward Nimby.

Nimby touched his hand.

"Got it," Dug said. "Like quantum physics, the 'spooky' connection between the two aspects of a divided photon. What happens to one is reflected in the other, instantaneously, though there is no apparent association between them. Even Einstein had a problem with that, because—"

"Dug," Kim murmured.

He smiled. "Okay. The point is, there can be devious connections between two things having a common origin, such as bits of light or Queen Irene. The Xanth Xone folk associate with their Land of Xanth counterparts, but it's not direct."

"So they can't just say 'Better half, send help,' and have it understood," Kim said.

"Right," Dug agreed, for he now had the full import of Nimby's thought. "But in quantum physics, sometimes you can do on a mass scale what you can't do in a single instance. If many Xanth Xone equivalents send a message, some may get through."

"Like scattershot," Kim said. "Got it. So what's the message?"

"It has to be masked," Chlorine said. "So as not to be obvious, and thus alert Dearth."

"Who?" Kim asked.

"Sorry. Demon $E(A/R)^{TH}$, or D. Earth. We don't know whether he is watching the GigaGrid, but better not chance it. So it has to be something that isn't obvious, but will be understood in Xanth."

"Coded," Dug agreed. "Seeming innocent, to those who don't know the background. But an immediate alert, in Xanth."

"Okay," Kim said. "So what's the message?"

"To GM: Nimby eats dust," Chlorine said.

"To Giant Motors? What do they—" Kim paused. "The Good Magician! I get it. But is that enough?"

"It contains the problem and the solution," Chlorine said. "In your vernacular, as we understand it, eating dust is to be in trouble."

"Close enough," Kim agreed. "But what's the solution?"

"To fetch magic dust, which carries the magic of Xanth. If some of that can be sent to Nimby, he will recover some of his power, and be able to do what he needs to.''

"Oh, I see. In Xanth, Nimby is the source of magic, but he's in Edsel's Mundane body, so lacks most of his magic. But with the dust, it would be like a little bit of Xanth. An island in Mundania.''

"Yes. With that, he would be proof against Dearth. For a while. And could continue his exploration without concern.''

"Got it," Kim said, echoing Dug's comment. "Let's get the message out.'' She typed in the address, and made her way to the Xanth Xone, doing it for Chlorine because she was much faster. **This is Salmon Ella with a public message, non spam, for all Xanth Xone regs. Please send these four words to your namesakes only: "GM—Nimby eats dust."** She looked up. "Anything else?''

"Better clarify that it isn't done via the keyboard,'' Dug said.

"Oh. Yes.'' She typed again. **This is afk effort.**

"Will they understand?'' Chlorine asked anxiously.

"We'll have to hope they do,'' Kim said. "We can't clarify it online, because that could alert Dearth, but they'll be discussing it privately, and a number should catch on and spread the word. Then they'll go to it with a will. What each wants most is to have a genuine contact with Xanth. They should enjoy making the effort, even if they don't get through.''

"How will we know they're doing it?'' Chlorine asked.

Kim laughed. "No problem there. They're already doing it. Look.'' She turned the screen so that Chlorine and Nimby could see it.

Mela Merwoman: I sent it. I think I got through.

Electra: I tried; don't think so.

Draco Dragon: We winged monsters are taking off.

Chlorine: Couldn't make contact. Will try again. :-)

"That's me!'' Chlorine said, with a mixed thrill.

"That's why she couldn't get through,'' Kim said. "You're not in Xanth at the moment.''

"Yes. So she's honest. What's that punctuation?''

"You read it sideways. It's a face. The colon is the two eyes, the dash is the nose, and the end-parenthesis is the mouth.''

"Oh, it's smiling!''

"Yes,'' Kim said. "They can smile, or frown, or make variant expressions. Some get pretty sophisticated. It's a way of conveying emotions in lieu of the facial expressions we can't see. What this means is that they are getting on it, and word is spreading.''

''But if they're writing about it, on the screen, won't that alert Dearth?''

Kim nodded. ''Probably so. But he won't be able to do anything about it, because there will be too many to catch. He can't shut down the whole GigaGrid.''

Nimby touched Chlorine. ''Actually he *could* shut it down,'' she said. ''Because electrical effects are part of his power. But Nimby thinks he won't, because he can't be sure this isn't just a game similar to others the Xoners play, and there would be quite a reaction if the whole Grid collapsed. Dearth doesn't like to be obvious, any more than Nimby does; it's bad Demon form. He prefers to let the ants play out their antics on their own.''

''The Demons see people as ants?'' Kim asked.

''When they notice them at all,'' Chlorine said. ''Except for Nimby. When he had to participate as a mortal creature, and win one tear of love or grief, he got to know some of us, and now he accepts us as people in our own right.'' She smiled at Nimby, loving him. ''But the other Demons would step on us without knowing or caring. We're just an infestation in their territories.''

''Well, at least we know where we stand,'' Dug said, shrugging. ''Now we've set the ball rolling, we can get on with our camping trip.''

Chlorine looked at Nimby, who nodded. ''Yes. We can have the fun we planned on, knowing that Dearth won't be able to interfere.''

They rode and drove to the nearby mountains, surveying the situation. The mountains were impressive. They would be able to disappear into their green forest and get the feel of Mundane nature. That was part of what Nimby really wanted. They would come out here in the morning with their camping gear, and have days and nights in the wilderness.

They returned to the motel and relaxed. They watched the Mundane gourd; Nimby paid special attention to the news, learning everything he could about this realm. They finished on a public service channel, which had a nature program about the pollution of the sea.

''Why do they despoil it?'' Chlorine asked. ''Xanth is so much nicer.''

''People are short sighted,'' Dug said. ''And corporations care for nothing but making more money. But folk are beginning to be aware, and things are starting to be done.''

Chlorine managed to get through her insulin shot without too much discomfort or messiness. "But this is a pain," she told Nimby. "I'd rather be rid of it."

Nimby looked at her.

She nodded. "Yes, why don't you abolish it? When you get your magic, it wouldn't be hard to get rid of the diabetes, and maybe trim down some of the fat on this torso. As appreciation for letting me use this body. It would be a nice gesture."

Nimby nodded.

Later, when they were alone and in their room, and she stripped away her clothing, she had another thought. "I wish panty-magic worked here in Mundania. It gives a girl confidence. For instance, I could just whip away my skirt, like this, and freak you out, unless you clamped your eyes shut just barely in time. But as it is, I can't impress you at all." She went through the motions, and sure enough, he did not freak out. Of course he wouldn't have, being who he was, but still, she would have liked to make the effort.

But she did after all make an impression, putting Nimby in mind of the stork, and this time their summons was more competent than before. That was an achievement, because drear Mundania did not enhance it by magic. They had to do it all themselves.

Next morning they rode out to the mountains, checked in as hikers, and set off with their loads of gear along the Apple-aching Trail. The scenery was beautiful, and every detail was special. It had resemblances to Xanth, except for the lack of magic. They had to use a special salve to keep the biting bugs off; there was no spell to banish them. There were no dragons, griffins, or harpies in the sky, only birds, and small ones at that.

Late in the day they camped, pitching cozy mini-tents and watching the colored sunset. "I had forgotten how much fun this was," Kim remarked.

"I hadn't," Dug said. "It was the first time I got you into the sack."

"That, too," she agreed.

"Why would he want to put you in a bag?" Chlorine asked.

Dug and Kim laughed. "Mundane men have this quaint notion that women should be kept, so they try to stuff them into sacks," Kim explained.

"And for some reason the women don't like getting stuffed," Dug agreed. "It's called the war of the genders."

"And we're winning," Kim said. "Fortunately the men don't yet know that."

Chlorine shook her head. "Mundania is a strange place."

"Well, it's not Xanth, but it's bearable on occasion."

Kim set up her little computer. "You can use that with no connection?" Chlorine asked, surprised. "I thought that without magic, it wouldn't work alone."

"No magic. It's a notebook. With a good battery and satellite link, no problem." Sure enough, her screen lighted and print appeared. She moved through the linkages. "The O-Xone's back! We can check in again."

Chlorine checked in, leaving her message: all is well. Then they closed, as Kim said it wasn't good to run the computer too long on batteries. But, reassured, they relaxed. Dearth had not caught on, and they were not under siege. It had perhaps been a false alarm. Still, Chlorine was glad they had made the effort of contact through the Xanth Xone. If Dearth was aware, that might be the reason he was letting it go, realizing that he couldn't entirely block the connection to Xanth.

In the night it rained. It was a sudden, booming thunderstorm, with sharp winds that brought down branches, and the rain was torrential. The tents were well pitched, but a fluke of drainage softened the ground and let a peg on Dug and Kim's tent pull free, and their tent collapsed. In the darkness, in the storm, they couldn't do much about it except huddle under the canvas, and they kept reasonably dry.

But in the morning they discovered that some baggage had gotten exposed to the rain, and soaked through. The clothing would dry, but the notebook computer had been shorted out and was inoperative. It would have to be taken to a shop for repair before it could be used again.

The computer had been put in a corner of the tent nearest the washed out peg. The coursing water had made a channel that oriented on that corner with eerie precision. Almost as if nature had intended to nullify the little machine.

"Dearth," Chlorine said grimly. Nimby nodded. They had relaxed, foolishly, and now they were in trouble. For Chlorine knew that this was merely the second step, after the O-Xone interruption, of a program of isolation and containment by the Demon $E(A/R)^{TH}$. He intended to trap Nimby here, and surely had other mechanisms to enforce that.

Nimby pointed at the sky. There overhead was a shape in rainbow colors, but it was no rainbow. It was a full circle, with two lines bisecting it, forming a cross: ⊕

"The symbol for Earth," Chlorine said. "It is the Challenge. Nimby must get out of Mundania within three days of this moment, or he has lost."

"And Dearth has already handicapped him by taking out our computer contact," Dug said. "Demonic timing."

"Of course. Now Dearth believes he can win."

"I think we are not going to enjoy the next few hours," Kim said. Those were surely true words.

10

Robota

Edsel really liked the way Pia had warmed to him during the challenges. And all because he had shown some respect for her mind. If only he had realized that that was what she wanted all along, they would never had drifted into marital difficulties.

"Wait for us!" Breanna called. She and Justin were coming through the now unguarded portal. "How did you ever do it? We just saw you talking, and then you were through."

"Sex appeal and quantum physics," Edsel said.

"We distracted them," Pia clarified. "The guardians were only clones."

"For sure," Breanna said uncertainly.

They turned to enter the castle proper, now that they were safely beyond the wall. A woman was coming toward them. "Oh, there's Wira!"

The woman paused as they approached. "Hello, Breanna and Justin," she said. She turned to the others. "And you must be Edsel and Pia. I am Wira, the Good Magician's daughter in law."

"Wira can't see you," Breanna said. "But she can hear you."

"You're blind?" Edsel asked before he thought. "I mean, aren't there healing springs—" He broke off, afraid he was being crude.

"I am naturally blind," Wira said. "So can't be healed. But I am happy here, and Humfrey and his designated wives are nice."

"Designated whats?" Pia asked sharply.

Wira smiled. "The Good Magician has had a long life. He married and lost five and a half wives, then got them all back together. Now they take turns being with him, and the current one, Rose of Roogna, is here this month."

"Rose of Roogna?" Edsel asked. "Isn't that the name of the capital Castle?"

"Yes. She lived there for a long time, until she married Humfrey. She grows magic roses. She is especially nice." Wira turned and led the way through the castle.

A comfortable gray haired woman met them. Her hair was coifed to resemble a rose flower. "Hello. I am Rose. Let me feed you before you see Humfrey."

They sat down to a meal of rose hips and rosé wine, along with rose potatoes and red gravy. There was rose scented bread with rose petal jelly. It wasn't the most conventional food, but it was good. Rose was a good hostess who seemed genuinely to enjoy their company though they were strangers to her; that was an art not every person had.

"The next step you two must take alone," Breanna said. "Justin and I would only be in the way."

Then Wira conducted Edsel and Pia up coiling stairs to a dingy cubbyhole. A gnomish man hunched over a monstrous tome.

Edsel let Pia talk, as this was really her mission.

She stepped forward. "Good Magician—how can we get rid of the Demon CoTwo?"

The little man looked up. His set features softened as he oriented on Pia; she had that effect on men of any age. "My dear, you can't. Ask another Question."

"But this is the one I need!" she protested, her lower lip beginning to tremble. "I've got to have it."

"Please," Wira murmured nervously. "Don't argue with him. It makes him grumpy."

"I don't care if it makes him explode," Pia said, sounding hysterical. "The trees are drowning, and we've got to save them."

Edsel stepped in. "Maybe I can finesse this," he said quietly to Pia. This came under the heading of supporting her completely. Then, to

Humfrey: "What she means is, there is a crisis we want very much to alleviate, and we hope you will be able to provide us a means. Is there some way we can accomplish our objective?"

The Good Magician oriented on him. The gnome's direct gaze was disconcertingly savvy. "Well put. What you require is the magic locket, which is one of the stray artifacts with imbued talents from the ancient city of Hinge. Hitherto only bracelets have shown up, but now so has the locket. Put the Demon CoTwo therein, and it will lessen his power sufficiently to eliminate the melting, without putting all Xanth into deep freeze."

"Magic locket?" Pia asked.

"You have seen it," Humfrey informed her gently. "The half demon children have it. Borrow it from them for your purpose. Now consult with my assistant to arrange your Service."

"That may be complicated," Edsel said. "You see, we—"

But the weathered old eyes had already returned to the tome. The Good Magician had tuned them out.

"This way," Wira murmured. They followed her out of the cramped study and down the stairs to another chamber. A man and woman, each in the neighborhood of thirty, stood to meet them as they entered.

"This is the Good Magician's assistant, Magician Grey Murphy, and his wife, Princess Ivy," Wira said. Then, to the others: "Edsel and Pia of Mundania, here as exchange visitors."

"Glad to meet you," Grey said, advancing to shake hands. He was a nondescript person, who would have been unremarkable except for his magic. "I was raised in Mundania myself. I was frankly glad to get away from it, not just because of Ivy."

The princess smiled. She had long greenish yellow hair and blue eyes. "I visited it, but do prefer it here in Xanth. Sit down; we must talk."

They took seats on the large toadstools in the room. "We are supposed to see about our Service for our Answer," Edsel said. "But we can't stay in Xanth for a year, much as we might like to."

"Humfrey knows that," Ivy said. "He always knows, and things always come out well. Your service can be performed in as little as a day, but it is vitally important."

Pia began to relax. "A day we can handle. But why would anything important be left to Mundanes? We hardly know anything about Xanth, really. We depend on our Companions to keep us out of trouble."

"Breanna and Justin have not deserted you," Ivy said. "This just happens to be something rather special and private."

"And especially suitable for Mundanes," Grey said. "Because you have so little direct connection to Xanth."

"This is a peculiar qualification," Edsel said.

"It is a peculiar mission," Grey said earnestly. "Are you familiar with the concept of temporal paradox?"

"You mean traveling back in time and murdering your grandfather?" Edsel asked.

"Yes. Any change to a person's own present status would be as difficult. But here in Xanth the rules are different. We can, in our fashion, travel in time, and we don't necessarily honor the laws of paradox. That's what makes this mission so awkward."

"You want us to travel in time?" Pia asked, alarmed.

"Not you," Grey said. "Me. But I am concerned that I may do something that changes Xanth's present situation, and might not know it."

"How *would* you know it?" Edsel asked. "To you in the present, whatever existed would seem to have always been the case."

"Exactly. I might retain a memory of the other situation, but no one else would believe me. And if I did something that caused Ivy not to exist—" He shuddered.

"Whatever would possess you to take such a risk?" Pia asked. "Assuming it's possible, which I doubt."

"I must bore you with a bit of spot personal history," Grey said. "My father is Magician Murphy, who makes things go wrong. My mother is Sorceress Vadne, whose talent is topology. Several centuries ago Murphy tried to wrest the throne of Xanth from the legitimate king, for which he was retired to the Brain Coral's Pool for indefinite storage. Vadne resented Millie the Maid's appeal to the Zombie Master, and topologically converted her to a book. For this she too was banished to the Pool. During the Time of No Magic the two escaped Pool confinement and made a deal with Com Pewter: he enabled them to go to Mundania, where they could not be apprehended. But there was a price: they had to give their future child to Pewter, for lifelong service. I am that child."

"But how could you be committed to such a thing?" Edsel asked. "You didn't even exist."

"People of honor fulfill their deals," Grey said. "Pewter performed a real service for my parents, that enabled them to live good lives in Mundania, and enabled me to exist. We recognize that debt.''

''But people can't be traded for favors,'' Pia said.

Grey shrugged. ''Those who feel that way should of course refuse to make such deals. But if they do make them, they should honor them.''

''So you serve Pewter?'' Pia asked, unpleased.

''No. My service was pre-empted by that to the Good Magician. Since this is a permanent position, the matter has become moot.''

''So you found a way to wiggle out of it,'' Pia said.

''Technically, yes. But I do feel I owe Pewter something. Hence our present agreement. I will perform a significant service for him, that only I can do, to make up for the service he lost. Because of the delicate nature of it, he is amenable to this, and will consider the deal my parents made to be complete.''

''Plea bargaining,'' Pia said.

''Or accepting reality,'' Ivy said. ''Pewter knows he's never going to get Grey full time, and this is a lot better than nothing. Grey's good will is essential.''

''And the Good Magician goes along with this?'' she asked.

''He prefers to have me free of potentially awkward obligation. This will free me.''

Edsel was getting quite curious. ''Just what is this significant, critical thing you will do? That maybe involves paradox.''

''I will conduct a creature of Pewter's creation to Xanth's past, so she can learn something Pewter wishes to know. The journey would be extremely difficult to accomplish without my assistance, because my talent of nullifying magic is necessary at some points. However—''

''You could change Pewter's past—and therefore his present,'' Edsel said, catching on. ''You might even cause him not to exist.''

Grey nodded. ''This is not a mission a person would send an enemy on. As it is, I do feel I owe him a favor, and I am amenable to acquitting it in this manner. He knows he can trust me to do my best to accomplish it, without trying to nullify him. I have my own reasons to see that the present situation is maintained.'' He glanced at Ivy, who smiled back.

''How do we fit in?'' Pia asked.

''We need to provide more background first,'' Ivy said.

''The danger of inadvertently changing the present is unavoidable,'' Grey said. ''I will not do so intentionally, but the effect could be just as severe if I made a mistake. But it will be very difficult to avoid that risk, because not only will I be in the past, where the consequences of my actions will not be immediately apparent, but when I return to the present, others may not believe that any change has occurred. So it probably will not be possible to correct it.''

''I'd be extremely nervous,'' Pia said.

''I am. But this is a necessary risk, if I am to acquit my obligation. So we hope to establish a safeguard. We believe that though regular Xanthians will not be in a position to know whether any change has occurred, Mundanes who have no historical connection to Xanth may be more objective. They should be able to see any changes, because they are not affected.''

''That's us!'' Pia said.

''How?'' Edsel asked.

''Com Pewter can set up a liaison, a mental connection between us, so that the two of you will be able to tune in on what the two of us in the past are doing. Then if you see Xanth changing around you, you can notify Pewter, who will send in another person to go to the past to try to change it back, or get me to change it back. If you see no change, we will know that I have succeeded in avoiding incidental mischief.''

''And that reassurance is just as important,'' Edsel said. ''To know you have succeeded cleanly.''

''Yes. The consequences of failure would be no less horrendous for being unknown. Without that assurance, we couldn't risk the mission.''

Edsel whistled. ''I wouldn't care to risk it in any event.''

''Pewter has assessed the risk, and believes that it is minimal, with these precautions. We have to assume he is correct.''

''And I guess we'd better go along with it,'' Edsel said. ''Because there aren't many Mundanes traveling in Xanth at the moment.''

''And we do owe for our Answer,'' Pia agreed.

''So how does this work?'' Edsel asked.

''We will go to Pewter's cave, where he will use his power of reality alteration to establish a connection between the two of us and the two of you. You will be comfortable; in fact you will be able to walk around and talk with each other, as long as you remain with Pewter's sphere of influence. You will know whatever we do, as if you are seeing it yourselves.''

''Even when you—have natural functions?'' Pia asked distastefully.

''The other person, with whom you will identify, will not have natural functions,'' Grey said.

Edsel shut his mouth, sure that no comment on Pia's own nature was intended.

"Not have—?" Pia asked.

"She's a golem," Ivy said. "Made of metal and cloth. Animated for a purpose, alive, conscious, but not fleshly. Her name is Robot A. We call her Robota."

"And what will she be doing in the past?"

"Com Pewter is studying the processes of weather," Grey said. "He is vulnerable to electrical effects, such as lightning, and wishes to learn how to control them. Robota has been crafted to have the capacity to comprehend magical weather, but needs to observe it in action. Therefore she is to be sent to observe the Storm King, who governed Xanth before King Trent took over in the year 1042. He had great power over the weather, and she can learn more from him than perhaps any other person. Because talents do not repeat in exactly the same form, this is the only person who can show her this. So she will go there to study weather."

"You are risking Xanth's very history so that Pewter's golem can study weather?" Edsel asked.

"Weather is important to us all," Ivy said. "Now that Pewter is a nice machine, he will use the information for beneficial purposes."

"We could use some more information about hurricanes," Pia said. "They do millions of dollars worth of damage every year."

"Less so when there's an El Niño," Edsel said. "But that does other damage, and we understand it even less."

"Since our weather has magic components, it's more complicated," Ivy said. "So we do feel it's a worthy mission."

Edsel nodded. "The weather affects history too. Sometimes drastically."

"Now we realize that much of this observation will be dull," Grey said. "But you will be able to skip over parts. It will be like—" He paused, evidently searching his distant memory of Mundania for a suitable analogy.

"Fast-forwarding a video recording past the commercials," Pia said.

"Exactly," he agreed, smiling at her. "I haven't seen a video in—in thirteen years." He shook his head. "How time flies!"

"When you're having fun?" Ivy inquired.

"Of course," he agreed quickly.

Edsel and Pia laughed. "Those two are definitely married," Pia said.

"Indeed we are," Ivy said. "And here come our children. They are three years old now."

Three little energy balls burst into the room. One was in a green dress. She ran into Ivy's embrace, and Edsel saw that her greenish blond hair and blue eyes matched those of her mother. Another was in a brown dress; she ran to hug her father, and her brown hair and brown eyes matched his. The third wore a red dress; her red hair and green eyes matched neither. She paused to gaze at the visitors, then went to hug Pia, and that was where her green eyes matched.

Pia accepted the hug; she couldn't do much else. But she seemed uncertain. She had never had much to do with children; they were by her definition incompatible with sex appeal.

"This is Melody," Ivy said, setting her child on her lap. "The three have a joint talent."

Melody began to hum. A vague disturbance appeared in the center of the room.

"This is Harmony," Grey said, setting his child on his lap. "Whatever they sing and play together—"

Harmony produced a little harmonica and began tootling on it, in harmony with her sibling's humming. The disturbance became an opaque cloud with projections, in the shape of a model castle.

"And you have Rhythm," Ivy said to Pia. "She resembles her cousin Dawn, physically. The three together make things real."

Rhythm produced a little drum and beat on it with her fingers, providing a cadence. The music became better defined, though hardly expert.

The shape in the center became a castle made of candy. It was rather like a child's drawing, with the walls somewhat askew and the gates uneven, but there was no doubting the cookies and pastries and the gumdrops that formed its substance.

"Of course this is illusion," Grey said. "They aren't up to solids yet. But in time they will be able to make a real castle of candy."

"But there's no chocolate," Pia said.

All three girls focused. The castle melted a bit, then firmed up as solid chocolate.

"Oh, you little darlings!" Pia exclaimed, hugging Rhythm. But that broke the child's concentration; she lost the beat, and the castle collapsed into a pile of chocolate rubble. Then it dissipated as the rest of the illusion crashed.

"Nevertheless impressive," Edsel said. "Congratulations, girls."

All three little princesses tried to blush. All they achieved was patches of red on their foreheads, but surely that too would improve as they matured in body and talent.

"But now we must go to see Com Pewter," Grey said. "I'm afraid we shall have to leave the children here with Wira."

The three looked unhappy. Then they began to hum, play, and beat, and a dark thundercloud formed.

"We have transportation," Edsel said quickly. "Para, the duck footed boat. Plenty of room for them."

Ivy considered. "Well, in that case—"

The cloud dissipated and sunlight replaced it. The room was closed, without a skylight; the beam appeared from nowhere. The three girls jumped down and ran for the door.

"They will be a handful as they age," Edsel murmured to Pia as they followed.

"For sure," she agreed faintly, looking bemused.

They went outside. There were Justin and Breanna, with Para. "Boat!" "Duck!" "Foots!" cried the three children respectively, running to overwhelm the boat with attention. Para seemed to like it.

There was just room for the six adults, with the children scrambling around the edges. "To Com Pewter's cave, please," Grey said. The boat started moving, but it was somewhat slow and clumsy. There was too much weight for the ten feet to handle comfortably.

"I will Enhance you," Ivy said. She put a hand on the side of the boat.

The craft steadied, and the motion became smooth and swift.

"That's her talent," Breanna explained. "Enhancement. She can make anything do better."

Edsel was interested. "If I may ask, what's your talent?" he asked Grey.

"I nullify magic. Of course I don't use it unless there is a magical threat."

"Danger ahead," Pia said tersely.

"Her talent is to know what's inimical," Edsel said. "Just as mine is to modify or deflect other talents. We'd better check."

"There appears to be a break in the path ahead," Justin said.

They looked. It seemed that a recent storm had washed out the magic markers, and part of the enchanted path had been erased. A fire dragon was lurking there, waiting to pounce on whoever entered the unprotected section.

Para halted. Grey got out of the boat and walked to the bad section. The dragon pounced, seeming about to devour him. Then the dragon fell over, whimpering, its tail twitching like that of a wounded snake.

"These morsels are not for you," Grey told it. "Go and hunt elsewhere, and your powers will return."

The dragon struggled back to its feet and limped away. As it did so, it recovered, and soon was fully functional again. It turned to face Grey, inhaling. It was about to blast him from a distance.

"I wouldn't," Grey said calmly.

The dragon reconsidered. It turned about and departed. "Good decision," Ivy said. "Dragons are magical creatures, and will soon die without their magic."

Grey found the scattered markers and replaced them along the sides of the path. "These are depleted," he said.

Ivy went there and touched each marker. "She's Enhancing them," Breanna said. "So they'll be as good as new."

Edsel was impressed. Neither Grey nor Ivy had magic that showed ordinarily, but when they had reason to use it, it was powerful. That was of course why they were called Magician and Sorceress.

The journey resumed. "This robot golem I'm to identify with," Pia said. "Exactly who and what is she?"

"Robota," Grey answered. "This requires some background. Seven years ago, there was a Game of Companions, wherein two Mundanes visited, and one won a talent."

"I know," Pia said. "That was Kim. We know her."

"That was when Dug helped the Black Wave find a good place to settle in Xanth," Breanna said.

"Yes, in 1092. That game required considerable cooperation from a number of entities, among which was Com Pewter. In exchange for that assistance, he was given a number of magical parts, from which he and his mouse Tristan assembled Robota. She is endowed by her creator with a portion of his magic ability to change local reality. She can do it only in relation to herself, however, and even so her power is limited. That might be considered her talent. She also has a remarkably analytical mind, oriented on weather, as she is a weather golem. This mission will be the completion of her training and education. Thereafter she will be to weather what Grundy Golem is to languages.''

''Grundy?'' Pia asked.

''He was made from wood and string,'' Ivy said. ''But later the Demon $X(A/N)^{TH}$ made him real, and he married Rapunzel. Their child, Surprise, can do almost any magic once—and only once. Grundy is a translation golem, so he can speak to and understand any living creature, including insects and plants. It would put him in contention for Magician status, if he were a man.''

''But you said he was made real. So isn't he a man now?''

Ivy was surprised. ''Why yes, I suppose he is.''

''And how am I to identify with a creature who isn't alive?''

Grey stepped into the dialogue. ''In Xanth, the distinction between living and nonliving can be obscure.''

''For sure,'' Breanna said. ''Consider the zombies.''

''Robota is animate,'' Grey continued. ''She is not flesh, but she is conscious and motivated.''

''But if she's a machine—'' Pia said.

''Machines are people too. Your connection will enable you to see through her eyes, hear through her ears, and feel through her hands and feet. You will not have to think of her as alive, if you prefer not to, but we feel its not a relevant issue.''

Pia let it go, but seemed unsatisfied.

Meanwhile they were moving rapidly through the forest. It seemed that Com Pewter's cave was not really far from the Good Magician's Castle, and the enchanted path facilitated travel. Before long, they approached the area.

An awful noise sounded. ''Ooo-gah!''

''That's the invisible giant,'' Grey explained. ''He guards the cave.''

Pia sniffed. ''What is that bleeping stench?''

''He doesn't wash often enough,'' Ivy said. ''But soon we'll be in the cave.''

The ground shook. ''Ooo-ga!''

''He has a heavy tread,'' Breanna said. ''But he won't step on us. He knows us.'' She lifted her hand and waved upward. ''Hi, Giant!''

''Hi!'' returned from the sky, deafeningly.

''You look great as ever,'' Breanna called.

The invisible giant laughed. The sound rolled around the landscape, crashing off mountains and flattening valleys.

They came to a hole in the wall. Para ran in, and they were surrounded by darkness. Then it opened into a chamber where a collection
of junk lay, with a glassy screen sticking up in the center. The boat
stopped and they got out. The children clustered around the screen.
"Hello, Com Pewter," Grey said. "We have come with observers to
handle the mission."

The screen lighted. HELLO, MAGICIAN GREY MURPHY. WHO?

"Two Mundanes who will not be affected by changes in Xanthly
circumstance."

EXCELLENT.

"Here are Edsel and Pia Mundane," Grey said, introducing them.
"On service for the Good Magician. They have almost no prior experience of Xanth, and will return to Mundania soon."

EXCELLENT, the screen repeated. I AM AWARE OF THEIR IDEN-
TITIES, BECAUSE I MAINTAIN THE O-XONE. THERE IS A MESSAGE
FROM CHLORINE: THEY SUFFERED AN INTERRUPTION IN CON-
TACT, BUT LATER IT WAS RESTORED. THEY ARE SATISFACTORY.

"That's a relief," Edsel said.

A puzzle pattern appeared, on the screen, evidently for the amuse-
ment of the children.

Grey turned to Ivy. "Why don't you and the children return for us
this time tomorrow?"

"We will," she agreed, kissing him. She turned to the Companions.
"Do you wish to remain here or return with us?"

Breanna hesitated. "I think we'd better stay here. Just in case."

"May we use the boat, then?"

"Sure, if Para wants to go," Breanna said. "He has more than returned the favor we did him."

Ivy departed with the children. Now two new figures appeared. "I
am Tristan Troll," the tall ugly one said. "Pewter's mouse."

The other was a tiny woman who resembled Ivy, as an elfin princess.
"And I am Robota," she said. "Pewter's golem."

Pia looked down at her. "You look alive."

The small figure fuzzed, and reformed in full human size, looking
more than ever like Ivy. "It is mostly illusion. I am a creature made for
a purpose, given the abilities I need to fulfill that purpose. For example,
I have been programmed to speak three Mundane dialects, English,
French, and Italian."

"You speak English very well," Pia said, evidently startled.

Robota laughed. "I am not speaking it here. You are not speaking it here."

"But of course I am," Pia said. "It's the only language I know."

"When you enter Xanth," Grey said, "You speak the human dialect of Xanth. All people do, whatever their original languages. It happens automatically. It is part of the magic of Xanth."

"It's true," Breanna said. "It happened to all the members of the Black Wave when we came to Xanth. When you try to talk across the magic boundary, it's like gibberish."

Edsel was as surprised as Pia. "We were never aware of any change."

"There is no need to be," Grey said. "But when Robota and I pass through Mundania, we will not be intelligible, and will need to handle the local dialects."

"I will translate for you," Robota said. "And speak for you, using your voice."

"Fortunately we won't be there long," Grey said.

"Why go there at all?" Edsel asked. "I thought you were to travel back in time."

Grey smiled. "That is the most convenient way it is done. The interface between Xanth and Mundania is temporal as well as spacial. We shall leave in our present time, and re-enter in the time of the Storm King. Robota is attuned to the key times."

"This is weird," Pia said.

BUT FEASIBLE, the screen printed.

"Like the Adult Conspiracy," Breanna muttered.

"So what do we two observers do?" Edsel asked.

"You will be made comfortable here," Tristan said. "Pewter will provide for any special needs you have. Simply tell me, and it will be arranged."

"My credulity is straining," Pia said. "I think I'd like to go home."

Tristan didn't blink. "Describe your home."

Justin smiled. "You will like this."

"Well, it's a garden variety house," Pia said. "We each have an office, so I can do the accounts and he can do the programming without getting in each other's way. We have colored carpeting on the floors, and pictures on the walls." She continued to describe their house in greater detail, evidently feeling nostalgia.

Edsel noticed what she did not: as she spoke, the house was forming around them. She hadn't clarified that their two offices were in different rooms, so here they were side by side, alcoves in the same room, but otherwise correctly appointed. There were pictures of flowers and lakes by her desk, and pictures of his Lemon motorcycle by his desk, plus a sexy pinup calendar.

Pia finally noticed. "Yes, that's it, in a way," she said. "But it's all illusion, of course."

"No, this is temporary reality," Tristan said. "This is my master's power."

"And it's some power," Breanna said.

"Reality? Of course not," Pia said. She walked to her desk and slapped at the chair, probably expecting her hand to pass through without resistance. Instead it struck the chair.

She stared. Then she touched the desk, more carefully. Then she lifted a picture from the wall. "It's real!"

"For sure. I told you."

Edsel walked to his section. His things were real too. He tried to modify it, using his magic talent, but nothing happened.

"Ordinary magic can not overrule Magician caliber magic," Tristan said. "Com Pewter is supreme in this cave, except for Magician Grey, of course. But if you wish anything changed—"

"No, this is just fine," Pia said. "It really is pretty much like home."

"Then perhaps we should begin," Grey said.

"If the two of you will touch the two of them, the connection will be established," Tristan said to Edsel and Pia.

"Wait!" Pia cried, alarmed. "Do we lose our souls or something?"

"I assure you, this is not the case," Tristan said. "This is merely a link between you, so that the two observers will always know what the subjects are experiencing."

"And do they also know what *we're* doing?" Pia asked sharply.

"No. This is one way only. My master has been as yet unable to develop the magic required for two way temporal communication."

"That a relief," Pia said. Edsel agreed, though he didn't say so.

They went to stand before Grey and Robota. Edsel extended his hand to Grey, and Pia extended hers to Robota. When Edsel's fingers touched Grey's he felt an electric tingle. That was all.

"That's it?" Pia asked, sounding almost disappointed.

"Close your eyes and look," Tristan said.

Edsel closed his eyes and tried to see. He saw himself standing there, with his eyes shut. Startled, he opened his eyes, and for a moment suffered a double image. Then the view of himself faded, and his vision was normal again.

"I was seeing through your eyes!" he said to Grey.

"Yes. The magic sends to you. Then you can tell Com Pewter, especially when there is anything alarming."

"I don't like to ask this question," Edsel said. "But I think I must. Suppose you die?"

Grey smiled. "That is unlikely in Xanth, because of my magic, and Robota of course can't die, though she could be destroyed. But it is possible in Mundania, and I admit I am nervous about that aspect of our journey. If it happens, your awareness will go blank. Then I regret that it will fall to you to advise the others."

"Advise me," Tristan said. "I will advise the others."

"I hope that doesn't happen," Edsel said. "This is becoming much more serious than I expected."

"We believe that the mission can be safely accomplished," Tristan said. "In any event, there is no personal risk to the two of you. It would not be ethical to subject you to that."

"Yet you are subjecting Xanth to the risk of serious change."

Grey gave him a straight look. "Not if you are sufficiently vigilant."

Edsel shut up. He would do his best, though he sincerely hoped that nothing went wrong. His knees felt a bit weak.

Com Pewter's screen lighted. DO IT.

Grey nodded. "Perhaps I should carry you, at this stage, Robota."

"Yes."

Grey picked up the golem and tucked her into a shirt pocket. He turned to the exit tunnel. He took several steps, then paused, turning back. "If I discover a problem I don't believe we can handle, I will signal you, like this." He lifted his two hands in a gesture as of prayer. "That will mean to send help."

"If we see that, we'll tell Tristan," Edsel agreed. "But I sincerely hope it's not necessary."

"I hope so too," Tristan said. "Because I am the one who will have to go there, and I do not feel competent, as a troll."

"I know the feeling, as a Mundane," Edsel said.

Grey turned again and walked on out of the cave.

Edsel, suddenly uncertain about the connection, closed his eyes and concentrated. He saw a light, growing, and realized that it was at the end of the tunnel. It was the opening, as Grey approached it. Then daylight was around him. "The connection is working," he said, relieved, as he opened his eyes.

"I know," Pia said.

Grey closed his eyes again—and found his vision sailing up into the sky. He stumbled, almost falling, until someone steadied him. It was Breanna. "Something's wrong," he said.

"For sure. I hope you're not sick."

"Perhaps you are seeing the invisible giant picking them up for transport," Tristan said.

Oh. Edsel felt foolish. "Yes. I forgot about the giant."

"Perhaps it would be easier if you retired to your office and sat down," Tristan suggested.

Edsel was feeling giddy. "Yes. Grey's images and mine don't mesh perfectly. It's like motion sickness." He walked to his den and took his chair. Pia did the same with hers.

Now Breanna talked to Tristan. "It's going to be a long wait. How about some solitaire?"

"Perhaps we can connect with Terian and Com Passion," Tristan said, sounding pleased.

Edsel tuned them out and closed his eyes again. Now he saw the Land of Xanth coursing by below. It was a patchwork of jungle, lake, and field. He realized that the legs of the giant must be between him and the land, but they were completely invisible, so it was like low level flying. Soon they approached the boundary at the northwest region, what in Mundania was called the Florida panhandle.

The land came up. Grey was being set down. He turned and waved, probably to the departing giant. Maybe the giant waved back.

Grey turned to look at the nearby sea. It was changing color from blueish to greenish. Then, suddenly, Grey ran west, away from Xanth. Mundane foliage surrounded him.

"Are you all right, Robota?" Grey inquired, patting his pocket.

"I'm fading," she answered. "But I will not lose my magic entirely. Keep me near your ear so I can translate for you."

Grey walked on. The scenery did not look like Florida. Edsel opened his eyes. "Are they in the right place? I don't recognize the landscape."

Tristan looked up from his card game. "They are in the land you call Italy, circa 1885 if I have your numbers correct."

"1885!" Pia exclaimed, opening her eyes. "You mean, like a century ago?"

"Perhaps I can clarify this," Justin said. "In terms of the Xanth time they are visiting, it is about seventy-five years, when the Evil Magician Trent first transformed me into a tree for trying to oppose him. But when he was thereafter exiled, he emerged in Mundania of southern Europe near the end of the nineteenth century, your time. He returned to Xanth twenty years later, and became King. Grey is following his route, as it is easier to do that than to establish a new temporal route."

"Clear as mud," Pia said.

"There is no fixed connection between Xanth and Mundania," Tristan said. "A person can step from Xanth into any time of Mundania, and return into any time of Xanth, if he knows how. Thus that is merely a stepping stone."

"From Xanth now to Italy then," Edsel said. "From Italy then to Xanth then. Only not exactly the same then."

"That's close enough," Pia said, rolling her eyes.

Edsel closed his eyes and tuned in again. So did Pia.

Grey approached a settlement by the sea. He spoke gibberish to a native. The native responded. "Robota is speaking for him, in his voice," Pia reported. "He is holding her up near his face so it's not obvious. It's Italian. He—she's asking for the road to France."

"You can understand Italian?" Edsel asked, amazed.

"No. I can understand Robota. *She* understands Italian."

Grey negotiated to get a horse to ride, and set off. Mountains loomed ahead. "But this may take days!" Edsel protested.

"For him, yes," Tristan said. "But when he returns here, he will do so within a day of his time of departure, so you will not be unduly delayed."

"But how can I follow days, in hours?"

"You fast-forward past the dull stuff," Breanna said.

"This is weird," Pia said.

"Ain't magic wonderful," Breanna said, laughing.

Edsel tried it. Lo, suddenly he was looking at southern France. At least the mountains were behind and the landscape looked vaguely French. In a moment Pia confirmed it.

Skipping ahead, they found Grey joining Evil Magician Trent's Mundane army. Grey was able to do this because Trent didn't know him back then. In fact, it was before Grey had been delivered, so no one in Mundania could have known him.

Edsel took a break. He stretched and walked out to join the others. They were playing quadruple solitaire with illusion cards, freely interfering with each other's layouts and evidently having a great time. Justin and Breanna formed one team, and Tristan and Pewter the other, the troll/mouse making the moves per the machine's printed instructions.

Breanna looked up. "Oh, hi, Ed. Everything okay?"

"They're passing through Mundania, and there is no problem. In fact it's dull; I'll be fast-forwarding soon."

"For sure." Breanna slapped an illusion card down across the layout. "Trump."

Angry swirls of colored light crossed Pewter's screen, his way of showing frustration. Then they cleared. "Double," Tristan said, putting down a card for the machine.

"Raise," Justin said, placing one of his cards.

HIT ME Pewter's screen printed.

Breanna laid down three cards. "Meld."

Tristan picked one up. "Kiss mee."

"Just what kind of solitaire *is* this?" Edsel asked, baffled.

"It's one we invented, called Kiss Mee Donkee," Breanna explained. "It's sort of eclectic."

"So I see." Edsel still could not make head or tail of the play. "You know, Com Pewter could play better if he had a joystick and keyboard. Considering the nature of Xanth, those would probably give him joy and the key to new insights."

Pewter was interested, so Edsel described those devices in greater detail, and the others saw about making them. He returned to his study and resumed tracking Grey. Pia remained in her chair with her eyes closed, either locked into the past or asleep.

They marched east, back toward Italy. But Grey went ahead, because he needed to be in Xanth before Trent got there. He used his magic to nullify the deadly shield that was now there, and the familiar magic landscape returned.

Robota came back to full animation. She was a golem, but used illusion to change her appearance and her reality adjustment to magnify her size. Now she resembled an elf, still much smaller than Grey, but able to keep up with him on her own. Edsel assumed that Grey looked like himself, but Robota now resembled an elfin Pia, quite pretty.

They spent a night on the path to the North Village, as it was a fair hike from the border. The path was not enchanted, and there were dangers, but Grey nullified them. Robota was metallic in essence, and could hardly be hurt by routine monsters, but she was practicing the ways of living femininity, so as to be able to fool the Storm King.

They found a mush room that was big enough. The mush was mostly on the outside, and the room mainly inside, so it worked well enough. They brought pies in, and Grey ate one while Robota emulated him. ''I can take bites in my mouth, but can't keep them there,'' she said. ''What should I do with them?''

Grey considered. ''Maybe make spot illusions to conceal them, and set them down.''

''But then there will be a growing pile of pie bites on the table.''

He considered again. ''Maybe make spot illusions of bites, and of bites missing from the pie.''

''Yes!'' she agreed, pleased. She practiced, and soon had a reasonably realistic mode of eating. When the pie was finished, she quietly moved it elsewhere on the table, and let it revert to complete, as if it were a new one.

''And my clothing,'' she said. ''Do I have it right?''

''I'm not sure exactly what the elves of this time wear,'' Grey said. ''But maybe you can represent yourself as one from a distant tree, with different conventions.''

''Yes. I shall be Silica, a princess of the Mineral Elves.'' She shifted her outfit to a dark gray blouse and skirt.

''That should do,'' Gray agreed.

''Now to be realistically female, how much here?'' she asked, indicating her bosom.

''Well—''

''Say when it's right,'' she said. Her bosom expanded.

''Ah—'' he started, evidently uncertain how to handle this.

It became full, then large, then huge, then so large it burst out of the blouse and threatened to fill the room.

''Let's start over,'' Grey said quickly.

The monstrous breasts vanished, and the slightly filled blouse reappeared. The bosom started expanding again. ''When!'' Grey said, stopping it at a reasonable magnitude.

After that they covered the legs, until she had a rather nice set under a tastefully brief skirt. ''And don't show your—''

"I know," she said. "They freak men out." Then she reconsidered. "But I think I'd like to do that, some time."

"Not on this mission," he said firmly. "We can't risk mischief."

Grey slept, and Edsel's window closed. But Pia's continued. "She's experimenting with poses," she reported. "Breathing deeply, crossing her legs."

"She doesn't sleep," he said. "So she has time to work things out."

Pia opened her eyes and looked around. "What time is it in real life?"

Breanna looked up from her card game. "Early evening. You've been at it a while."

"Can we pick them up when we want to?" Pia asked. "Like in their morning, when it's our morning?"

"Yes," Tristan said, playing a card. They seemed to be playing a new, different game of interactive solitaire, with Pewter using his new joystick to deal smiley-face cards. Edsel decided not to inquire.

"Does this suite have a bedroom?" Pia asked.

A door appeared. "It does now," Tristan said.

Pia got up and opened the door. "Is it private?"

Tristan considered. "Technically, nothing is private in this cave. My master governs all of it. But apart from that context, it is private."

Pia nodded. "Then come on, Ed."

Edsel was glad to comply. He joined her in the bedroom, and found it was very like their own bedroom at home. It was almost as if they were back in Mundania.

"Do you know what Robota's doing now?" Pia asked as she joined him in bed.

"No. My window is closed."

"She's practicing wiles."

"But Grey's asleep."

"Yes. I think she knows better than to try them on him when he's awake; he's faithful to Ivy. But now she's pretending. She wants to be a real woman."

"I suppose it's sort of sad, being an animate creature of metal."

"Yes. She does have feelings; I can feel them. She knows she exists for a purpose, and that purpose isn't to be a normal woman. But because she has to emulate one, she has the emotions, and that becomes painful."

"I never thought about the morality of making robots or golems before," he said. "But does seem cruel."

"Too bad she can't be real."

"Grundy Golem became real. Maybe if she does a good job on this mission, she will be similarly rewarded."

"I hope so." Then Pia proceeded to put him into the kind of rapture only she could manage.

In the morning they emerged from the bedroom to find that another bedroom had been formed for Justin and Breanna. Edsel wondered how far the girl had managed to take the former tree this time. He knew that Pia had been encouraging him, but old inhibitions died hard. He felt guilty for the thought, but would have loved to snoop on their nocturnal activity.

Tristan appeared. "Is everything in order?"

Edsel started to answer, the realized that the question was actually about the time travelers. He closed his eyes and tuned in.

Grey and Robota were walking along the path. "Yes, they seem to be headed south, after a safe night."

Edsel and Pia had a Mundane breakfast of cereal and fruit and cocoa. It was amazing how Pewter could shape reality within his cave. Then they tuned in again on the time travelers.

They were approaching a female centaur, who was bare breasted, in the fashion of her species. Now Edsel knew that Grey did notice such things, for the image remained firmly framed in his vision. "Hello," he said. "I am Grey Human, and this is my companion Silica Elf."

"I am Cassie Centaur," the centaur replied. "Or if you prefer, Cassie Girl." She became a human woman, suitably clothed. "My parents suffered an encounter at a love spring, so I am a crossbreed."

"My talent is minor prophecy," Grey said, completing his introduction.

"Mine is to go in and out of the Void."

"That is remarkable," Grey said. "I would not care to go near the Void. But I would have thought your talent would be the ability to change between your two forms."

"No, that's inherent. Most crossbreeds assume aspects of both parents; I must be one or the other, in turn. So it is independent of talent. Some of the mertaurs have talents too."

"The mertaurs?"

"They are quite rare, so it's not surprising you haven't encountered them. Centaur/merfolk crossbreeds, with human heads and arms, equine bodies, and aquatic tails. I'm going to visit them now."

"We wish you a good visit. We are going to the North Village to see the king."

"You are on the right path. Proceed on south."

They separated amicably and went their ways. Robota was pleased because her identity had not been challenged. Centaurs were intelligent, observant folk, so that was a good sign.

Edsel took several small jumps forward, bypassing the hours of dull walking. Pia kept pace with him, so they wouldn't get out of phase with each other.

Grey and Robota entered the North Village. This was where the Storm King lived. But before they approached the rather meager palace, they checked in with the village elders, Roland and Bianca. These were, Justin explained as he and Breanna emerged from their bedroom, the parents of Bink, who had recently been exiled from Xanth for lacking a magic talent.

Grey and Robota needed an introduction to King Aeolus, and Roland and Bianca were the ones to do it.

"I am a traveling man with the talent of minor prophecy," Grey said when Roland answered the door. "This is Silica, of the Mineral Elves, whom I am protecting." Robota was in regular elf form, about a quarter the height of Grey, but proportioned exactly like a human woman, with not too much bosom. "She is interested in studying weather, and would like to meet the Storm King. So we come to you, as Village elders, to ask for an introduction to the King."

Edsel opened his eyes. "Is this ethical?" he asked.

"For not sure," Breanna said. "What's happening?"

"Grey is claiming to have a talent of minor prophecy. This is the second time he has done so."

"That is his cover story," Tristan said. "You will understand that they can under no circumstances tell the truth, for that would lead to immediate chaos as every person sought to know his personal future, and Xanth would be changed irredeemably. Neither can they avoid identifying themselves, for that could arouse suspicion. So they must have persuasive false identities."

"But this is lying."

Pia looked at him. "When did a lie ever stop you, Ed?"

"What are you talking about?"

"When you wanted to get a girl into bed."

"That's different!"

"Perhaps this is not a fit subject for discussion at this time," Justin said.

"Why not?" Breanna asked. "I'm interested. It's okay to lie when—?"

"I apologize!" Edsel said. "I'm sorry I brought up the subject."

"I guess lying in a good cause is okay," Breanna said doubtfully.

"Oh?" Pia said. "The end justifies the means?"

"Well—"

"The end of getting a girl into bed?"

"You have a point," Breanna said. "It's not right."

"But the alternative would be to completely change Xanth's present," Tristan said.

Pia and Breanna looked at him. "Oh, that," Breanna said.

Edsel wanted to get off the subject. "Why don't we agree that lying is wrong, but that what Grey and Robota are doing is role playing. They must maintain their roles, as the truth would either be not believed, or would have devastating consequences."

The others considered, then exchanged nods.

"What is happening?" Tristan asked.

Edsel and Pia closed their eyes. "And the King banished him," Bianca was saying. "Because he couldn't demonstrate any magic."

Edsel repeated that to the others.

"She's talking about Bink," Justin said. "He was believed to have no magic. Actually he has Magician-caliber magic, but it is indefinable."

"He will return," Grey said reassuringly. "I can't tell exactly how or where, but I foresee his return, in good health, and acceptance in Xanth."

"Oh, that's such a relief!" Bianca said.

"Is she trusting, or desperate?" Pia asked.

"Desperate," Justin said. "By all accounts she was a fine person and loving mother. Her talent was the replay: she could in a spot area set time back five seconds, so that a scene could be briefly replayed. It was very useful when someone misstepped or hit his thumb with a rock. Roland's talent was the freeze: he could make a person stop in place, not even breathing, until freed. As a couple, they could be formidable, but they never abused their powers."

The appointment with the king was made. Edsel and Pia skipped ahead to that. They didn't seem to be able to return to any prior scenes, so learned to be cautious about fast-forwarding. But so far there was no indication of any trouble. No one questioned the identity of the time travelers, and they were making no waves.

But Edsel was uneasy. He knew that sometimes the simplest things could go drastically wrong. In this case, the wrongness could be extremely subtle and extremely unfortunate. He refused to be lulled into complacency.

That afternoon, in the past, Robota got to meet Aeolus the Storm King. He was an old man, feeble, and surely not much longer for kingship.

"I am Silica, of the Mineral Elves," Robota said, flashing her most winning smile. She was getting it down well; it almost lighted the room.

"And who are you?" Aeolus asked Grey.

"I am Grey, with the talent of minor prophecy. I am helping Silica find her way through the human kingdom."

Justin nodded when Edsel reported that. "Xanth elves associate with particular elm trees, and their strength is inversely proportional to their distance from their home trees," he said. "They are super-strong near their own elf elms, but very weak when they are too far from them. An elf maiden would need help in the human domain."

"The King is inquiring their business with him," Pia reported.

Edsel tuned back in. Robota was answering. "I am studying weather, as it affects our activities. Please demonstrate a storm for me."

The Storm King's answer was gruff. "No."

"But I need to observe weather magic, so I can understand it."

"My talent is not a parlor game," Aeolus said. "I invoke it only when there is legitimate need."

Robota argued, but the King would not budge. "The truth is that his talent faded with age," Justin said. "He seldom invoked it toward the end."

"Did you tell them that?" Edsel asked.

"Oh, yes, they know," Tristan said. "But the King still has some power, and she can analyze its nature when he uses it. Then my master will be able to duplicate it with full power. So they will do their utmost to get him to demonstrate it."

"Get on it," Pia said, her eyes closed. "This is getting heavy."

Edsel closed his yes. "A wiggle swarm to the south?" the King was asking incredulously. "There hasn't been one of those for decades."

"Nevertheless, I see one coming," Grey insisted. "You could destroy it with a solid storm."

"Why should I believe the word of a stranger?" Aeolus asked.

Grey spread his hands. "I can't prove that my prophecies are correct until they come true. But in the past they have been reasonably accurate."

"Well, if a wiggle swarm comes, we'll see about it," the King decided. "I'm not at all sure a storm will blow wiggles away; they can drill right through stone."

Edsel reported that, doing ongoing narrative as he listened; he was getting better at it. Pia corrected him on details, as she saw the same scene through Robota's eyes and ears.

"That king may be old, but he's not stupid," Breanna remarked.

Then Grey found a prophecy that made an impression. "I see Evil Magician Trent returning with an army to conquer Xanth."

"Oops," Breanna said. "If he warns the Storm King, won't the King stop the invasion, and Trent will never conquer Xanth, and all history be changed?"

"Not so," Justin said. "Trent didn't take Xanth by force. Aeolus died, and they gave Trent the crown."

"Oh," Breanna said ruefully. "I keep forgetting that you lived Xanth history. You were there."

"And you are here now," Justin said. "You were well worth waiting for."

The Black Wave girl tried her best to blush, with imperfect success.

The Storm King seemed much more alert to this threat than the one from the wiggles. He walked to the wall where a magic mirror hung. "The border," he said.

A picture formed in the mirror. It showed a group of men out beyond a shimmering border. They were setting up cages on the other side of that shimmer, which Edsel realized was the deadly magic shield that prevented anyone from crossing, before Trent took power and shut it down.

"There *is* something happening out there," Aeolus said. "I had better prepare."

"So will you demonstrate your talent?" Robota asked, favoring him with her most winning smile, and a rather nice flash of elfin bosom.

Old and feeble as the King was, he was not completely immune to the wiles of lovely women. "Yes. Wait here."

The King departed the chamber, through a door that opened magically to let him pass. Immediately Robota tried to follow, but the door balked her. Then Grey touched it, nullifying its magic, and they went through.

Aeolus was opening a magic strongbox. He reached inside to lift something out, but his hands came up empty. Yet there was a faint sparkle.

The King straightened up and turned—and saw Grey and Robota standing there. "You saw!" he said, chagrined.

"What did they see?" Edsel asked, mystified.

"We don't know," Tristan said. "This is new to my master."

Then Grey caught on. "Your soul is in that box!" he said.

"But why?" Robota asked.

The king looked frightened but canny. "I will tell you, if you will promise not to tell anyone else."

"Not within fifty years," Grey promised, and Robota agreed. He was aware that the information was being transmitted fifty-seven years to the future. Also, spreading a truly significant secret might change Xanth history, and they couldn't afford that.

"That's good enough." Aeolus took a deep breath. He was standing up straighter, and looked better, now that he had his soul with him. "This is a soular cell, made by Magician Yin/Yang centuries ago. It prevents aging and death for the person who stores his soul inside. I don't need to have my soul with me all the time, so I store it here so I won't die."

"But you're already pretty old," Robota said.

"Yes. I got this box only a year ago, and it can't undo the age I suffered before then. But I can remain my present age for a long time. Unfortunately, my talent remains with my soul, so when I need to invoke it, I must recover my soul for the occasion."

"So you're not really senile," Grey said. "Just soulless."

"That is correct. I pretend senility in order to avoid onerous tasks."

"Well, demonstrate your talent, and we will depart and never see you again," Robota said.

"Will a small storm do?"

"Certainly." She smiled engagingly.

Aeolus concentrated on the center of the room. In a moment a cloud formed. It thickened and swirled. Then a little bolt of lightning shot out, and there was a crack of thunder. A small rain shower followed.

"Wonderful!" Robota exclaimed, clapping her little hands. "Great demonstration."

The storm dissipated. The Storm King walked back to the soular cell.

Aeolus made a clutching motion at himself. Something sparkly lifted from his body. He crammed it into the box and pushed down the lid. He had put away his soul.

He turned toward them. "Now you will go, and be silent," he said.

"Yes," Grey agreed.

They left the chamber with the king, so this time Grey did not need to nullify the door. Then the Aeolus bid them farewell, and they walked out of the palace. "You got what you need?" Grey asked Robota.

"Yes. Now I understand the secret of weather magic. My master will be able to duplicate it."

"Then walk with me, and do not argue."

"Argue?"

"When I do something surprising."

Perplexed, Robota agreed.

They walked north, out of the North Village. But the moment they were out of sight of it, Grey picked her up and stepped off the path into the brush. "Revert to golem size," he whispered.

She did, and he put her in his pocket. Then he forged on through the brush at right angles to the path. There were needle cactuses, thornberries, and tangle trees in that trackless jungle, but he nullified them as he passed through.

"What is he doing?" Pia asked.

"This is a mystery to us," Tristan said. "He is supposed to bring them right home."

Grey circled the North Village, bearing west and then south. There he found a small little-used path, and followed it farther south.

As the day grew late, he found a thick thicket between two thin thinets, and used his nullifying magic to penetrate to the center, where he was well protected and effectively invisible.

"Now what is this all about?" Robota inquired in his ear. "You didn't need to go to this much trouble to get me alone, you know."

Grey surely smiled. "The Storm King is without a conscience."

"He seemed nice enough to me."

"The conscience resides with the soul. The soulless have no decent limits, as with the demons or the animated inanimate."

"Now wait a moment! I'm animated inanimate."

"And so you have no conscience. Fortunately you have not yet discovered how dastardly you could be, if you thought of it. I hope you will continue to act in a decent manner."

"You mean I can't seduce you?" she asked, disappointed.

"That's right. A woman of conscience would not try to seduce a married man."

"But why not?"

"That comes under the heading of conscience. To a person of conscience, that which is feasible is not necessarily that which is appropriate."

"I don't understand."

"Precisely. But if you do well, one day you may became real, and have a soul, as Grundy Golem does. You will want to be prepared for its limitations."

Robota considered. "You're right. I do want to become real. So I will study conscience, now that I have studied weather. But you will have to help me, because my master never said anything about it."

"Com Pewter is animated inanimate, too, and so without conscience. Fortunately there are some limitations established in his programming. What about Tristan?"

"He's funny. He won't cheat at cards even when it seems he could, and he doesn't do anything illicit even when he's away from our master's control."

"Tristan has a conscience. In fact, he has one of the finest consciences of his kind, and is a fine model to emulate."

"You mean I should act like him?"

"Yes, with due allowance for your gender."

She sighed. "This will be horribly restrictive."

"It's worth it."

"So why did you bring me here, since it wasn't for illicit purpose?"

"The Storm King wants to hold on to power as long as he possibly can. He doesn't know he is going to die soon, making his retention of the kingship moot. We discovered a secret of his. He will seek to eliminate us."

"But we promised to keep that secret fifty years."

"He judges us by himself. He expects us to break that promise. So he will seek to eliminate us before we do so."

"How can he do that?"

"By arranging to have us ambushed and killed on our way home."

"But he can't kill me; I'm not alive."

"He doesn't know that. In any event, he could have you taken apart and scattered."

Robota nodded. "That would do it. Especially here in the past, where my master can't recover the pieces."

"So we must hide from him. We arrived at the North Village from the north, and departed it to the north. He will assume that we live somewhere north, and will send his scouts out to intercept us. They will hardly think to look well away from the paths amidst the dangerous jungle."

"And when they don't find us to the north, they will spread their net wider."

"Yes. But they will have little chance to find us if we are careful, and if we stay well ahead of them. So we must postpone our departure from Xanth until the search dies out."

"But won't that mess up our return to our own time?"

"No, we'll re-enter Xanth just when we should. This merely prolongs our stay here."

"What of the observers?"

"They will have to fast-forward by most of this. I regret inconveniencing them, but I had not anticipated dealing with a soulless king."

"What's for supper?"

Grey looked around. "I didn't think of grabbing any food before coming here."

"I can go out and find something for you; I'm small enough and hard enough to handle this thicket."

"Why should you bother? You don't feel hunger yourself."

She shrugged. "Isn't that what a person of conscience would do?"

"Yes. But—"

"So I'm learning." She climbed down his shirt, dropped to the ground, and went out in search of food.

"This is getting interesting," Pia said, opening her eyes. "Let's take a break, then fast-forward."

"Agreed," Edsel said. For though the time travelers had spent a day in Xanth, the observers had spent much less time. In fact, their times were not synchronized; the two in the present could go through any amount of past adventure as fast as they wanted, by skipping ahead. But they did not want to skip too much, too freely, lest they miss something vital and be unable to backtrack to see it. They missed nothing during their breaks, but could miss everything during an ill-advised fast-forward.

"Robota spoke of seducing Grey," Pia said. "He talked her out of it. But is it physically possible? I mean, she's a golem made from metal. She doesn't even have a—a place.''

"It is physically possible," Tristan said. "For two reasons. First, she can change her own reality, to an extent, so can form a place. Second, metal is no necessary bar to such activity, just as the fact that my girlfriend Terian is a literal mouse is no bar when we meet physically. Magic makes us compatible. It's a variation of the accommodation spells the elves and imps use when they wish to associate with large folk on an equal basis. Even all-metal folk, like the brassies, can be remarkably soft when they wish to be, so Robota has that ability too.''

Pia seemed somewhat taken aback. "Golems have more potential than I thought," she said.

That surprise was true for Edsel too. Even seemingly simple forms of magic were turning out to have intriguing aspects.

In due course they resumed the observation. Edsel was finding it increasingly easy to identify with Grey Murphy, who seemed like a fine person. He suspected that Pia was finding the same with Robota, who had arranged to look like her in her elfin form, and in her golem form too. That was a considerable compliment, especially because it seemed to be unconscious.

Grey and Robota continued south to the Magic Dust Village. This settlement, Justin explained, had lost most of its men to the call of the nearby Siren. A few men had been grabbed by a tangle tree near the path, and rescued in injured condition. But the injured ones kept trying to follow the Siren's song. The village was run by a tough female troll named Trolla.

"A troll," Pia said. "But aren't you a troll, Tristan?''

"Yes. We are not all bad, just as full humans are not.''

"For sure," Breanna agreed. "No species is all bad, not even zombies.''

Grey and Robota joined the villagers, she now in her natural golem form, because the king's men would be looking for an elf. When the Siren sang again, Grey was unmoved.

"How do you resist the Siren's call?" Trolla asked.

"It's my talent," Grey said. "I can nullify—''

"He has selective deafness," Robota interrupted. "He hears only what he wants to hear.''

Grey, realizing that he had almost made a careless mistake, shut up.

Edsel was attuned to his mind, and could follow his thoughts with increasing facility.

"My word," an old wife of the Village said. "I'd swear my husband and all my children had that talent."

Grey considered, and concluded that he would not be changing history if he spared the men from the tree. He went to the tree alone at night and touched its trunk. When it tried to grab him, he nulled it. "You will never again molest a man following the Siren's Song," he informed it. "Otherwise I will do this." He nulled much of the trunk for a moment.

The tree got the message. It left the men alone. But it remained dangerous to women. Fortunately they had the sense not to go near it. They assumed that the Siren had made a deal with the tangler, so that she could capture more males.

Grey and Robota remained a few days at the Magic Dust Village, but Grey became increasingly uncomfortable, because there were so many women there who missed the company of men. They were becoming rather obvious about their attraction to him, and some were quite alluring.

Lovely music and singing filtered though the forest. "I think we should go see just what is happening with the siren," Grey said.

"You are succumbing to her song!" Trolla said, alarmed.

He smiled. "No. I can shut it out. But as long as the Siren remains, there is a danger to the village. Maybe I can talk her out of singing."

"That would be nice," Trolla said. "Better yet, we would like to have our men back."

"For sure," Robota agreed. The others laughed when Pia reported that.

They followed the path through the jungle, Robota sitting on Grey's shoulder and holding on to his ear. The motion of his body caused her to lean outward and inward, her bosom colliding with his ear every so often. "That's not accidental," Pia murmured professionally. "She's keeping her options open."

"Keeping her what's open?" Edsel asked.

The others smiled. They were getting used to him.

"Of course we can't really change the Siren," Grey told Robota. "That would alter history. But we can talk to her, and perhaps make things easier for the Magic Dust Villagers."

"They seem like nice folk," she agreed. "I could study conscience with them."

"You could indeed. They are doing a difficult job, dispersing the magic dust so that it doesn't pile up too thickly and distort the magic of Xanth. All types of people are working together in harmony, all motivated by their sense of duty. An excellent model.''

It was a good path. It led them toward the sound of the singing, to the shore of a small lake. There was a island in the middle. On the island's tiny beach was a stool, and on the stool sat a lovely female figure, facing away from them, playing a dulcimer.

There was a bleat, and suddenly a sheep-like animal charged toward them. ''That's a battering ram,'' Grey said. ''Dodge it.''

''But you could nullify it.''

''I believe it has an encounter with Bink, not long hence. I don't want to change that encounter, lest—''

''Lest history change,'' she concluded. ''Now I understand.''

The ram came at them. Grey jumped nimbly to the side, and it ran right on by. Before it could brake and turn, it collided with a pineapple tree. A pineapple dropped, detonating under the ram's tail, and shrapnel flew out. The ram, reasonably battered, ran on.

The music continued. ''It has a pretty melody,'' Robota said. ''But I don't find it compelling.''

''I do,'' Grey said. ''But I can nullify its magical component. That is the Siren.''

They found a path across the water, and followed it toward the figure. The path faded behind them, leaving open water; it was one-way.

The Siren heard them and turned, ceasing her playing and singing. She had hair like flowing sunshine, and a tail like flowing water. Her bare breasts were spectacular.

''She can summon me anytime,'' Edsel breathed.

''Well, you're an idiot male,'' Pia retorted. She pursed her lips. ''But she does have formidable architecture.''

''The Siren is seventeen years old at this stage,'' Justin remarked. ''She has a teenaged figure.''

''That's the best kind,'' Breanna said.

''Indubitably.''

''You must be the Siren,'' Grey said.

''Why so I am, handsome man,'' the mermaid said, inhaling. ''Are you going to stay a while?''

''I, ah, already have company,'' he said, indicating Robota, who remained on his shoulder.

"I'm sure the golem girl can share you. What can she offer that I can't?"

"Legs," Robota said, flexing hers.

"Really?" The siren drew her tail from the water, and it split and became a fine bare pair of legs. She stood, setting her dulcimer on the stool.

"We came only to talk," Grey said quickly. "You seem to have been causing some mischief in the neighborhood."

"But all I do is divert myself by singing and playing my dulcimer," the siren protested. "It gets so lonely."

"Couldn't you go elsewhere to divert yourself?"

"No. Our parents left me and my sister the Gorgon here, making us promise never to leave the lake. So I remain, hoping for company. But it never remains."

"Gorgon?" Robota asked.

"That's her name. She's lovely, like me, and has almost as sweet a disposition. But we got tired of each other's company—I mean, we're both female—so she went to another island nearby. The trouble is, though I play fair and let men go on to meet her too, she never sends them back. It's generating some stress between us."

"You don't know why?" Grey asked.

"Well, I never thought she was selfish, but I'm beginning to wonder."

"They are truly innocent," Justin explained. "When they reached the age of—of—"

"Stork interest," Breanna supplied.

"Um, just so. At that stage their magic talents also matured, and they could no longer be safely kept at home. So they were deposited on the islands of the lake, to fend for themselves. Which, unfortunately, they were more than capable of doing, despite their innocence."

"So then you lure more men, with your music," Grey said. "And the same thing happens."

She pouted prettily. "Yes. I would like to marry and settle down, but I have to let them meet my sister, because we are supposed to share evenly, and then I lose them."

"Well, I may not be an authority, because I'm from Mundania," Grey said carefully. "But I think there are better ways to meet men. Perhaps I can persuade your sister to send one back to you."

She clapped her hands. "That would be wonderful! I have so much to give, if only there was someone to take."

"She's not fooling," Edsel commented. "That bare figure—"

"We know," Pia snapped. She tended to get snappish when encountering women with fuller bosoms than hers.

Grey and Robota followed the one way path on to the Gorgon's island. "What are they up to?" Pia asked. "That creature's dangerous."

"I believe he wants to persuade the Gorgon not to turn *every* man to stone," Tristan said. "But this is chancy, because the Gorgon significantly affects Xanth history, especially after she encounters Magician Humfrey, and this must not be changed."

"Grey knows that," Breanna said. "He lives at the Good Magician's castle. He knows the Gorgon personally."

"Then she'll recognize him!" Breanna protested.

"No, dear," Justin said. "She does not know him at this time. Later she may remember him, but that's much closer to the present, and shouldn't have much effect. Still, I confess I am not at ease about this encounter."

"Ssst!" Pia said. "The golem's on it."

"Is this wise?" Robota asked as they walked. "The Gorgon will marry the Good Magician, after he makes her deadly face invisible."

"I won't interfere with that, of course," he said. "I merely want to unstone some of the men from the Magic Dust Village, so they can return there to work and comfort their women."

"The Siren's song will just lure them away again."

"True. But at least they will have some time with their families, making things better without changing history significantly."

"I think you're risking paradox," Robota said.

"No I think it will be all right."

"In fact, I think you have been foolishly smitten by the lovely innocence of the Siren, and want to see the Gorgon in her teenage youth."

"What makes you think that?"

"I am objective as only a machine can be, and female besides. Turn aside, Grey."

"I think she's right," Pia said. "He is after all a man. There's only so much bare female flesh they can handle before their foolish minds overload."

The others looked at Edsel. "I fear she's right too," he said. "That

siren is one luscious creature, and she has made it plain she wants a man
to love. Grey has lost his objectivity.''

"Do we have to send in help?" Tristan asked nervously.

"Not yet," Edsel decided. "It hasn't happened yet. Maybe he'll
come to his senses before he does something really stupid.''

But Grey demurred, forging onward. He seemed to be beyond reason.
Edsel winced, watching it. Men *were* foolish about women. This was the
danger they hadn't anticipated.

"Remember," Robota said, perhaps resigned to likely disaster.
"Sight of the Gorgon's mere face turns men to stone. All stone, not just
one little part of them the way the sight of other women does." She
hugged his head, pressing her bosom against the side of his face.

"She's trying to distract him," Pia said. "And for once I agree. If
she seduces him, there won't be a change in history.''

"I'll be careful," Grey said carelessly.

They passed through a region of the lake where tall trees grew up
through the water, forming a natural screen. They rounded a turn, and
something moved. Grey instantly exerted his talent—and accidentally
nullified the path across the water. He fell in with a splash. Robota
laughed, clutching on to his hair. "Serves you right," she said. "Maybe
this will shock you into some common sense.''

"You're right," Grey said, treading water in a more conventional
man. "I've got no business meeting the Gorgon. What was I thinking
of?" He was swimming now, perforce.

"Maybe this," Robota said, pressing her bosom against his ear again.
"Or this." She spread her knees. "Swim to shore, and we'll get out of
here.''

"Right." He swam to the nearest shore.

A hand reached down to help him climb out and up the steep bank.
He looked at his rescuer—and turned to stone.

Pia screamed. Edsel fell off his chair. Grey had been caught by surprise, not thinking to nullify any more magic, and had accidentally gazed
at the face of the Gorgon. The ultimate disaster had happened.

11
FANTA SEA

After a moment, Pia recovered enough to help Edsel gasp out the nature of the catastrophe.

"Grey—stoned?" Tristan repeated, stunned. "We never anticipated this."

"For sure," Breanna said, not smiling. She looked as white as her brown face could get. "We were so concerned about him changing history, we never thought of how history could change *him*. What'll we tell Ivy? She'll be Poison Ivy when she hears about this, even when it's not the time of the month."

"Women in Xanth have times of the month?" Pia asked. "I thought—I mean, with the stork and all—"

Breanna glanced to make sure no males were close enough to hear. "Between storks, they can get out of sorts, about once a month," she said. "Men don't know. But what I really meant was—"

"I know. This is awful. She loves Grey."

DO NOT PANIC, Com Pewter's screen printed. STONING IS NOT PERMANENT.

"It isn't?" Pia asked, foolish hope flaring.

"All the stoned men recovered in the subsequent Time of No Magic," Justin said.

"That's a relief," Edsel said, looking more than relieved. "I thought he was dead."

"I will have to go to rescue him," Tristan said with grim determination. "When I get him out of Xanth, the magic will relent, and he will be restored. He is not dead, merely enchanted."

Pia grabbed on to something. "What's this time of no magic?"

"It occurred about a year later," Justin said. "When Bink mistakenly freed the Demon X(A/N)TH and the Demon departed, taking his magic with him."

"But the Demon X(A/N)TH is still here," Pia protested. "In the form of—"

"It was temporary," Justin said. "The Demon returned after about a day, and the magic was restored. But the stoned men remained whole; the Gorgon's spell had been interrupted, and could not restore itself. It was an incidental benefit of a very awkward period."

"Then—" Pia said, working it out. "Then all they have to do is wait for that, and Grey will be all right."

The others circulated a surprised glance. SHE IS CORRECT, Pewter's screen printed. NO RESCUE MISSION IS NECESSARY AT THIS TIME.

Tristan looked twice as relieved as Edsel had been. It was clear that he did not want to travel into the past, and risk disturbing history himself. Yet he had been ready to. The troll had courage.

"Quick, fast-forward," Breanna suggested. "See if they work it out themselves."

"No!" Justin said. "Resume at exactly that time, to see how Robota reacts. That may be important."

"Yes!" Pia shut her eyes and tuned in. It was obvious that Edsel couldn't, for now.

"Hello," Robota said.

The Gorgon stared at her. "Oh—I thought you were a man."

"Not exactly," Robota said. "I was climbing on this statue of a man; maybe you confused us."

"That must have been the case. I thought I saw a swimming man."

"Our eyes do sometimes deceive us," Robota said. "Is there another path away from here?"

"Yes, that way." The Gorgon pointed.

Robota took the path and made her way back toward the Magic Dust Village. "She shows no regret at Grey's fate," Pia reported. "She's just going about her business."

"She's a golem, without a soul," Tristan reminded her. "She can emulate caring, but can't actually experience it. Since she is alone, she must see no reason to emulate it."

Robota reached the village. "He got stoned."

"I don't understand," Trolla said.

"He made a mistake, and will not be returning. So I have come to join your community."

"You are welcome," Trolla said. "Provided you are willing to work hard."

"Yes."

So Robota settled in, in her natural golem form, and helped the villagers disperse the magic dust. She worked hard, and soon was accepted by the others. She did them favors when she could, and became increasingly decent as she studied the others to learn the ways of it.

Pia opened her eyes. "What I don't get is why Grey went so crazy, there toward the end. I mean, I thought he was a pretty level-headed married man."

"He is," Justin said. "But the Siren's song—actually it's her dulcimer that carries the magic—is among the more remarkable lures of Xanth. Grey surely underestimated its power to affect him."

"And perhaps rationalized to believe that he remained in control," Tristan said. "Men do that."

"For sure!" Breanna agreed. "The biggest part of the Adult Conspiracy is that women are the true rulers of Xanth."

"That song was pretty alluring," Edsel said. "If I'd been in control, I'd have gone to her right away. But that wasn't all. When she made legs, they were really something."

"Oh?" Pia inquired, mildly annoyed. "I've got legs." She hoisted her skirt to better display them.

"And those bare breasts," Edsel continued.

Pia was moderately annoyed. "I have breasts." She pulled her blouse tight.

"And that touching sweet innocence."

Pia was silent, and really annoyed.

Breanna stepped in. "Well, we girls have sweet innocence, until we get corrupted by men."

"Indubitably," Justin agreed. Pia smiled to herself; it was clear that he was the relatively innocent one in that relationship.

"Had we known that they would encounter the Siren, we would have prepared them better," Tristan said. "But that was not on the schedule.

Obviously the Siren did affect Grey somewhat, enough to distort his judgment. Robota tried to dissuade him, but males in that state can be difficult to dissuade.''

"Like alcohol," Edsel said. "The one person in the group who thinks he *hasn't* taken too much is the drunk."

"Let's hope that Robota does the right thing," Tristan said. To that they all agreed, as Pia closed her eyes and fast-forwarded.

A year passed. Then five travelers came, searching for the source of magic. There was the Good Magician Humfrey, looking the same as always. There was his son Crombie, in the form of a griffin. There was Chester, a powerful centaur. There was Bink, who was Ivy's grandfather. And there was Grundy Golem, not yet made real.

The villagers welcomed them with open arms, wings, and whatever else offered. Nymphs, sprites, and buxom human maids surrounded Bink. Fairies, elves, gnomes and minionettes mobbed Humfrey. Centaur fillies rubbed shoulders with Chester. Two griffin cows attended Crombie Griffin. And Robota went after Grundy Golem.

"But isn't he married to Rapunzel?" Pia asked, disturbed.

"Not at this time," Justin said. "Rapunzel is locked in an ivory tower on the Gold Coast, I believe; it will be several years before Grundy rescues her. He is at this stage without marital encumbrance."

"Without what?" Breanna inquired dangerously.

"A figure of speech," Justin said hastily.

"I know what it means. You think marriage is an encumbrance?"

"I did not mean to imply that. I merely—"

"Robota is having a ball," Pia reported. "She kissing Grundy, and he's kissing her back."

"They are the only two golems in Xanth, I think," Tristan said. "So they may be entitled to celebrate."

"They certainly are celebrating," Pia said. "You're right: she does have a place, and she's getting pretty soft."

"Oh, phooey," Breanna said. "I can't keep my mad while they're doing that. Come here, Justin."

Pia noted the girl's ways with a certain professionalism. If she hadn't succeeded in seducing her man yet, she was bound to accomplish it soon. It made Pia more interested in doing something with Edsel, for all that there was by now little novelty in it. But now was not the time. Not when there was a better show on.

Pia watched the activity of the golems with some interest. Robota had evidently done some thinking on the matter, and was straightforward in her approach. She continuously complimented Grundy, and showed him flesh, which she crafted to be extremely well proportioned, and she eagerly acceded to his every notion. Yet it seemed that he was using her too, because he had no more soul than she did. The result was a rather uninhibited session that surely would have alerted any golem storks in the vicinity.

Then the Siren's song came again. All the males perked up, listening.

"It is the Siren!" a fairy screamed.

The women sang, trying to drown out the summoning sound, knowing the effect it had on males. But it was not to be denied. The males drew away and headed for the sound. They passed right by the tangle tree, which let them be. Until Crombie Griffin, who was then a woman hater, balked and pecked at the tree. That led to an amazing encounter.

"They are fighting the tangle tree," Pia reported. "Magician Humfrey is using his magic against it. And the Village women have gotten courage and are coming with torches. Robota is among them. Oh, this is a Grade A fracas!"

"A tragedy," Justin said. "That poor tree."

The tangler was a fearsome opponent, but the combined force of men, women, and magic was too much for it, and it was destroyed. But the Siren's song sounded again, and the men resumed their march toward it, to the women's great disappointment.

"What happens to them?" Pia asked, her curiosity aroused. "I can't tell, because Robota remains with the Village."

"This is known to history," Justin said. "They passed the battering ram, and the pineapple tree. Then—" He paused.

"What happened?" Edsel asked.

Justin resumed, reluctantly. "Chester shot the Siren. Through the heart."

"But she was no threat to them," Pia protested.

"The Good Magician had healing elixir," Tristan said.

"Yes," Justin said. "As it turned out, the men concluded that the Siren was not a menace to them, after they destroyed her magic dulcimer. They gave her elixir, restoring her, and spent the night there. Then they went on to see the Gorgon. The Good Magician was able to handle her by making her face invisible. They liked each other. Right from the first."

"He had great power of magic, and she had great power of beauty," Tristan said. "That is a feasible combination."

"Thereafter, they—" Justin resumed.

"Oh, I see," Pia said, closing her eyes and fast-forwarding. "They returned to the Magic Dust Village."

But though the Villagers welcomed the men, they did not stay. They accepted a local guide, and pushed on into the Region of Madness. Robota remained at the Village. After further adventures, summarized by Justin, the men reached the Demon X(A/N)TH. Then—

"Robota's finally moving," Pia reported. "She's following the trail to the Siren and Gorgon, though both of them have lost their powers."

"She anticipates the Time of No Magic," Tristan said. "Now if she just does the right thing—" Robota made her way to the Gorgon, who had not yet made up her mind what to do. "Things are going to become very strange," Robota told the Gorgon. "For a day there will be no magic. Then there will be magic again, and your power will be restored. Your face will be visible again, and as time passes you will be able to stone women and plants as well as men."

"But I don't want to stone anyone," the Gorgon protested, shedding invisible tears. "Once the Good Magician made me understand what I was doing, I was appalled."

"Then you must go to Mundania, where you will have no magic power," Robota said.

"Mundania!" the Gorgon repeated, horrified.

"It's the only way. Maybe we can guide you there. When the magic returns."

"I don't know," the Gorgon said. "Everything I know is here."

"What do you have here? You can't interact with any man, and the women are not likely to be friendly. Go to Mundania where you can live in peace, until you decide what else to do with your life."

"I suppose so," the Gorgon agreed doubtfully. "But I already know what I want to do with my life. I want to marry Magician Humfrey."

"Then go to Mundania, mature some, figure things out, and return when you're ready."

"I shall," the Gorgon agreed with sudden decision.

"When the magic stops, all these statues will return to life," Robota said. "And I will lose much of mine. I am stuffed with magic dust, so I will retain some animation, but I'll need Grey Murphy. So I will join him now."

She found Grey's statue, and climbed up to perch on its shoulder. She waited.

Pia fast-forwarded. Suddenly the scene changed. "It's become a blur!" she said.

"That must be the Time of No Magic," Tristan said. "It came suddenly, and even the magic dust lost most of its potency, when the Demon X(A/N)TH left the area entirely. So Robota may be worse off than she was in Mundania."

"She is," Pia said. "But she's hanging on."

Grey Murphy recovered. He found himself at the edge of the lake, his legs still in water. "But I can't connect," Edsel said.

"Because there is no magic," Tristan said. "We are dependent on Robota's limited awareness."

Robota clung weakly to Grey's head. "Time No Magic!" she gasped without breath. "Help me, Gorgon!" She collapsed.

"I was stoned!" Grey exclaimed, catching on. He put Robota in his pocket, where she was able to peek dimly out. Mostly, she just listened.

Men were milling around: the other restored statues. Fortunately they didn't know what had happened to them, or they would have gone after the Gorgon with mayhem in mind. She was nevertheless frightened of them.

Grey put his arm around her. "Come with me. We need to get somewhere else."

"Out of Xanth," Robota said faintly.

"Too long a trip," Grey murmured to her. "Too dangerous. There will be crazed beasts all around."

"Then find somewhere safe," she said.

He pondered. "Maybe I can reach Com Pewter's cave. That's safe."

"But—Paradox," she said.

"I don't think so. I don't exist in this time, and Pewter can keep a secret."

Robota evidently lacked the strength to protest further. She just watched from the pocket.

Grey and the Gorgon forged through the jungle. Everywhere, trees were drooping, and animals were suffering. They had never before experienced the absence of magic. Grey would not be able to stop them by nullifying their magic, but they were too distracted to be a menace to him, other than accidentally.

Pia fast-forwarded until they reached the cave. Pewter was inert; he could not animate without magic. Grey and the Gorgon, having walked most of a night and day, lay down on the floor of the cave and slept. It was cold, and they had no blanket, so they held each other for warmth.

After a time, Robota stirred. She hauled herself from Grey's pocket. She pulled a sodden handkerchief out after her. She crawled across to the Gorgon, and laid the handkerchief across her face.

The Gorgon woke. ''What—?''

''The Magic—returning,'' Robota said. ''Cover face.''

''Oh.'' The Gorgon spread the handkerchief. The spell of invisibility had been banished by the absence of magic, and would not be mended by the magic's return.

Then the magic returned. Com Pewter came to life, his screen lighting. Grey Murphy's eyes opened, and he stared full into the handkerchief. ''What?''

''Look away!'' Robota cried with renewed strength. ''Gorgon!''

He did so with alacrity. Robota had just saved him from getting stoned again. He got up and faced Pewter's screen. ''Change reality,'' he said urgently. ''Make the Gorgon's face invisible.''

WHO ARE YOU? the screen demanded.

''I will explain. It's important. Null the Gorgon first.''

Grudgingly, Pewter did. The Gorgon's threat disappeared, and she returned Gray's hanky.

''Now I will tell you the truth,'' Grey said. ''But you must forget, and make the Gorgon forget, after we leave. I will tell you why.''

STRANGER HAS MUCH NERVE.

Then Grey told Pewter why. ''That's the first time I've seen a machine surprised,'' Pia commented.

''Now will you help us leave Xanth safely?'' Grey asked.

YES. THEN I WILL SEAL OFF THIS MEMORY UNIT UNTIL YOU INVOKE IT IN YOUR TIME.

''Good. Now we could use some food, and better clothing.''

Pewter generated a well stocked table of food, and they fell greedily to. Robota talked with Pewter, explaining how he had made her, in the future, and providing details of their mission Grey had skipped.

Then two more people arrived at Pewter's cave. They were bedraggled, having evidently struggled through the nonmagical jungle most of the way before the magic returned. One was a middle aged man, the other a rather pretty young woman. They stood blinking at the gloom.

Grey looked at them—and froze. "I forgot!" he whispered. "We must get away from here."

The Gorgon and Robota looked at him. "Why?" the Gorgon asked. "Aren't they people seeking refuge, like ourselves?"

"Yes! But they are my parents. His talent is to make things go wrong—and they just went wrong for us."

"Oh, no!" Robota said. "Paradox."

The man heard them. "There are people here," he said, surprised. "And food." The two of them lunged to the table, too hungry to resist.

Grey looked as if he were going to faint. Then Robota came to the rescue. "Pewter can erase the memory," she said.

Grey sighed with sheer relief. "Yes!"

"Hello," the man said. "We are two strangers in need of sustenance. May we join you?"

"Yes," Grey said. "We shall talk. Then Com Pewter will help us all to go to Mundania, and erase your memories of this meeting."

"Why?" the woman asked, around a mouthful of pie.

"Because this is Robota, a golem from the future." Robota smiled and inclined her head. "And you are Magician Murphy and Sorceress Vadne."

The Magician leaped to his feet. "How do you, a stranger, know that?" he demanded.

"Because I am your son you just signaled the stork for, Grey Murphy."

Both of them stared at him. "How can this be?" the man demanded.

"I am also from the future, on a mission to what is my past. I will be delivered to you in Mundania, and grow up with you, before we all return to Xanth."

"We can't be in Xanth," Vadne said. "They would put us back in the Brain Coral's Pool we just escaped."

"You will be pardoned, and become productive citizens of Xanth. And I will marry a princess. Until I undertake this mission, fifty six years from now."

They doubted, but slowly the came to believe. "My son!" Vadne exclaimed, coming to hug Grey. It was odd, because she was slightly younger than he.

"That's so touching," the Gorgon said, blowing her invisible nose.

Robota turned to Magician Murphy. "If I were real, would I be shedding a tear now?"

Murphy brought out a handkerchief and wiped off her wet face. "Yes."

The scene blurred. Pia had to open her eyes so she could wipe her own face.

"But you hardly know Grey Murphy," Breanna said. "And you never met his folks."

"It's like a wedding," Pia said. "You just have to cry."

Soon she returned to the observation. Grey, Robota, and the Gorgon had retreated behind a screen, and the memory of Magician Murphy and Vadne had evidently been wiped. The two bedraggled figures stood at the entrance to the chamber.

GREETINGS, INTRUDERS.

"Who are you?" Murphy demanded.

I AM COM PEWTER. YOU ARE NOW IN MY POWER.

Actually that was no sure thing, because Murphy's talent was to make things go wrong. But the two worked out a deal: Pewter would help them get safely out of Xanth, if they gave him their just-ordered son. They agreed.

Then Pewter put them into temporary stasis and addressed the others.

GREY, YOU CAN AND WILL GUIDE THEM SAFELY OUT.

"I can and will," Grey agreed. "Otherwise I would jeopardize my own existence." He glanced around. "I will guide the Gorgon out, too."

YES. I WILL NOW WIPE HER MEMORY.

"No!" the Gorgon cried. "Please! I beg of you. I promise never to tell. Let me remember this wonderful scene, and the way Magician Grey has helped me."

Pewter paused.

"It makes sense," Robota said. "She will be in Mundania, and later will return to marry the Good Magician, who knows everything anyway. So it shouldn't make any difference."

AGREED.

"Oh, thank you!" the Gorgon cried. "And thank *you,* Robota! I will remember this favor." She paused, considering. "But never tell."

Then they organized for the trip to Mundania. Grey, Robota, and the Gorgon made an entry, and were introduced to Magician Murphy and Vadne as their guides to Mundania. The party of five set off.

The walk took several days, but was without event. They took the invisible bridge across the Gap Chasm and followed the trail north through the North Village. They disguised themselves, and no one recognized them. When they reached the border, Grey did not have to nullify the deadly shield; it had been taken down, on orders of King Trent. But they forgot one thing: to tune in the color of the water of the sea near the border. So they did not come out where Trent and his army had been, but in a different time and region of Mundania.

"That's all right," Grey said. "The border interface automatically registers you as you pass through it, and at such time as any of you return, you will return to the same time in Xanth that you left. Except that it will be as much later in Xanth as the time you spend in Mundania." He did not explain about the time traveling aspect; he and Robota were a special case.

The Gorgon's face reappeared as they left the magic. She was just as pretty as her sister the Siren, and had just as good a figure. "That's all right," she said. "I will make do."

They ascertained that this was the region they had passed through before, that spoke Italian. "I can teach you a few words," Robota said.

The Gorgon considered. Then she smoothed her skirt and inhaled. "I will pretend to be a mute girl, in need of a good man's protection. Do you think that will work?"

Grey considered her statuesque face and figure. "I believe it will. Still—"

"Thank you." She walked away, into the heart of drear Mundania.

Vadne nodded. "She will surely succeed."

"Now where do the two of you wish to be?" Grey inquired. "There are different sections of Mundania, speaking different languages and having different customs."

They considered. "You seem like an honest young man," Magician Murphy said. He no longer knew Grey as his son, because of the memory wipe, but they had spent several compatible days together. "Take us to a region you feel will be good for us."

Grey paused, and Pia knew why: he didn't dare change his own history. Robota whispered in his ear: "Where you lived."

So he watched the changing color of the sea, and brought them to the region and time within a year of where he had been delivered, which was fourteen years after the Gorgon's time, and on another continent, where English was spoken. The stork might find it a challenge to make a delivery outside of Xanth, but history indicated that it would succeed.

Grey explained the problem of language, and Robota told them a few useful words so they could get started. "As I understand it," Grey said, "when Xanthians go to Mundania, they are not challenged; the Mundanes seem to believe that they have always been there. But they do need to learn the conventions."

"He did not say where he learned that," Justin remarked. "But it was surely from his parents—the very ones he is now addressing."

They came to a crossroads. Three roads led away from them. Murphy and Vadne took one, and Grey and Robota took another. But Vadne hung back a moment. "Thank you. We will name our son after you," she called.

Startled, Grey didn't answer. "Thank you," Robota called back in his voice, and nudged him with her knee so that he got moving. They were at the fringe of magic, so she had fair animation.

"That's playing it close," Edsel commented. "I think we might find a paradox hidden somewhere in there, if we looked hard enough."

"Don't look!" Breanna said.

Tristan smiled. "It does seem that this meets the technical situation of not changing the future."

When they were alone, Grey reversed course and went back the way they had come, right back into Xanth. Robota oriented, and they entered just one day after their original departure.

The invisible giant was waiting for them. He picked them up and brought them rapidly to the cave.

"Why didn't the giant carry them from the cave, when they were leaving Xanth?" Pia asked.

"The giant might have remembered," Tristan said.

Then Grey and Robota entered the cave. "Did anything change?" Grey asked.

Pia exchanged a glance with Edsel. She had forgotten about that aspect toward the end.

"Not that we know of," Edsel said. "You did a nice job of covering your historical tracks."

"When my parents walked in, I thought we were lost," Grey admitted. "But then I realized that I was not overlapping myself, because I did not yet exist. I had merely been signaled for."

"And when you got stoned, *we* thought you were lost," Pia said. "But Robota carried through."

"I had to," Robota said. "I could not handle the return alone. Also, it was what a souled person would have done."

Pewter's screen lighted. DID YOU GET THE WEATHER DATA?

"Yes," Robota said. "And so much more. I have learned to emulate a conscience."

"For sure," Breanna agreed.

Grey turned to Edsel and Pia. "I believe that completes your service for the Good Magician. You are now free to go." He turned to Com Pewter. "And I believe it also completes my obligation to you, according to the terms of our agreement."

AGREED.

"And you may now open the closed file, and recover your personal portion of the adventure."

The screen dissolved into a pleased swirl of color as Pewter did just that.

"Hello," Ivy called from outside. "We're back. Are you?"

"Yes, dear," Grey called.

"Oh," Pia said, suddenly remembering. "Were Demon Ted and DeMonica here yesterday?"

"Why yes," Robota said. "We played together. But they departed before you arrived."

"Did they have a magic locket?"

"Yes, that was what we played with."

"Where did they go?"

"Demon Vore took them to the Fanta Sea. They love that."

"What is that?" Edsel asked.

"It's a pond where folk can find their wildest dreams."

"I hope they didn't stay there," Edsel said.

"They should have been home by the end of the day," Tristan said.

ONE MORE THING, Pewter's screen printed. CONTACT WITH THE EXCHANGE COUPLE HAS BEEN LOST AGAIN.

"That's nervous business," Edsel said. "They could be in trouble."

Pia agreed. "We had better wrap up our business in Xanth and try to make the exchange back."

I SHALL CONTINUE TO MONITOR THE O-XONE, Pewter printed.

Pia bid farewell to Tristan and Robota, whom she had really come to like, and they left the cave. There was the duck footed boat with Princess Ivy and the triplets.

They rode back toward the Good Magician's Castle, telling the story. It was of course Grey's story, but Edsel and Pia were able to fill in many details and reassure Ivy that he had done nothing untoward during his adventure.

"Except sleep with the Gorgon," Pia said mischievously.

Ivy raised a brow. "Oh?"

"Well, you have to understand," Edsel said. "She was eighteen and lovely then."

"And innocent," Breanna added.

"To keep her warm," Justin said.

Ivy laughed. "I'll ask her, next time she's the Designated Wife." But Pia suspected that she did not find the joke as funny as the others did.

They reached the castle and dropped Grey and Ivy and the triplets off. "Now we need to find those demon children," Pia said.

"Probably best to start with their parents," Breanna said. "Nada Naga should be able to round up DeMonica any time."

"Where can we find Nada Naga?"

"I believe she's visiting her home now," Justin said. "That would be Mount Etamin, north of the Gap Chasm."

Para set off. He knew the way there.

Progress was swift, thanks to the duck footed boat. Soon they were crossing the Gap Chasm, using the invisible bridge: the same one she had seen through Robota's eyes in the past, when she and Grey were guiding his parents and the Gorgon to the Xanth border. The Gap was as awesome as before, descending a mile or so into gloom. They had crossed the chasm when the harpies carried them south, but it seemed more formidable now that they seemed to be floating close to its maw. Suppose there were a break in the bridge, a section out?

Pia closed her eyes, feeling unpleasantly giddy. Soon they were back on solid land, to her relief, and forging along a new path. "Oh, we're coming to the Library," Breanna said enthusiastically. "I love this place."

"You like to read?" Edsel asked.

"Not exactly."

Pia looked at her. What did she mean?

They came to a section where the tree trunks resembled the spines of books, complete with print. Two, close together, formed a gateway. In front of it was an armored knight on a steed galloping in circles.

Para halted. "What's that?" Pia asked.

"That's Sir Q Lation," Breanna answered. "Hi, Q! Feeling smart today?"

"Very well rounded, thank you," the knight replied courteously. "Do you wish me to show you around?"

"No, thank you," Breanna said. "We're going straight through, this time."

"As you wish." The knight guided his armored mount to the side, and Para waddled on through the gate.

Just inside was an ogre stamping his big hairy feet. They left little marks on the pile of cards beneath. "That's the date stamper," Breanna said. "Hi, can I have a date?"

"For sure, paramour," the ogre responded with something like a smile. He tossed her a card with a date on it. If there had been any doubt before, now it was clear that Breanna had been here before.

Then there was a solid man sitting at a desk shaped like a huge tome. "Hi, Dick," Breanna said. But the man stared stolidly ahead, not deigning to answer. "That's Dick Shunary," Breanna explained. "He won't speak a word to anyone, though he knows every word in the book." She did not seem annoyed.

After a moment, Pia got it: shun. In dic*tio*nary. A verbal pun.

"Let's see, there's a map in here somewhere, if we can find it," Breanna said. Para wove along different paths, searching. They came to a glade with a pattern of grass and sand, like a miniature golf course. "Atlast."

"At last what?" Pia asked.

"We finally found the map." She indicated the pattern, and Pia realized that it was indeed a map, with the sand marking paths.

"Atlas," Edsel murmured. "Atlas at last."

Oh. Pia could have done without that.

They followed a path to a number of warriors doing a dance of victory. "That's the Conquer Dance," Breanna said.

"Concordance," Edsel murmured. He had more of a mind for this nonsense.

Beyond the dance was a dead tree. A feline snoozed in its bare branches. "Catalog," Edsel said.

"Can't we just get on out of here?" Pia inquired, pained.

"It does get rather wearing," Justin agreed. "Magic is the main thing that distinguishes Xanth, but surely its second attribute is puns."

They passed a tree with dampish small fruit. "Dew date," Breanna said happily.

Then there was a dolorous researcher poring over a several volume set. "Sigh Clopedia," Breanna said.

"I do love her," Justin said. "Even here."

Breanna faced him. "Shut up or I'll use the card file on you."

"Card file?" Pia asked, unable to stop herself.

"It trims the edges of the King, Queen, Jack, and so on," the girl explained with a straight face. "And there are some book jackets." Pia looked. Sure enough, there were shivering books with warm jackets.

They passed a moving picture of young women dancing and removing items of apparel. "Para!" Breanna said severely. "I told you not to go by the film strip."

"That's quite all right," Edsel said, watching avidly.

The boat veered, taking them by a high building. "What's this doing here in the library forest?" Pia asked.

"It's a story collection."

"You walked into that one," Edsel said.

They peered up to the thirteenth floor, where spirits flitted in and out of the windows. "Don't tell me, let me guess," Edsel said. "That's a ghost story."

"Enough!" Pia cried. "Get me out of here!"

"She really means it," Edsel warned Breanna.

"Yes, she's series," the girl agreed.

If Pia had had a pillow, she would have whammed them with it. Fortunately the exit loomed. There was only one insubstantial plant barring their way. "Through that mist tree," Breanna told the boat.

Edsel opened his mouth to say something smart, but caught Pia's dagger of a glance.

"We found our way out because we have the indecks," Breanna said, patting the interior of the boat.

Index. The female dog was still doing it.

But now they were out of the library and back in normal magic jungle.

"Do you know, I once met a lady who gave nothing but opposites," Justin remarked innocently. "Her name was Anti Nym. I believe she would have felt at home at that library."

"But we don't really need the library," Breanna said. "We can see the paper view." She held up a roll of paper.

Pia knew she was going to hate herself, but she had to ask. "Paper view?"

"You pay for each time you see it."

"That does it!" Pia screamed. She jumped out of the boat, landed off-balance, and whirled into the soft side of a cow-like creature. The thing made a soft, sickly "Mooo!"

"I—I'm sorry," she said, recovering her balance. "I did not see you." The cow looked so sad that all her anger dissipated.

The boat halted, and she climbed back in. "Moo-sick soothes the savage beast," Edsel murmured.

Pia tried to summon back her rage, but was worn out.

"Actually, it is the savage breast that is soothed," Justin said.

"She's got two of those," Edsel agreed smugly.

"And they are most elegant," an elephantine creature remarked, leaning over the boat to stare at her blouse.

"Pay no attention to the sycophant," Breanna said. "It flatters everybody with equal insincerity."

"We are approaching Mount Etamin," Justin said.

Pia was relieved—until she saw the dragon circling the peak. In a moment the dragon spied them, and swooped down.

Breanna seemed unalarmed. She stood carefully in the boat. "Hi, Draco!" she called. "It's us—Justin and Breanna. And friends. Coming to see Nada Naga."

The dragon waggled with wings and veered off. Pia was not entirely reassured. "What would have happened if we had not been friends?"

"He'd have toasted us," Breanna said, shrugging. "But I wouldn't have let us come here if I hadn't known it was safe."

"Draco is an honorable dragon," Justin said. "He has a very nice collection of gemstones in his nest. I believe he is the only dragon to possess some black beryls."

Para ran up to a tunnel and into the mountain. Soon it opened into a lighted cave. A huge snake loomed, forming the head of a human being. "Who are you, and what is your business here?"

"Breanna of the Black Wave, Justin Tree, Edsel and Pia of Mundania, and Para Boat," Breanna said. "We need to see Princess Nada Naga about her daughter, DeMonica."

The naga guard rolled his eyes. "Has that demon child gotten into more mischief?"

"Not exactly. She has something we need. A locket."

"Wait here." The human face disappeared, and the serpent slithered through a hole in the wall.

Soon two other snakes returned. The big one formed a lovely human head with a small golden crown. ''Hello, Breanna,'' the princess said.

''Hello, Nada,'' Breanna said. ''Edsel and Pia are Mundanes, here on an exchange program. They need to borrow the magic locket Ted and Monica found.''

The small snake formed into DeMonica. ''It got boring. We left it in the Fanta Sea.''

Oh, no, Pia thought. They were going to have to search for it.

''Can you show us where?''

''Sure. I think.''

Breanna hesitated. ''Is it safe for Mundanes in the Fanta Sea?''

''It is if they are careful,'' the Princess said. ''Why don't you take Monica along, and bring her back here when you find it?''

''Thank you,'' Breanna said. ''Hop in, Monica.''

The child performed a huge hop and landed in Pia's lap. ''Hi, Pia,'' she said cutely, and kissed her on the cheek.

Pia hugged her. This sort of thing was getting easier with such cute children. ''Hi, Monica. How did you get so sweet?''

''I gave my sour to Ted. For today.''

The others laughed. The boat turned around and set off. Monica remained on Pia's lap. Pia loved it; there was just something about the child. Pia had never wanted to have children, but after meeting this one, and Ivy's three, she was changing her mind.

''Now just what is this Fanta Sea?'' Edsel asked. ''I mean, I know that wild dreams appear there, but what kind of dreams are they?''

''All kinds,'' Breanna said uneasily. ''The truth is, I don't much like the Fanta Sea. But if that's where we have to go, then that's where we have to go.''

''Good dreams or bad dreams?'' Pia asked. If Breanna didn't like that region, chances were that Pia wouldn't like it either.

''All kinds,'' Justin said. ''It is a place where actual dreams escape from the realm of the gourd. Normally they are disciplined, organized by the gourd crews and carried by the night mares to sleepers who deserve them. But at the sea they are undisciplined, and can do what they want. Even the good dreams may not be welcome, when they have no outside controls.''

''Good dreams unwelcome?'' Edsel asked. ''I'd love to be swamped by good dreams.''

But both Justin and Breanna looked dubious. Only the child agreed. "Yes. Fun."

"I'd like some clarification," Pia said nervously. Xanth was a land where face values could be very literal, but still needed to be handled with caution. Why should a child enjoy something that adults were wary of?

"It is somewhat awkward to explain," Justin said.

"We're here," Monica said. "Go straight ahead, quack-foot."

Pia looked ahead. It seemed to be an ordinary lake, with brush around the edges and reeds growing in patches. Para ran into it and started swimming.

Breanna looked to the side. There on the bank was a cemetery memorial stone. She shuddered.

"That's a dream?" Pia asked.

"For sure. That's serious."

"It's a grave stone."

The girl nodded. Then Pia smelled a pun. Grave stone—serious rock. "Are you pulling my leg?"

"Not this time. Honest. That stone reminds me of my dead mom."

"Your mother's dead?"

"No. But I used to dream she was, and I knew because I saw that stone. It scares me to pieces."

Pia saw that the stone was moving along beside the boat, paralleling their progress. "Can you get rid of it?"

"I used to be able to wake up. But now it's out here in my waking state."

"There is a way," Justin said. "It is possible to make the dream spooks cancel each other out. What is necessary is to lead one into another, so that they collide. This requires some maneuvering, but is feasible."

"What happens if one catches you first?" Edsel asked.

"Dreams can't cancel people, because then there would be nothing to see them," Justin said. "They are mere phantasms."

"But they sure can scare you," Breanna said. "That's what they do. That's their magic. They make you feel whatever they want you to feel, and you can't escape it."

"So we have nothing to fear but fear itself," Edsel said.

"Or other emotions," Justin agreed.

"I'm too young to be scared by grownup things," DeMonica said proudly.

Meanwhile Pia was watching the grave stone. "That thing is moving closer."

"I know it," Breanna said tightly. "I'm afraid that if it catches me, my mother really will die." She was not joking; her face was distraught.

"I believe I see another," Justin said. "But I don't recognize it."

Pia looked. It was a tropical tree, seemingly growing out of the water. "It's just a palm tree," she said. "No threat to me."

Edsel looked. "Oh, no," he breathed. "It's mine."

"What's its threat?" Pia asked.

"It's a joke my brother Bentley played on me when we were kids. He told me about it, and I thought it was real. It's a Na Palm tree."

"I don't believe I am conversant with that variety," Justin said.

"That's because it didn't exist in Xanth, until this moment," Edsel said. "It's my bad dream. It has barrel-like fruits that explode on contact, setting fire to anyone near."

"Oh, a variety of pineapple tree."

"Maybe so. But it terrifies me." Indeed, Pia had never seen Edsel so scared.

"Tree go bang," Monica said, intrigued.

Pia saw that the tree was coming closer. It did have deadly-looking fruits. She remembered the description of napalm: it soaked its victims, and burned their skin off, and wouldn't stop. It was one of the most horrible weapons in existence. She didn't want to experience it even in a dream.

"You said we can make them collide," Pia said. "Let's do it."

"Only their subjects can lead them," Justin said.

"But neither Breanna nor Edsel look capable of doing much," Pia pointed out.

"Yes, that is the inherent irony of the situation. However, we can guide them." He spoke directly to Breanna. "Call that stone to you, dear."

"I just want to get away from it!" the girl shrieked.

"I love you. Trust me."

Breanna looked almost white with fear. But Justin took her hand, and she fought for control. She looked at the gravestone. "C-come," she whispered.

The stone moved toward her, much faster.

"Me?" Pia asked Justin.

"If you would. We must have both orient on us."

Pia leaned toward Edsel. "You heard him, Ed. Call it to you."

Edsel stared at her with dilated eyes. "The thing will destroy me!"

"No it won't," she said firmly, though she had some private doubt. "Summon it."

"I can't!"

"Yes you can. I'll help you." She kissed him on the mouth. "Do, it Ed." She hated using her power over him this way, but she had to motivate him to do what he had to do.

He stared at her, his emotions of fear and love warring on his face. She smiled at him. Then he turned, slowly, and gazed at the tree. "Come, you horror, come," he whispered.

The tree responded with alacrity. Suddenly it was bearing down on them.

"Hold on, everyone," Justin called. "Para—now!"

The boat had evidently been waiting for this directive. He leaped forward so suddenly that Pia fell backward off her seat.

And behind them, the rushing gravestone crashed into the charging tree. There was a ball of fire, followed by dissipating smoke. The two dream monsters were gone.

"But there will be more," Breanna said, recovering. "For all of us."

"Monica, find that locket," Justin said urgently to the child.

"That way," Monica said, pointing to a nearby tiny island.

The boat veered. But another shape appeared, and it wasn't the locket.

"Oh, no," Justin breathed.

"What is it, dear?" Breanna asked.

"It's a morph."

"Morph," Edsel said. "As in morphine, a pain killer, or morphing, changing form?"

"Both," Justin said with impending dread.

"But those are two different things," Pia protested. "One's a shot, the other's a movie and ad gimmick."

"Both," Justin repeated weakly. "It's an injection that causes folk to change shape involuntarily. I've seen it attack animals and ruin their lives. They get addicted to change, but can't handle the new forms. It's going to get me, and make me change back into a tree, or worse, right when I want so much to remain as I am.''

"Now I feel your pain," Breanna said. "I don't want you to change."

"Changing forms is fun," Monica said innocently.

"But it's only an emotional thing, isn't it?" Pia asked. "Not really physical?"

"An emotional tree could not embrace Breanna," Justin said, his eyes locked on the approaching hypodermic shape.

"We have to get rid of it, for sure," Breanna said.

But meanwhile Edsel had spotted something else. "Book shape at nine o'clock," he said.

Pia looked—and froze. "That's the awful cook book."

"What's scary about a cook book?" he asked. "You never cook anyway."

"That's *why* I never cook," she said tightly. "It burns me."

An errant glance bounced around the boat. "A cook book burns you?" Breanna asked after one and a half moments.

"It's another experience from childhood," Pia explained, unable to look away from the horrible book as it nudged closer. "My mother was cooking in our apartment, on a hotplate, and she had a cook book out. I saw the hotplate and asked what it was, but she thought I meant the book, and said 'It's a cook book.' So I tried to pick it up—"

"And you burned your hand," Edsel said.

"Now I understand," Breanna said. "That book out there is steaming hot. You could cook on it."

"For sure," Pia agreed faintly. "I'm terrified of cook books. I know it's stupid, but I can't touch one of those things."

"And that morph better not touch Justin," Breanna said. "It's our turn to maneuver, Edsel."

"For sure," he agreed.

Now the two of them focused on their partners, reversing the prior case. "Justin, call in that morph," Breanna said.

"It's going to stick me!"

"Pia, call that cook book," Edsel said.

"It'll burn me!"

"Call it!" Breanna and Edsel said together.

With extreme reluctance, knowing that the others were right, Pia pried open her mouth and said "Come, you awful thing." And the hot book accelerated toward her.

"Come, needle," Justin whispered.

"Go, Para!" Breanna cried.

The boat shot forward. There was a crash behind it. And Pia's horror eased. Two more awful fantasies had been destroyed.

But another was already appearing. It looked like a vertical column, but it wasn't supporting anything. "What is that?" Edsel asked.

Pia, recovering, looked. The thing did not fill her with horror, so she knew it wasn't hers. That was a kind of relief. "It looks like a rug," she said, "A rolled carpet."

"A carpet!" DeMonica cried, her voice a wail. "That shouldn't be here."

"You mean it's yours?" Pia asked, surprised. She had thought the half-demon child to be immune.

"I gotta get outa here!" Monica shrilled, and scrambled for the far side of the boat.

"Wait!" Pia exclaimed, catching her. "You can't run on water, and anyway, it'll follow you."

"Let me go! Let me go!" the child screamed, struggling. But Pia drew her in close and held her firmly.

"What's the problem?" Breanna asked, and it wasn't any routine query.

"Let me go!" Monica shrieked.

"The child needs calming," Justin said.

Pia did not know the first thing about calming a child. She had never wanted anything to do with children, who had in the past struck her as irrelevant nuisances. But she tried. "Take it easy," she said, hugging the little girl.

"No!" Monica was starting to change her form, oozing out of Pia's grip in slow demonic fashion.

Pia shifted her hold, but it was hard to hold on to a shifting squirming squiggling form. She was losing the contest.

"We must discover the nature of the threat," Justin said insistently.

Pia saw the rolled carpet looming closer. It was angling now, as if making ready to unroll on the water. "Monica!" she said, taking another hold. "What's about that carpet?"

But the child was beyond listening. She wanted only to get away, and try to flee, though she drown in the attempt.

"Kiss her," Breanna suggested.

Pia hauled Monica in and kissed her on the forehead, trying to emulate motherly fashion. The child burst into tears and clutched her. "Don't let it get me!"

"I won't," Pia promised, though she had no idea how to keep that promise. "But you must tell me: what's its secret?"

"It's going to roll me up!" Monica cried wetly. "I'll smother."

Now it was coming clear. Suffocation inside the rolled carpet. Someone must have threatened the child with that once, and it had become a buried fear. Maybe the carpet was illusory, but its terror could still stop the child's breathing. It was tilting farther, showing its hollow interior. "Is there another spook in sight?" Pia inquired desperately.

"No," Edsel said.

Pia hugged the child closer. "Then find another way to abolish it."

Edsel turned to Justin. "Is there any other way?"

"Sometimes. If there is a pun that can be changed. But there seems to be nothing funny about being smothered by a rolled carpet."

"Yes there is," Edsel said. "Carpet tunnel syndrome."

"You got it!" Breanna said. "But how can it be changed?"

Pia was discovering, to her surprise, that she rather liked comforting the child. She had never tried it before, but holding the little girl seemed meaningful. Monica was taking comfort, though as yet they had no certainty of saving her. The carpet was unrolling, making ready for its prey.

"There has to be some other variant," Edsel said. "Carpet— carpal—"

A bulb flashed over Pia's head. "Car pool tunnel thin dome!" she exclaimed.

The carpet apparition seemed to groan. It changed form, becoming a thin glassy dome with a tunnel through it, wide enough for several cars. No way to smother anyone in that. Disgusted, it faded.

"You saved me!" DeMonica said, giving Pia a heartfelt extra hug, and then a wet kiss.

"Well, I had to, dear," Pia said, feeling a tear at her eye.

"I love you."

"And I love *you*," Pia said. Now she was sure: she wanted a child of her own. She had never realized before how precious they could be.

"You never punned before," Edsel said, amazed.

"I guess I never had to." She let the child go. That job was done, but she would never forget that joy of holding the little girl close.

"There's the magic locket," Monica said, as brightly as if she had never been scared. Children did recover from things rapidly. "On Soft."

Pia looked. She saw the locket hanging by its chain from the neck of a chunky standing man. The man was facing the other way, but the locket was against his broad bare back.

"I can get it," Edsel said.

"No, this is my mission," Pia said. "I'll get it." She appreciated his offer, but suspected that she could more readily charm the man to give it to her.

Para reached the isle and waddled onto land. Pia stepped out and approached the man. She noticed that his back was flat and covered with small print. "Excuse me," she said.

He turned. For a moment she was afraid he was completely naked, but his front side was garishly clothed. "Yes?"

"I—I'm Pia. I need that magic locket."

"Welcome to it. I am Softcover. I was holding it for DeMonica."

"Softcover?" she asked.

"My soft paper back is hard to cover."

Now she made the connection. Paperback—hardcover. He was in fact a standing, talking book. Not a cookbook, fortunately; cheap adventure fiction. She smiled fetchingly at him. "Thank you so much, Mister Softcover. Will you give it to me?"

"I am unable to reach it. You must take it from me."

So did he want to make her embrace him? Well, if that was the price of it, she could do it. She stepped in close, reached her arms around his arms and chest, caught hold of the chain, and lifted it up and over his head. It was a stretch, and at one point she was pressing fairly firmly against him, but he didn't move. She brought it down, and had possession. "Thank you," she said, smiling again.

"You are welcome."

Now she saw that his arms were actually the soft covers of the book, with the hands painted on. He could not move them other than to open and close them. So he had not been deceiving her.

She turned and stepped back into the boat. "Now let's get the bleep out of here," she said briskly.

The boat splashed into the water and moved rapidly back the way they had come. But another shape was coming toward them. It looked like a winged woman. Whose fantasy was this one?

"Willow!" Monica called happily.

"Willow!" Breanna echoed. "What are you doing here?"

The winged girl came to land in the boat. "Hello Monica, Justin, Breanna. I think I have business with your friends."

"Oh. Okay." Breanna turned to Edsel and Pia. "This is Willow Elf. Sean Mundane's wife." She turned back to the girl. "And these are Edsel and Pia, from Mundania."

"Yes. The Good Magician told me to find them here. I need the magic locket."

"Now wait a minute," Pia protested. "*We* need this locket, to stop the Demon CoTwo. The Good Magician knows that."

"Yes, of course," Willow agreed. "But as soon as you finish with it, I must take it to Mundania, to help Nimby."

"Nimby's in trouble?" Breanna asked, alarmed.

"We fear so. He has very little magic there, because he is using a Mundane body rather than his own, and we think the Demon E(A/R)TH is trying to trap him there. Messages came to several folk, saying Nimby Eats Dust. The Good Magician takes them most seriously. So we must get magic to him soon."

"This is serious," Justin said.

"Yes. I need to fill the locket with magic dust, so that it will carry the magic to him. Then he will be able to re-connect with you and return to the land of Xanth."

"While we return to Mundania," Pia said, surprised to hear a tinge of regret in her voice. Despite all its complications, she was coming to like it here. For one thing, there was her sixteen year old body. It had been wonderful having it, and using it to impress men. "We'll give you the locket as soon as we finish with CoTwo."

Willow frowned. "It would be better if I borrowed it now, to fill it with magic dust."

"You can't fill it," Monica said. "It's bottomless."

Willow nodded agreement. "I mean, to put enough dust in it to help Nimby."

"But we need it now," Pia said, distrusting this.

"I will bring it back to you. I simply need to take it to the Magic Dust Village."

"How long will that take?"

"No more than half a day," the elf said. "Most of that will be flying time."

Pia was pained. "Isn't there a faster way?"

Willow considered. "Actually, there is, now that I remember it. Pearl lives near here."

"Pearl?"

"Her talent is summoning magic dust. With her help, I could do it in an hour."

"Go to Pearl," Pia agreed, handing over the magic locket.

"Thank you. Where can I most readily find you, then?"

"At the snow mountains."

"I will be there." Willow spread her lovely wings and took off.

"This is bad news," Breanna said. "If Nimby gets trapped in Mundania, all of Xanth will be in trouble."

"We shall deal with CoTwo, and then the locket will go to rescue Nimby," Edsel said. Then his glance strayed. "My!"

Pia looked. She saw a troupe of shapely nymphs dancing across the surface of the water. "Whose horror is that?"

"Mine," Edsel said. "Only it's no horror. I've always dreamed of going to a show like that."

Pia eyed the figures disapprovingly. They had very well fleshed legs and very short skirts. There were five of them, with hair matching skirts: blue, red, green, yellow, and black. "This is going to freak you out?"

"For sure," Breanna said. "When they get close and do a high kick, so as to show their pretty colored—"

"I get it. So is there another horror to collide with them?"

"I fear so," Justin said. "Over there."

Pia looked the way he indicated. Her blood tried to curdle. It was a formless hump that sent a dreadful chill through her.

"What is it?" Breanna asked.

"It's my personal monster," Pia said. "The thing I want least to encounter."

"What is that?" Justin asked.

"I don't know. Just that I've got to get away from it."

"How can you be afraid of something you don't know?" Monica asked.

"I think I'm afraid of it *because* it's unknown," Pia said. "It's something I simply can't face."

"Well, we'll crash it into the dancing nymphs," Breanna said. "But you'll both have to summon them, so they'll collide where we were."

"Glad to," Edsel said. "Come, nymphs."

Pia opened her mouth, but the words wouldn't come out. She just couldn't summon that unknown horror.

"Hey, we have to get them aligned," Breanna said. "Bring the hump! Only you can do it."

"I *can't*," Pia moaned. "I just can't."

"Then we have a problem," Breanna said. "The nymphs are upon us. Para, dodge!"

The boat dodged to the side, but couldn't escape the nymphs. They intercepted it and spilled onto the seats, going for Edsel. One of them tumbled head under skirt into Pia, giving her a phenomenal flash of green panties. Of course that didn't freak her out, because she was female, and because her main attention was taken by the more distant lump pursuing her. But she knew Edsel was another matter.

The nymph rolled on into Pia—and through her. It was an illusion. But those bright, full panties would take men out regardless.

"Justin," Breanna said urgently, "maybe you'd better—before one of them flashes *you.*"

"I didn't want to use this, but I see I must," Justin said with regret. He drew from a pocket something that to Pia's peripheral vision looked like a big letter D. He flipped it at the cluster of nymphs.

There was an explosion. Pieces of nymph and skirt and panty flew out in every direction, dissipating, but Pia didn't feel anything physical.

"Hey, what happened?" Edsel asked, blinking.

"Justin destroyed them with his dee-tonate," Breanna said. "It blows things up. He set it for illusions, so it blew up only the illusion."

"But I was just about to see them do the high kick," Edsel complained.

"And it would have freaked you out five-fold," Breanna retorted. "A one panty freakout is over as soon as eye contact is broken, but when there are several, the effect is geometrical. You'd have been out for days, and we can't afford that."

"Oh." Edsel looked both disappointed and sheepish.

"But Pia's spook is still coming," Justin said. "And we can't stop it."

"We'll just have to run for it," Breanna said. "Maybe it can't go beyond the edge of the Fanta Sea. Go, Para!"

The boat lurched forward. They reached the bank, and the boat heaved out of the water and across the land. Were they safe?

Pia faced back, watching, because she had no choice. For a while they gained on the horror, but then it floated off the water and over the land. It was still coming.

"Well, we'll figure out something," Breanna said uncertainly. "Keep going, Para. To the snow mountains."

The boat ran along at an excellent clip. Slowly the pursuing apparition lost ground, and finally disappeared behind a turn in the forest. Pia's gaze was freed. But she knew the thing had not given up. It would pursue her until it caught her.

"The locket!" Breanna exclaimed. "You can put it in the locket."

"An illusion?" Edsel asked.

"For sure. That locket takes in anything you ask it to, and won't let it out until you say so."

"But Willow has the locket," Pia reminded her.

"Oh, bleep! I forgot. Well, we'll just have to stay out of its way until we get the locket back."

Para made excellent time, and before long they were rising through the foothills of the mountains. Pia could tell, because the hills were shaped like giant feet.

But this also slowed the forward progress of the boat. The pursuing hump was floating, and had no problem with climbing; it came back into sight, slowly closing in.

"It's going to catch us," Breanna said. "Before we get there, and before Willow brings back the locket."

"What can I do?" Pia wailed.

"There is only one way to deal with inescapable terror," Justin said. "That is to face it and conquer it."

"But I *can't* face it!"

"Then it will destroy you," he said regretfully.

"But it's not physical," Edsel said. "It's just emotion."

"Emotion suffices," Justin said. "It can wipe out the mind. It is called insanity."

"So if she flees it, and it catches her, she's doomed," Edsel said. "But if she faces it down, maybe she'll make it."

"That is the situation."

"Maybe not," Breanna said. "Has anyone ever tried to intercept one of those things? I mean, someone it's not aimed at?"

"I do not believe so. But—"

Breanna jumped out of the boat, caught her balance, and stood in the path of the spook. "Come on, spook," she cried. "You've got to get through me first."

The thing loomed up—and passed right through the girl. Breanna couldn't touch it.

Pia knew what she had to do. "If I can't escape it, I might as well face it," she said. She got out of the boat and stood beside a small pond. This was not courage, but desperation; she was quaking.

The hump sailed toward her, followed by Breanna. But the girl stopped when she saw Pia. This was something that only Pia could tackle.

Pia hoped she looked brave from a distance. It certainly wasn't the case up close. Her heart was pounding, her hands were shaking, and she knew her eyes were dilated. The only thing that stopped her from turning to run away was her certainty that it would catch her and be even worse than if she faced it.

The thing loomed close. It slowed, orienting on her. It began to assume the form of a person, or rather, a horrible parody of a person. "Who are you?" she demanded timorously.

The shape continued to clarify. It became female, with a shapely body, a heart shaped face, green eyes, and long dark brown hair. It looked weirdly familiar. In fact—

She looked at its reflection in the pond. Beside it was her own reflection. The two figures were the same.

She was terrified of herself?

She was indeed terrified, and it was her image. But behind the fever of her fear, a certain animal cunning lurked. Were things really as they seemed? Or was this apparition fooling her in a way she did not understand?

She peered at the thing, and saw that its face was colored. Did that mean something? It was black. What did that mean? Red might be rage, green might be jealousy, blue might be sick, yellow might be fear, but what was black? She was sure it had nothing to do with race; Breanna of the Black Wave had abolished any such concern. It had to be an emotion—she felt it almost overwhelming her—but which one?

"What are you?" she asked.

The figure moved closer. Its face began to show the highlights of a skull. But it wasn't death, just a comparison to death. Something she'd rather die than do. Or, rather, admit.

"What awful secret do you hide?" she asked desperately.

The figure reached for her. She knew it would blast her mind if she didn't counter it. But how could she do that if she didn't know what it was?

Desperately she reviewed her concerns, frustrations, and fears. She couldn't think what it was. But there was something much worse than a cookbook. So bad that she couldn't recognize it even when it stared her in the face. What *was* this black emotion?

Then she did something extremely nervy, for her. She reached out and touched the thing's hand.

Suddenly the emotion clarified. It was Guilt! She was so horribly guilt-ridden for something that she couldn't even face it. But now she had to, lest she be destroyed by it. What was her guilt?

Then, slowly and painfully, it came to her. Her guilt was about Edsel! And his friend Dug. For she had been Dug's girlfriend, and tired of him, supposing Edsel to be more entertaining. So she had flashed a bit of this at Edsel—the figure's blouse faded to show breast and cleavage—and a bit of that—it showed high thigh. And in a moment she had captured his fancy. Then all that remained was to engineer an exchange. It had been almost too easy. So Dug was without girlfriend, and Edsel was with her. And Pia was satisfied.

But it had been dirty. Dug was a fine man, eminently undeserving of such treatment. Oh, he had found another girlfriend, in Kim, and was happy now. But that did not ameliorate Pia's guilt for the way she had treated him. She should have been up-front, told him how she felt, assured him that it was no fault in him, and wished him well. Instead she had covertly dumped him.

And now, long after she thought she had buried it forever, that guilt had returned to haunt her. To overcome her. The girls of Xanth thought that there was shame in accidentally showing their panties. They didn't know what real shame was!

The irony was that there was nothing she could do about it. Dug was better off with Kim than he had been with Pia—and Pia was worse off with Edsel than she had been with Dug. She had been doing neither Dug nor Edsel any favor. She wasn't worth their company. She would be doing them both a favor by getting the bleep out of the picture.

"You win," she said to the awful figure. Then she turned and leaped into the pond.

In half a moment she realized that even in this she had messed up. First, she couldn't drown herself, because she was too good a swimmer and the pond was too small. Second, the water was only knee deep. She had gotten soaked for nothing.

Para was there, floating to her rescue. But Pia waved him away. "I guess I really can't escape," she said. "I have to deal with it." The odd thing was that she was feeling better now, despite her bedraggled condition. She felt better than ever, physically, and more confident emotionally.

She saw the others in the boat. Breanna dipped her hand in the water, and opened her mouth, but Justin cautioned her, and she was silent. They were leaving Pia alone to settle this herself, in whatever way she could.

She stood and strode out of the pool toward the figure. "I know what I have to do," she said. "I have to stop burying, stop running, and handle my guilt. I have to learn from bad experience. I can't change the past, but I can change the present and the future. I can stop being so stupidly shallow and start being a better woman. I can make sure that I never wrong a good man again." She turned to look at Edsel. "And I can bleeping well do everything I can to make our marriage work."

She turned back to face the spook. "I can do all the things I wouldn't do before. I can learn to cook, I can do the laundry, I can—" She paused with dawning surmise. "I can have children, and be a mother. I can do the whole family bit. So that I have nothing to feel guilty about any more."

Then she walked right into the figure. "So do your worst, spook. I'm ashamed of how I was, but I don't have be that any more."

But the figure was gone. It had dissipated as she touched it. She had banished the spook.

Para came up to her, carrying the others. "That pool," Breanna said. "Do you know what it is?"

"Not deep enough," Pia said. "I'm a mess."

"It's a healing spring," Breanna said. "We didn't realize, before."

"A healing spring?" Pia asked blankly.

"Whatever injuries or whatever you have, it makes them better."

"The only problem I have are physical and emotional," Pia said. "My diabetes and my attitude. And I'm fixing the second."

"I think it fixed the first," Breanna said. "How are you feeling now, physically?"

"Great! Never better. But diabetes isn't something a mere splash in a pool can fix."

"Why not?"

Pia considered. "Well, I don't know. But if I discover that I can get along without insulin shots, *then* I'll know." She turned to Edsel. "Meanwhile, I'll do what I can. Ed, the marriage is on."

"On?" he asked, looking as if he expected this to be a joke.

"And we'll do it your way. With children and home cooking."

"I—I don't understand."

He had been too far away to overhear her dialogue with the guilt spook. She climbed into the boat and hugged him. "You will. But right now you'll have to settle for me wet."

"Any way you want!" he agreed enthusiastically. "Here's a towel." He started drying her off, somewhat ineffectively.

"Wrap her in a blanket," Breanna suggested. "Meanwhile, we had better get on into the mountains."

"For sure," Breanna said. She looked around. "Monica, time to get back in the boat."

The child came running back from the bushes. "Look what I found!"

"First in, then tell," Breanna said.

The boat resumed his trek, while Edsel swathed Pia in a voluminous blanket so she could get out of her clothing and get thoroughly dry. She knew this wasn't the occasion to go naked again.

"So what did you find?" Breanna asked DeMonica.

"A slug."

"Yuck!"

The child laughed. "No, not a real slug. A fake slug. That pretends to be a coin or something. See, it takes any shape I want." She held up a tiny dark disk. In her hand it shaped itself into a thimble, then a star.

"Hey, that's clever," Edsel said. "Can I make it work too?"

"Sure." The child delighted in teaching the man how to do it. Edsel had always been good with children; it was Pia who hadn't wanted any. Until now. If by any chance they had succeeded in getting the stork's attention, she would keep what it brought her. Of course this was Xanth, and they were in borrowed bodies, so it didn't count. But the principle was there. In Xanth or Mundania, she knew Edsel would be happy to cooperate.

It was getting on time for her shot, but she didn't feel the need. She pricked her finger and did the blood test, and it showed she was perfect. Could she really be rid of her ailment? That seemed too good to be true. Yet she continued to feel great, physically, and good mentally too. It was as if the healing spring had healed her emotions as well as her body. As if it had made her whole.

They came into the region of snow. It was smaller and higher than it had been; more snow had melted. That meant that more water was flowing down to flood the valley. The Demon CoTwo needed to be stopped immediately. Which was of course why they had gone for the magic locket.

"The locket!" Pia exclaimed. "Where's Willow?"

"She must have been delayed," Breanna said. "She wouldn't stand us up deliberately."

"But what if CoTwo comes?"

"Don't speak his name!" Breanna said.

Too late. A dark swirling cloud formed. "Did I hear my name?" the voice of the demon came.

"We're in for it now," Breanna said darkly.

"You got that right, Blackwave darling," the demon said, as his tawny body took muscular shape. "Didn't I tell you to stay away from here?"

"I'll distract him," Edsel said, jumping out of the boat. "You get out of range."

Para turned, ready to flee.

"Not so fast, quackfoot," CoTwo said, reaching out to hook a huge finger into the back so as to hold the boat in place. "I think you would make excellent kindling."

"I'll distract him," Pia said, scrambling out, her blanket still around her. "To stall for time."

The demon gazed down at her. "What have we here? A shrouded nymph?"

"A shrouded *woman,*" Pia said bravely. She opened the front of her blanket.

"Well *well!* Aren't you the shapely one. What are you up to, sensual creature?" He lifted his finger from the boat, and it scooted away. But then he aimed a blast of air at it, and boat and remaining occupants tumbled headlong into the river.

But Pia couldn't help them. She had to distract the demon long enough to give Willow time to bring the magic locket. How could she do that? She knew only one way. "I—I'll dance for you," she said.

"Indeed you shall," CoTwo agreed. He reached out, caught the edge of her blanket between thumb and forefinger, and jerked. The blanket whipped away, and set Pia madly spinning.

She caught her balance. Now she was naked, for there had not been time for her clothing to dry; the blanket was her clothing. She didn't even have her panties on, so couldn't freak out the demon, assuming that demons could be so freaked. But she had to carry through.

She started to dance, making her hips shift and her flesh jiggle. She had the best shape of her life, and it seemed the best health of her life, thanks to her sixteen year old body and the loss of her diabetes. She could impress any man—but the demon was not exactly a man. Could she distract him long enough?

She whirled and bounced and lifted a leg fetchingly, giving it her all. *Where was Willow?*

"You're pretty good," CoTwo said. "In fact I think I'll keep you."

"Keep me?" She didn't like the sound of that.

"You came back when I sent you away. You are trying to stall me so your friends can escape. But you do have an interesting shape. So I will subject you to a fate worse than death."

She had been too successful in diverting him. Now he wanted her for storkish purposes. Pia tried to run, but the demon's arm stretched out impossibly long, and his hand became huge. It caught her around the torso, not hard but very firm. It lifted her into the air, so that her bare legs dangled.

As with the Guilt monster, she could not escape. She had to tackle it directly. But she knew that vowing to be a better person would not have much effect this time. So she pretended confusion. "Worse than—?"

"Are you a masochist?"

"No way!"

"Excellent. Because I am a sadist. I am going to bind you in chains, and whip you, and force you unwillingly to serve my pleasure at your great discomfort dozens of times a day until I tire of you. Then I'll break you and throw you away."

If he had intended to frighten her, he had succeeded. Pia screamed. She couldn't help it, though she knew that was what the demon wanted.

CoTwo smiled. There was nothing nice about it. "Yes, scream, my fair little toy. Scream in anticipation, because the reality will be much worse." The arm contracted, bringing her closer.

As she tried dizzily to free herself, her eye caught a glimpse of something in the sky. It looked like a bird, a plane—no, a winged elf. Willow was arriving!

All she had to do was stall a little more. Pia forced a sexy smile. "No, I'm sure the reality will be much better. You're quite a figure of a creature."

"Don't try to fool me, precious. I will make you scream in physical and emotional pain." The huge fingers contracted cruelly, showing that this was no bluff. She was already hurting.

"But—but don't you want me smiling?" she gasped. "Obliging your every foolish whim?"

"Obliging, yes. Smiling, no. I like my toys to suffer."

"Not so fast, hot stuff!" It was Edsel.

CoTwo looked. So did Pia. Edsel was advancing on the demon, holding the magic locket before him. She remembered that the locket had to be close to the object before it could be invoked. Could Edsel get close enough?

The demon dropped Pia like a squeezed sponge and focused on the man. "What do you propose to do about it?" CoTwo demanded.

"I am going to put you inside this magic locket," Edsel said evenly. "Just as soon as I get you into its range."

"Ed, don't tell him that!" Pia cried from the ground. But she was being foolish, because he already had told, giving away the element of surprise.

"Fascinating," the demon said. "That really *is* the magic locket. I thought it was lost centuries ago along with the other Hinge artifacts. Where did you find it?"

"Demon Ted and DeMonica found it," Edsel said, carefully aiming the front of the locket at CoTwo. "We recovered it from the Fanta Sea. It's the one thing that will stop you, because when invoked, it puts whatever it is aimed at within, and even a demon can't escape. Once you are safely inside, you will stay there, and only a little of your substance will remain outside. Not enough to warm Xanth much. The mountains will cool, and the glaciers will grow again, and the valley below will no longer flood, and the trees will prosper."

"What are you—an environmentalist nut or something like that?" CoTwo asked derisively.

"Something like that," Edsel agreed. He was close to the demon now.

"Don't dally, Ed," Pia cried. "Just do it!" Needless delay was sheer folly, when dealing with a brute like CoTwo.

"It won't work," CoTwo said.

"Oh? Why not?" Edsel held the locket up and opened his mouth, about to invoke it.

The demon's hand swept through the air so fast it left a glowing blur-streak. It snatched the locket from Edsel's hand. "Because now I have the magic locket," CoTwo said triumphantly.

Pia screamed. She hated seeming like a helpless damsel, but that was what she had become.

"No," Edsel said, looking horrified. "What are you going to do?"

"What do you think, foolish mortal? The same thing you were going to do to me. I'll conjure you into the locket. Then I'll make your girl-friend scream and scream as I ravish her. When she has suffered so much that she can't scream any more, I will break her in half and put her into the locket for you to enjoy. What do you think of that?"

"I can't stand it!" Edsel cried, turning to run away.

CoTwo leaped forward, bearing the locket. He aimed it at Edsel at close range. "In!" he said as Pia screamed again in sheer despair.

There was an implosion as the locket took in substance. A cloud of smoke puffed around, obscuring the scene.

Pia burst into tears. Not for herself, but for her lost husband. "Oh, Ed—you were so brave, and I'm so undeserving. I'll never forget you or stop loving you."

The smoke dissipated. There stood Edsel. "That's great," he said.

"Ed! You're free!" She wasn't sure she could believe it. She ran to hug him. "What happened? How did you—?"

"Well, I outsmarted him. I—"

But as he spoke, a horrible suspicion suffused her. Could this be the demon, emulating Edsel, to torment her further? She had to know.

"Ed, who was I with, before I was with you?"

He looked at her, surprised. "What has that got to do with the price of beans in Mundania?"

"Just answer. Please."

"Dug, of course."

But the demon might have eavesdropped on prior conversations, and picked that up. "How did you get me?"

"We made a bet. My motorcycle against his girlfriend. I won. So—"

"It really is you!" She hugged him again, and kissed him ardently. She couldn't remember ever before being so relieved.

Willow Elf flew down. "I hate to interrupt, but I need the locket."

"For sure," Edsel said. "But I'd better adjust it first." He bent and lifted the locket from where it had fallen, and used his fingernail to pry off the front panel.

"What are you doing?" Pia asked, amazed.

"Well, I figured I couldn't get close enough to CoTwo to conjure him in, so I faked him out. I used Monica's slug to put this fake front on the back, so it was actually facing the opposite way it seemed to. Then—"

"So he conjured himself inside!" Pia said. "Instead of you. That was brilliant, Ed. When he grabbed it, I thought—"

"That was the idea. You really helped, Pia, because you believed." He handed the locket to Willow. "Now it's right. Remember to point it the right way when you invoke it."

"For sure," Willow agreed, smiling. Then she spread her wings and ascended.

Para Boat waddled up, carrying Justin and Breanna. "We need to get back to Com Passion's cave, and let Para go," the Black Wave girl said. "He's done more than enough for us."

Ed looked at Pia. "You know, I just love holding a bare damsel like this. But maybe you'd be warmer in the blanket."

"For sure," she agreed, kissing him again. "Oh, Ed, I love you. I really do, now."

"Ugh," DeMonica said. "Are you two going to get mushy?"

"For sure," they said together, laughing.

12
WEATHER

T he storm seemed to have cleared the air. They packed
their gear and rolled up their sleeping bags and started
back along the trail. Their camping excursion would have
to be cut short; they needed to get to a computer terminal and to the O-
Xone before Dearth struck again.

"Let me make sure I have this straight," Kim said. "All you need
is to connect with Ed and Pia via the Modemode, and switch back, at
then it will all be over?"

"Yes," Chlorine said. "Once Nimby is back in his own body, in
Xanth, Dearth can't touch him."

"But couldn't Dearth do something awful to Ed, for vengeance? Like
stepping on a nuisance ant?"

"Dearth wouldn't bother. Nimby is all that matters. Once he escapes,
the game is done, and Dearth will pay no further attention."

"Are you sure? That's not the way a human person would react."

"Demons aren't human. It took Nimby time and concentration to
learn any human things, like dreaming. It doesn't come naturally. He
wouldn't have done that, if he hadn't gotten so closely involved with
human folk, because of his wager. No other Demon has done that. They
remain indifferent to antly affairs. It's just not in a Demon to care what
happens to Ed or Pia, one way or the other, when their bodies are no
longer host to our spirits. They will be perfectly safe."

"That's a relief," Kim said.

"But while Nimby and I remain here, Edsel and Pia's bodies are definitely at risk," Chlorine continued grimly. "Nimby would lose considerable status if his host body were killed while he was in it."

"Killed!"

"As you said: stepping on an ant. Actually the body wouldn't die as long as Nimby remained confined in it, but—"

"But can that happen?" Kim asked with a shudder. "I mean, if it's only weather that Dearth controls?"

"Weather can become ugly."

"The weather is beautiful right now."

"But consider last night," Dug said. "The way that storm came up, and washed out the one peg to collapse our tent and waterlog our computer. That impresses me."

"It should," Chlorine said. "Demons have enormous power, when they choose to exercise it. So we need to reach the O-Xone and revert identities as soon as possible."

"Before Dearth realizes," Dug agreed. "Like an ant avoiding a trap, unnoticed."

"Yes." But Chlorine, alerted by Nimby, doubted that it would be that easy.

They hiked to the base camp, where their car and motorcycle waited. They loaded the gear. Then Dug and Kim got into the car, and Nimby and Chlorine got on the motorcycle.

The cycle's motor started right up, but the car didn't follow. They looped back to check.

"Dead," Kim called. "Storm must have shorted out the battery."

The folk of a neighbor car approached. "Need a jump?" the man asked.

" 'Fraid so," Dug said. "Thanks."

The man had jumper cables. Kim explained the process to Chlorine as the men did it. "The cables connect the good battery to the dead one, and provide current to start the motor. Then it recharges its own battery as it runs."

But it didn't work. Dug's car remained dead.

"I think you have a worse problem," the man said. "Better call Triple B."

"I guess we'll have to," Dug agreed. "But thanks for the jump." To the others, he said "They'll come fairly promptly, but we'll still have to get the car towed and fixed, and that could take longer."

They consulted. "Maybe you two should get on back to town," Kim said. "We're going to be delayed several hours, by the look of it. You can go to a library and use their connection, and switch back before we get out of here."

Chlorine looked at Nimby. He shook his head no. Then he touched her hand.

Oh. "Nimby thinks Dearth is trying to separate us. We will be relatively vulnerable without our knowledgeable Companions. It is better to remain together."

Dug and Kim exchanged a look. "That could be," Dug said. "And we don't want to put you into any unnecessary risk."

"We must advise you that there is risk to you, as long as you remain with us," Chlorine said.

"But maybe less than there is to you if you are alone," Kim said. "So we'd better stick together."

Dug considered. "I wonder. I think there is risk in delay, and risk in separating. Maybe we should call a taxi, just to get this done in a hurry."

"But maybe Dearth has anticipated that," Kim said. "In which case we would be playing into his hands. I wonder—can Nimby sense the larger situation? So as to know what course is best?"

Chlorine checked. "He can't fathom the intention of Dearth, but can focus on the likely route that help will come to us from Xanth, if we can't reach the O-Xone on our own."

"Maybe try that, while we wait," Dug said. "I think this is a bit like a chess game. We need to see more of the board before making our next move."

Nimby agreed. So Dug went to call Triple B, while Nimby sat in the dead car and focused his ambient Awareness on NoName Key, where a person from Xanth would most likely pass through to Mundania with magic dust. If any of the Modemode folk got through to the real folk in Xanth.

And the news was good. "Willow Elf has passed through," Chlorine said. "Carrying a locket of magic dust. She has joined the Baldwin family. They are setting out to bring it here."

"But how will they find us?" Kim asked.

"They have the address of Ed and Pia's home," Chlorine said. "They will go there."

"So that's where we should be going, as soon as we can," Kim said.

Chlorine looked at Nimby. "Yes." But she wasn't speaking the truth, because Nimby indicated no. Because Dearth was now listening, and would block whatever they tried to do.

The BBB help arrived. The car had to be towed; it refused to respond to the mechanic. This was an interesting process whereby the truck connected to the car and hauled it along by its nose.

They waited while the repairs were made at the garage. There was a place to eat nearby, called a diner, so they went there. "This has delayed things several hours," Dug said. "But with the car going again, what's to stop us from just driving home?"

"And waiting for the Baldwins to arrive?" Kim added.

Nimby merely smiled.

"Then what about going to a local library and lumbering on, going to the O-Xone, and exchanging back from here?" Dug said.

Chlorine knew the answer to that. "The others have to be there to make the exchange. If we go there, and Edsel and Pia aren't there, it will be for nothing, and Dearth will make sure we can't go there again later. We have to go at an appointed check-in time."

"But we've been checking in different times," Kim said. "So have they, evidently. So—"

"Breanna had an Ear," Chlorine said. "That's what you would call a field unit, for spot communication only. They could have been anywhere in Xanth. But now they must report physically to Com Passion's cave, to enter the ambiance of the O-Xone. Xanth is more limited in this respect than in Mundania. We trust they are on their way, and will remain there until we connect."

"So it's better late than early," Kim said, comprehending. "Because chances are there will be only one chance; after that Dearth will catch on and interfere."

"Exactly."

Dug nodded. "So between times, we might as well travel, so as to get more convenient access."

"And get the magic," Kim said.

As they left the diner, it was as if night were falling, though it was only mid afternoon. Clouds loomed high and broad, moving to cut off what remained of the sky. A considerable storm was forming.

"And we couldn't get moving to escape it before it formed, because of the time it takes to fix a washed out car,'' Dug said, understanding. "Dearth knows what he's doing."

"I've never seen such a dangerous looking storm-cloud,'' Kim said, awed.

Nimby touched Chlorine's arm. "Nimby wants you to know that if you leave now, while we remain here, the storm will not follow you. You can escape what is apt to be exceedingly ugly weather.''

Dug and Kim spoke together: "No."

"Spoken like true Companions,'' Chlorine said. "But you will pay a price."

"Let's get moving now,'' Dug said. "But maybe you'd better park the Lemon and ride in the car with us. It'll be safer."

Nimby shook his head. "We'll ride it back,'' Chlorine said. "You told us how Edsel values it. We must return it to him in good condition."

Dug looked again at the brooding cloud. "You do have a point, but this could be dangerous. We could have it garaged here, to keep it safe. Cars are safer in storms."

But Nimby would not yield. Chlorine knew that he had his own reasons, perhaps beyond her understanding, but surely valid.

The Neptune was ready. "It's amazing how much damage a single storm can do, sometimes,'' the mechanic said.

"Well, it's not a new car,'' Dug said.

"This was independent of age. This car has been well cared for, but somehow the wiring—I've never seen this particular failure before. It's a fluke."

"Just so long as it won't happen again."

"Guaranteed. It's better than new now."

Dug and Kim did what they had to, to settle the cost of the repair; they had something called insurance that made it easier. Then they drove the car out of the repair shop.

Nimby and Chlorine climbed on the motorcycle and joined them. "Maybe Pia should ride in the car,'' Kim called. "It's going to be wet on the Lemon."

"No, I'll stay with Ed,'' Chlorine called back.

The storm looked worse than ever. It frightened Chlorine, but she clung to Nimby. She was not going to let him face it alone.

The Neptune turned south and followed the highway out of town. Most of the traffic was streaming the other way, into town, as Mundanes caught on that the weather was truly threatening. They were doing the sensible thing and heading for cover.

A gust of wind caught them. The cycle veered, then corrected course. Nimby had progressed from beginner to full competence at a rapid rate, and now could handle it very well. But she wondered why he had chosen to ride the Lemon, when he could have ridden in the safer car. Was it to spare the Companions some risk? She suspected not; there must be some way in which the motorcycle enhanced his own chances.

Lightning cracked close by, and thunder boomed out from it. Chlorine remembered Cumulo Fracto Nimbus, once the worst of clouds, and the show he could put on. But this was in drear Mundania, and that made it more frightening.

Rain came down, first a few big drops, then a pelting of medium drops, then an almost solid sheet of small ones. In one and a half moments they were soaked. The road looked slick and slippery. But Nimby pressed on, following the car. Chlorine shivered, and hated what it was doing to her hair. But what had she expected?

Lightning struck a tree ahead of the car, and a large branch crashed onto the road, blocking it. The Neptune's wheels skidded as it braked, and it almost didn't stop in time. The Lemon stopped beside it.

Chlorine was in contact with Nimby, so knew what he wanted her to know. "Clear the branch; we'll distract the storm!"

"But we must stay with you!" Kim called back.

"We'll return soon." And they were off, riding back along the road.

Nimby lifted one hand, reaching behind his shoulder. Chlorine realized he wanted to talk more specifically. She touched his hand with hers.

His thought came, but she couldn't believe if at first. "You want me to drive this thing? But I don't know how."

His further thought came, instructing her in the rudiments. He was serious. He needed time to think, to spread his Awareness, to find something he needed. But he couldn't pause, because the moment he did, the storm would catch him with a bolt of lightning. It wouldn't kill him, but could kill her, and knock out his body, costing them valuable time. If his body was unconscious, away from the Companions, it might be days before they got together again, and Dearth would win.

The notion appalled her, but she would have to try to do it. To give Nimby the time he needed to be Aware. It was almost the only magic he retained, and he had to have the chance to use it.

But to control the motorcycle, she would have to get in front. How could they change places, without stopping?

She drew her feet up, setting them on the saddle beside Nimby. Then she clung to his shoulders and lifted her bottom, standing behind him, bent over his head, hanging on as the wet wind tore at her body. Then she hauled one foot up and over his shoulder, and the other. Now she was standing in front of him, reaching under herself to clutch at his shoulders, her panties in his face. If he had been a normal man, in Xanth, he would have freaked out and they would have sailed into a tree. She slid down his front to land in his lap. Then he slid back, and she took over the handlebars and pedals. He put his hands on her hips, and did not move again. He was tuning out.

She was controlling the machine! All she had to do was keep it going without spinning out of control and crashing, until Nimby was through sensing. She didn't have to race, but in the driving rain the handling was treacherous. She tried to keep going straight, but veered to the left. She leaned and steered right, and veered too sharply right. The wheels went into the puddle that lined the side, sending up a spray and dragging; she felt the machine slow. But she managed to get it back into the center and straightened out.

Then something in the road loomed. Maybe a piece of branch, or an animal. She swerved around it, and veered too far left, into the puddle there. Again the water went up in a sheet, and the cycle slowed. She had to watch her reactions. But she was getting better control. Her confidence was increasing. This wasn't so bad.

Lightning struck right ahead. The flash blinded her, and the crack of it deafened her. She could neither see nor hear—but they were still hurtling forward.

She didn't have time to panic. She knew where the road was, and if she kept their balance, it would be all right until she recovered her senses. If she could just go straight. Was she going straight?

She felt the motorcycle slowing. That meant she had drifted to the side. But which side? She had to turn back into the road, but if she turned the wrong way, they would go off the road and crash. She didn't dare go wrong—but which was right?

She used her ears which were starting to recover. The splashing seemed worse on the left, and the motorcycle seemed to be trying to drag that way. So she fought it, going straight, because she wasn't quite sure. Better to forge on through water than to turn the wrong way.

Her vision was returning around the glare blindness. She saw the road on the right, and moved that way, recovering speed. She had been correct! She was back in control. Then she wondered: had that lightning bolt been intended to strike them, and missed because she had gone too slowly? Or had it been *meant* to blind her, so that she would have to stop or crash? Would there be another?

Chlorine nerved herself and accelerated. She steered to one side, and then the other. She wanted to become a more elusive target, just in case. She also squinted, hoping to avoid any further blindness. However, Dearth did not seem to be trying very hard to stop them, maybe because they were going away from home. When they eventually turned back south, it was bound to get worse.

Nimby squeezed her hips. He was tuning back in! ''You want to take over?'' she asked over her shoulder, and put one hand back.

He touched her hand: yes.

She was concerned how to change places again, as reversing her moves would be tricky. But he simply moved up, and she lifted to sit in his lap, his arms going around her to take over the handlebars. He had control now, and knew where he was going.

He swerved, splashing through the puddle and onto a dirt trail that was now mud. The wheels slued and skidded, but the machine remained upright. The trail was sloppy, but navigable. Chlorine couldn't have done it, but Nimby seemed unconcerned.

Soon they went cross-country, zooming across a soggy field and up a wet slope. They intersected another road and followed it to a farmstead.

Nimby slowed the machine, and held his hand toward her. Chlorine touched it, and received a mindful of information. As she assimilated this, Nimby guided the Lemon to the farmhouse and stopped.

Chlorine got off. Then Nimby rode on, so as not to make a stationary target for lightning. Chlorine knew what she had to do.

She marched up to the farmhouse door and knocked. It opened after a moment, revealing a mature woman. ''Girl, you're soaking!'' the woman exclaimed. ''Come in and get dry.''

''Thank you, but I must go out again in a moment. I must talk to your husband.''

The woman led her to a warm stove. The radiating heat was wonderful. A mature man approached. ''I'm Farmer Jones. What's a slip of a girl like you doing out alone in weather like this?''

''I am Pia,'' Chlorine said. ''My party is stalled on the road because of fallen wood. We need a pulley to haul it off. I would like to trade for yours.''

"I've got a spare block and tackle, but it's too heavy for you to handle.''

"My—my husband Edsel is on the motorcycle. He can handle it. Our friends in the car are blocked; that's why we need it.''

"My college son John can load it for you.'' The farmer nodded at a younger man behind him.

"Thank you. That will really help.'' She smiled at John, putting as much reward in it as she could muster in her bedraggled state.

"What do you have in mind to trade?''

"A—a dragon. I mean a giant reptile. Bones. Very old. On your land. We will show you where.''

"What do I want with snake bones?'' the farmer demanded.

"Dad, she's describing a fossil,'' John said. "Maybe a dinosaur.''

"Is that good? Why should I trade a good block and tackle for news about something I've already got on my land?''

"Might be worth it, Dad. Dino fossils are valuable, and hard to find. The bones could get washed away in the storm before we ever saw them.''

The farmer pondered briefly. "Okay, you go look at them, and tell me if it's worth it.''

"Nimby—I mean, my husband will show you where,'' Chlorine said. "But you'll have to ride with him on his motorcycle.''

"This grows interesting,'' John said, pulling on a raincoat. "I'll do it.''

"You can wait here, and have some hot soup,'' the farmer's wife said.

"Wonderful,'' Chlorine said blissfully.

John went to the door. There was the sound of the motorcycle arriving, by no coincidence; Nimby's Awareness made such timing feasible.

"Oh,'' Chlorine said. "Edsel doesn't talk. But he understands. He'll show you.''

John nodded and stepped out into the weather. Chlorine settled down to a bowl of steamy soup. It was sheer rapture.

The farmer's wife tried to offer Chlorine dry clothing, but she demurred; she would soon have to go out in the rain again. But she thanked them sincerely for the temporary warmth of the stove and the soup.

Soon there was the sound of the returning motorcycle, and John entered. "It's true, Dad. It's a dinosaur for sure, and we'd have missed it. We'll need to shore it up, to keep it from washing into the river. Thing could be worth thousands. We'll find out when this freak storm ends and I can call my paleontology prof at college. But it sure as hell is something. Also, that's a Lemon he's riding; only good folk have those. Give them the tackle."

And so Chlorine found herself back on the Lemon, trying to keep the bulky block, tackle, and rope in place. They headed south.

The storm abruptly intensified. Dearth obviously was tracking them, and had been biding his time until they tried to head south again.

Nimby seemed unconcerned. He gunned the motor, following the road at high speed. Chlorine hardly dared look, for fear she would see disaster looming. She reminded herself that Nimby was not the mute dragon or man-form he seemed, but the Demon $X(A/N)^{TH}$, one of the overwhelmingly powerful figures of the cosmos. The fact that he lacked most of his power here did not mean that his intellect was diminished; he knew what he was doing, and where things were. He had surveyed the whole area, during his time of introspection, and now had a virtual map of it in his mind. Now that he lacked most of his magic, she was able to see the power of his other qualities, such as his Awareness and his learning ability. If she hadn't loved him already, she would have been falling in love with him now. She was nothing, owing everything to him, but he was such a superior creature.

He turned his head to glance briefly back at her, and winked. Oh— she had forgotten that he could read her thoughts! That was part of his Awareness, especially when he was so close to her.

But that reminded her that here in Mundania she was neither her natural homely, dull, unhappy self, nor her enhanced lovely, smart, nice persona. She was an ordinary person in the body of a Mundane woman. But she at least had the wit to know her limits, and to follow without question the guidance of the one whose limits were immeasurably beyond hers. She trusted Nimby, and wanted to share his fate, whatever it might be. He did not have to read her thoughts to know that. He made her seem like a princess in Xanth, while he made himself seem like nothing much, but the reality was vice versa. She never forgot. If her fate was to die in Mundania, she wanted to do it in Nimby's company.

Lighting cracked ahead, and a small tree fired out sparks and toppled onto the road. Nimby hardly paused; he simply guided the cycle overland around the base of the tree and back onto the road. He had barely been slowed.

Dearth must have been infuriated, because the storm intensified. Thunder became continuous, and the darkness of the massive cloud formation was countered by the brightness of repeated lightning flashes. Chlorine thought of Fracto throwing a fit. Nimby was getting to Dearth, and that was good.

More trees came down, crisscrossing the road so thickly that it was pointless to try to use it. Nimby didn't; he rode through the forest, winding between the standing trees and brush, sluing around puddles and rocks. In places the foliage was so thick that it seemed impossible to penetrate, but somehow Nimby guided the Lemon through it without even scraping. That map in his head made his course clear, however opaque it might seem to her.

The tackle tried to dislodge; she felt it shift as they whipped around a turn. She reached back with one hand to take hold of it. Nimby was getting them where they needed to go; she had to see that they got there with their payload.

Something odd happened. There was a funny quality to the air around them. Her long brown hair lifted of its own accord, spreading out around her head like a dark halo.

The cycle suddenly braked, skidding across the forest floor. It spun around. Chlorine screamed. But they did not fall over. Instead they paused, then took off back the way they had come.

Lightning cracked behind them. The burst of heat shoved them faster forward. Dearth had struck directly at them, but Nimby had anticipated it and maneuvered out of the way just in time. It seemed he could tell when and where lightning was about to strike.

That halo of hair—that must have been a signal. In Mundania things didn't just happen magically; they had to be prepared for. Those few seconds were enough to allow Nimby to get clear.

The Demon Earth was doing his worst, and they were escaping it. They did have a chance. She realized that she had been somewhat fatalistic about that; now her hope was growing.

They slid through ridges and channels, across fields and through more forest, and then arrived back where Dug and Kim were waiting with the car. They had used a tow rope to haul the branch clear with the car, so were ready to move. The block and tackle weren't necessary after all.

Chlorine realized that though Nimby could sense what was around him, he could not see into the future. The tackle would have done the job, if the car hadn't been able to.

Nothing had happened to Dug and Kim in the interim; even the rain had abated. It was Nimby Dearth was after, no one else, and Chlorine realized that Dearth might not even be aware of others. So Nimby had enabled them to clear the way, just by being absent.

They loaded the tackle into the car, and resumed their journey south. This time the motorcycle led the way. The rain increased, and the wind, but no trees came down. Dearth evidently realized that they now had the means to haul trees out of the way, for the tackle could multiply their pulling power several fold. So the tackle finessed the trees; the mere threat of it stopped that ploy.

But now it was afternoon, and they would not get home today unless they drove in the night. The storm was extremely dark ahead; Dearth was saving his worst for last.

Nimby lifted one hand, signaling the car, then rode into a motel lot. He stopped, and the car pulled up beside it. Nimby touched Chlorine's hand, imparting information.

"You stay here for the night," Chlorine said, getting off the cycle and stretching her legs.

"But we can drive a couple more hours before night," Dug protested. "And into the night, to get home. We don't have to stop."

"Nimby knows," Chlorine said. "Stop here, eat, sleep early. We'll need to resume in the wee hours."

"Okay," he said dubiously.

Chlorine turned back to the cycle—and it was starting to move. "Wait for me!" she cried. But Nimby just waved and drove away.

"I guess he means for you to stay with us," Kim said sympathetically.

"I suppose so," Chlorine agreed, concealing her hurt. She knew Nimby was protecting her, by giving her a chance to eat and sleep in peace while he distracted Dearth, but she hated being apart from him.

They took a motel room and turned on the TV while taking turns showering and cleaning up and changing to dry clothing. Chlorine saw the ongoing news and was appalled. It showed scenes of devastation. A freak storm had laid waste the region, and the Chat-A-Hoot-Cheese River and its tributaries were flooding. One of the flooded rivers crossed their route south. The bridges were closed.

"We're not going to get across that in the next two days," Dug said grimly. "Not with a car."

"Nimby knew," Chlorine said, beginning to appreciate why he had halted their drive south.

Kim emerged from the shower, wrapped in a towel. She was a lanky girl, but self assured. "Look at that!" she exclaimed as the TV picture showed a bridge getting washed away. "Where is this disaster?"

"On our route south," Dug said, heading for the shower. "Freak storm, they say."

"Freak storm, my eye," Kim said. "That's Dearth going after Nimby."

"Yes," Chlorine agreed. "That tree across the road was just to delay us while the storm flooded the area between us and home. Nimby stopped it with the tackle, but too much time was lost. But Nimby has something in mind."

"It's like a chess game," Kim said. "Ploy and counter-ploy. We're just pawns, not seeing the larger strategy until it's too late."

"Nimby will find a way," Chlorine said bravely.

Kim patted her hand. "I'm sure he will." But Chlorine knew fake optimism when she heard it.

The rain was only moderate in this region. They went out to eat, and got gasoline for the car, and turned in at eight at night. Chlorine had a bed to herself. She missed Nimby, but knew that if he returned here to be with her, the storm would intensify and the motel might well be struck by lightning and burned down. So Nimby was protecting them all.

"It's an irony," Dug remarked from the other bed. "We Companions are supposed to keep Nimby out of mischief in this unfamiliar land. Instead he's keeping *us* out of mischief."

"Nimby's very smart," Chlorine said. "And he's been studying conscience. Demons don't come with consciences; they're like machines or golems in that respect. But Nimby's trying to learn how to love, to dream, to have conscience—all the things the souled creatures do. So this is practice for him."

"I'd say he's getting there," Kim said. "Okay, we've got the alarm set for two AM. Let's sleep."

"Shux," Dug said. "I thought we were in for six hours of hot love."

"Six *minutes,* swiftie," Kim retorted. "Then you're done, ready or not."

"You are a hard taskmistress."

"No, a soft one. For five and a half minutes. After that I turn into a brassie lassie."

Now Chlorine really missed Nimby. The brassies were Xanth folk made of brass. Their women could be surprisingly soft when they wanted to be, but were otherwise metal hard. Kim was obliging Dug's interest, but had set a time limit well within a normal man's capability. She was a nice person. Chlorine knew that if she set Nimby such a limit, he would manage to signal five storks in five minutes. That was an advantage of not being human.

She closed her eyes, imagining Nimby's performance. And thought she felt his answering nudge. Probably imagination, because of his lack of magic here. But maybe he was tuning in on her, and shared her vision and feeling. She wished they could signal the stork and have it deliver, but of course that would never happen unless Nimby wanted it. He had given her so much, she was ashamed even to think of wanting more. Of being a normal family, with all the joys and travails of raising children.

The alarm went off, startling her awake. They scrambled out of their beds and lined up at the bathroom, getting ready. Twenty minutes later they were outside, two in the car and one waiting for the motorcycle.

It came. Chlorine got on behind Nimby, and they were on their way somewhere. She wondered where he had been all night. Probably riding around in random patterns, never pausing, so that Dearth could not pin him down. Fortunately Nimby did not need sleep; when they lay together for the night, and she slept, she knew that his Awareness was reaching out, exploring all Xanth. But what about Edsel's mortal body? That must be getting tired. So where were they going now?

Not south. Nimby followed roads and trails to the side. Dearth was aware—it seemed he always know where Nimby was, once he tuned in—and the weather worsened. But it was apparent that a storm could not be generated instantly, and Nimby, taking an unexpected direction, was staying just ahead of it. Still, this was not leading home.

They drove some distance, and dawn came. Still Nimby led them in the strange direction.

They took a side trail. This soon became waterlogged. The flooding had reached this far, drowning out the road. Chlorine saw a bridge ahead that was above the water, but the approach was impossible.

Nimby turned off the motor and came to a stop. He touched Chlorine's hand.

She got off and went to the car, which had stopped with its tires deep in standing water. "The road goes through, and crosses the river. Thereafter it's mostly high ground. If we cross here, Dearth won't be able to flood us out later. But it will stop your motor. Turn it off. We'll make a winch. It will be slow, but can be done."

They didn't question this. They shut down the motor and brought out the block, tackle, and rope. Nimby walked the Lemon out to a stout tree, then anchored the block to it. It was a special design, that could be set to increase the pulling force considerably. This required a lot of rope, but they had it; Nimby had planned well. Then he tied one rope to the motorcycle and the other to the distant car. He rode the cycle along a dry ridge—and it hauled the car slowly through the water.

Chlorine remembered that there had been an example of such a pulley in one of the movie previews they had seen on the second day in Mundania. Nimby had studied that, and learned. There had been motorcycles, too, she realized. Now he was using what he had learned then. Nothing passed him by.

Then Nimby disconnected and walked the Lemon to another tree, farther along. He repeated the process. After several such stages, the car was through the deep puddle and back on dry land, at the edge of the bridge. It had been towed through the water without having to struggle to keep its motor dry. Apparently water didn't hurt a motor that wasn't running, at least not in the same way as it had in the mountains. Unless it was guided in the night by the malign power of the Demon E(A/R)TH.

They let the motors dry briefly. Then they started them, without difficulty, and rode across the bridge. The water was rushing tumultuously under, but the bridge supports and structure were solid. Evidently this was a little known crossing that Dearth had not thought to wash out. Now it was too late.

Was Dearth angry? So it seemed. This time clouds did not form and thicken; the opposite was the case. The terrain warmed and dried. Steam rose from the scene. Then smoke. Then fires broke out. Smoke rose into the sky. What was happening?

Nimby touched her hand. "Volcanic activity?" she asked, amazed. "Are there volcanoes here?"

Not hitherto. But Dearth was angry, and the power of the earth was his as well as the powers of the air and water. This region would see its first volcano, if Nimby didn't get away from here soon.

But Nimby was already moving away from it. Their two vehicles raced past the spreading fires and left them behind. The volcano, too, was too late; Dearth had not had time to raise it to sufficient power, thanks to Nimby's sudden change of direction. Even so, there would be new weather headlines for the local newspapers. Chlorine wondered again where Nimby had been during the night—but obviously it had not been near here. So he had surprised Dearth, and gotten through another barrier.

Nimby signaled the car again. They pulled over to the side of the road. Nimby touched Chlorine's hand.

"Nimby needs time to be Aware," Chlorine announced. "We have caught up to his prior plan, and now he needs more information. But we can't afford to pause; Dearth will strike. We have an hour of clear road ahead. Nimby must ride in the car, and Dug can ride the Lemon."

"Got it," Dug said. "It's been like magic, getting through. We want more of that." He took over the motorcycle.

Nimby got into the back of the car, with Chlorine. Kim drove. As they moved out, Nimby leaned back and closed his eyes. Chlorine thought he was sleeping, but he took her hand.

Suddenly she was sharing his Awareness. She saw the Land of Mundania extending as her perception rose from the car, like a bird flying upward. The trees, houses, roads, lakes, and fields spread out in the manner of an unfolding map. There were tiny cars on the roads, moving in various directions. She realized with a start that this was not a picture; this was reality. This was what was happening in this region of Mundania right now.

There was another river, also flooding, with its bridges closed. They had circled around one such impediment, but now were heading into another. Well, they had almost two days to get home, and if it took one day to get around this one, they would still be in time.

The scene flew south, to the peninsula of Xanth, called Florida in Mundania. It dropped down to another swollen river, crossed it, and oriented on a town beyond. On a motel. Into that motel, searching out a particular unit. Into that unit.

There was a figure Chlorine recognized: Sean Baldwin Mundane. With a young woman who looked somewhat familiar—oh, it was Willow Elf, without her wings. Her Mundane version. And Sean's little brother David Baldwin, now age fifteen. And his cat, Midrange. They had visited Xanth three years ago. Chlorine knew them well, for she and Nimby had been with them when the Ill Wind came to Xanth.

Willow carried a locket. Chlorine recognized it, from Nimby's

Awareness: it was magic, holding any amount of anything, and at the moment it held a few oddments, a lesser demon, and a bucket of magic dust.

Magic dust! She had for the moment forgotten. That was what Nimby needed to have some power of magic in Mundania. His body in Xanth was the source of all magic, but here he was Mundane. Until he got that dust. Sean and Willow were bringing it to him, but had been stalled by the flooded rivers. They could not get across.

Did Dearth know this? So far he had given evidence of watching only Nimby, but he surely could watch anyone he chose, here in his dreary land. So he was not only blocking Nimby's progress, with imperfect success, but blocking Sean's progress, with better success. Because Sean did not have Awareness; he could not fathom the devious ways to circumvent the barriers.

That river would take days to subside. How could Sean and Willow get through? They had Sean's car, but the bridges were closed. The bridges were in place, but deemed to be unsafe during the flood. No one was allowed on them. Maybe someone could sneak across by foot, but then he would be without his car. What could they do?

Willow perked up, cocking her head. She heard something, or sensed it. She touched Sean's arm, and whispered something to him. She had felt Nimby's Awareness! Chlorine knew this only because Nimby did. Contact had been made. Willow was of Xanthly origin, so was better attuned to magic, even this very slight magic of sensing.

But what good was it? No one could cross that river from either side. Not until the three days of the Challenge were long since over. Nimby had gone around one block, but used up a night doing it, and the block at the other end he could not do much about. So the essential nature of this contest suggested that Nimby would lose. Did it mean that Sean's party would give up its effort to bring the magic locket to Nimby?

Then the scene faded. The vision was done. Chlorine opened her eyes. Nimby did not. He had gone to sleep. Or at least his body had, and that was surely good.

Chlorine told Kim what she had seen. "So the Mundane Baldwins are trying," she concluded. "But they can't reach us, and we can't reach them. Even if one party managed to cross its river, the other river is keeping the other back. We are kept apart by parallel rivers. So it looks as though Dearth has won."

"Is Nimby concerned?" Kim asked.

"I don't know. He's asleep." No need to clarify that it was really Edsel's tired body sleeping.

"He probably got no rest last night."

"So what do we do?" Chlorine asked, near tears.

"We move on south. Maybe we'll get a break."

"A break?"

"Like finding a boat to cross the river."

"Dearth would sink it."

Kim shrugged. "It's not over till it's over."

They continued south. When they reached the city, there was no way to go south beyond it.

Nimby woke. "We have gone as far south as we can go," Chlorine said.

He touched her hand, then returned to sleep. "Turn left," she told Kim. "There is a motel there with a room free." The motels were crowded now, because of the number of people caught unexpectedly away from home. Finding a room for the night would be difficult.

Kim turned, and Dug on the motorcycle followed. They drove along the side road.

"There," Chlorine said, pointing.

"But it says No Vacancies," Kim protested.

"Try it anyway."

They drove to the front office. Kim got out and went in. She emerged moments later with a look of vague awe. "They thought they had no vacancies, but then they got a cancellation, so we got it."

"Nimby knew," Chlorine said.

"How could he know the future? I mean, you explained about the Awareness, but that's all in the present, isn't it?"

"I think he knew the people were canceling in the present. They just hadn't yet notified the office."

So they had a good room. This time Nimby joined them. The storm hovered, but did not intensify; Dearth seemed satisfied to keep the two rivers flooded, knowing that they represented a formidable barrier. He knew where Nimby was, and where Sean's party was; as long as they remained separated, victory was just a matter of time.

Nimby went to bed and slept.

"We'll go get pizza," Dug said.

Chlorine sat beside the bed and watched Nimby. Surely his body was tired, and needed the rest. But he didn't even seem to be worried. Was he bluffing? But with the two parties unable to meet, he had to lose. Should he at least be trying to get across the river, on the chance that Sean would get across his river?

"Whatever the end of this, I love you," she murmured. "You are my everything, Nimby." For at least she had had three years of the wonder of him. And perhaps she would have more, if all Nimby lost was status. She didn't want him to be hurt, but she hardly cared about his status, as long as she could be with him. But she was afraid that if he lost that status, he would leave Xanth, and that would be the end of everything.

Dug and Kim returned with the pizza. They turned on the TV and watched the weather news. It wasn't good. They chatted about incidentals, staying away from the obvious subject.

Nimby slept on.

Finally Chlorine joined him, lying beside him, holding his hand. He was unresponsive. Was that just because his body was dead tired, or was it worse? Could Nimby have given up?

In the morning Nimby joined them at a restaurant across the street for breakfast. Finally Dug broached the awful matter: "Two days are gone. What do we do?"

Nimby touched Chlorine's hand. "We relax," she said. "We read a book."

"Read a book?" Kim asked. It was evident that her patience was fraying.

"I saw a little library just down the street from us," Dug said. "We could go there."

Kim glanced at him, but refrained from making a sharp comment. "Well, it will pass the time, I suppose." As if they had too much time on their hands. Chlorine shared their gathering depression. Were they just supposed to dawdle here, waiting for the end?

They finished breakfast and went to the library. But as they entered, the lights went out. "Oh, another power failure," the librarian said. "I'm so sorry." Her name tag said MARY LOU MATTHEW.

Kim looked around. "You have a computer system."

"Yes, for the patrons to use to go inline," the librarian said. "They love it. But the power's been so erratic the last two days, we can't use it."

They knew why the power failed. Nimby could escape the moment he reached the O-Xone, if he had access to the Grid at the right time.

The formal check-in time was in the next half hour, but Dearth would make sure the power didn't return until well after that, or when Nimby left the library. Things were quiet now only because Dearth was in control of the situation, but Dearth wasn't taking any chances.

They looked at books, as it was light enough without electric lights. Nimby took one about quantum physics, and read it avidly. Chlorine remembered that Dug had discussed the matter. Nimby tended to follow up on anything that attracted his interest, so now he was completing his knowledge of that subject. Chlorine preferred to look at a book of pretty pictures.

Then Nimby touched her hand. Mystified by his request, she got up and went to the library's bathroom. It had a window to the back. She loosened the latch and opened it. "Here," she said out the window.

Something leaped up, landing on the sill. Startled, she drew back. It was a nondescript cat.

Then she recognized it. "Midrange!" she said. "What are you doing here?" She picked him up. Nimby had known he was coming.

She carried the cat into the main section of the library and set him down beside Nimby. Nimby reached out to Midrange's collar. There was a chain with a locket. Nimby took the locket in his hand, without removing it from the cat. He touched Chlorine's hand, and she felt a thrill of power. It was the magic dust within the locket; Nimby was drawing on it without even having to open the locket. Something in her body changed. In fact she felt three pulses of change.

Chlorine stared. So did Dug and Kim. "Is that what I think it is?" Kim asked.

There was a sudden roll of thunder outside. Dearth had just caught on.

Nimby got up, briefly touched the hands of Dug and Kim, and went to the computer terminal, carrying Midrange, who seemed more than satisfied. Chlorine knew how that was. He touched the unit. It came on.

Lightning struck the building. But the library evidently had an arrester, because there was no damage. Dearth had been caught by surprise, and couldn't act swiftly enough.

Kim caught on. She leaped to the terminal and started typing. The screen came on. "But there's no power!" the librarian protested.

"Now there is," Dug said. And indeed there was, for Nimby was powering the system magically. None of them saw fit to mention that detail, however.

Chlorine sat at the adjacent terminal, joining in. This one was also working, as the current flowed throughout the system. Dug came to type for her.

Kim led them straight to the O-Xone. They entered it, and the hall became real around them.

Edsel and Pia were there in Breanna's Leaf. So were Breanna and Justin. "We were afraid you wouldn't make it," Pia said, coming to hug Chlorine.

Chlorine had had a similar fear, but didn't care to admit it. "Nimby knew."

"For sure," Breanna said. "We sent the locket out, but heard there was really bad weather in Mundania. We figured we knew why. When the Baldwins reported trouble getting through, we were really nervous."

"Midrange Cat got through with the locket," Chlorine said. "I think the magic leaked out and affected him, giving him extra intelligence. He knew where to go." Suddenly she realized why Nimby had been sleeping so much: his Awareness had been following the cat, guiding Midrange throughout. "The Demon E(A/R)TH was watching the humans, not the cat, so he slipped though." She glanced at Kim. "You'll have to see that Midrange gets back to his family, with our gratitude."

"We will," Kim said.

Nimby touched hands with Edsel, and Chlorine touched Pia. Her orientation changed; now she was looking the opposite way.

Nimby touched Chlorine's hand. Suddenly she had important new information. She turned to Pia. "I have some news for you. Nimby is pleased with the way you and Ed cooperated, and has given you three gifts."

"Oh, we don't need any gifts," Pia protested. "Being in Xanth was such a wonderful experience for us." She glanced at Edsel. "We're going to stay married, and have children, and I'm going to study the environment. I have gained so much!"

"Then I hope you are pleased with the gifts, for they have already been given," Chlorine said. "First, your body has been restored to its form at age sixteen, as it seems was your wish in Xanth, and will be easier to maintain that way."

"Oh!" Pia exclaimed. "I thought that was only during the adventure. It was a foolish wish, anyway."

"It's really meant for Edsel," Chlorine said.

"I like it," Edsel agreed.

"Second, your diabetes is gone."

Pia's mouth dropped open. "No more needles? I thought that was only in Xanth too. The healing spring."

"No more needles. Third, you will receive a visit from the stork."

Pia was astonished. "You mean—even though we were in Xanth, with your bodies?"

"Perhaps," Chlorine said. "We used your bodies similarly. Because of your association with Xanth at the time, your child will have a magic talent, when visiting Xanth."

Pia seemed about to faint. "That really gave her something to think about," Kim said, smiling. "I envy her." Kim's smile, though genuinely warm for her friend's good fortune, had a tinge of sadness she tried to mask.

"You, too, will receive a visit," Chlorine told her. "With similar magic."

"A—? But that can't be! I mean—" Kim hesitated, unaware that they knew about her problem in that respect, and her secret heartache. "I mean, we were in Mundania the whole time."

"The storks deliver as Nimby tells them to. The two of you were extremely helpful, and are deserving."

Now Kim was the one about to faint. "You mean, I really will have—a baby?" Her underlying sadness was transforming to abiding joy, and it was mirrored in Dug's face.

"As will I," Chlorine said. Then, startled, she looked at Nimby. "I will?"

Everyone laughed. Then the three women came together and hugged each other.

"This is wonderful but weird," Breanna said, looking on somewhat enviously.

Nimby touched her hand.

"But my turn will come," Breanna added, awed. "And be worth waiting for." Behind her, Justin's eyes widened in surprised surmise.

But after a moment of thought, Pia got serious. "I don't want to seem ungrateful, but I don't think I want these—these gifts."

Kim winced. "Pia, this isn't exactly something you can turn down. Nimby is—"

"I know who Nimby is." Pia faced him. "I appreciate all this, Nimby. I really do. But they are selfish things. I've been selfish all my life, but in Xanth I discovered that I don't like that style. I want to—to

do something useful with my life. So with all due respect, take back
your gifts. I do want to be beautiful, and free of illness, and now I do
want to make a family, but I would trade them all for the ability to
accomplish my new purpose, which I think is to save the great old trees
of Mundania, just as I helped save them in Xanth. And I guess that's
something I'll just have to do by myself. I think I can do it all, the hard
way."

Nimby looked at Edsel.

"No argument here," Edsel said. "All I wanted was Pia back, and
I think I like her even better this way."

Nimby extended his hand to Pia. She stepped forward and took it.
Nothing showed, but Chlorine knew that there was a pulse of magic.
They were all in magic, all the way out to the library terminals that
Nimby's magic was animating.

Then Pia stepped back. Nimby touched Chlorine's hand.

"You now have additional intelligence, courage, and persuasive-
ness," Chlorine told Pia. "These qualities will help you to accomplish
your purpose."

Pia smiled with genuine gratitude. "Thank you so much, Nimby.
These gifts I will use well. I will always treasure my time in Xanth, but
my true mission is in Mundania."

Nimby turned away. The job was done.

The others bade each other quick farewells. Then the four Mundan-
ians departed, and Nimby and Chlorine went back toward Xanth, leaving
Justin and Breanna in the Leaf.

"Wait till Pia discovers that those last gifts weren't in exchange for
the first ones, but in addition," Chlorine murmured. "And wait till Edsel
discovers your influence on his Lemon motorcycle, when Midrange hides
the magic locket in it."

Nimby didn't reply, but he smiled. He was learning about niceness,
too.

Author's Note

N o, it's not true that a woman in a southern state accidentally got her skirt torn, so that her panties were exposed, and left a trail of seventeen freaked-out men. That doesn't happen in Mundania, where there is no magic. Anyway, she was riding on the back of a Lemon motorcycle at the time, so hardly anything showed. In any event, this novel is fiction. And no, that Lemon is not for sale.

Some of my readers do seem to have difficulty distinguishing fantasy from reality. It's that trace of magic dust that wafts out from between the pages when they first open a Xanth novel. Nothing to be much concerned about; it gradually wears off, in the course of years. When they lose the last of their imagination, they are ready to be adults in Mundania.

This novel is special for a reason having nothing to do with its merit: with this title, I now have had published one or more books beginning with each letter of the alphabet, from *Alien Plot* to *Zombie Lover*. They aren't all Xanths; they scatter across fantasy, science fiction, martial arts, autobiography, and history. But it was Xanth that wrapped it up, as I tackled the more difficult letters: X, Y, and Z. No, I don't plan to go through the alphabet again; once was enough. But I regard it as one of the nicer meaningless accomplishments.

Readers often inquire where I get all my ideas. In the case of Xanth, that's easy to answer: most come from my readers. They are constantly sending notions ranging from simple puns to full novels, and I dutifully note them and see where and how I can use them. I had more than two hundred reader notions piled up when I started this novel. I used more than 150, but didn't come close to catching up, because more were piling in while I wrote the novel. It's like trying to bail out a leaky boat. Some just don't fit in with the current story. Some I used this time go back several years. Many I use, but am unable to do full justice to. A number have had to wait until I can give them proper play, such as having a particular character have an adventure. So to those of you who hoped to see your notions here, and do not see them, I'm sorry, and maybe next time. As of this novel, I have caught up with the feasible notions through the year 1996, and about half those for 1997.

Readers also inquire where I get my names. That answer is easy: I collect books of names. In 1965, before we had our first surviving child (we lost three stillborn in the first decade of our marriage; life can be drear in Mundania), I got the twin (no pun) booklets ''3000 Names for Boys'' and ''3000 Names for Girls,'' which are very good. I deducted them as a business expense—the whole 50¢—because they were indeed for business: naming my characters. For example, that's where I found Colene, the depressive girl in the Mode series. It's a variant of Colleen, Irish for Girl, but I like the spelling better, because Colene is no ordinary girl. Later when we did have children of our own, we got ''Names for Boys & Girls'' free from the hospital. We also bought ''Let's Name the Baby,'' and all of these served well for characters. In 1991 Lori Tomlinson sent me *The Baby Name Personality Survey,* which describes the popular impression of first names, which seem to derive mostly from celebrities who cast the shadows of their personalities across their names. For example, Linus resembles the kid in the comic strip ''Peanuts,'' or will be a scholar like Linus Pauling. That sort of perspective is ideal for my purposes. Then in 1996 I got *A Dictionary of First Names,* published by the Oxford University Press, which is naturally the most authoritative. Yes, of course I'm prejudiced; I was born (delivered) in Oxford, England, seven weeks before another genre writer, the late John Brunner. Yes, I knew him; he was very good, his most notable novel being *Stand on Zanzibar.* Anyway, that ''Dictionary'' has 443 pages of names. Yes, my name is in it; it's a variation of Peter, meaning ''rock.'' It says the modest popularity of the name Piers may derive from Langland's medieval poem *Piers Plowman,* and symbolizes the virtues of hard work, honesty, and fairness. I can live with that, though I was actually named after a character in the Jalna series of novels my mother was reading at the time. No, I never read any of them myself, but it does seem fitting that fiction gave me my name. There may after all be a trace of magic in Mundania.

But the point is, where did I get names like Edsel and Pia? And I have to say, not from these books. Oh, they are there, in some of them, but my inspiration was elsewhere. I go to the name books only when I haven't thought up something better on my own. Back when I wrote *Demons Don't Dream,* I needed a couple of humorously incidental names to flesh out Dug Mundane's background: his best friend, and his girl-friend. I remembered the car Ford made and named after the son of Henry Ford, Edsel. It was supposed to be a great new success, fabulously researched, designed, and promoted, and was in fact a marketing flop, a sort of sinking *Titanic* of the auto industry, which one wag said looked like an Oldsmobile sucking a lemon. I love it when the high-paid experts belly-flop, showing how little they really know. Pia was inspired by a more recent and less unkind image: the starlet who married a billionaire, Pia Zadora, a cute girl but not favored by critics for her acting ability. I have considerable sympathy for folk not favored by critics; maybe if I had another hundred thousand words to play with, I could document why I regard critics as Edsel types. So the name Edsel was meant to vaguely suggest disaster, and the name Pia to suggest cuteness without much else. A lovely couple. But of course when I made them main characters for this novel, I got to know them better, and learned more respect. That tends to happen when you get to really know anyone you once held in contempt, and is surely one of the fundamental lessons of life: it is ignorance that breeds prejudice.

I proofread my novels, but it is my theory that errors grow on the page after the proofreading. Ask any other writer if it isn't so. But this time I caught a bad one before it escaped. I use the Dvorak keyboard, which has the vowels on the home row on the left side, and the most used consonants on the home row on the right side. It's a better layout than QWERTY, but it's hard to get on a computer. My wife, who was a programmer in the stone age of computing—the 1960's—has to get into the works to change the key assignments, and it is a struggle, and the keys remain marked wrong. So I have learned to ignore the marks and type by touch. But I do make some errors. The O is next to the E, and, well, I discovered that when I had referred to the peephole of the gourd, that double-E came out as a double-O. Never mind what it spelled; I corrected it in a hurry.

One of my contributors, listed below, is Natalie Tran. She gave an interesting history to one of her suggestions. Her class was on a three day field trip, and naturally got bored during the interstices. They had just seen many fascinating tide-pool creatures. One of the supervising mothers was an actress, and she invented a game called "Anemone Enemy." There was one Anemone and one Enemy standing before a Judge. The only way they could be distinguished was that the enemy had a pencil hidden on her body. The Judge had to figure out which one was the Enemy. Behind the Judge was the Jury, who distracted the Judge by singing loud and out of tune songs, such as "Puff the Magic Dragon" twisted into a horrible racket. A Judge who guessed correctly was given a set of purple anemone earrings. I wonder—doesn't a real trial sometimes seem almost as crazy?

Here, at any rate, are my credits for reader suggested notions, some of which may not have turned out the way the suggestors had in mind, and some of which did not turn out the way I expected. I hope I have not garbled any names. They are roughly in order of their appearance in the novel, except when one reader suggested several.

Chat Room Consultant: Tammy Bender aka Dragonfly-29. MUD Consultant: Marisol Ramos. Grundy Golem speaks computer languages; Mode M; people ensnared in chatlines; Talent of becoming what is needed; Siamese triplets—Heather Oglevie. Xanth underwater setting (I may return to this in a future novel; it's an example of not doing a notion justice)—James Shaw. Brass coast—Mike Burkholder and Aaron Batista. Prince Dol, talent of turning the inanimate living—Sean McDonald. Xanth theme park—Nikki Tomson. Xanth Wave from the future— (there's another notion deserving more) Justin "Virus" Chiang. "Through the Gourd" Home Page—Jessica Grider. Diabetic cured in Xanth—Kimberly Putz. Talent of seeing one day future; to create solid illusionary creatures—Sarah Curran, Chris "Mud" Robinson. Isle of View II—Andrew Cowell. Restling, Boxing, Socker—Vasudev Mandyam. Description of DeMonica—Monica Ramirez. B-rate, Jeanie Yus with IQ vines—Katie Green. Joy stick, sad stick—Andrew Graft. Magic Locket; magic bracelets from Hinge; super vacuum cleaner—Billy Banks. Cloud shaping, walking on water, 6" levitation—Jeremy & Cameron Grey. Making things sink into the ground—Mike Ward. Conjuring mint plants, making things slippery, conjuring eggs, amplify noise, making paintings come to life, summoning birds, thickening and thinning, hearing anything close by—Chris "Mud" Robinson. Talent of making a shield around oneself; Heal other folk's injuries—Abby Everdell.

Fracto assuming human form—Jilana Conaway. Talent of learning—
Kiel VanHorn. More & Less twins, talent of turning into humanoid
crossbreeds—Sean McDonald. Talent of turning things transparent so
that their ideas show—Jake Watters. Waxing the moon's green cheese—
Jessica Mansfield. Returning things to their original state—Pedro Leon
de la Barra. Pet roc, E Coli, Salmon Ella, Chocolate spiders—Barbara
Hay Hummel. Bringing statues to life—Matthew King. Glaring dag-
gers—anonymous. Controlling the emotions or moods of others—Al-
exandra Roedder, Chris Robinson, Mike Ward. Laika—Emily Ratsep.
Bowling, sock-her balls—Chris Swanson. Putting wings on anything—
Chelsea Bagwell. Modifying or deflecting talents—Joshua T. Fesmire.
Chin-chilla, Speaking things real, His story/her story, Anti Nym—Don-
ovan Beeson. Chili powder, Cook book—Dorcas Bethel. Know-ledge—
Michael G. Till. Window pain—Miguel Ettema. Dinomite—Robert
Meyerson. Thyme being—Alex Gordon. Leprechauns in Xanth—Tracy
Ann Romano. Rusty, who makes metal rust—Rusty Balcum. Straight
jacket—Chris Swanson. Simon says, and it happens—Jessica Mansfield.
Brandon Risner, Ass fault, Toad lily—Jessica Sager. Raccoonnaissance,
tailgator—Wanda Remenaric. Scholar ship—Terry McNamee. Lake of
Pollux oil—Jason Randle. Chess nut—Nath Aiken. Elena Human, Polly
Esther, Anemone—Natalie Tran. Intermission, firedrake's iron lung—
Andrew Graff. Handi Harpy—Sarah Curran. Girl who relates to dragons—Heather Davis. Shaunture Centaur, with talent of mispronuncia-
tion—Bryce Weinert and Kristine Courtnage. Mundanes named after
colors—Kristin Gardner. Sigh-press tree—Alan Little. Earth, water, air
ants—Rick Raddue and his brother. Alexandra, were-dolphin—Alexandra Roedder. Gabriel, visiting Mundane boy—Gabriel McDermott.
Brothers who can turn self to ice, or anything else to ice—Larry Horn-
baker. The Land of Xanth being nice female—Dana Bates. Centaur Magician who knows the talents of others—Rachel Rempel. DeMonica and
Demon Ted growing up and marrying—Bethany Ayers. Diluted love
elixir and finder spell—Karla Sussman. Roller skates—Ron Leming.
Roses levitate own colors—Jefferson Kohler. Ally Horse—Christy
Weese. To save Hugh Manatee—Tom Pierce. Thera pea—Betty Schaef-
fer. Lie-lack bush—Margaret Pavlac. Ruler takes control, Pie & Ears—
Michael Burkholder & Aaron Batista. Chemis-tree—Jane Burkowski.
Water chestnut tree—Jill Conto. Adder does math—Melissa Stephens.
Pitchforks—Nicole Adkins. Hall minotaurs—Joe Barder. Bi-noculars—
Gordon Johnson. Captivi tree, Brain storm—Vincent Tardo. Bed Making

Adult Conspiracy—Tiffany Stull. Attire—Chris Efta. Seal—Jessica Mansfield. Fireweed—Marshall Porter McConahy. Lack toes intolerant—Andrew Crawford. Quack doctor—Anita Haviland. Dot—Scott Edwards. Changing gender at will—Richard Barnhart. Reverse wood lives backwards—Ray Koenig. Owen Cossaboon—Sharon Kresser. Thimbleberries—Jessica Mansfield. Sting-ray—Billy Exton. Cir-cuss for harpies—Nicole Taylor. Waller & Wallette building walls—Thomas L. Bruns. Air compressor—Chris Efta. Canteen—Rikki Goren. Hand book, Ill literate, High piers, low piers—Dorcas Bethel. Butter knife—David Simons. Roll-playing game—Jonathan Ulrich. Human race—Michael Meilstrup. Cy Centaur, Cy Clone—Gary Roth. Christopher Christopher—Christopher Humphries. Story of Grey and Robota—Erin Schram and daughters Sharayah & Fiona. Joystick and keyboard for Com Pewter—Spencer Lease. Cassie Centaur—Becca Steel. Mertaurs—Jason B Rollins. Poison Ivy—Chris "Mud" Robinson. Fanta Sea—Greg Rimko. Library puns—Mary Lou Matthew. Paper view—Rusty Balcum. Moo-sick soothes—Sharon Ellis. Sycophant—Ursula Flinspach. Draco Dragon's black beryls—C B Hutchings. Dream realm monsters loose—Tom Koonce. Grave stone—Adam W Ellis. Na Palm tree—Bentley Gettings. Morph—Kyle Johnson. Paperback person—Kelly English. Carpet tunnel syndrome—Karla Sussman. Car pool tunnel thin dome—Tim Alsop. Talent of summoning magic dust—Elizabeth Pearl. Dee-tonate—Dee Lahr (I bought my left handed bow from her; I think she's related to Dee Light, Dee Lectible, or Dee Licious, because she lives in Kiss Mee). Fun Gus—Michael Kenny. Moon Shine—Mark A Godbois.

Many readers inquire about Jenny Elf, who derives from Jenny Gildwarg, paralyzed at age 12 by a drunk driver. I haven't said much because not much has changed. At this writing, in Jamboree 1998, Jenny is 21 and remains mostly paralyzed. Drunk drivers are still given mostly wrist slaps. I still write to her every week. Jenny Elf, in Xanth, got married last novel, and is now a princess, and isn't in this one because the year following marriage is nobody else's business. Presumably the stork will have one more visit, in due course.